DIFFERENT DEVILS

CONNECTED BY A CAR. DIVIDED BY THEIR SINS

JEFF RABKIN

Agent Contact:

CarbonDog Publications

Menifee, California 92584

carbondogpublications@gmail.com

BOOK ONE
MAKING THE EXCELA

M onarch Motors had just finished its newest manufacturing plant outside Atlanta, Georgia. The sprawling facility, which covered 3.5 million square feet, employed 8,300 people and employed 789 robots, which produced 1,400 cars daily.

One of those newly assembled cars was Monarch's newest automobile, Excela. The Excela was Monarch's entry into the high-end luxury market, and its engineers spent years developing the latest technology. The "Grade Logic" transmission detects if the car is traveling up or downhill and uses the most efficient gear ratio to maximize power and save on fuel. It has an engine sensor that measures the outside air temperature and pressure. The sensor sends this information to the fuel-air system, which calculates the most efficient amount of fuel going into the cylinder head. This increases the power and also saves fuel. The Excela is also the first mass-produced automobile to use a "brake-by-wire" braking system (BBW) developed for Formula 1 race cars. This system eliminates the need for hydraulic brake fluid. BBW uses a sensor that measures the force with which the driver presses the brake pedal. The sensor information is sent to an electric pump, which applies pressure to the brake pads. Production costs and pricing were critical issues. Monarch wanted a luxury car but needed to keep the price down. They built the car using the frame from one of their other models. Designing and manufacturing frames is expensive, so having a ready-made frame was a substantial cost savings. The seating is made of imitation Nappa leather, the same leather Rolls-Royce uses in its cars. Nappa is a leather made from lamb hide that has not been altered. During processing, it keeps the hide's natural surface and grain intact. Monarch's Nappa utilizes cowhide processed to resemble Nappa. It features a polyurethane base to minimize the effects of the sun and heat. It is luxurious but affordable and built to last.

GROVE PARK IS one of the roughest parts of Atlanta, with more violent crimes than any other part of the city. Kids growing up there were faced with two choices: you were either going to sell drugs or take drugs. If someone was going to sell drugs, they had to join a gang. If they were going to use drugs, robbing and stealing was necessary to afford them. This neighborhood is where Javon Waters, his wife, Mary, and their eight-year-old son, Quentin, rented a three-bedroom house. The house blended in with the other homes on their street. The only distinction was that it was in better condition than the others. The house sat on a small lot with shrubs in front and a driveway leading to a small garage filled with lawn equipment and boxes.

Javon Waters was 28, a Black man who stood nearly six feet tall and always wore a baseball cap. He worked at Miller's Fabric Mill, a 60-year-old company that produced bulk linen. Javon's job was to ensure that the massive spinning machines, transforming cotton fibers into thread, operated smoothly. It was a skilled position that paid well. The linen was shipped to Vietnam and Taiwan, where it was returned to the States as pants and shirts. His wife, Mary, had a small beauty shop in the utility room at the back of their rented house. She had a sink, a hair dryer, and the tools of her trade arranged on a small table. Between her regular customers and the occasional "word of mouth" client, Mary made a nice contribution to the family finances. Two days before the July Fourth holiday, Mary was in the kitchen when Javon came in. Holding a small box, Javon said, "I picked up Quentin's birthday present today. I hope he likes it." Mary turned from the sink and saw the box. "Oh, he's going to love it. Grand Prix Racing was what I saw him looking at in the store. He'll love it. Besides, it'll keep him at home instead of outside. There was another damn shooting today."

"Well, that's bad. It's a good thing we're getting close to leaving here. The house downpayment is shrinking every day."

"Leave his game next to the hairdryer. I'll wrap it up later today. He's gonna just love it."

Javon arrived at work one morning and heard some disturbing news. After clocking in, he headed to the employee break room to check if there were any donuts left. Vendors vying for Miller's business always brought donuts. One of Javon's co-workers, Ray Cruz, was talking to a group of employees seated at one of the tables. He was telling the group that someone in Washington had developed a conscience regarding the use of child labor to produce clothing from Asia. Ten-year-old children worked ten hours a day in a sweatshop sewing shirts. They earned 10 cents for each shirt, which would sell for twenty-five dollars in the U.S. Members of Congress recognize a good thing when they see it. Who doesn't want to protect children? Soon, the terms "tariff" and "embargo" began to circulate. The media was exposing the offending countries. Everyone was on board.

Javon and the employees knew where Millers' customers were located. Millers' fabric was the same fabric handled by ten-year-olds thousands of miles away to the east. Everyone at the company was worried about how they might be affected by the outrage back home. It didn't take long for them to discover just how concerned they should be. Millers had lost many of its customers and was downsizing rapidly. The major U.S. clothing manufacturers were pulling up stakes and moving their operations to factories that were monitored for child labor and were more politically correct. As a result, the clothing maker's manufacturing costs increased. They stopped buying from Millers and sought cheaper fabric elsewhere to make up the difference.

Three days later, Javon came to work, more nervous than usual. Millers has laid off dozens of its employees over the past week, primarily administrators and support staff. Javon believed his job was secure because it involved maintaining the machines, requiring skill and training. However, he was preparing for a pay cut. His pay was cut all right, all of it. He didn't possess enough seniority to keep his position, so he joined many of his co-workers in searching for another job. Javon sat in his car, parked in Miller's employee lot, half an hour after he was let go. He cried uncontrollably. He had never been without some form of work since he was nine years old.

"What am I going to do? He wailed." "What am I going to do?"

Javon felt the weight of his situation, much like the statue of Atlas bearing the weight of the world. Images of Mary and Quentin flashed through his mind. Finally, he pulled himself together.

"I'll think of something," he said to himself. "I have skills. I'll find something." He started the car and drove out of Miller's employee lot for the last time.

Javon didn't tell Mary that he'd lost his job. He was the family's main source of income, and he felt embarrassed. He blamed himself for losing his paycheck. He knew the trouble Millers was in and should have been looking for a new job much earlier. Ever since he could remember, Javon worked for his money. He recognized the irony that he lost his job because children thousands of miles away were working to help their parents, just as he supported his parents while growing up. Javon's earliest memory was getting paid to knock on doors and hand out discount flyers from John Johnston's grocery. He was nine years old.

After losing his job, Javon didn't change his routine at home. He continued to wake up at the same time each day, leave for "work" at the same hour, and return home every evening with fabricated stories about his workday. He would say things like, "The new fabric dye was difficult to mix," "They finally got a bigger refrigerator for the break room," and "I got into an argument with the new gal running the spindle." When he shared these stories, Javon felt as if he was still working. It helped ease the tension. He spent his "workday" at the library, either on a PC searching for a job or reading a book. The book provided an escape from his reality.

Two months after losing his job, Javon's work fabrication was working well. Mary didn't suspect he had been let go. Quentin was in fourth grade at Jefferson Elementary and was doing well, with grades consistently better than those of his classmates. Mary had expanded to a second hairdryer and was earning more money. Javon spent his days searching for a job—any job. The only problem with his "still going to work" scheme was time, and he was running out of it. His unemployment benefits were set to stop next month, and his secret bank account was getting low. Javon and Mary had an understanding: Mary had complete control over the money she earned, and the same applied to Javon. They contributed to a joint bank account for their expenses, a college fund for Quentin, and a down payment fund for a house they hoped to buy someday. Mary was unaware of Javon's secret bank account, where he deposited money skimmed from his paycheck. The couple had been putting money aside for a home they could call their own. He wanted to surprise Mary with the money he had skimmed and have enough for the down payment. Each month, Mary would see that the down payment fund still wasn't enough. When Javon knew that they truly had enough, he planned to surprise her with the funds from his secret account. He had spent years stashing money into this account and was close to covering the down payment until he lost his job.

Every Wednesday, Javon's "workday" began at 6:30 a.m. He got out of bed, dressed, and was out the front door by 7. Mary used their only car to run errands and shuttle Quentin around, so he took the bus. He took the same 7:15 bus he always took to Millers. Of course, he wasn't going to Millers. He got off two stops later and caught the bus going downtown. After three stops, Javon got off at Pearl Street and entered the Silver Dollar diner. "The Silver," as it was called, resembled an oversized Airstream travel trailer from the outside. Upon entering through the front door, a long aisle stretched down the center of the diner. To the right of the aisle was a countertop with round vinyl seats on posts, while tables for four lined the left. At the rear was a table that seated six, and that's where Javon headed. Sitting at the table were five of his former co-workers.

Bob Holt was seated in the chair next to the empty one where Javon would eventually sit. Beside Bob was Tyreece "Ty" Hill. On the other side of the table sat Jim "Jimbo" Hanover; next to Jimbo was Frankie Carlotta. Ray Cruz was positioned next to Frankie and directly across from Javon's chair. They all used to work in the same department at Millers and called themselves The Breakfast Club. They had been meeting here since they lost their jobs to stay in touch and share job-hunting ideas.

The Breakfast Club started as their Wednesday night poker game while they worked at

Millers. Poker in the evening gave way to breakfast in the morning. Javon was relieved that Wednesday night poker was no more. He worried Mary might mention one of his fabricated work stories, and the jig would be up. His explanation for not playing poker anymore was that he kept losing and would rather put every extra dollar into their down payment fund. Bob was close to retirement and had plenty of savings. His wife worked as a city accountant. Bob joined the breakfast club because he enjoyed spending time with these guys, and it gave him a reason to get out of the house.

"Hey, Frankie. Any news on your dealer's exam?" Bob asked.

Frankie was trying to get a job in Atlantic City at the casino where his cousin worked.

"I took it two weeks ago and still haven't heard back. I'm thinking about giving my cousin a call. Maybe he can put in a good word to help me out."

Jimbo chimed in. "You should consider moving to Vegas. There are way more casino jobs there."

Frankie said, "Can't do that. Carol likes being close to her parents and doesn't want to move the kids to the desert. Besides, my cousin Riki says I can make more money in Atlantic City."

"I heard Millers might start hiring again." Everyone turned to Ty.

Ty said, "Millers got a contract with Celina Military to supply fabric for the tents they make for the Army."

Nobody believed him. Ty was known for making up stories about the company's business dealings. He was always reminiscing, and he didn't like change.

"Nope, Celina has been buying from Dalton forever. There's no way Millers is getting that business," Ray said emphatically.

Dalton Textiles was Millers' main competitor, and they were also downsizing.

Javon asked Ray, "How are you and Marie doing with the new baby? Is he walking yet?"

Ray replied, "Not yet, but he's getting there. Little Ray will be running the hundred-yard dash before long." After a moment, he continued, "Sorry, guys, but I need to leave early. Marie is taking Little Ray to the doctor for a skin rash and wants me there. I told her I would fit the appointment into my busy schedule."

With that, Ray stood up and walked to the exit door up front. For the next hour, the remaining five club members discussed everything from winning the Powerball lottery to what to say or admit in a job interview.

Two weeks later, Javon entered the Silver Diner for the weekly breakfast club meeting. He had missed the last two weeks because Mary and then Quentin had come down with the flu. He still had to go to work each day and felt guilty about having breakfast with the guys, so he stayed away. Instead, he looked for jobs online at the public library. Not having any luck finding a job online, Javon spent most of his days hanging out in the Home Depot parking lot, snagging day labor jobs from the construction contractors visiting the store. Chuck Harrington typically had the most work for him—minimum wage, cash, and off the books. Two days after receiving his last unemployment check, he felt more desperate than ever to find a job that would pay what he needed. Panic had set in. After two weeks away, Javon returned to the diner, walking down the aisle toward the big table at the end. When he reached halfway, he noticed the table was occupied by unfamiliar faces. Then, he spotted Ray sitting alone at a table near the window. Ray waved and motioned to one of the empty chairs.

"What's up?" Javon asked. "Where is everybody?"

Ray frowned. "It's just you and me, bro. Frankie got his Atlantic City casino job, and Bob decided to retire officially. He and his wife are moving to Phoenix. Jimbo went to work in his brother's heating and air business. I have no idea where Ty is."

"Jeez," Javon replied. "I'm gone for two weeks, and everybody disappears."

Ray said sadly, "Everybody is moving on except us."

Javon asked how little Ray was doing. "Did he get over his skin rash?"

"That developed into an infection. The infection's gone, but not the medical bills. On top of that, my unemployment ran out."

"You and me both."

Ray's voice cracked with emotion as he said, "I don't know what I'm going to do. Marie has to take care of little Ray, so she can't work. I'm two months behind on my mortgage and making trips to my church's food bank."

Javon sympathized. "I know. My stash of money is getting lower by the day. I'm not making enough money with my Home Depot gig, and every time I turn around, Quentin needs new clothes. He's growing so fast. Mary maxed out her Walmart credit card, buying Quentin's clothes and school supplies. I've maxed out my three cards, keeping the car running and cash advancing myself. I'm waiting for the bank to start banging on my front door, looking for their minimum payment." He continued, "On top of that, I think Mary is getting suspicious. She keeps asking questions about Millers and my job."

Ray lowered his voice to a whisper and leaned forward. "I have something I want to talk to you about."

"What's up?"

Ray said, "This is totally between you and me. I have a way we can both make some serious and easy cash."

Javon's eyebrows furrowed. "Things serious and easy, and money's involved usually means something illegal, and I'm not going there."

Ray lowered his voice, "Just hear me out. It's not what you think. No robbing or stealing is involved, just driving from point A to point B."

"Driving what, exactly?"

Ray leaned in closer and lowered his voice even more. "Coke, my cousin-"

Javon cut him off. "Coke? Are you serious? No way and no how. You get thrown in jail for that shit. No, sir, not me."

"Keep your voice down," Ray whispered. "Just listen to what I have to say. I ran into my cousin Hector last Saturday. We had a family cookout to celebrate my sister's five-year cancer remission. We talked about some things."

HECTOR CRUZ WAS A MEAN INDIVIDUAL. He stood well over six feet tall and had long, greasy black hair. He was also covered in tattoos. Hector was finishing up a nickel at Ware State Prison in Waycross, which houses nearly fifteen hundred inmates and is reserved for Georgia's most dangerous criminals. Hector was incarcerated for putting his girlfriend in the hospital, nearly killing her, after holding her hostage for six hours. He received a three-year sentence for that, with an additional two years for putting his fist into a rival prison gang member's face. The offending gang member nearly died. After five years, he was returning to society.

Hector was an "enforcer" for La Sangre (The Blood), one of the most feared gangs in Mexico. They trafficked cocaine for the Sinaloa cartel, and Hector kept that fear alive within the prison walls. He grew up with crack-addicted parents, both of whom were involved in public assistance scams to feed their habit. Hector didn't care about school; his role was to act as a lookout for police and rival gang members near the crack stash house his gang operated. The gangs in his neighborhood dedicated as much time to robbing and killing each other as they did to selling drugs to a captive audience. A month before Hector was set to be released, Don "Pappa" Gonzales approached him. He earned the name Pappa due to his age, although nobody dared address him that way. Gonzales was serving a life sentence for killing an undercover cop during a drug deal gone wrong and was La Sangre's leader inside the prison. "You've done well for me these past years," Don Gonzales said. "Your loyalty to La Sangre is unquestionable. La Sangre is family above all else, and you are a trusted member of Nuestro Familia."

Hector replied, bowing slightly, "Mucho gracias, Don Gonzales."

"A man named Diego Garcia will contact you in the next couple of weeks. He has some work for you."

"What kind of work, Don Gonzales?"

"Diego will tell you what he needs." With that, Gonzales left.

———

BACK AT THE DINER, Ray told Javon, "Hector told me he drives a truck from Miami to Atlanta every two weeks. He's a mule for La Sangre."

Javon frowned. He knew all about La Sangre. Everybody in Grove Park did.

Ray continued, "La Sangre has the concession for the Sinaloa cartel in Colombia. Sinaloa delivers its coke to Miami. La Sangre then takes it from Miami to Atlanta."

Atlanta is home to the world's busiest airport, Hartsfield-Jackson. It has hundreds of passenger flights each day going all over the globe. It's also a major freight hub. FedEx, UPS, and DHL all have a significant presence there.

"Hector says he delivers his load to a warehouse near the stadium."

"Like I said before, I'm not interested. I'm especially not interested in driving to Miami."

Exasperated, Ray said, "Will you shut up and let me finish?" "Hector has drivers in passenger trucks take the product from the warehouse to the freight terminal at the airport."

Javon moves in a little closer.

"La Sangre has a TSA supervisor on the payroll. The TSA guy pays another agent to tell him when it's safe to bring the driver in past security. The supervisor puts in a call to Hector's driver, who's parked near the terminal entrance. The driver gets through security and delivers the load to the freight terminal. That's it.

Javon says quietly, "It still sounds pretty dicey."

"Hector's paying these drivers five thousand bucks a trip."

That gets Javon's attention. "Five grand?"

Ray responds, "You betcha. Some of these guys make twenty grand a month, and it's becoming a problem for La Sangre."

"How is that a problem?"

"It looks suspicious that the same faces are driving through security in different trucks. The blow is coming into the warehouse faster than they can get it out. They need more drivers—drivers they can trust. Hector says he can get us jobs driving to the airport. Five grand, mi hermano. F.I.V.E."

Ray leans back with a smile.

Javon sat back and said, "It sounds tempting, but I'm still going to pass. I have a gig with this contractor I met at Home Depot. The guy's name is Chuck, and his company just landed a contract to renovate an office building downtown." He continued, "I'll be prepping the floors and walls for the electrical wiring. I can make double if I bring my own tools. Maybe I'll start my own contracting business." Javon smiled.

"Well, good luck with that," Ray said sincerely. "I'm going to take my cousin up on his offer."

What Ray doesn't realize is that Hector is offering jobs to other people. If they don't start making room in the warehouse, La Sangre will put things on hold in Miami, and Hector will take a significant pay cut. Hector doesn't know that his employee search has attracted the attention of the Juarez cartel, Sinaloa's and La Sangre's bitter rival.

JUAREZ, Mexico, sits on the other side of the Rio Grande River from El Paso, Texas, and is considered to be one of the deadliest cities in the world. People in rival gangs were killing each other faster than an Indy race car. Bodies hanging off bridges and roadway overpasses with ropes around their neck and signs pinned to their shirts announcing what gang killed them were a common sight. Severed heads and limbs thrown into trash dumpsters were everywhere. Car bombings were considered an art form. Gang members took great pains to inspect their cars before getting in and starting them. Bombers had to be very creative in hiding their work. They were paid well.

The second largest business in Juarez, next to drugs, was guns. The cartels were armed with weapons that did a lot more than shoot a bullet. The illegal arms trade did a lot of business with the cartels. After all, they had the money, and they paid in cash. AK-47s and M4 Carbines were the standard weapons carried by most cartel members. The cartels were also using belt-fed Gatling guns, drone bombs, land mines, and 50 caliber Barretts sniper rifles. As if this wasn't enough, they were adding FGM-148 infrared-guided, shoulder-fired Javelin anti-tank missiles to their arsenal. The Javelin missile would lock onto and follow a tank's heat signature, allowing the person firing it to escape after pressing the launch trigger.

Julio Gomez was an up-and-comer in the Juarez cartel. He stood a little under six feet and had black hair cut very short. When he was eleven, Julio left his home in the Aldama section of Juarez to join the Juarez cartel. Aldama is a violent neighborhood. In addition to the drug business, it also has one of the highest incidents of domestic violence in Juarez. Julio's father, Pablo, was a drunk who could never hold a job. He took his employment woes out on Julio and his mother, beating them regularly.

One night, his wife, Manuela, was late getting dinner on the table. It was late because she had to wait for her neighbor to come home and "borrow" some food. The refrigerator was always empty. Enraged, Pablo ripped the towel rack off the kitchen wall and beat Manuela to death. Julio fled.

The Juarez cartel, unlike Sinaloa and La Sangre, confined its activities to the city. Its leader, Marco Ledesma, kept a tight grip on the cartel's territory. He had an armed wing of the cartel called La Linea. La Linea's primary function was executing people he deemed unreliable or traitorous. La Linea was responsible for many of the bodies hanging from the bridges in Juarez. Julio's job was following the people La Linea had targeted. Nobody would think a child was part of a hit squad. Juarez was full of children begging in the streets.

Julio would follow the unlucky person and phone in his location to his boss. The boss would then dispatch a death squad. At night, Julio helped hang the body under a bridge. He placed a rope around the victim's neck while the others in the squad pulled the body out of the truck bed and hung it under the bridge. When Julio turned fifteen, he stopped following people and started killing them

Sinaloa was expanding and needed another border town to move its cocaine and Fentanyl from Mexico to the U.S. The world's biggest consumer of illegal drugs. The cartel had already claimed Tijuana and set its sights on Juarez. Sinaloa started by devising a plan to assassinate Juarez's leader, Marco Ledesma. Part of this plan was to hang Juarez soldiers' bodies off bridges with signs on their shirts announcing their presence. The bodies were bait for any disgruntled Juarez members looking for a change in their fortunes. The war between Juarez and Sinaloa was at a fever pitch.

Julio was becoming very good at his job. He transferred the skills he acquired from tracking victims and turned himself into a one-man hit squad. His boss would provide Julio with a person's name, confident that they would be dead in short order. Julio was brutally efficient in executing his orders. His nickname within the cartel was "La Muerte" (The Death).

VALERIA SANCHEZ WAS in her kitchen on Monday morning, preparing breakfast for her children, nine-year-old Adelina and her seven-year-old brother, Enrique. Valeria was a rather plain-looking, heavyset woman of thirty-three with brown hair. It was clear that Adelina took after her mother. In contrast, Enrique resembled his father, Ricardo, who was very handsome with jet-black hair. Their house was in a gated community filled with professionals from all walks of life. Living in a gated community was almost a requirement for anyone involved in Mexican politics. Ricardo served as the chief of staff for Thiago Rivera and a deputy in the Mexican Congress, running for senator. Thiago was a strong supporter of efforts to loosen the drug cartels' grip on the Mexican government through corruption and intimidation. He had been targeted for assassination on several occasions. One such attempt occurred several months ago when Thiago and Ricardo were about to enter Thiago's SUV; it exploded prematurely, slightly wounding them and killing the driver. Valeria wanted Ricardo to leave politics for obvious reasons, but Ricardo resisted, saying, "If people don't stand up, what kind of future will their children have?"

Ricardo entered the kitchen, sliding his tie knot to his neck and saying, "Buenos días, mi familia." The children looked up from their cereal bowls, smiled, and said in unison, "Buenos días, Papa."

Valeria said, "Ricky, Camila can't sit with the kids tonight. You'll have to go to the fundraiser by yourself."

He replied, "Valeria, you know how important this is. There are going to be many important people there—people who will support me when I run for Thiago's seat in three years. I, I mean we, need to project me as a devoted husband—which I am—and a family man."

"The fundraiser is for Thiago, not you.

"Yes, it is, but I, we—need to be seen with him. People need to get familiar with my name and face. Being chief of staff is behind the scenes. Nobody knows who I am."

"I understand that, but it doesn't change the situation with Camila."

Before he could reply, a car horn sounded outside. Ricardo said, "Azul is here. I need to go. I'll be home after the fundraiser." With that, he kissed each child on the cheek, did the same with Valeria, and left.

Ricardo entered Thiago's office space in a building next to the Legislative Palace. Thiago had a staff of eight people, and Ricardo's job was to manage them and make sure they kept Thiago's carefully crafted message in the public eye. One of those staff members was Mario Mendoza, Ricardo's deputy, thirty-four, tall with black hair and a closely shaved beard. Mario's good looks made him a magnet for any single woman who saw him, and Mario wasn't shy about taking full advantage of this attention. He seemed to have a new girlfriend every eight or nine months. Although Mario grew up poor, his devoted parents ensured he received an education and avoided falling into the clutches of the Juarez Cartel. Mario's older brother, Castel, was the opposite. The easy money and power of the Cartel attracted him like a moth to a bright light.

When Ricardo entered his office, one of three in Thiago's space, Mario stopped in the doorway holding a cup of coffee and said, "I just got off the phone with Ethan Herrera. He won't be at the fundraiser tonight."

"Damn!" Ricardo said.

Ethan Herrera was a wealthy man who made his fortune mining Mexico's vast copper resources. He used his money to buy favors and ease environmental restrictions around his mines. However, he was having second thoughts about Thiago's chances of winning a Senate seat in the upcoming election.

Mario said, "It's not good. We were counting on him."

"I know," Ricardo said sadly. "Now we don't have enough money for those television ads. We need those ads. If we don't have them, that gives Martinez another edge."

Videl Martinez was the current occupant of the Senate seat that Thiago was after. He had held the seat longer than any other member. He was old, and there were rumors that his staff was covering up his frequent mental lapses, often forgetting what reporters had asked him. He may have memory problems, but his constituency never failed to come through come election time. This time, however, he faced a formidable rival; the polls showed Thiago was making it a tight race.

Mario said, "Well, Martinez is old and needs a wheelchair. I think we should make that a central theme in the campaign."

"I don't want to get in the mud with that. We need to focus on vision and accomplishments, not beat up the old guy. Besides, Thiago isn't getting any younger either."

Mario replied, "People don't understand vision and don't care about accomplishments if it doesn't affect them."

"Well, be that as it may, we're staying on message."

"Okay, you're the boss." Mario turned and left.

Ricardo sat back and thought about Mario. "That jerk. He hasn't paid any dues, and he's telling me how to run the campaign? I don't think so. I know he's angling for my job. I've seen him brown-nosing Thiago. Well, we're going to win this election, and when we do, his ass is gone."

****

Mary had just said goodbye to her last client of the day. It was three o'clock, and Quentin was in his room on the floor, drawing pictures on a yellow notepad. Mary stood in the doorway and said, "Quent, why aren't you playing your video game?"

Quentin looked up and said, "It's only fun when you're playing with somebody, and Glen got grounded and can't come over."

"What are you drawing there?"

"Different cars."

"Can I look?"

Quentin took the pad and handed it to his mother. She looked at the drawing and said, "Quent, this looks really good. I didn't know you could draw so well." Noticing something, she pointed to the picture and asked, "What's this?"

Quentin glanced at what his mother pointed to and replied, "That's an air scoop. I wanted the car to look like one of those race cars on TV. The race cars daddy watches."

Mary thumbed through Quentin's other drawings and said, "Quent, these are really good. Can you draw anything besides cars?"

"I can, but I like cars. I'm going to draw one for a car company and send it to them. Maybe they'll like it enough to turn it into a real car."

Quentin smiled when his mother said, "You're very talented, Quent." He stopped smiling when she continued, "Maybe Glen getting grounded wasn't such a bad thing."

Mary returned the pad and went to clean her "Beauty Salon," as she liked to call it. It was almost four when she finished cleaning. Today had been a good day; she had six clients. One of them was Delores White. Delores told Mary that her neighbor, Jan Stephens, had recently been laid off from her job at Millers and was planning to become a notary. She expressed how good an idea she thought it was and mentioned she was considering doing the same. Mary didn't respond because she was thinking about Javon. He hadn't said anything about Millers laying off people. Something felt different about him, but she couldn't pinpoint exactly what it was. Two hours later, Mary heard the front door open and Javon announcing himself. He entered the kitchen and saw Mary stirring a pot on the stove, and said, "That smells damn good. Biscuits in the oven and gravy on the stove. I'll bet we're having fried chicken tonight. Damn girl, you know I can't get enough of your fried chicken—or you."

Mary turned to look at him, smiled, and said, "Well, listen to you. Mister hot to trot. I haven't made this in a while. The chicken was on sale, so I bought enough for tonight and some more for the freezer."

"Where's Quent?"

"He's in his room. I found him drawing on a notepad this afternoon. Did you know he could draw so well? He had all kinds of car drawings in that pad."

"Well, I knew he liked cars. You know how he makes me go to that big car show at the convention center every year. Nothing like spending hours looking at cars you can't afford."

"Delores White came over for her hair today. She told me her neighbor, Jan Stephans got laid off from Millers. Is Millers laying off people? Do you know anything about that?

Caught off guard, Javon said, "That's a lot of questions." He lied, stating, "I don't know who Jan Stephens is. She might be in the offices next to the plant. I don't know about any layoffs. She probably got fired and is telling everyone she was laid off."

"For someone who works there, you sure don't know a lot of things. If Millers is having problems, you need to find out. This is serious. I'm not playin', Javon."

"I'll head over to the personnel office tomorrow and ask about Jan. Probably won't tell me anything, confidentiality and all that." Changing the subject, he said, "How about I make the mashed potatoes? You can start the collard greens. You know how I love your greens. Extra bacon, please."

MARIO SAT at the table in the kitchen where he grew up, his brother Castel seated across from him. Their mother, Guadalupe, was preparing la comida for them—something she did every Sunday after church. The meal she made today was much smaller than those she cooked when her boys were growing up and their father was alive. Those meals were filled with cousins, aunts, uncles, and grandparents. Now, it was just the three of them. Castel looked at Mario and asked, "How's the election going, mi hermano? When will you be President?"

"Yes, when will you be President?" their mother chimed in.

Mario replied, "I'm not running for President. My boss is running for the Senate, and the polls say we're tied with that old man, Martinez."

Castel asked, "Tied? How can you be tied? Martinez can't even remember where the bathroom is."

"Some people don't like change."

Castel said, "If your boss wins, will you be promoted?"

"I hope so. My other boss, Ricardo Sanchez, is going to run for Thiago's seat in the next election."

"So, if Thiago wins, you'll take your boss's job? Sanchez's job?"

"I don't know. He might decide to stay with Thiago after the election. He'll be the Chief of Staff for a senator. That'll give him more visibility and influence than if he leaves."

"Influence?"

"Thiago isn't really a policy guy. He likes being important and all the perks that come with it. He likes the attention and the free vacations. He depends on Sanchez to advise him on what to vote for."

Their mother interrupted the conversation by placing a large bowl of pozole on the table. "Enough politics talk. Eat your food. I made enough for your wives and niños. Oh, I forgot. You boys aren't married."

When Castel left his mother's, he remained in his car parked in the garage of his mansion-like home. He reflected on what his brother had told him. All this time, he believed Thiago Rivera was the thorn in the cartel's side. He now realized that Ricardo Sanchez was behind Thiago's anti-cartel rhetoric

MARY WALKED into Althea's Beauty and Supply and sat in one of the empty chairs in the waiting area. It wasn't lost on her that she had clients needing their hair done, but she had to go to Althea's to get hers done. She also purchased supplies from Althea's. Mary dreamed of owning her own salon one day, where she wouldn't need to go elsewhere; one of her employees would take care of her. Her daydreaming was interrupted when she heard Althea Gibson say, "Hi, Mary. Are you still taking my clients?" Althea was one of Mary's closest friends. Standing by the reception counter, she heard Mary reply, "You have enough clients. All I hear from mine is their complaints about not being able to get an appointment here." They both laughed, and Althea said, "You have good timing. My two o'clock just canceled. Let's get you in my chair before you steal any more of my clients sitting there." When Mary was seated, she said, "I'm surprised you're not busier. When I called, I didn't think I would get in today."

"Things have been slow. Two of my clients got laid off from their jobs at Millers."

Mary asked, "Is one of them Jan Stephens?"

"No. Who's Jan Stephens?"

****

One day, Julio walked from the kitchen to the living area of the tiny apartment he shared with his girlfriend, Mirabelle, and turned on the TV. He noticed a small white envelope under the door as he approached the recliner. He sighed and picked it up. Julio knew what it contained and cursed that his Saturday had been ruined. He opened the envelope and pulled out a small card. The name "Ricardo Sanchez" and an address were written on it, along with a picture of the man. Julio didn't recognize the name or the face. It didn't matter. He rarely knew who his victims were and did as he was told. He went to his computer and opened Google Maps. He entered the address from the card and switched to "satellite view." The screen displayed a large house at the end of the street, which dead-ended at a very large hill. Behind the hill was a large open field stretching across the housing development. On the other side of the field was a shopping center, with the center's parking lot meeting the edge of the open field.

Mirabelle Flores had known Julio since they were children growing up next door. She had grown into a beautiful woman, loved Julio, and followed him when she was old enough to leave home. Although she disapproved of Julio's occupation, she understood it was the only way for him to survive in such a violent place. She was in the kitchen cooking breakfast when she said, "Julio, I saw that envelope by the door. You promised me we were going to El Paso today so I could get my mother her birthday present."

"I know. We can still go, but I need to get ready for something. I won't be long."

"I mean it, Julio. My mom's birthday is Thursday. This is the only day I have to get her gift."

"I know, mi amor, I promise."

Mirabelle's heart raced, and anxiety washed over her when she saw the envelope on her way to the kitchen. She had never grown accustomed to Julio's occupation. Every time he left their apartment, she wondered if he would return.

Whenever Julio left her, she thought about her father and brother. One day, when she was ten, her father took her older brother, Gael, with him to see his friends. At least, that's what she had been told. She didn't know that Gael, who was eleven, had been involved with the Juarez Cartel, and their father, Miguel, had discovered it. Miguel was heading to the gas station where he knew Gael's friends hung out after school. The Cartel used the gas station as a collection stop for the money earned from their operations. Miguel was going to confront the men who ran the gas station. As luck would have it, when Miguel parked his beaten-down truck, two cars came screeching into the station. Members of a rival gang poured out of the cars and began shooting. It was a robbery in progress. When the people inside the station started firing back, Miguel was hit in the chest as he was getting out of the truck. The bullet shoved him back into the truck. He looked down at his chest and then glanced over to Gael. Gael's head was slumped down, and blood was trickling down his ear.

Growing up was challenging for Mirabelle. Her mother, Juanita, worked two jobs to cover the rent and bills, leaving little time for Mirabelle's upbringing, like most mothers provide. As a result,

Mirabelle grew close to Julio; they faced difficult situations and found comfort in each other's company, serving as a refuge from the violence surrounding them. Mirabelle felt relieved when Julio escaped from his abusive father, convinced it was only a matter of time before one might kill the other. After leaving his father, Julio would stand on the corner five houses from Mirabelle's home and wait for her. He walked with her to school and did the same on the way back. As long as they were together, the violence faded from their minds. As they grew older, Mirabelle felt a sense of sadness for Julio. He never seemed truly happy. He wasn't afraid of the violence; he was the violence. It didn't change her feelings, though. She loved him more than anyone could ever love someone.

Julio finished breakfast, walked out the door, and entered his car. He took out his phone, entered the address into his Google Maps app, started the car, and left, listening to his phone's directions. He planned to conduct some initial surveillance to see what he was up against. He drove into the shopping center and parked at the far end of the lot, adjacent to the field shown on Google Maps. Julio opened the glove compartment and retrieved his Vortex 5000—wide-angle rangefinder binoculars. Leaving the car, he walked across the field and up the hill in front of his target's house. When he reached the top of the hill and lifted his binoculars, the rangefinder flashed 628. Six hundred yards was an easy distance, he thought. Julio watched the house for the next two hours until he saw his target: a large blue Chevy Suburban pulling into the drive-way. The rear doors opened, and two children piled out. The driver and a female passenger then exited the vehicle. Julio took the photo from the envelope and compared it to the man he was looking at. No doubt, this was his man. Julio entered his apartment after his reconnaissance of Ricardo Sanchez. Mirabelle was lying on the couch, reading a book. Relief washed over her when she saw him. She softly said, "Thank you, Jesus."

The next day, Sunday, Julio pulled into the shopping center parking lot before dawn. He reached into the trunk and retrieved a Barrett .50 caliber sniper rifle. He mounted a Vortex 150x scope, heard it click into place, and began walking to his perch. For three and a half hours, Julio patiently waited for his target to appear. At around 7:30, he noticed people leaving their houses and driving away. There was no mystery about where they were headed. It was Sunday, after all. He shifted his focus back to the target's house and the blue SUV parked in the driveway. Julio patiently waited. It had been almost fifteen minutes since he'd last seen a car leave any house on the street. Finally, his target's front door opened. Two children dashed toward the SUV, their parents hurrying behind them. Somebody's late for church, Julio thought.

He brought the scope to his eye, placed the crosshairs on the father's head, and followed him to the driver's door. The family was piling into the SUV as his target went to open his door. Julio gently pressed the trigger and waited. He wanted the politician seated and stationary. The trigger pressure increased as soon as the driver sat down and closed the door. The crosshairs were squarely centered on his head. When Julio noticed the SUV start moving backward, he adjusted his aim and pulled the trigger. Almost instantly after the rifle sent its steel-jacketed high-velocity bullet, he saw the driver's window shatter, and the driver's head exploded. The windshield sprayed red. The SUV slowly rolled down the driveway, hit the curb in front of his neighbor's house across the street, and stopped. Julio kept looking down the scope and saw the passenger door fly open and the mother stumble out. The left side of her face and neck were red with her husband's blood, some of it dripping from her chin. She was screaming and frantically opening the rear door to protect her children. Julio stood up and started walking back to his car. He was hungry and thought about breakfast.

Monday morning, Julio's boss, Jorge Amos, sat at the counter of La Cocina restaurant, eating breakfast and thumbing through the news on his phone. He smiled at what he saw, and said to himself, "Killing that pendejo in front of his family going to church was perfect. I can always count on Julio to get the job done."

IGNACIO PEREZ WAS a top lieutenant in the Juarez cartel. He was in a bitter power struggle with Jose Alvarez. They were both in line to become one of the underbosses of the cartel. He knew he was at a disadvantage for promotion. Everybody liked Alvarez. Perez needed an edge and decided that eliminating his competition was the only option. He had to be secretive, though. He could not be suspected, and even a hint of involvement would mean death and his hanging from a bridge. He trembled at the thought but decided he had no choice. If Alvarez became underboss, his first order would be to kill him and hang him from a bridge. Cleverly, he devised a foolproof plan to eliminate Alvarez.

Julio was more than surprised to receive a call from Ignacio Perez; he couldn't believe that someone like Perez even knew him. A mix of excitement and wariness washed over Julio when Perez requested to meet with him without informing anyone else. Julio was a good soldier and respected Perez's request. Perez instructed Julio to meet him at a cantina across town called Tino's at 9 PM. It would be dark by then, and Tino's was far enough from prying eyes. As Julio approached the cantina, his heart pounded harder than a jackhammer. He had never felt this nervous, and he started sweating. Upon entering the cantina, his eyes immediately scanned for potential threats. He knew how people could emerge from nowhere and cause death. He did it all the time. At the back of the cantina, Julio spotted a man sitting at a table, gesturing to him and pointing to the empty chair across from him. The man appeared to be in his early fifties, wearing a straw hat and sporting a gray mustache. Unbeknownst to Julio, Perez's heart was also pounding like a jackhammer. He was on his third bottle of cerveza. Julio approached the table and took a seat.

"Good evening, señor. Perez," Julio said.

"Good evening, Julio," Perez replied. "Thank you for coming."

Julio began to relax. "No thanks needed. I'm always at your command."

"Marco Ledesma asked me to speak to you in the strictest confidence," Perez said, starting to calm down.

When Julio heard the name "Marco Ledesma," his heart began to pound again. What's happening? he thought. Ledesma? Is this a joke? His mind raced, searching for possible reasons why he was sitting there.

"I'm deeply honored, sir; how can I serve you?"

Lowering his voice, Perez replied angrily, "We have a traitor in our midst, and Señor Ledesma has asked me to take care of it." Flattering and deflecting attention from himself, he... went on, "Señor Ledesma is aware of your service and talents and asked for you specifically to help him with his problem.

Julio leaned in closer. He couldn't believe what he was hearing.

Perez spoke forcefully, "What I am about to tell you stays here. Nobody must ever know we spoke. Is that clear?"

"Of course, Señor Perez. I always follow my superior's orders."

"Bueno," Perez went on, "Señor Ledesma has become aware that Jose Alvarez has been talking to his counterpart in Sinaloa, Miguel Marquez. They are plotting to kill Ledesma and take control of our business."

Julio wanted to ask how they knew this but did not dare.

"Alvarez is a traitor, and Señor Ledesma wants him removed. Your job is to remove him." Perez sat back and watched Julio take it in.

After a moment, Perez stood up to leave. "Julio, your talents are very well known. "Señor Ledesma wants you to kill that piece of shit, Alvarez. Make it look like Sinaloa's work."

With that, Ignacio Perez walked away.

Outside, Julio looked calm, but inside, he was ready to faint.

———

IT WAS STARTING to get dark. Javon anxiously waited in his usual spot in the Home Depot parking lot where he looked for day work, when Chuck pulled up in his truck. He rolled down his window. "Hey, Javon. How're you doing? Sorry I'm late. I got busy at the job site and lost track of time." Chuck reached over to the passenger seat, picked up a stack of papers, and handed them to Javon.

"What're these?" Javon asked.

Chuck replied, "The two on top are for the IRS. They set you up as a "Sole Proprietor" company and assign a Tax ID for you. The bottom three are for the state registering your business, your contractor's license, and your city business license."

Javon frowned and took the forms. "What do I do with them after I fill them out?

"Once you fill them out, get them notarized. Make sure to get them notarized. They won't be accepted if they aren't notarized. Mail them to the address on the form." Chuck reached into his shirt pocket and pulled out a piece of paper. "Here's a list of the tools you'll need. "And the address of the job site. We start in two weeks. Have you thought of a name for your new business?"

"Waters Contractors," Javon said with a smile. "I thought about 'Waters and Son,' but my boy Quentin is going places when he grows up. He's gonna find his own path and not follow me."

"Sounds good to me. Listen, I gotta go. Let me know when you get your licenses, and I'll see you in two weeks." With that, Chuck drove off.

When he looked at the list of tools, Javon's eyes bulged. This is some expensive stuff, he thought. Even if I drain my stash account, I might not have enough. Maybe Ray can front me some cash. He's probably rolling in money with his coke thing. Javon glanced at the list again and took the bus home to get the car. He returned two hours later with the family car and the remaining balance of his stash account. He'd gone to the bank and emptied it. Javon walked up and down the aisles, putting tools into his cart—a hammer drill here, a battery-powered grinder there, everything on Chuck's list. Standing in line to pay, he started to feel anxious. What if I don't have enough cash? He wondered. I added every-thing up, but I don't know what the sales tax is gonna be. Damn. I should get an employee discount for as much time as I spend here. When the clerk totaled his tools, he was $18.34 short. He scanned his items, deciding which one he could buy later. Suddenly, he remembered the twenty-dollar bill he always kept in his sock. When he was a kid, passing out flyers for Johnston's Grocery was a one-dollar bill.

Rolling his shopping cart to his car, Javon realized he had a prob-lem. Where was he going to hide these tools from Mary? Thinking it over, he decided to come clean to Mary about his charade of losing his job. Javon figured that once he started work and got his business license, he'd probably get more sex than he could handle. Javon unloaded the tools from the shopping cart and placed them into the trunk. Then he grabbed Quentin's blanket from the back seat and covered the tools with it. That'll work, he thought. Tomorrow is Friday, Mary's busiest day. It was also Carol Stinson's turn to drive her daughter and Quentin to school, so Mary won't need the car. He thought, I can drop these tools off at Ray's tomorrow and stash them there until I start work in two weeks. Ray will probably want to be my business partner when he sees what I'm up to. Maybe not. He's likely buried in cash. He shut the trunk and got in the car, grinning from ear to ear.

When Javon got home, he noticed a car in the driveway. He parked on the curb and walked over to the strange vehicle. He noticed the Alabama license plate and immediately became agitated. He said out loud, "That dumbass fool. What the hell is he doing here?'" Javon was referring to Mary's brother, Marvin. He couldn't stand the guy. Mister, I got it better than you." Marvin was always bragging about how great he is and how you're not." That jerk had to park in MY driveway," Javon fumed as he entered the house.

"Hey, Dad, Uncle Marvin is here!" Quentin exclaimed, running up to him. "He's going to stay over tonight!"

Terrific, Javon thought.

"Hey, dude. What's up?" Marvin called from the recliner where he was sitting.

Pissed that Marvin was in his chair, Javon replied, "Nothing much, man. What brings you here?"

"Company business. We're bringing on a new distributor here. I'm here to evaluate their systems. Didn't Mary tell you I was coming?"

"Must have slipped my mind."

Mary entered the living room holding a large spoon. "I told you last week he was coming," she said, irritation in her voice.

"Look what Uncle Marvin gave me!" Quentin held up the latest model iPad.

"Wow, that's really nice. Did you say thank you?" Javon asked, glancing toward Mary.

Mary and Javon knew an iPad would help Quentin in school; they just couldn't afford one.

Mary raised her voice, "Of course he did. Now it's time for dinner. I canceled two hair appointments to cook, so you'd better eat every crumb." She turned and walked back to the kitchen.

After dinner, Quentin rushed to his room to explore his new iPad. Mary cleared the table while Javon and Marvin moved to the living room. Javon dreaded the thought of listening to Mr. Moneybags brag about how wonderful his life was. An hour later, Javon announced that he had a long day ahead and was going to bed.

Mary said, "I had six customers today and have eight for tomorrow. I need some sleep, too. Marvin, I'll make up the couch for you."

"Thanks, sis. I have to leave at five, so I'll say my goodbyes now. Thanks for the hospitality," Marvin said, grinning.

Javon replied flatly, "It was great to see you, Marvin. I'm sorry you have to leave so early."

When morning arrived, Javon got out of bed and glanced at the clock. It was just after six. On his way to the kitchen, he saw that, true to his word, Marvin had left. He noticed no effort had been made to fold the blanket and sheet he used. After getting his coffee, Javon thought about his car. He planned to move it off the street and park it in his driveway. He opened the door to go outside and saw that his car wasn't where he had parked it on the street in front of the house. He noticed shards of glass sparkling in the street where he was sure he had parked it. He shifted his gaze to the driveway and saw nothing but an empty space. Marvin's car was not there. Javon started to feel hot. It was like he touched the power line leading into his house. Panic began to consume him. Approximately 19,500 cars have been stolen in Georgia this year. Javon's made it 19,501. He started running up and down the street, frantically searching for his car. Thoughts of his tools and his new business flooded his mind, and images of his new tools and filled-out paper forms flashed in his mind. He began yelling, "NO, NO, NO!" After several minutes, exhausted from running, Javon crumpled to the ground, wailing. When he finally found the strength to rise and start walking back to the house, he realized the inevitable: He was going to have to call Ray.

JULIO STAYED at the table after Perez left the cantina. He thought about what had just transpired. He wasn't being asked; no, he was being told to kill one of the senior leaders of the Juarez cartel. Juan Alvarez was one of Marco Ledesma's senior lieutenants and a good friend. It was a given that Alvarez would be promoted to Underboss. He was very popular with all the cartel members. Killing him was going to be a very difficult task. Julio rose from the table and stepped outside. He took a long walk, contemplating how he would kill Alvarez. It soon became apparent that eliminating Alvarez would be the toughest job he had ever undertaken. As he considered the task ahead, confidence surged within him, and he held his head high. He was La Muerte. Killing was his business, and business was good. He continued his stroll but felt something small and faint tugging at his confidence. What could it be? He wasn't certain. Julio glanced at his watch and cursed. Mirabelle was probably worried about him. He looked at his phone and saw that Mirabelle had left more than a few voicemails. He had turned his phone off before entering the cantina.

Juan Alvarez had two different homes. A palatial hacienda approximately thirty-five miles from Juarez and a smaller house in the wealthy Campestre neighborhood of Juarez. The hacienda was at the end of a four-hundred-yard driveway coming off a private road. A fifteen-foot gate faces the road, and a large guardhouse is at the entrance. There was another smaller guardhouse just before entering the parking area and a ten-car garage on the left side of the main house. A long promenade connected the main house to the garage area. The promenade had arches held up by marble columns with alabaster ornaments at the top. The house was almost 20,000 square feet and filled with all manner of luxury. As visitors entered through the front door, they were greeted by an eight-foot crystal chandelier, trimmed with 24-karat gold, hanging from the thirty-foot ceiling. Persian rugs adorned the floors, and sweeping staircases led to a seven-hundred-square-foot banquet room and a larger, better-equipped kitchen than a five-star restaurant. A fifteen-foot stone wall surrounded the entire estate, while a narrow path meandered from the garage to a building resembling a guest house. However, this building wasn't meant for guests but served as the nerve center for the state-of-the-art security systems that safeguarded Alvarez, his wife, and their three children. It buzzed with activity like a beehive. The security house operated around the clock, staffed by a two-man rotating team. They communicated with seven security personnel, also on a rotation, who patrolled the outer grounds and perimeter of the main house alongside their Belgian Malinois dogs. Infrared sensors were installed throughout the estate to detect body heat from anyone foolish enough to enter uninvited. Motion and vibration sensors were placed around and beneath the estate's surrounding wall. As an additional precaution, a two-man sniper team kept watch from the roof of the main house. During the week, Juan Alvarez stayed at his house in Juarez, where he conducted his business. The house was a fortress, complete with an underground escape tunnel and an armored SUV waiting to whisk Alvarez away from any danger.

He used this SUV to commute from the house to his hacienda. En route, he was accompanied by two identical SUVs filled with security personnel and weapons. Back at the hacienda, the security building controlled a bomb-carrying drone that flew overhead. None of this mattered to Julio. He wasn't the danger coming from the outside; he was the danger coming from within. Julio was a well-known and respected member of the Juarez cartel, and he would use this notoriety to his advantage. No amount of security would protect Jose Alvarez from him.

The next morning, Julio began to devise his plan. He knew he couldn't penetrate Alvarez's defenses, whether at the house in Juarez or at the hacienda. He traveled in armored vehicles, so that option was also off the table. Or was it? He knew the vehicles were virtually impenetrable to bombs. Even if they were vulnerable, he would never get close enough to plant one. Also, the vehicle was thoroughly searched before Alvarez got in. To top it off, there were three identical SUVs. Which one to choose? After some deep thought, Julio grinned. He would have one of Alvarez's security detail bring the bomb to Alvarez inside his Juarez house.

WORKING ON HIS PLAN, Julio called his good friend, Danny Ortega. Ortega was one of the cartel's most creative bomb makers. Ortega once had a target's phone explode as he answered a call.

Without naming his intended target, Julio shared the details of his plan. Ortega informed Julio that he would have something for him the following week. Ever reliable, Danny called as promised. He told Julio to meet him at their usual spot: the Plaza Sendero shopping mall parking lot. He had something that would impress even the most skilled bomb maker. Julio drove into the parking lot and spotted Ortega's car already there. He parked his car and got into Danny's.

"What's up, bro?" Danny fist-bumped Julio.

Julio replied, "Thanks for helping me out with this. It's much appreciated."

"No problem. I love these specialized requests. They get my creative juices flowing."

"So, what did you come up with?" Julio asked excitedly.

With a confident smile, Danny reached behind his seat and presented Julio with four 16-ounce paper cups held in a cardboard container. The cups and containers came from El Pollo Feliz, a popular fast-food chain in Juarez with eighteen locations around the city, one of which was just a block away from Jose Alvarez's house.

"What the hell is this?" Julio asked, holding one of the cups.

Danny replied proudly, "That's one of the bombs you requested. Notice it's a little heavier than you would expect?"

Julio lifted the carrying box with both hands, moving it up and down to check the weight. "It does seem to weigh more than it should, but not by much," he remarked.

"That's because the cups have a false bottom. I put one ounce of plastic explosive in each cup. It's my special blend. The cup has a micro-pressure switch that activates when the cup is filled with ice and soda. The cup goes boom when your guy drinks about a third of his soda."

Amazed, Julio said, "I knew you were good, but holy shit. This is genius!"

Ortega added, "When the cups are full, you can hardly feel the extra weight."

"What if only one of the cups explodes from drinking? Nobody drinks enough from the other three."

Danny replied confidently, "As long as any of the drinks are within thirty feet of the others, the exploding one will set off the others."

Julio smiled and said gratefully, "Thanks, man. You've totally outdone yourself. This is genius. Listen, I have some errands. I'll let you know how things work out." He exited the car and got back in his own.

Driving back to his apartment, Julio realized he had a problem—a very big problem. He knew one of Alvarez's crew made a lunch run every Friday to El Pollo Feliz. He discovered this when he started planning his attack. Walking back to the house from the restaurant, one of Alvarez's crew would carry a large paper bag in one hand and grip the handle of the soda carrier in the other. Julio's problem was getting the soda cups inside the restaurant and into the hands of Alvarez's errand boy. By the time he arrived home, Julio had devised a solution: He would bribe and threaten one of the restaurant employees.

"Here's more money than you'd make in ten years, but if you don't follow through, you won't live to spend any of it, including your family." He smiled at the thought of terrorizing an innocent employee.The next day, Julio walked into the restaurant near Alvarez's house. He approached one of the employees and spoke softly to the pretty woman behind the counter. El Pollo Feliz had employed Juanita Castro for the past two years. She listened to Julio as he took a thick envelope from his back pocket. Julio spread the envelope open so Juanita could see the contents. She gasped and placed her hand over her mouth. She had never seen so much money, and it astonished her. She didn't hesitate or need any threats; she was ecstatic about this strange request. She had no idea what was going on and didn't care.

WHILE JULIO WAS TALKING to Juanita, Mirabelle was at the back of the grocery store where she worked. Her best friend, Ana, was helping her with the weekly inventory and deciding what needed to be ordered from the store's main warehouse. Ana was the same age as Mirabelle and had grown up in the same neighborhood. Glancing at Mirabelle, Ana put her clipboard down and said, "Mir? What's going on?"

"What do you mean?"

"Mir, you haven't said a word since we came back here."

Mirabelle put her clipboard down and replied, "Ana, Julio has been acting strange the last couple of weeks."

"Mir, speaking from experience, he's probably seeing someone. Los hombres son cerdos!"

"Ana, not all men are pigs. Julio certainly isn't. I asked him if he was seeing anyone, and I could tell by how he answered that he wasn't."

"You know what he does. You should find someone normal.

"I've known Julio since we were kids. He's a good person. He's only doing what he does until he can get enough money so we can move to California."

"I don't know, Mir. What would he do when you move? He doesn't exactly have any employment references."

"He has a cousin who lives in San Diego. He works for a big landscaping company and told Julio he could get him a job working there."

"So what did he say when you asked if he was seeing someone?"

"He told me his bosses were giving him something difficult they wanted him to do, and it was harder than he thought."

"I still think you should find somebody normal."

HECTOR WATCHED as the Beach King Air turboprop approached the hastily prepared landing strip that his crew had constructed the week before. The landing strip was situated near Redland, Florida—a tiny backwater town devoid of prying eyes.

Hector grumbled as the large aircraft came to a stop. The cargo door at the rear opened, and a tall man wearing a cowboy hat exited the plane and walked toward Hector.

"Buenos días, señor Hector," he said, approaching with a wide smile. Pepo Salazar worked for the Sinaloa cartel and was responsible for transporting the cartel's cocaine and fentanyl from Mexico to Miami.

Hector replied angrily, "What the hell is this?" gesturing toward the plane.

"It's our newest airplane. It can carry almost twice the product as the other plane."

"Are you serious?" Hector shouted. "I'm having trouble moving what I already have. I can't have you guys sending more."

"Not my problem, bro. La Sangre has the concession with Sinaloa to move our product once it's delivered here. If you can't manage that, then we have a problem."

Hector resigned himself to the situation and told his men standing by their truck to move it and start unloading the plane. "I'm done with this crap," he mumbled to himself, walking away.

Hector found himself in a tough situation. The warehouse in Atlanta was nearly full, and no one was being paid, including him. Sinaloa kept sending him more product without considering his ability to move it. He was responsible for getting the product onto the freight planes at the airport, but he couldn't keep up. Hector wasn't foolish. He knew that if his bosses discovered how much coke was sitting in his warehouse, they would replace him, and he understood what that implied. Coke meant money, money that wasn't going to La Sangre. He needed to change his circumstances. Hector had decided to go into business for himself. He planned to move anyone's product from Atlanta to wherever they wanted, regardless of the cartel involved. He had the airport connection, and he would use it as leverage. If La Sangre wanted to keep things moving, they would need to go through Hector. The same applied to anyone else. Once he had La Sangre taken care of, he would reach out to the Juarez cartel. They had been trying to move into La Sangre's and Sinaloa's operations since they caught wind of La Sangre's airport connection. Juarez would jump at the opportunity to do business with Hector. The prospect of the mountains of additional cash Juarez would bring made Hector smile.

Several weeks later, Hector and Ray stood in the new warehouse Hector had purchased. It was located in the same industrial complex as his existing one but was much larger. The warehouse was plain-looking and blended in well with the surrounding buildings. It featured two large garage doors—one in the front and one in the rear. Trucks would drive through the front door to be loaded and exit out the back.

"This is great," Ray said. "When do you think it will be ready to start sending trucks to the airport?"

Hector replied, "It's going to take some time. I need to find more drivers, and I'm waiting to hear back from my friends in Juarez."

Hector had reached out to his old cellmate, Luis Alaverea, who was still incarcerated, to contact a Juarez gang member at Ware. They would relay Hector's offer to one of the higher-ups in Juarez. This was a very risky request for Luis. Prison gangs were very territorial. Communicating with a rival gang member without permission is a serious violation. Hector understood the rules inside; he could easily overlook them since he wasn't there anymore. Luis decided it would be best to seek permission from Don Gonzales.

———

SITTING at a table in Hector's warehouse office, Ray asked, "Have you decided on that thing I talked to you about?"

"Yes, I have. It's not a good idea to involve outsiders in our business. It's never a good idea."

"I get it, Hector, but this is different. I used to work with this guy. We both got screwed when we lost our jobs. He's not looking for anything other than making a few bucks to get back on his feet."

Hector contemplated Ray's words. He was desperate to clear out "the old" warehouse and fill the one he was standing in. He also knew that bringing in a stranger posed a serious security breach. If they found out, La Sangre would punish him severely for it.

Screw those La Sangre and Sinaloa assholes, he thought. I'm not working for you anymore. I'm the one calling the shots now. Hector said to Ray, "Alright, bring him tomorrow night. He can ride with you. Show him how things work. If he screws up, that's on you, and I don't have to tell you what that means. Cousin or no cousin."

Ray patted Hector on the back. "Thanks, man. This is going to work out great. You get another driver, and I get to help out a friend." Ray pulled out his phone to call Javon.

JULIO SAT at one of the outdoor tables of the Starbucks across the street from Alvarez's house, staring at the front door. He wore a baseball cap and sunglasses in an attempt to hide his appearance. He doubted he was succeeding in his attempt at anonymity and was drenched in paranoia. Julio was convinced Alvarez's henchmen were at the window, pointing at him. He had given Ortega's cups to Juanita over two hours ago and was growing more nervous by the minute. It was past one, and no one from Alvarez's house had made the usual lunch run. He would wait another hour before retrieving the cups. Suddenly, as if his thoughts were being read, the front door opened, and a man wearing a fedora walked out and spoke to the guard at the security gate at the end of the small driveway. Julio watched the gate open and saw Fedora walking towards El Pollo Feliz. His heart began to race like a drum in a marching band as he watched Fedora enter the restaurant. A few minutes later, he emerged carrying a large bag in one hand and a cup holder with the deadly drinks in the other. Julio sighed with relief. Fedora passed through the security gate and headed into the house; thoughts of something going wrong flooded Julio's mind. The bombs didn't go off. Worse, they were discovered, or he was being set up. He scanned the area for anyone behaving suspiciously. The stress became overwhelming. Julio decided that there was nothing he could do at this point. His plan either succeeded or failed, and sitting here wouldn't change that. After a few more moments, he got up to leave and walked to his car, which was parked several blocks away. He had just reached his car when he heard a massive explosion. A smile crept onto his face as he opened the car door. Julio quietly murmured to himself, "Way to go, Danny. I owe you one."

JAVON WAS ALREADY SITTING at the table when Ray entered the Silver Diner. He sat down across from Javon.

Ray asked, "You ready, man?"

Javon replied nervously, "Ready as I'll ever be. I really appreciate you helping me out, man. I still can't believe I'm doing this. If Mary found out, she would leave me in a heartbeat and take Quentin with her."

"Dude, it's so easy, and Mary isn't finding anything but money in your bank account. I've already made four runs and have twenty grand to show for it."

The prospect of getting that kind of money instantly shifted Javon's thoughts from the consequences of what he was getting involved in to the money he would have and using it to start his own business.

"I'm in. What's next?" Javon asked.

"We're going to the warehouse. My cousin wants to check you out. He knows you're an outsider, but I vouched for you. Hector trusts me."

With that, they both got up, left the diner, and got into Ray's car. Forty minutes later, Ray pulled into a parking space four blocks from the warehouse. "We're walking from here," Ray said, getting out of his car. Javon opened his door.

They walked the four blocks and stopped in front of a door of the nondescript warehouse. Ray looked up at the camera, watching them, and waved his hand. There was a loud buzz, and the door opened. Holding the door was a scary-looking dude with tattoos on his face and probably everywhere else on his body. He had a Glock 19 semi-automatic pistol strapped to his side. Javon's eyes bulged when he saw the gun. He thought, "It's getting real now. What the hell am I getting into?" He followed Ray into the warehouse. Looking around, Javon thought the warehouse didn't seem all that special. It was just a big space with a twenty-foot ceiling. There were shelves on the walls, but only a few had boxes on them

"Follow me," Ray commanded.

Ray walked to the back wall and waved at the tiny pinhole camera under one of the shelves. There was another loud buzz, and Ray pulled the shelf with the camera toward him. As if by magic, a portion of the back wall opened to reveal another large room. It was filled with wooden crates and boxes stacked on top of each other, almost to the roof.

"Holy shit!" Javon said. "Are all of those crates filled with coke?"

Ray replied, "You bet. Hector wants this stuff out of here as quickly as possible. That's why you're here."

They walked through the warehouse, navigating a narrow path between the crates. The path led to an open door. They entered a small office and saw Hector on the phone, yelling at some unfortunate person on the other end. Javon took in what he was seeing and grew agitated. He became even more agitated when he saw the AK-47 rifle propped up against the wall. Hector finished his call and slammed down the phone. Asshole!" He yelled. "I'm going to kill that puta when I catch him." Turning his attention away from the phone, he looked at Javon while talking to Ray.

"So, this is your friend from work?"

"Yeah, cuz, this is Javon", Ray replied

"You didn't say anything about him being an outsider. He's black." After a pause, he looked at Jevon and said, "No offense, man. We usually only work with our own, if you know what I mean."

Javon began to sweat. The moisture started beading on his forehead.

Ray countered, "He can drive a truck. He can help you move product just as good as anybody else, and he knows how to keep his mouth shut."

Looking at Javon, Hector said, "Well, we'll see about that. Ray will fill you in on the details."

"Yes, sir", Javon said meekly.

Hector chuckled, "You hear that, cousin? He called me, sir. I like that. It shows respect." Looking straight at Javon, Hector spoke in a menacing voice, "Now let me tell you what else to respect. I don't tolerate screw ups. If you screw up, you're going to find yourself with a bullet in your brain. Then you'll get cut up and your parts put in trash dumpsters around town. Comprende?"

Javon nearly collapsed upon hearing this. He wanted to get out of there as quickly as he could. The sweat on his forehead began to trickle down his face.

DEFENDING JAVON, Ray said, "C'mon, cuz, you don't have to be like that. He's okay. We already talked about this."

Hector smiled, "Alright. Your truck is ready. Take him with you and show him what's what. My TSA guy at the airport clocks in at seven tonight. You know the drill." He turned his attention back to his phone and started dialing another unfortunate person's number.

Ray and Javon left the office and headed down another path through the crates. They arrived at a door leading into a large garage with two box trucks inside. The lettering on the outside of the trucks read, "Rodgers Wholesale Plumbing Supply." The rear liftgate was rising on the truck nearest the garage door, with one of the warehouse crates on it.

A man wearing a blue baseball hat holding the handle of a pallet jack impatiently waited inside the truck to load it.

Ray pointed to the crate being loaded and said, "That's fifteen million dollars worth of 'yeyo' going into that truck." Yeyo was the cartel term for coke.

"Seriously?" Javon asked. "That much cash for what's in the crate?" Thoughts of Hector and his gun faded away. "Maybe I should stick around instead of just making a couple of runs with that kind of money." Ray frowned. He didn't have the heart to tell Javon what his situation really was—what he had signed up for and didn't know about it. Ray knew the score. You can come in, but the only way you're leaving is with a noose around your neck hanging from a bridge with a sign pinned to your skin. It's pinned to your skin because you're naked with your dick and balls stuffed in your mouth. He would wait for a more opportune time to break the news to Javon. Ray said morosely, "Get in. Time to make some money."

It was a twenty-minute drive to the airport. Ray barely spoke. He would only speak the minimum required to answer Javon's barrage of questions. Ray was depressed. From the start, he should have told Javon what he was getting into. This wasn't some part-time gig he could walk in and out of. Javon was so desperate after his car and tools were stolen; Ray just wanted to help him. Maybe he half-believed Hector would let Javon leave after a couple of runs since he was an outsider. Ray knew the score, what he was getting into, and the consequences of disobedience. He deeply regretted not being upfront with Javon, but it was too late now. Ray came out of his thoughts as he pulled the truck to the side of the access road leading to the airport's cargo terminal. The terminal gate was ahead, off to the right. He got out and lifted the truck hood, pretending there was engine trouble. If a cop pulled up, he would say his company was sending a mechanic. He got back inside the truck and explained to Javon, "We wait here until the TSA guy ties a white handkerchief to the gate. When he does that, we know it's okay to pull up and be let in. We're looking for a Consolidated Freight plane with the tail number N904DE." After about fifteen minutes, Ray and Javon spotted a figure in a TSA uniform tying a white cloth to the gate fence. Ray jumped out of the truck, closed the hood, and then jumped back in and started the engine. "Showtime," he said. He pulled the truck up to the gate and handed the guard an air freight manifest for Consolidated Freight along with a Bill of Lading. The TSA guard made a show of examining the paperwork and pointed to another access road leading to Consolidated's terminal. Ray put the truck in gear and started down the access road.

They drove for about a quarter of a mile, passing the huge freight terminals of other carriers. Consolidated's was the second-to-last one on the left. In front of the terminal's hangar sat a Boeing 747-400 cargo plane, illuminated by the mercury vapor lights surrounding it.

Ray checked the tail number and drove up to the loadmaster, who was directing a multitude of forklifts coming and going from the terminal's loading platform. Ray got out of the truck and handed the loadmaster his paperwork. The loadmaster made a show of reading the documents. A faint smile appeared as he thought about the twenty-five thousand dollars he had just earned. He passed the papers back to Ray and instructed one of the forklifts to pull the crate out of Ray's truck and load it onto the plane. Driving back the way they came, Javon said, "That's it? That's all we have to do?"

Ray responded, "That's it, man. Time to get paid."

Half an hour later, they pulled into Hector's warehouse.

"I'll meet you back at my car," Ray said as Jevon exited the truck.

He was sitting in Ray's car when he saw Ray come out of the warehouse. He got into his car and handed him a white envelope. Smiling, he spoke to Javon, "Here you go, man."

"What's this?"

"It's your half for tonight's run."

Javon opened the envelope and gasped. "How much is in here?"

"Twenty-five hundred bucks."

"That's enough for me to buy my tools again!" he said excitedly.

Ray didn't say anything.

"So, the next time, I'll go by myself and make five grand?"

"You got it. Hector wants you back in two weeks.

Javon considered telling Ray he wasn't going on another run, but the thought of making another five thousand dollars changed his mind. He felt elated, but that elation quickly turned into dread when he considered having to deal with Hector by himself.

AFTER BLOWING up Alvarez's house, Julio returned to his apartment and immediately turned on the TV. News of his handiwork was on every channel. He switched off the TV after several minutes. He just wanted to confirm that the bombs had exploded in Alvarez's house and didn't need any further information. The next day, Julio was grabbing lunch from a street vendor near his apartment. Just as he unwrapped his torta, his phone rang. He glanced at the caller ID and saw it was his buddy, Danny Ortega.

Julio thought, He's probably figured out that it was his bombs that killed Alvarez and is freaking out. That's okay. Once I explain that it was Ignacio Perez who ordered the hit and Marco Ledesma gave permission to do it, Danny will calm down. He answered the call and heard Danny yelling.

"You messed up, man. You really messed up!"

Julio responded calmly, "Hold on. Just hold on. I know why you're calling. I'm sorry I wasn't truthful with you about what I was going to do with the bombs. I was ORDERED to kill Alvarez." Julio went on to recount his meeting with Perez.

Ortega spoke with panic in his voice, "Alvarez isn't dead. He was at his hacienda when the house exploded. Alvarez's goons just paid me a visit. They knew I made the bombs. Sorry, dude, I had to tell them I made them for you, but I didn't know what you were using them for. I swear, Julio, they were going to kill me. They told me Perez was behind the attack, and I would end up like him if I didn't tell them what you said to me."

"What do you mean, end up like him?

"Perez is dead. He's probably hanging from a bridge somewhere. Watch out, Julio. They're coming for you."

Julio hung up and looked up the street at his apartment building. His head was on a swivel, scanning everyone around him for potential threats. He thought, "I stuck to the plan. Am I being set up? Why is Danny so freaked out?" Not taking any chances, he quickly walked back to his apartment and went inside. He moved the couch and pried open the panel he had cut into the wall. He reached in and pulled out a small backpack. This was his "go bag." It contained a change of clothes, fake glasses, fifty thousand dollars in hundred-dollar bills, assorted IDs, and forged passports that matched the IDs. He grabbed the backpack and bolted out of the apartment.

When Mirabelle came home from work, she noticed the couch had been moved away from the wall and saw a hole in it. Her hand flew to her mouth as she gasped. She yelled from the doorway, "Julio!?" She rushed into the apartment, calling out his name. Terror gripped her as she dashed to the bedroom, fearing Julio was dead inside. When she didn't find him, she began to calm down. She pulled her phone from her back pocket and called Julio. To her immense relief, he answered. "Julio! Something happened in our apartment. Are you okay?"

"Yes, mi amore. I had to leave quickly. I'm sorry if I scared you."

"Julio, what's going on? You've been acting strange for weeks, and now I come home to this? Did you do something? Should I be afraid?"

Trying to soothe her, Julio replied, "No, of course not. I would never get involved in something that might hurt you. I talked to my bosses, and everything is fine. I have to be away for a while, but everything will be good. I promise. I'll call you as soon as things settle down. Don't worry." Mirabelle ended the call. "Maybe Ana is right. I should find someone normal."

LUIS APPROACHED DON GONZALES, who sat at one of the large metal tables in the common area of Ware prison, inside cell block D. Luis asked, "You wanted to see me, Don Gonzales?"

Gonzales replied, "Yes, I need you to get in touch with Hector. Sinaloa is sending him a man from our good friends in the Juarez cartel."

"Sinaloa?" Luis asked incredulously.

"Yes, apparently, this guy, Julio Gomez, tried to kill someone named Alvarez, who is a lieutenant for the leader of the Juarez organization. There's some kind of power struggle happening inside Juarez. Another lieutenant, a guy named Perez, was behind the hit on Alvarez. Gomez is Juarez's top Sicario. He's a very skilled assassin, though not so skilled this time. Alvarez found out about Perez's plans and had him killed, but Gomez managed to escape. He's looking to stay alive and switch sides. He wants to offer his skills to La Sangre.

"Nothing like a little cartel infighting. Too bad for them," Luis chimed in.

Gonzales continued, "Juarez has been trying every way it can to gain control of our airport connection and set up its own operation. This guy, Gomez, has all sorts of contacts inside Juarez and knows what they're up to and how they plan to take over Hector's operation."

"I guess Juarez is about to find out that their best sicario is now ours. We... "

Gonzales interrupted Luis, saying, "No, they are not going to find out anything. Your job is to inform Hector that Gomez is coming, and he needs to work with him. Julio has to learn about our operation and tell us how to protect it from Juarez trying to take it. Tell Hector what we discussed and never mention this again. Under no circumstances can Juarez discover that we have their man. Now, go." Luis stood up and walked toward the prisoner's wall phone next to the guard station. Halfway there, he remembered he had already used his call for the day. He'd have to call Hector tomorrow.

DIEGO GARCIA MET Julio at the same Taco Bell where he had met Hector when he was released from Ware. Julio entered the restaurant and spotted a man with a red bandana stuffed in his front pocket sitting at a table in the rear of the dining area. Julio had been instructed to look for someone with a red bandana. He didn't approach the man. Instead, he went to the counter and ordered a meat and bean burrito with a large orange soda. After getting his food, Julio sat at a table in the front of the dining area, facing red bandana. Julio wasn't there to eat; he was there to observe. He didn't trust anyone, especially people he didn't know. Julio had eaten half of his burrito when he looked up and gave a slight wave of recognition toward Diego. He got up with his tray and drink, walked over, and sat at Garcia's table. Diego said, "Pretty clever, dude. You blended right in. Nice touch, pretending not to know me. I didn't catch on until you waved your hand. I'd probably be a dead man if your hand had held a gun."

"Look before you leap," Julio replied.

"My name is Diego. That was some serious trouble you got yourself into back in Juarez."

Julio spoke dismissively, "Not my fault. Perez was one of Ledesma's top guys. I do what I'm told. It's their problem that one of their cholos is a traitor. They might cut me some slack, given the circumstances. I'm not interested in finding that out; that's for sure. I'm gone. I don't want anything to do with assholes who don't have their shit together."

"Can't argue with that. Alright, we need to go." Diego stood up. "We're going to meet Hector, and I'll give you a heads-up. Hector is a lot to take in when you first meet him." They got into Diego's car and drove out of the parking lot. Diego didn't notice the blue Toyota truck parked three cars over that had started its engine and began to follow them.

JAVON WAS GETTING ready to make his twelfth run to the airport when he saw two people he didn't recognize walk into Hector's office. Javon kept telling himself he was going to quit, that this would be his last run. But those thoughts vanished every time he got back in his car with an envelope containing five thousand dollars. He had to figure something out if he wanted to start his own business. He couldn't do that while working with Hector at the same time. Hector didn't give him a schedule; he had to be available whenever he received a text on his burner phone. He couldn't tell Chuck he needed to leave the job site to deliver fifteen million dollars worth of coke to the airport and would be back in three hours. He could say to Hector that he was done, but damn, look at all this money. Mary was becoming suspicious of his comings and goings at all hours. He only made things worse by buying a new Monarch SUV to replace his stolen car. "That was really stupid", Javon thought. "First, I don't have any cash, and now I have too much, if that's even possible." Unbelievable!

Diego knew Hector was in his office because he could hear him yelling into the phone halfway down the hallway. Diego and Julio exchanged glances, and Diego shrugged. "That would be Hector," he said, opening the office door. They walked in just as Hector slammed the phone down. Talking to himself, Hector said, "I'm going to kill that piece of shit. He's a dead man hanging from a bridge." Julio and Diego looked at each other again. Hector turned his attention away from the phone and looked at Julio.

He smiled and said, "Señor Gomez. ¿Cómo estas?" He got up to shake Julio's hand. "I've heard a lot about you. I can use a guy like you. We have a big operation here, and it's going to get a lot bigger." Since Hector learned Julio would be coming to join him, he started scheming. He was about to make new enemies when he parted ways with La Sangre and Sinaloa. Someone like Julio could take care of those enemies. "Please, take a seat," Hector said, gesturing to one of the chairs in front of his desk. He told Diego to leave and close the door behind him. For the next two hours, Hector filled Julio on how things worked. He didn't want to share his plans with Julio, but he showed him the new warehouse and needed Julio to set up its security.

Julio spent the following three weeks observing how Hector managed his operation. He made multiple trips to the airport with Ray and took time to learn how Hector paid the TSA agents. He identified several major inefficiencies, which he discussed with Hector.He also installed the security system in the new warehouse and prepared it to start receiving product from Miami and transferring crates from the old warehouse. Julio called Mirabelle every Sunday to let her know he was okay and to share what he was doing at his new job. He always dodged the question whenever Mirabelle asked him when he was coming home. One day, Julio walked into Hector's office to deliver the good news.

"All set, boss. The new place is ready to go. We can start on the tunnel after you buy the building behind us. When do you want to start moving the crates?"

"You're done?" Hector asked.

"Sí, I have the security system up and running, the hydraulics are working for the loading dock lifts, and the fire suppression system is ready for testing."

"Perfect." Hector paused for a moment and then said, "Close the door; I want to talk to you about something." For the next hour, Hector outlined his plans to take over La Sangre's Sinaloa concession in Miami. He also asked Julio about approaching the Juarez cartel and bringing them into Hector's new venture. Hector said, "That's it, man. What do you think?"

Julio replied, "It sounds great. Have you considered that La Sangre and Sinaloa aren't going to agree with this? They're going to come at you hard. Really hard."

"That's where you come in. We're going to need your talents to send a message. Coming at us hard is a bad idea and won't work."

Julio asked, "We? Us?"

"Julio, you've done an excellent job turning this place around and setting up the new warehouse. I couldn't have asked for more. I've decided to make you a partner and give you ten percent of the pie."

Julio gasped, "Really? A partner with ten percent? Dios mío, Hector! I can't believe you're doing that for me. Shit. A month ago, I was running for my life with nowhere to go, and now look at me. I'm going to be rich!"

Hector chuckled, "We make a great team. We're going to be bigger than La Sangre and Sinaloa combined.

"You bet we will," Julio said.

"Okay, Julio, let's start moving these crates into the new place."

ANA WAS in her Aunt Sofia's kitchen, helping her bake the cake for her cousin's promotion party. When the cake was in the oven, Ana left her aunt and started walking home to the same house she grew up in. Halfway there, she called Mirabelle. When she answered, Ana said, "Mir. My aunt Sofia is having a party for my cousin on Saturday. He got a big promotion at work. I want you to come."

"Ana, is this another one of your schemes to set me up with somebody? You know, Julio and I love each other."

Lying, Ana said, "It's nothing like that. You wouldn't like him. He's too involved with his work. I know you love Julio, but I thought you'd like to get out of your apartment."

"I don't know. I was planning on taking Antonia's shift at work. I need the extra money now that Julio is away. Besides, I already told Antonia I would take her shift."

"Antonia's shift doesn't start until four. The party is at noon. You can still work."

Thinking about being around people enjoying themselves, Mirabelle said, "Ok. You're right. I'm getting tired of being in this apartment. Work, home, work, home. It's beginning to get to me."

Saturday, Mirabelle approached the front door of Ana's aunt's house. She heard the sound of music and people talking coming from the backyard. Deciding not to ring the doorbell, she walked around the side of the house to the back. There, she saw that the backyard was full of people talking and laughing. Next to the house's back door, she saw a large table filled with food and a smaller table with her cousin's cake. She scanned the backyard, looking for Ana, but didn't see her. She walked through the open back door and saw Ana putting beer cans into a large cooler. Maribelle said, "Hi Ana."

Ana turned her head and said, "Hey, Mir! You came!"

"You were right. I needed a break from my cat and that apartment. This is a big party."

"Everybody is someone's cousin. I can't even remember everyone's name. Here. Help me take this outside. It's heavy." They both grabbed the cooler's handles and took it outside. As soon as they put it down, people started taking the cans inside.

Ana said, "Well, that's going to last about ten minutes." Suddenly, remembering her motive for asking Mirabelle to the party, she said, "Come here. I want to introduce you to my cousin."

Ana took Mirabelle's hand and walked to the large barbeque grill several yards from the cooler. Three men were gathered around it, with one cooking carne asada, hamburgers, and chorizo on the grill. Ana tapped one of the men on the shoulder and said, "Mario. This is my best friend, Mirabelle." She turned her head to look at Mirabelle and continued, Mirabelle, this is my cousin Mario Mendoza. He's going to be President one day. Mario looked at Mirabelle, smiled, held out his hand, and said, "Pleased to meet you, Mirabelle."

She took his hand and said, "It's nice meeting you. Congratulations on your promotion. Who do you work for?"

Mario smiled and replied, "I am the Chief of Staff for Thiago Rivera. He will be President one day soon, and so will I."

Ana said, "Excuse me. I have to go check the cooler. It probably already needs refilling."

Ana quickly left with a slight smile, leaving Mirabelle and Mario to get acquainted. Mirabelle looked up to the much taller Mario and said, "So, are you going to be Mexico's President also?"

Mario replied with a smile, "Someday. I'm working on it. Will you vote for me?"

"Well, I'm not sure. Why don't you tell me why I should vote for you?"

"Why don't we sit over there, and I'll tell you?"

Throughout the party, Ana kept an eye on her cousin and friend. They seemed oblivious to the people around them. She looked at her phone to check the time. Mirabelle was going to be late for work.

Javon was at home when he received a text from Ray. Hector wanted them to come to the old warehouse ASAP, but no reason was given. Javon knew Hector and the new guy were working on getting the new warehouse ready; it probably had something to do with that.

"Damn," Javon said. "Mary's not going to like me leaving just before dinner. This is only going to make her more suspicious." He walked into the kitchen.

"Mary, I need to go to the shop. One of the spindles broke, and I have to fix it. Shouldn't take long."

Mary, with her hands on her hips, replied, "Damnit, Javon, this is the third time you've had to leave just before we sit down to dinner. What's going on with you and that job?"

"It's a good thing, Mary. The fact that they call me when there's some kind of emergency shows my value. It's another bargaining chip for a promotion and raise," he lied.

Mary turned back to the stove. "Well, sometimes, being with your family and having a present father is more important than some broken whatever at work."

"It's probably another bearing assembly wearing out. I'll be back before you even notice I'm gone."

Javon entered the old warehouse and began walking toward Hector's office. He wondered where everyone was and why the overhead lights were off. "I thought this was some important meeting," he muttered to himself. Since all the crates had been moved to the new location, Javon could see Hector's office as soon as he stepped into the back section of the warehouse. He approached the door and saw Hector, who appeared to be sleeping with his head resting on the keyboard of his PC. "What the hell?" he exclaimed. Javon started to speak to Hector when he noticed a red liquid coursing through the keyboard and dripping onto the floor. Confused, he struggled to process what he was seeing. Glancing to his left, he stumbled back against the door. He saw Ray lying on the floor with a hole in his forehead and a pool of blood surrounding his upper body. Javon began to hyperventilate, trying to get control of himself. He didn't understand what he was seeing. Just as he started to turn and run, he froze when he saw what was in front of him. He was looking at the barrel of a suppressed Sig Sauer 9mm pistol. Julio was behind it. Javon closed his eyes just before the hollow-point bullet left the gun.

"Piece of crap outsider," Julio said, looking at Javon on the floor. Javon's forehead had a perfectly round hole that was the exact size of the bullet that made it. Blood squirted out as his heart made its last few beats. Julio reached into his back pocket, pulled out his Iridium Satellite phone, and dialed a number. When the call connected, Julio said, "It's done. Juarez now controls La Sangre's Sinaloa concession. La Sangre's crew is dead, and the TSA agents at the airport are ours.

"Excellent. I knew you would be successful. We'll start getting things moving on our end." Jose Alvarez ended the call. Julio walked out the front door of the old warehouse and spotted the blue Toyota that had followed him after leaving the Taco Bell a few weeks earlier. Danny Ortega parked and got out.

"All done?" Ortega asked.

Julio replied, "Yeah, it's done. I left a few loose ends in there."

"No problem. I have just the solution." Ortega opened the camper shell on the truck and pulled out eight shoeboxes. Each shoebox contained one pound of C4 plastic explosive connected to a deto-nator and a burner cell phone. Each phone was set to receive a conference call. They each took four and began placing them around the warehouse. Twenty minutes later, they got into the Toyota and started driving away. When the Toyota's odometer indicated they had traveled two miles, Ortega pulled over to the side of the road, retrieved a burner phone from the center console, and called a number. Seconds later, they heard a thunderous boom. When Julio returned to the motel room he'd been staying in since his arrival, he called Mirabelle. He was surprised she didn't answer.

Julio had become suspicious right after his cantina meeting with Perez. There was no way someone as high up as Ignacio Perez would meet directly with a sicario and be so secretive about it. He quietly began gathering information about Perez. Apparently, not so quietly, because shortly after he started asking questions, he was summoned to meet with Alvarez at his hacienda. A black SUV was sent to pick him up. He was shown into Alvarez's library, where he saw Marco Ledesma conversing with Alvarez. Without any introductions, Ledesma asked Julio what he knew about Perez and why he was asking about him. Julio recounted, in detail, his meeting with Perez at the cantina. When he finished, he noticed Alvarez and Ledesma exchanging glances but saying nothing. After an uncomfortable silence, Ledesma said, "Thank you, Julio. You can leave us." Just as Julio got into the black SUV to take him home, one of Alvarez's assistants approached him and said, "Señor Alvarez wants you to return to the library."

A week later, Julio returned to Alvarez's hacienda and laid out an elaborate plan. They would use Alvarez's "failed assassination" to seize La Sangre's Miami connection and make it their own. This would provide the Juarez cartel a significant expansion inside the United States and severely weaken their rival, Sinaloa. The most crucial part of Julio's plan was Don Gonzales's willingness to betray La Sangre and help Juarez, tricking Hector into accepting Julio. Gonzales was getting old. He knew things were changing inside La Sangre, just as they were inside Ware prison. He was being shoved aside. Helping Juarez would be his way of showing La Sangre and Sinaloa that he was still in charge. He still wielded power.

THE LAST GUESTS attending Javon's funeral reception had finally left Mary's house. It was late evening. Quentin was asleep in his room while Mary found herself alone, sitting in a chair, still in disbelief. How could Javon be involved with drugs? Not just drugs, but a cartel? What on earth was going on with him? What am I going to do? How is Quentin supposed to grow up without his dad? How was she going to cope without her husband? These were the questions swirling in Mary's mind between bouts of immense grief. She had no answers, nor did the authorities, regarding how Jevon became involved with a drug cartel. People from the Atlanta police, the FBI, and Homeland Security all questioned her extensively. She felt as though she was being interrogated and that they suspected she was somehow involved. They obtained a warrant and searched her house from top to bottom, making a mess of everything. She and Quentin had to go to a neighbor's house while strangers ransacked her home. After an hour of being lost in thought, Mary rose from her chair and peeked in on Quentin, sleeping in his bed. She worried more about Quentin's grief than her own. She silently closed his door and went to her bed, knowing she needed rest. When Mary woke the next morning, she was filled with determination. Javon was gone, and the reason didn't matter. Quentin mattered. He didn't have a father, but he did have a mother who was going to raise him. She would do whatever it took to ensure his success in life. She wasn't going to wallow in grief at Quentin's expense.

Several months after Javon's funeral, Mary received a letter from Citizens Federal Bank addressed to Javon. She looked at the letter and initially thought it was a credit card solicitation. She and Javon had never done any business with Citizens Federal. She started to throw it away but reconsidered, thinking she could use another card as a safety net. Inside was a letter informing Javon that his safety deposit box was due for renewal in thirty days. The yearly renewal fee was $650, and the bank branch where the box was located was listed at the bottom of the letter. The next day, Mary drove to the bank branch and presented the letter to one of the tellers. Mary asked the female teller, "Can you tell me what this is about?"

The teller replied almost sarcastically, "It's a renewal letter for a safety deposit box."

Mary said, her voice tinged with anger, "Yes, I can see that. This is addressed to my husband, who died recently. We've never done any business here. Why would you send him this notice?"

Changing her tone, the teller replied, "I'm so sorry. That's terrible. You have my deepest sympathies." She continued, "Your husband does have a box here—number 1175. Its yearly renewal is due next month."

Mary asked, "Can I see it? Can I open it? I don't know anything about this."

The teller said, "Yes, you can. But first, you'll need to fill out a release of liability form and provide a notarized copy of his death certificate. After we receive those, the bank can release the box to you."

Mary was back at the bank the next day with documents. She spoke to a different teller this time and said the same thing she told yesterday's teller. The teller summoned her boss, explained the situation, and gave him the papers that Mary had brought.

"Hello, Mrs. Waters. I'm Tyler Wilcox, the assistant manager. I'm so sorry for your loss." He reviewed Mary's papers and said, "Everything is in order here. Let me get the master key and open your box for you." Tyler returned a minute later and escorted Mary to the Safe Deposit area in the bank. He located Javon's box and inserted his master key. He turned the key and slid the box out, placing it on the table in the center of the room.

Tyler said, "Here you are, Mrs. Waters. I'll leave to give you some privacy. Again, my deepest condolences. With that, Tyler left Mary staring at the box before her. Her hands trembled as she opened the lid. She gasped when she saw the contents, which were stacks of hundred-dollar bills. Her knees nearly buckled at the sight. "Javon, what the hell are you doing?" she thought. "Where did you get all this money?" She raised her head and quickly scanned the room. Noticing no one, she pulled out one of the stacks and examined it. The paper wrapper around the stack had $5,000 printed on it. Mary gasped again. She closed the lid and returned the box to its slot. Mary left the room and headed to Tyler's office. Tyler looked up from his desk. "Hello, Mrs. Waters. Is there something I can assist you with?"

"Yes, Mr. Wilcox. I have a problem, and I don't know what to do. May I show you?" Tyler stood up from his desk and accompanied Mary back to the box. She removed it from its slot and placed it on the table. Opening the lid, she looked up at Tyler.

"That's quite a lot of money," Tyler remarked. "How can I help you?"

"I don't know anything about this. I don't know what to do with this money. I can't just put it in my purse."

"I understand your concern. I have a solution. Please come back to my office." Tyler took the box and walked back to his office. He picked up his phone and summoned one of the tellers to come to his office. When the teller arrived, Tyler said, "Hi, JoAnn. Can you assist Mrs. Waters? She needs to convert this money into a cashier's check."

"Of course, Mr. Wilcox. I'd be happy to help." With that, Tyler began removing the cash from the box. Mary watched him, becoming more agitated with each stack placed on the desk. After finishing, Tyler said, "That's fifty-three thousand dollars, Mrs. Waters. Would you like the cashier's check made out to you?"

Mary whispered, "Jesus, Mary, and Joseph. Javon, what did you do?" Then, speaking louder, she replied, "Yes, that will be fine."

JoAnn left to get the check. Tyler then pulled out a white envelope with the name "Mary" written on it from the box. "I think this is for you," he said, passing the envelope to Mary. She opened the envelope and saw it contained a letter. She reached to pull it out but decided to read it when she was alone. After getting her cashier's check, Mary walked back to her car. She got in and immediately pulled out the letter.

My darling Mary,

I'm so sorry you're reading this. I love you and Quentin more than anything in this world. The only thing I ever cared about was making you and Quentin safe and happy. I had such plans for us. I ruined everything. Please know I intended to make a better life for all of us. I screwed everything up. The letter continued to tell Mary about his job loss, his business dealings with Chuck from Home Depot, his conversations with Ray, and his involvement with Hector. He explained how he tried to leave Hector as soon as he had enough money to replace his stolen tools and how Ray warned him that Hector would kill him if he did.

The money in the box is for you. It cost me my life with you and Quentin, and I know you will use it for something good. It came from a bad place, but it's going to a good place. I love you so much and am so sorry I left you and Quentin.

I love you always, Javon.

Mary placed the letter on her lap and cried uncontrollably. Her shoulders heaved with each wail. She stayed in the parking lot for almost twenty minutes before driving home. When Mary pulled into her driveway, she remained in her car for another twenty minutes, lost in thought, before getting out and entering the house. She found Quentin sitting in his dad's chair, looking at his iPad. He didn't greet her when she came in.

Mary spoke softly, "Hey, Quent. What are you doing? Are you working on your schoolwork?"

No response. Mary went over to him and knelt, looking him in the eye. She said in a gentle voice, "Listen, Quent, your daddy's gone. He left me the same as he left you. We only have each other now. Uncle Marvin will visit us a lot. I know how much you like him, and he loves you. He loves you the same as I love you. Now, I need to make supper. I'm going to make your daddy's fried chicken. We're going to set a place for him at the table and pretend he's late like he always was. Does that sound good?" Quentin raised his head, looked at his mother, and nodded his head up and down.

After supper, when Quentin was asleep, Mary went to her room, sat on the bed, and looked at the check she had received from the bank. She placed it on the bed, reread Javon's letter, and cried quietly. Minutes later, she composed herself and went deep into thought. Suddenly, she stood up. She put Javon's letter in her nightstand drawer and closed it. She said to herself, I'm sorry, beyond words. But I'm not going to let this situation hurt my baby boy. I'm going to finish raising him until he's a man, and he's going to be a good man. I swear by all that's in heaven. The streets aren't going to get my boy.

TWO WEEKS AFTER MEETING MARIO, Mirabelle was taking inventory at work when Ana approached her. She said, "So, Mir, how are you and Mario getting along? Has he asked you to marry him yet?"

"Ana, we just met two weeks ago."

"Well, I talked to Mario, and he seems quite smitten. He never talked about his other girlfriends like he does you."

"I have to say, he makes me think about him a lot."

"Mirabelle, the important question is, how good is he in bed?"

Mirabelle, "It's been only one time, but what does this smile tell you?"

"Ooo, Mirabelle, how lucky are you? What's going on with Julio?"

"I don't know, Ana. I haven't talked to him since Mario's promotion party. I think you were right. I need a normal person. Being with Mario, I didn't realize what normal was. I've always been with Julio. Mario makes me feel safe."

"Well, I guess so. Ever since his boss was killed, Mario has had security people following him everywhere."

"Tell me about it. Every time we go out, there's people with guns watching us. It's hard to talk in the car with those people listening. It is kind of cool, though. I feel really important."

"Well, you can't avoid Julio forever. You're going to have to talk to him sometime."

"I know. He sent me a text this morning. I haven't texted back, but I think I'll call him tonight."

After work, Mirabelle was home feeding her cat, Kyro. She had picked up and put down her phone more than a few times, trying to get up the nerve to call Julio. After a half-hour of this, she finally dialed his number." Julio picked up after the second ring and said, "Mirabelle, why haven't you returned my calls or texts? Are you okay?"

"I'm sorry, Julio-"

"Mirabelle, I thought something happened. I asked Carlos to check on you. He said you wouldn't talk to him. What's going on?"

"Julio, I'm fine. I need to tell-"

"I've finished my work here. Mirabelle, Atlanta is a beautiful city. It's clean and much nicer than Juarez. You're going to like it here. We'll have money and our own house in a nice neighborhood. Our Niño's can play in the backyard. It will be wonderful for us."

Feeling the tears well up, she said in a shaky voice, Julio, I'm not moving to Atlanta."

"What do you mean?"

Crying now, Mirabelle said, "Julio, I'm sorry. I've met someone, and I want to stay here. I'm sorry."

"Met someone.? What do you mean you met someone?"

"He's Ana's cousin. I met him at a celebration for his job promotion."

"Mirabelle, we've been together since we were children. If there was something wrong, if I did something, why didn't you tell me?"

"I'm sorry, Julio. I can't live in your world anymore. It's too much violence. You scared me so much when you left to go to Atlanta. Mario makes me feel safe. His world isn't violent."

Julio said angrily, "Mario? Is that his name? Mario. What's he do that makes you feel so safe? You were always safe with me. What does this Mario have that I don't?"

"Julio, you kill people. Your world is filled with violence. Someday, somebody might kill you. Every time you leave, I wonder if you'll come home, just like this time when you left. I can't live like that anymore. I'm sorry, Julio. I still love you, but can't be with you anymore."

Julio was red with anger and had a vice grip on his phone when he said, "Violence? Do you think my world is violent? Is Mario violent? No? Well, he's about to find out what violence is. I am an excellent teacher of violence. You can tell your Mario, school is in session!"

With that, Julio disconnected the call, leaving Mirabelle in tears and shock. She began to panic. Knowing Julio's nature, she thought, "Oh my God. What have I done? He's going to kill Mario. She grabbed her phone and called Mario.

Julio hurled his phone against the motel room wall and screamed," Mirabelle, I'm going to kill you and that pendejo. You're both dead!" Three days later, Julio opened the apartment door he and Mirabelle had shared, and had so many memories. He noticed immediately that all of Mirabelle's things were gone. She had moved out. He entered the bedroom and saw a note on the dresser. He picked up the note and read it. My dearest Julio. I am so sorry. I have hurt you, but you must realize that getting angry and hurting people is not the way for us to move on with our lives. I have always loved you and always will. We have shared a bond since we were children, which can never be broken. It is time for us to walk different paths, and I hope you understand. Please don't be angry. Go and find someone who will make you forget about me. Remember, I will always love you, Julio. Mirabelle.

Julio screamed with rage and tore the note into shreds. He went around the small apartment, breaking and throwing things until exhausted. Finally, he sank to the floor and cried until his stomach hurt. He fell asleep and woke to find the apartment dark. When morning arrived, Julio set out to seek his revenge. His first stop was to find out who Mario was. It didn't take him long to see he worked for an important politician recently elected to the Mexican Senate. Worse, he was the brother of Castel Mendoza. Julio knew Castel very well. His stature in the Juarez Cartel was the same as his boss, Jorge. This gave Julio pause. He could handle killing someone who worked for a politician, but killing the brother of a medium-ranking cartel member was something else. It was then he decided that Mirabelle was the one who needed to go. She had betrayed him. She had turned to another man. She had abandoned him. She would be the one to pay for her mistake.

Julio spent the day figuring out how he could kill her. He didn't know where she was staying, but he did know where she worked. He took a Glock G17 handgun, got in his car, and drove to Mirabelle's work. When he arrived, he was told that Mirabelle no longer worked there. Frustrated, he drove back to his apartment. He decided that killing Mirabelle would require planning. After some digging, he found out where Mario lived. She was probably living with him. Puta (whore), he thought. He got back in his car and drove to Mario's house. When he arrived, he was stunned at what he saw. Mario lived in an exclusive condo high-rise. It wasn't the high-rise that got his attention; government security personnel were everywhere.

Julio said to himself, "I guess killing that politician had some unintended consequences." He quickly realized getting to Mirabelle was going to be a very difficult thing to do. When he returned to his apartment for the second time that day, he sat in the recliner in front of the TV, deep in thought. An hour later, a calendar alert chimed on his phone. He looked at it and saw that Mirabelle's birthday was in two weeks. He was ready to throw the phone at the TV when he realized something. Her birthday was a week before her father's. Mirabelle would always visit her father's grave on his birthday. She never failed to do so. Visualizing the grave, Julio knew how he was going to kill the whore.

DANNY ORTEGA WAS PUTTING the finishing touches on his latest creation, a car bomb disguised as a gear shift knob for a Jeep Cherokee, when his phone rang. He looked at the caller ID and saw it was Julio. He picked up and said, "Julio! How are things in Atlanta?"

"Hey man. I'm here in Juarez, taking care of some business. Thanks again for helping me out back there."

"No problem. It was fun. I got to try out my new cell phone transmitter. What's up?"

"I need you to make something for me."

Danny said warily, "Okay, what is it this time?"

After telling Danny what he needed, Julio drove to Juarez Lawn and Garden and bought a bag of grass and weed killer. Then, he went to Castle Crest Memorial Park, where Mirabelle's father was buried. The exclusive cemetery had a winding drive that snaked through the lush, well-maintained grounds. Her father could rest in such a beautiful place because Julio had paid for it, or, to be precise, the cartel had. When he arrived at the gravesite, Julio took the grass killer and spread it around her father's grave as well as several adjacent graves. The directions said the grass and weed killer takes three days to work. Satisfied, he drove back to his apartment. A week later, Julio was eating a bowl of cereal at seven in the morning when his phone calendar alerted him that Mirabelle's

father's birthday was in one week. The alert served as a reminder
for him to call Danny and check his progress. He dialed Danny's
number and was sent to voicemail. Danny returned the call two
hours later and said, "Julio, I'm sorry, man. I had something come
up, and I'm going to be a little late getting to what you asked me
for."

"How late? I need that, like yesterday. It's really important I get
that."

"I can have it ready the day after tomorrow."

That was cutting it close. Mirabelle would be visiting her father's
grave in six days. It didn't leave much time for him to do what he
needed to do. He said, "Okay, Danny. That'll work, but no later.
Call me, and we'll meet at the usual spot." Julio was in the Plaza
Sendero shopping mall's parking lot two days later. He'd been
waiting impatiently for Danny to show up for almost thirty
minutes. When he arrived, Julio got out of his car and into
Danny's. He said, "It's about time, Danny."

"What do you mean? I said eight o'clock, and I'm only a few
minutes late. What's the big deal?"

"Okay, never mind. Show me what you have."

"It's in the trunk. C'mon, I'll show you."

The pair got out of the car, and Danny opened the trunk of his car.
Inside was a jewelry box that once held a beautiful diamond neck-
lace. The box was wrapped in black electrical tape with a small
toggle switch on one side. Next to the switch was a tiny light that
turned red when the toggle was switched to ON. Danny gave the
box to Julio and pulled a small hand-held walkie-talkie from his
coat pocket. He said, "This is the transmitter for the box. You flip
the toggle, and the light will turn red. Select channel twelve on the
walkie-talkie and press the transmit button. Make sure you're at

least thirty feet away. The transmitter's good for a hundred yards. Got it?" Julio took the walkie-talkie, put it in his coat pocket, and said, "What about the battery? How long will it last after I turn it on?"

Danny said, "It's good for about five days. Not much longer."

"Thanks, Danny. Listen, I need to get going. I'll call you tomorrow."

"I'm sorry, Julio. I'm really sorry."

"Sorry for what?"

"For being late. For not having this ready until today."

Getting in his car, Julio said, "Don't worry about it. It's ok. I know; I rushed you. I'll talk to you tomorrow."

Julio sped out of the parking lot and headed to the cemetery. He had a little over an hour before it closed. When he arrived at the grave, he smiled at what he saw. The grass killer had done its work, and the groundskeepers had done theirs. When they saw the dead grass, they had taken a rake and hoe and removed the dead sod replacing it with new. The area around the affected graves had been disturbed enough to camouflage what he was going to do. He lifted the sod if in front of Mirabelle's father's grave and used his hand to dig a small hole. He took the jewelry box, flipped the toggle, saw the light turn red, and placed it in the hole. He replaced the sod and returned to his car.

The next morning, around eight, Julio parked his car several blocks from the cemetery. The cemetery opened at nine, and Mirabelle usually arrived by ten. He reached into the center console and pulled out the box and walkie-talkie. After leaving his car, he started walking to the gravesite. He couldn't have seen the Apple AirTag hidden behind the car's license plate. When he reached the grave, he looked around and noticed a large mausoleum thirty yards away. He hid behind it and waited. Forty-five minutes later, he saw two black SUVs pull up to the grave. The doors of both opened, and the passengers got out. Most of them were men with guns. He noticed Mirabelle holding the hand of one of the passengers without a weapon and assumed it was Mario. He smiled and thought, "Puta, time for you and your friend to go." He took the walkie-talkie out of his pocket, selected channel twelve, smiled, and pressed the transmit button. Nothing. He pressed it again. Still nothing. He checked if he had the correct channel. He did, and he pressed the button for a third time. Nothing. He cursed under his breath and threw the transmitter against the mausoleum. "What the hell, Danny?!" He took a circuitous route back to his car, cursing Danny all the way. He got in and picked up his phone to call Danny. Before he could press the first number, his car exploded into a fiery ball. Debris from the blast showered the street. Danny was in the passenger seat of a car parked up the street from Julio's. Jorge Amos was in the driver's seat. Jorge turned to Danny and said, "Good work. It's a shame that Julio was so blinded." Danny said, "Love can do that. That's for sure. Jorge added, "We need to keep that man Mario safe. He could be President one day."

2

BOOK TWO
ENTER THE EXCELA

Mary Waters wanted to donate the money Javon left her to her church, Grove Park Baptist Church, because she knew it could certainly use it. Then she realized Javon wouldn't have liked that. Javon lost his life over that money, and she wanted to use it for Quentin and herself. She rented a storefront near the Silver Diner, where Javon and the breakfast club gathered. She opened a beauty shop and moved her equipment out of the house to her new location. Between her existing customers and some word-of-mouth, she quickly needed to hire two employees to help her manage the growing volume of business she was getting. She used Javon's money to buy the additional equipment.

Quentin walked into his mother's beauty shop after work one day. He was employed at Sweeney Monarch Automotive, a small new car dealership five bus stops from Quentin's school. He worked in the service department and started work as part of his high school's vocational program. He had been working there for the last two years. Quentin was able to focus on his schoolwork because he avoided the street gangs in his neighborhood. In truth, it was the street gangs that avoided him. Javon's association with La Sangre was well known. Even though Javon was dead, there were rumors that his wife and son were still connected to the cartel. She drove a new SUV and opened that beauty shop. Where'd she get the money for that? Quentin was going to tell her about the job application he had filled out earlier in the day. He said, "I applied for a job at that new car plant they built in Columbus today. Today was the first day they started accepting online applications. The pay starts at twenty-five dollars an hour. Can you believe I'll make twenty-five dollars an hour if I get a job there? That's more than Dad made."

Frustrated, Mary replied, "I thought we talked about this. You're going to college. I didn't work this hard all these years for you to work in some auto plant."

Quentin said, "I've been working at Sweeney's for the last two years, Mom. Mr. Sweeney told me he could help me get a job at the new Monarch plant. Mom, I like cars. I like everything about them. I've been servicing them at Sweeney's. Now, I want to build them, and after I build them, I want to design them. Besides, I can get my degree online. A lot of colleges are offering online classes."

Mary said nothing.

"Monarch has that new car they're making. It has all kinds of new technology. I want to learn about that technology. I'm not going to be an auto worker; I'm going to be an auto designer."

Placing the shampoo bottles on the shelf, Mary replied, "Well, as long as you put it that way, I don't see no harm. You just make sure you get your degree. Your daddy wanted for you to get that, and so do I."

Six weeks later, Mary was helping Quentin load his car. He was moving to Columbus to start his new job at Monarch Motors. She felt both happy and sad at the same time. She was happy because her boy was beginning his journey through life as a man, but sad because both men in her life wouldn't be coming home for dinner every night. She was determined not to cry in front of Quentin. Putting his hands on his hips, Quentin said, "OK, that's the last of it." Quentin shared his mother's feelings. He was excited to be going out on his own but sad to leave his mother, whom he credited with raising him and keeping him safe from the streets. Mary gave Quentin a tight hug and said, "You make sure to call me when you get to your apartment. FaceTime me so I can make sure you're not living in a dump."

A WEEK AFTER MOVING IN, Quentin's phone alarm woke him at 5:30 AM. He reached over to the nightstand and grabbed his phone. Looking at the time, he felt a rush of excitement. It was his first day of work after orientation, and he would finally be on the assembly line. Quentin spent his first two weeks at Monarch in their employee orientation program. Since he would be working on the Excella line, Monarch had a training program specifically designed for employees involved in Excella production. When Quentin attended his first training day, he was surprised to find that all the other attendees were transfers from different parts of the plant. He was the only new employee. Mr. Sweeny must have had something to do with that, Quentin thought. Quentin's pride at being the only new employee assembling Excella's was short-lived. When he clocked in, he was driven by a golf cart to the end of the production line. Here, newly assembled vehicles left the line and were taken to their next stop: final inspection. His pride shifted to disappointment. He wouldn't be involved in the car's actual assembly. Quentin's job was to use a scanner gun to input the vehicle's VIN, located on a sticker on the driver's door pillar. A large touchscreen computer monitor beside the vehicle displayed the car's information, including make, model, trim package, paint color, and other technical details. Quentin would compare the screen information against the paperwork in the car after its final assembly. After comparing the paperwork, he would visually inspect the vehicle to double-check everything on the screen and the paperwork in his hand. Quentin would press a large green button on the touchscreen if everything was correct. This would indicate that the car was ready to be driven from the factory floor to the massive parking lot next to the factory. Quentin couldn't contain his curiosity. He was about to send his first car to its lucky owner. Quentin's pride re-emerged. Someone was going to drive home this new car was going to be a significant part of their life. It would take them to work, drive their kids to soccer games, and offer them Sunday afternoon rides through the countryside. It would take them on date nights to their favorite restaurant, serving as a status symbol for its owner, loudly proclaiming, "I have made it."

After completing his inspections, Quentin had an idea. He removed one of the pop rivets that held the driver's door trim to the metal frame. He went over to his workstation and tore a used form in half. Using a Sharpie, he wrote, "My name is Quentin Waters, and I helped make this car. I hope it brings you great joy." He noted the date and time, folded the paper, and placed it inside the door frame. He reattached the pop rivet and closed the door with a smile. His curiosity prompted him to press the white button on the touchscreen. Instantly, the screen displayed the vehicle's dealer and shipping information:

Patterson Auto Group, Beverly Hills, California.

———

MIKE CARAS TORE the letter in half and angrily tossed it to the ground. This was his fifth rejection letter since graduating from Palmer University, an online school where he earned his degree in

Finance Administration. His parents had to support five children and couldn't afford a four-year college for him. He set his sights on becoming a bond trader or stockbroker at an investment bank, where the real money is made. He wanted to buy everything he had dreamed about as a kid growing up in Culver City, a suburb of Los Angeles. Culver City is near the Paramount, Universal, and Keystone movie studios. Mike's father, Erick, worked at Keystone as a Production Specialist. He worked with producers and directors to find off-site filming locations and manage the stunt crew. Mike walked into the TV room of his family's house. His mother, Shelly, sat on the couch watching TV. Raising his hands, Mike said, "Well, that's number five. I have two more resumes out there, but I'm not very hopeful. What the hell is wrong with these people? I can't even get an interview. I know I could be one of their best-producing brokers. I just need someone to give me a chance to show them. Is that too much to ask?"

Shelly replied, still staring at the TV, "Don't worry. You're smart. You'll find something. What about that brokerage in Century City you were thinking about? What happened to them? Wolz something or other, wasn't it?"

"Dad's boss at the studio, Mister Sikes, told me about them. I checked them out and didn't bother sending a resume. Wolz Securities is small time. Harry Wolz only has a handful of brokers, and his client base is nothing but small-dollar investors. I'd be spending my days dialing for dollars, talking to older people who want to protect their retirement savings, and nothing more. I would end up selling savings bonds at two percent. No thanks.

Several days later, Mike received his sixth rejection letter. He hardly glanced at it before tossing it in the trash. He sighed and walked over to his desk in the corner of his bedroom. He placed copies of his resume and securities license in a FedEx envelope and addressed it to Wolz Securities, 1535 South St, Pasadena, California. Mike

thought that sending his resume by FedEx would help him stand
out from everyone else competing for the same thing he was.
"Gotta start somewhere," he said aloud, taking the shipping label
and placing it on the envelope.

TWO WEEKS LATER, Mike entered the offices of Wolz Securities
for his first job interview since graduating from Palmer. His
anxiety was through the roof as he approached the attractive,
blonde-haired receptionist. He noticed her name plaque on her
desk that read Donna Michaels.

"Hello, I'm Mike Caras. I have an appointment with Mr. Wolz
at 11."

Donna looked up from her computer, gave Mike a slight smile,
and replied, "Yes, Mr. Caras. Please take a seat. I'll let Mr. Wolz
know you're here."

After sitting in his chair for nearly twenty minutes, Donna said,
"Mr. Wolz will see you now." She pointed to her left and added,
"You can go through this door. His office is at the end of the
hallway."

"Thank you, Donna," Mike said as he stood up and headed toward
the door.

As he walked down the hallway, Mike noticed a large room
halfway to Wolz's office. It contained a row of workstations occupied by eight people glued to dozens of computer screens. It was a
loud, bustling place. Mike smiled at the thought of working in that
room, making money. When he arrived at Walz's office, the door
was open, and Harry Walz was sitting at his desk, talking on the
phone. Walz gestured toward one of the chairs in front of him.
Mike sat down and waited patiently for Walz to finish his call.

Harry Walz was sixty years old and spoke with a raspy voice from his cigarette addiction. His office smelled like an ashtray. Walz ended the call, picked up Mike's resume from his desk, glanced at it, and said, "Mike Caras, Jerry Sikes mentioned you. I've known Jerry for years."

Mike said, "I know Mr. Sikes from my dad's work".

Still examining Mike's resume, Harry commented, "I see you just got your securities license a few months ago. I don't see any work experience. Nothing in our line of work, anyway."

Mike said, "No, sir. This is my first opportunity."

"That's a good thing. I want someone with no experience—someone I can shape into the kind of broker I desire. I see dozens of resumes every few months, and they all convey the same message. Want to know what that is?"

"Yes, sir, I would very much."

"I see resumes filled with all sorts of experience. 'I worked at this firm for three years and that firm for two years.' That tells me they haven't been successful. They keep jumping from firm to firm, thinking something will change with a new job, or they were fired from the one they had. I don't want that kind of person working here. What do you think about that?"

"That's very good to hear, sir. You're looking for someone you can mold. Does that mean I got the job?"

Wolz laughed, "That's what I like—always ask for the business. The number one rule here is ABC: Always Be Closing. You never stop asking for the business. The second rule is the three-no rule. Once you hear 'no' three times, hang up and call the next one. You're wasting your time going for a fourth no. If you're communicating by email, there isn't a three-no rule. Emails and texts last forever. You never stop sending them."

Mike let a small smile cross his face and thought, "This guy's doing all the talking. He can't stop talking. I finally got a job. Harry just hasn't told me yet."

MIKE'S ALARM clock blared at him at precisely 4 AM. Los Angeles time. He arrived at work at five, giving him ninety minutes before the markets opened at 9:30 AM New York time. After working at Wolz for the past month, he was getting used to the early wake-up calls. Mike spent the early morning reviewing the stocks that Wolz's research department had provided him. These were the stocks identified as the easiest to sell. Mike's job was to call Wolz's existing clients and persuade them to buy—that's what he did all day—dialing for dollars. Now into his second month at Wolz, Mike had generated a whopping twelve hundred dollars in commissions. His manager, Tim Halpern, called him into his office one Friday afternoon. Gesturing to a chair in front of his desk, Tim spoke, "Have a seat, Mike. I want to give you a progress report."

"Yes, sir," Mike replied nervously.

"Mike, I'm going to tell it like it is. You're nearing two months here. Your non-recoverable draw ends at the end of your third month. We're paying you five grand a month, which we don't get back. After three months, you'll go on straight commission. Your paycheck will be drawn against your sales commissions. You understand that, right?

"Yes, sir. I know that."

"For two months, we've invested ten grand in you, and you've only given us twelve hundred back. You're in the red right now and have a month to get in the black. Understand?"

"Yes, Tim. I'm doing everything you asked me to. I'm here at five every day and don't stop calling people until eight at night. I don't eat lunch most days," Mike said defensively.

Tim softened his tone, "Look, Mike. I can see you're a hard-working guy. I always tell my people, keep doing what you're doing, and you'll keep getting what you're getting."

"What do you suggest I do differently?"

"That's up to you. That's why we hired you. You're a selling machine and need to figure out how to make it run."

Mike replied, defeated, "I understand what you're saying. I'll get my sales up."

After his talk with Tim, Mike walked down the hallway to his desk, frowning. Donna was walking in the opposite direction, holding a bottle of water, when she asked, "Why the glum look?"

"Tim just read me my rights. He's going to put me in cuffs and walk me out of here if I don't start producing more."

"Tim's an asshole. He thinks he's such a big deal. Nobody likes him."

"Well, at least it's Friday."

Hearing this, Donna raised her water bottle, smiled, and walked away.

It was Saturday evening when Mike's father, Erick, found him in the kitchen, poring over paperwork he had brought home from work. "What have you got there?" he asked. "Why aren't you out with Toni? It's Saturday night."

Mike replied glumly, "Just work stuff. I'm in deep trouble. I need to make some sales, and I'm not doing so well in that department. I want my own place, but how can I afford rent when I can't even buy a double latte at Starbucks?"

"That bad, huh?"

"Toni's going to leave me, and I wouldn't blame her."

"Well, here's something for you, and I'm sad to say it. Keystone took a big hit with its last movie. They lost a ton of money. I saw the employee screening before they released it. It's a terrible movie, but they tried to sell it anyway. Keystone is cutting its payroll by offering early buyouts to vested employees. People who take the buyout will have a bunch of extra cash. I'm thinking about it myself."

Mike looked up. "That sounds interesting. That sounds very interesting."

"Why don't you give me some of your business cards? I'll pass them around."

Two weeks later, Mike got a call from Jack Richardson, a friend of his dads from Keystone. Sitting at his desk, Mike said, "Hello, Mr. Richardson. How are you?"

Using the name everybody at Keystone called Erick's son, Jack replied, "I'm good, Mikey; I guess you're in the real world now. No more coffee runs for the filming crew."

Mike remembered, as a kid during the summer, his father paying him two dollars an hour to run errands at the studio. He replied, "Yes, sir, trying to make my way in this cruel world."

Jack chuckled. "It is cruel, I'll give you that. Listen, I took Keystone up on its offer to buy me out. I used most of the money to pay off some of my mortgage and credit cards. I'm thinking of investing, but I don't know much about it."

Mike sat up and said, "That's what my job is, Mr. Richardson. I can help you find a place to invest your money and get it working for you by earning a good return. It's called ROI: Return on Investment."

Jack replied enthusiastically, "That's what I want. A good return. How do I get started?"

"Why don't we set up a meeting so I can go over everything? I need to know how much you want to invest and your risk level. How aggressive do you want to be?"

"I want to be plenty aggressive."

"When can you stop by?" Mike asked.

Over the next several weeks, Mike's phone rang like never before. He was signing up clients faster than a Daytona race car. Most of them were ex-Keystone employees. He was finally making money. Every Monday morning, Tim held a sales meeting with Wolz's brokers before the markets opened. For brokers who were on the hot seat for low sales, these meetings were a source of extreme anxiety. This anxiety was called "Sundaynightis by those who worked there." Just like tonsillitis, it made swallowing difficult. Sunday evenings were very stressful. At the sales meeting, a co-worker would say, "Look at Reynolds over there. He's getting the ax, so you know he had a severe case of Sundaynightis last night." Tim approached the podium and said, "Okay, listen up, folks. We have another week until the end of the month. The month ends on a Wednesday, so we will be extending it until Friday. That gives you two extra days to work your magic." He looked at Reynolds. Pointing to a whiteboard on his left that displayed every broker's name and their commission numbers for the month, Tim continued, "As you can see, Mr. Caras here is running away with it. Way to go, Mike. Perhaps you can enlighten us on your success and how you achieved it," still directing his gaze at Reynolds.

Sitting in his chair, Mike spoke up, "It's pretty simple. Don't be an order taker. Have a conversation with your prospect and listen to what they say. You can tell if they want to be safe with almost zero risk or if they want to go all in." After a pause, he added, "I have a list of twelve stocks—six for safe and six for all in. I also have a list of mutual funds with the same numbers. I like pushing mutual funds because they're packaged products—a bunch of stocks rolled into one. Clients like diversity. They don't like panicking at the mention of one of their stocks in the news. They hear something, and the next thing you know, your phone is ringing, and not in a good way. Other than that, I can't add any more, except that mutuals pay terrific commissions." He turned around, grinning at his co-workers. The sales meeting droned on for another half hour before Tim wrapped it up. "Okay, folks. Market opens in a half hour. You heard the man. Mutual funds. Reynolds, I need to see you in my office."

TONI HARRIS MET Mike in third grade. They were each other's reading partners. As they grew older and started high school, they were attracted to each other like magnets. They were rarely apart. Mike thought she was so beautiful. How lucky am I? After high school, Toni worked as an administrative assistant at one of the more prominent law firms in Los Angeles. At night and on weekends, she took courses at the same online university as Mike. She wanted to be a lawyer, and her firm, Arnold and Little, would reimburse her expenses for law school expenses if she remained an employee for five years. She was entering her fourth year. Arnold and Little planned to hire her as an associate once she passed the Bar exam. With Mike's newfound success and Toni's job, they decided to move in together. They rented a two-bedroom apartment in a new luxury apartment and condo complex in Pasadena. The apartment featured granite countertops in the kitchen and bath, a large living room, and a patio with the San Gabriel Mountains as a backdrop. After the movers left, Mike and Toni stood in their living room when Toni spoke.

"Well, it looks a little sparse to me. We have almost no furniture. Let's see, we have a bed, a couch, EZ chair, and a TV." After a pause, Toni said, "We need to do something about that."

Mike replied, "Yes, we certainly do.

"I have just the solution," Toni said confidently.

The next day, Toni and Mike headed to Palm Springs, roughly a hundred miles east. In the car, Mike asked, "Remind me why we're driving all the way to Palm Springs to get furniture?"

"Palm Springs has tons of furniture consignment stores. Rich people change their furniture like they change clothes. They get tired of it and switch it out, selling it in consignment stores. You can find high-end furniture at a big discount. My friend Sandy at work told me about this."

"Clever girl," Mike said.

Thirteen months after moving into their apartment, Toni passed the California Bar exam. Her co-workers at Arnold and Little celebrated with a big "Congratulations" party at their headquarters on Friday afternoon. While Toni chatted with her co-workers, most of whom were on the tipsy side, Mike, probably the only one not drinking, took the opportunity to meet potential clients. He patted the stack of business cards in his suit coat pocket and approached a man who was impatiently waiting for the bartender to serve him his drink. Extending his right hand, Mike said, "Hello, I'm Mike Caras."

The man turned around and glanced at Mike's hand. After a moment's hesitation, he replied, "Well, hello to you." They shook hands. "I'm Will Patterson. My friends call me Willy." Raising his glass filled with ginger ale, Mike said, "Great party. Do you work here?"

"No way. I'm a client. A big client," Willy replied with a slight slur. He continued boastfully, "I own Patterson Automotive Group. We have almost three hundred car and truck dealerships nationwide, and we're expanding into Canada. I was here for a meeting and discovered this terrific party. Do YOU work here?"

"Not me; I'm married to the woman the party is for. She just passed the bar exam."

"More lawyers," Patterson grumbled, picking up his drink. "You a lawyer too?"

"Not a chance. I'm in the securities business. Wealth Management, as it were. I work at Wolz Securities."

Perking up and losing his slur, Willy said, "Well, isn't that interesting? My meeting here was with a bunch of bobbleheads. Patterson is going public, and the bobbleheads are helping us with that."

Mike almost dropped his ginger ale. Did he say what I think he said? Mike asked himself. His mind immediately began calculating how he could benefit from this guy. How could he turn this meeting into money in his bank account? Mike asked, "Do you have a card? I might be able to help you with the bobbleheads. I'm pretty sure my wife speaks their language."

Willy set his drink down, pulled a cardholder from his pocket, and handed Mike his card.

Taking Willy's card, Mike said, "Here, let me give you one of mine."

Willy accepted Mike's card and said, "Thanks. Listen, I need to go, but I would appreciate anything your wife could offer. These bobbleheads are driving me crazy. They're always talking in circles and charging me three hundred dollars an hour to do it. Hell, I probably paid for this party."

Mike smiled and said, "Yes, of course. I'm sure she'll be able to help you out."

Laughing, Willy said, "I'm going to drive home. I'm too drunk to walk."

Saturday morning, Mike got up early and went to the other bedroom in the apartment he'd converted into a home office. He opened the web browser on his laptop and looked up Patterson Automotive. Willy wasn't kidding. Patterson is a huge auto group. Mike became increasingly impressed as he scrolled down its website. He noticed a section about its pending public stock offering and that Arnold and Little were shepherding them through the process. An hour after Mike woke up, Toni emerged from her alcohol-induced sleep and smelled coffee and bacon. She walked into the kitchen and saw Mike at the stove.

Mike turned around. "Well, good morning, sunshine. You're just in time for breakfast. You probably want to start with some coffee, right?"

"A big cup of coffee," Toni said groggily. "Please tell me I didn't do anything stupid at the party."

"Quite the opposite. You were very popular. I went off on my own so you could be you."

Sitting at the kitchen table, Toni said, "Well, that's too bad. You could have taken my drink away. I feel horrible."

"Are you kidding? You brought back fond memories of sex with drunk girls in college," Mike said, grinning.

"Shut up and give me my coffee."

Pouring Toni's coffee, Mike said, "I had an interesting conversation with Willy Patterson. Know him?"

"No, the name doesn't ring a bell."

"He owns Patterson Automotive Group. It's a big company with car dealerships all over the place. Jackson Little is helping them go public."

"Ok, I remember the company, not Willy. It's a big project. Ron Harper is handling that. What did you and Willy talk about?"

"Other than fly fishing, he called your co-workers bobbleheads. He doesn't understand what they're doing. He's a little pissed."

"Doesn't surprise me. Ron's an asshole. Nobody likes him. He made partner last year and now thinks he owns the place."

Mike sat down at the table and said, "Patterson going public could mean some business for me. When they go public, some of their employees will get stock in the company. Those employees might want to cash in some of their stock and invest it in something else. Not keeping their eggs in one basket, so to speak."

Toni perked up. "I'm friends with Ron's assistant, Sandy. I'll see what I can find out."

After a weekend of recuperation, Toni came to work thinking about what Mike had told her. Like any good associate aiming to make a partner, Toni always looked for opportunities to help. She approached Sandy at her desk outside Ron Harper's office.

"Hey Sandy, that was quite a party last Friday. You looked like you were having a pretty good time." Toni said, standing in front of Sandy's desk.

Turning away from her computer screen, Sandy looked at Toni, "I'm lucky to still have a job. Mr. Asshole Ron posted a TikTok video of the party."

"No kidding? I need to check that out. Hey, listen, do you want to grab lunch? My husband, Mike, met Willy Patterson at the party. It seems Mr. Patterson isn't too happy with Ron."

"I brought my lunch today, but I can't pass up the chance to get some dirt on Mr. Asshole. Why don't we go to that new place? The one across the street."

"Sounds good to me. Stop by my office when you're ready." With that, Toni left Sandy and walked toward her office.

At the same time Toni was talking to Sandy, Mike strolled through the open door of Harry Wolz's office. After bringing in the Keystone Studio's business, Mike enjoyed a new standing in the office. He reported directly to Harry instead of Tim Halpern.

Mike said enthusiastically, "I have some interesting news I think you'll want to hear."

Wolz turned from the computer screen he was looking at and asked, "What would that be?"

Mike recounted his conversation with Willy Patterson at Toni's party. He also mentioned his wife was going to sniff around and try to learn more about what Arnold and Little was doing.

"Wow." That was all Wolz could say.

"Patterson's HQ is here in Los Angeles. Most of the people there will be getting stock. After the six-month waiting period, they can cash out if they want. They can diversify instead of just holding Patterson stock. That could mean a ton of business for us." Mike rubbed his thumb and two fingers together.

Wolz said, "Keep this between us. You know the rule. Once you start talking about a deal that hasn't happened, it won't happen."

"I know that rule all too well, but I'm pretty sure this will happen." Mike turned to leave but paused. "I'll let you know what Toni finds out."

———————

TONI WALKED into her apartment kitchen, exhausted from a long day at work. She found Mike toiling over the stove, grinding pepper into a skillet.

Turning around, Mike said, "Well, there she is. What took you so long?"

"That smells fantastic. What are you making?"

"Chicken Marsala and toasted garlic broccoli. How was your day?"

"It was fine until Ron Harper started in on me. He found out I was sniffing around his Patterson deal and blew up. Guys, a major asshole."

"Oops," Mike said, shrugging. "Were you able to find out why Willy's so pissed?"

"Willy shouldn't be upset. Ron is just doing his job. Ron wants to set the opening stock value at a hundred twenty-five dollars per share. Willy wants it to open at a hundred seventy-five. Willy knows one seventy-five is too high, but he wants to help his friends make a lot of money by short-selling the stock. They 'borrow' shares at one seventy-five, wait for the stock to drop, which it will, and then return the shares at the lower price, pocketing the difference."

Mike looked at Toni and said, "You sound like me." Turning back to the skillet, Mike continued, "I think the folks at the SEC might have a problem with that. Something about insider trading."

"That's what Ron keeps telling him."

"I'm going to do a little research, but I think there may be a solution that keeps everybody happy. But first, it's time to eat," Mike said with a smile.

Several days later, Mike was in his office, double-checking his notes before calling Willy. He picked up his phone and dialed Willy's cell. Willy was moving chairs on the main patio of his house when Mike called. He answered, saying, "Hey Mike, how are things?"

"Pretty good, Mister Patterson."

"Lose the mister. My name is Willy to my friends."

"Well, okay, Willy. I have some news you're going to like. I know you and Ron Harper are not seeing eye to eye."

"Damn right. The guy's an asshole."

"Yes, I keep hearing that, but in your case, he's not. If you want to set a high stock price to help your friends, you're going to regret it. The SEC will be all over you like white on rice."

"Yeah, I keep hearing that."

Sitting up, Mike said, "Here's what you can do to help your friends AND your employees. You create an ESPP, which stands for Employee Stock Purchase Plan. Having employees own a piece of the company is a good thing. You can offer a fifteen percent discount to employees who want to buy Patterson stock and enroll in the ESPP. Your employees are going to love you. Now, about your friends: set them up as independent contractors, not employees, and you can give them the same discount as the ESPP. Everyone is happy, and there's no SEC issue."

After a long silence, Willy said, "That's terrific, Mike. What a great idea. Why didn't that asshole Harper mention this?"

"Ron's a lawyer, not a securities dealer. We think differently."

"Can I ask a favor? Can you talk to Harper about this ESPP?"

"No need to. This is a company thing. Something you set up like a new employee benefit. I told you your employees are going to love you."

"I owe you big time, Mike. If I can ever do anything for you, just let me know. I can't thank you enough."

Lowering his voice, Mike said, "Well, there is something you can do for me, Willy. Let Wolz Securities manage your ESPP."

"Mike, that's a done deal. I'd be stupid not to. I'll have my HR people get in touch. I'm going to have them put all of this in our employee newsletter and mention you and your company as the administrators of the ESPP."

After hanging up, Mike rushed down the hall to tell Harry the good news. Thanks to Willy, Wolz Securities was going to be making some very serious money. Two months after his phone call with Willy Patterson, Willy called Mike.

Mike picked up and said, "Willy, how are you?"

"I'm doing great, Mike. My stock is at one eighty-six. If my friends had listened to me and short-sold the stock, they would have lost money. Thanks for stopping me from being a fool."

Mike smiled. "That's my job: helping people with their money."

"You definitely helped me. That's why I'm calling. I want to give you a car from one of my dealerships. Pick out any car you want. It's on me."

"That's really not necessary, Willy. I didn't exactly go broke setting up your ESPP."

"Not hearing it, Mike. I'm as serious as a heart attack. I have a

Monarch dealership in Beverly Hills. I insist you go there and pick out a car. Take Toni and decide on one."

"Willy, I really appreciate it, but-"

Chuckling, Willy interrupted, "Get the car, Mike, just pick one."

With that, Willy hung up.

The following Saturday afternoon, after Mike had spoken with Willy, he and Toni drove to Willy's Monarch dealership in Beverly Hills. Toni stepped out of the car and said, "Look at these cars, Mike. We would never buy one of these."

Toni was referring to the dozen Monarch Excella's lined up in front of the showroom.

"We aren't buying one. We're being given one. Seriously, who gets to come to a fancy car dealership and take one home for free?"

Before Toni could respond, she noticed a salesperson walking toward them, waving his hand. He said, before reaching her, "Beautiful cars, aren't they? Mike and Toni turned toward the voice they were hearing.

"I'm Carl. Is there anything you're looking for in particular? Do you have any questions?

Carl pointed to a blue Excella. "This is the new Excella. We just got them in. Everybody is talking about them. It's a beautiful car with state-of-the-art technology. Let me show you." Mike and Toni were captivated and listened to every word Carl spoke. Carl was the top salesperson at the dealership and knew a buyer when he saw one. He started calculating his commission right away.

Carl gestured toward the blue Excella. "Would you like to take a test drive?"

Toni stepped forward and exclaimed, "Yes. I would love to drive this."

Mike thought, "That's it, Toni. Don't show him how interested you are. It'll make bargaining harder." Then he remembered they weren't paying for it. He grinned.

"Wait here while I grab the keys." Carl raced inside.

Toni and Mike took turns driving the car, barely paying attention to Carl as he pointed out the vehicle's features. Carl noticed their eagerness to have a car like this and smiled. When they pulled back into the dealership, Carl spoke as they exited the car.

"Pretty nice, wouldn't you say?"

Mike replied, "It's a winner, that's for sure."

Toni added, "I love it. We're getting this one."

Carl beamed and thought to himself, "I knew they were buying. They didn't even mention the price. I'm definitely getting a full commission on this for sure." He gestured toward the door. "Why don't we go inside and start on the paperwork?" Sitting in his small cubicle office behind his desk, Carl spoke to Toni and Mike, who were sitting across from him, "I need to get your insurance information if you have that. I also need to know your method of payment. We have a finance department with some very good financing terms." Carl didn't mention the extra commission he gets from in-house financing.

Toni replied, "Oh, we're not paying for it. We're here to pick it up.

"Excuse me?" Carl said, confused.

Mike said, "Maybe we should speak to your boss."

Before Mike and Toni's new Excella left the service department after its final inspection, the service technician noticed a loose pop rivet on the driver's door. He went to his tools and retrieved a rivet gun, mumbling, "Damn, factory morons. Always making extra work for me. Can't even get a pop rivet to hold."

Mike agreed to let Toni have the car. She earned it; after all, his reward was a big increase in his client base. He could buy one for himself anytime he wanted.

MIKE HAD MADE a great deal of money by convincing the employees of Keystone Studios and Patterson Auto Group to invest their money with Wolz. However, there was both good news and bad news. The good news was that he received a two percent commission on the money they invested. The bad news was that he only received a commission whenever a stock was bought or traded for a different one. The employees at Keystone and Patterson were cautious investors who aimed to preserve their investments while also earning a good return. They were quite satisfied with an annual return between six and eight percent. They rarely traded after their initial investment and were content to receive their statements each month showing a decent return. Mike reviewed his clients' investments very carefully. He compared their return on investment (ROI) against his "System." His System consisted of two groups of stocks: Group A, which included stocks he believed would yield a high ROI, and Group B, which would provide a moderate ROI. If either Group A or B had a better ROI than his clients, he would call them up to inform them that they might get a better return by trading some stock. The challenge Mike faced was simple. His clients, mostly conservative investors, wouldn't trade unless he could show them an almost absurd increase in their ROI. Aggressive investors were just the opposite and would trade for even a tiny increase in ROI. Trading stocks for a client was referred to as

"Churn," and this is what Wolz based his commission on. Aggressive investors typically had a high churn rate, while conservative investors maintained a low churn rate. A significant part of Mike's income depended on his churn rate. Unfortunately, he had far more conservative investors than aggressive ones, and he needed to bring in new clients if he wanted to make "the big money."

One day, while going through his emails at his desk, Mike noticed something that sparked a question in his mind. His spam folder was always overflowing, yet a few blatant spam emails were still making it into his inbox. He tasked himself, Why were these spams not getting filtered out? He also pondered how he was receiving these "spammails" in the first place. He decided to find out; he clicked on one of the spam emails from his inbox. It was from a golf shop near his home. Mike enjoyed playing golf but had never visited "Hole-In-One Discount Golf." He picked up the phone and called them. He spoke with the owner, who informed him that he used a marketing firm named Digital Media and gave him their phone number. Before making the call, he opened their website on his computer. The site provided an overview of the company's services and listed the employees, their titles, and photos. He saw Don Wheelan was the president and founder. Mike decided to call him. After being on hold for several minutes, Don picked up.

"Hello, this is Don. How can I assist you?"

"Don, my name is Mike Caras. I work for Wolz Securities and am interested in learning about your company and the services you offer. Specifically, I'm looking into email marketing and how it might help my business. Is that something you provide?"

"Hi Mike, thanks for your interest in Digital Media. Yes, we can deliver a complete email marketing solution. We can either customize your email according to your instructions or design it in-house for your approval. We also offer database services to help you target potential customers. Can you tell me about your business and how you acquire customers?"

Mike described what Wolz offers its clients and how they acquire them. He admitted that most of his clients came by word of mouth, primarily from Patterson or Keystone employees. He didn't engage in much cold calling.

Don asked, "So, if I'm understanding correctly, you want to expand your business beyond your current client base, reaching individuals who aren't part of the companies you mentioned, right?"

"Yes, that's exactly what I want. I want to reach out to everyone with money to invest and inform them about my business and what I can do for them."

"Ok. Pretty standard for most businesses looking to grow," Don said. "Can I ask what your ideal customer looks like? Are they male or female? What's their age range, employment status, and income level? What type of person are you targeting to open your emails?"

Sitting up in his chair, Mike responded, "You can find people who fit those things? I can send emails to people who make over a hundred thousand dollars a year, who are over forty years old?"

"You can do a lot more than that, Mike. Our database service includes over two hundred and fifty million email addresses. We gather data from hundreds of different sources. It's no coincidence that after you visit Amazon looking for dog toys, you start getting emails from "Dogs Are Us." Your phone or computer holds a wealth of information about you. Every time you make a purchase online or use your credit card at the Thai restaurant, you're leaving behind crumbs, or more accurately, cookies, so marketing companies can track your information. It's collected when you use your email address as a username for a service you subscribe to anything online. If you choose one of those "Meal at Home" companies, you're telling a database somewhere that you prefer chicken over beef. Before long, you'll start receiving emails from Popeye's Chicken. Look at your current customer list; you can email anyone who resembles them.

"That's unbelievable. I just got a new car and started getting emails about extended warranty offers," Mike continued. "Nobody's safe, I guess. I found out about your company from an email sent by a golf shop I've never visited."

'Now you understand. Welcome to the new world."

"What about spam?" Mike asked. "My spam folder is always full, and I usually ignore it. They auto-delete after thirty days. I don't want my emails landing in the spam folder."

"That's easy. When you send an email, it contains large amounts of data beyond what you write. There's information in it that verifies it's you, not some robot sending the email. Internet providers use Spam Sniffers to check for the presence or absence of data in the email. There's also something called "email and domain reputation." You earn a good reputation score if you send, receive, or reply to emails consistently over time. Conversely, you'll have a low reputation score if you send large numbers of emails from a new email address that has no incoming emails. A bad reputation score can result from having a list of ten thousand email addresses, where five thousand are invalid. You can think of an email address's reputation like a credit score.

"How do you get around that? How can my emails avoid going to the spam folder?"

"That's a trade secret, but suffice it to say, we have a ninety-five percent success rate. We guarantee it."

Mike said, excitedly, "Well, sign me up. I want to start sending emails ASAP. What do you need from

Me?"

ARANYA (AMY) and Thaila (Tammy) Lin were identical twins. Tammy was born at St. Joseph Hospital in Burbank, California, four minutes before her sister, Amy. Tammy always referred to Amy as her younger sister. Amy despised the reference. Amy and Tammy had brown hair and hazel eyes, and they were stunningly beautiful. Early in their lives, they adopted English names because they didn't get bullied as much in school. The twins had a lot of fun with their identical looks. In elementary school, they would sometimes switch clothes in the bathroom. In later years, they would do this on double dates. They were inseparable—until they graduated from high school. Tammy was a better student than Amy. She wanted to be an aerospace engineer—literally, a rocket scientist. Tammy's good grades and high achievements in academic clubs earned her a full scholarship to UCLA. Amy set her sights on being a mother and raising a family. Amy would sometimes turn down a Saturday night party so she could babysit and earn some extra spending money or save it. Tammy was the opposite and spent every nickel that came her way. Her parents thought Tammy's desire to excel in school and her career choice were her way of differentiating herself from her twin sister. Tammy's spending was a mystery. The UCLA campus was near the Lin's house. Tammy wanted to concentrate solely on her studies and lived at home with her parents. Focusing on her studies was not the only reason she lived at home. Her scholarship did not include on-campus housing, and off-campus housing was too much to ask of her parents.

After high school, Amy couldn't wait to move out of her child-hood home. She was ready to explore her newfound freedom and was prepared to be on her own. She found a job working in a hospice care facility run by the hospital where she was born. Helping people in the final chapter of their book of life was something she found very rewarding. Too bad her paycheck didn't reflect that reward. Ever the thrifty person, Amy was able to afford a small efficiency apartment near work. Not having a car in southern California was an unspeakable hardship for many residents, but not for Amy. She didn't care about a car, but she did care about all the money she had saved by not having one. Thank God for Uber.

Amy met her future husband, Andy, at a Thai restaurant near her work. She would often get take-out after work and rush home before it got cold. Andy's real name was Arthit Bui. His parents, Niran and Chalita Bui, were immigrants from Thailand who had found their American dream when they opened their restaurant, Thai Orchid, twenty-two years ago. They always thought their only child would take over after they retired, but Andy had other ideas. He wanted to take his mother's recipes and make them available in the grocery store. He saw how hard his parents worked and wanted none of that. One evening, Amy was picking up her favorite meal at Thai Orchid when Andy approached her at the register. He had been lurking behind the kitchen door, watching through the window as his mother took Amy's order. Andy had made several false starts to talk to the most beautiful girls he had ever seen, but he always lost his nerve. He would come out of the kitchen pretending to look for something. He would see Amy and start to talk to her, but he always froze. He only managed to say hello before fleeing back into the safety of the kitchen. He tried and failed every time Amy came to pick up her takeout. Andy didn't notice that his mother took longer to get Amy's order than any other customer's take-out. For her part, Amy was getting tired of eating Thai food and wished the gorgeous hunk would stop hiding behind the kitchen door and ask her out. Andy's mother answered the phone the next time Amy called to place her order.

She made a not-so-subtle suggestion to dine in rather than take out.

———

TAMMY'S MOTHER, Anong, stood in the doorway of Tammy's bedroom with tears in her eyes.

"Mom, will you please stop crying? I'm moving almost right next door. It's not like I'm moving to Australia. You acted like this when Amy left. Look at how that turned out. You practically spend more time at her house than your own. Even Dad says that."

"I know, Tammy. Amy needs help with the kids. Andy is opening another restaurant, and Amy is helping with that. You're moving out. This house is going to be so empty."

"You're selling the house. Remember? You guys bought a condo in Palos Verdes. Remember? Life moves on. Besides, you should be happy. I got my degree and now have my first real job."

Wiping her eyes, Anong said, "Your father and I are so proud. You were always the smart one. I bet there are plenty of smart men at your new job."

"Give it up, Mom. For the thousandth time, give it up."

Tammy had graduated from UCLA with honors. She was at the top of her class with a degree in Aerospace Engineering. She received multiple job offers but chose NASA's Jet Propulsion Lab (JPL) in Pasadena. There, she would be part of a team designing a new satellite for the Air Force. The world was at her feet. She moved into a small, one-bedroom apartment in Altadena, a suburb next to Pasadena and close to her work. Her apartment was part of a larger complex with dozens of other residences. Shortly after moving in, Tammy recognized one of her co-workers from her job at JPL, Doris McKenzie. Doris was forty-two and newly divorced.

She and Tammy became fast friends. One day, they were in the JPL cafeteria eating lunch when Tammy asked her who the guy was paying for his meal at the register. Doris said, "That's Kirk Milhouse. He started working here a few months before you did. I think he was part of that group from SpaceX that transferred here. I know what you're thinking, and yes, he's single, but I've seen him talking to Alice Murphy quite a bit.

Tammy had no shortage of men asking her to lunch or anything else they could think of to spend time with her. Sometimes, she resented the way she looked. Guys wouldn't leave her alone. She used their attention as a filter of sorts. She became interested in the guys who weren't always bothering her. She didn't want to get married, but whenever she visited her sister's house, a pang of envy crept into her thoughts. The pang grew larger around the holidays. Amy had it all: a loyal husband and doting father, two wonderful children, and running her and Andy's own business. And the house, don't even talk about the house. Tammy marveled, like her sister, at how identical twins could be so different. After lunch with Doris, Tammy wanted to meet Kirk and see where things went. He worked in a different part of the JPL campus, so she had to be clever. She needed Doris's advice. Doris mentioned that the SpaceX transfers were a tight group and liked to get together after work on Fridays at Chamo's, a bar and restaurant near the Rose Bowl. "Well, isn't that interesting?" Tammy said. "Let's go to Chamo's this Friday. You never know who you'll run into."

Doris was thrilled to join Tammy this coming Friday. She hadn't had much fun since her divorce and couldn't wait. She had failed miserably, trying to get out and meet people socially. Her only conversations outside work were with her neighbors and store clerks. That Friday, Tammy and Doris walked into the bar area of Chimo's and saw it was packed with people. Tammy braced herself for the male attention she always got in a bar. Doris was no shield. She was completely invisible to the younger crowd. Doris went to get drinks while Tammy scanned the bar, looking for Kirk. She saw him talking to Alice Murphy at the far corner of the bar near the restrooms. "Bitch," Tammy said to herself. This was going to be more complicated than she thought. As if on cue, Alice left Kirk and started walking to the restroom. Tammy didn't hesitate. She pushed her way through the crowd and walked up to Kirk. Speaking loudly over the noise, Tammy brazenly introduced herself.

"Hi. I'm Tammy. I work at JPL. I've seen you a couple of times in the cafeteria."

"I've seen you in the cafeteria a few times myself. My name is Kirk."

Tammy leaned closer to Kirk so they could talk over the noise. "I started working at JPL a few months ago and haven't met many people outside my department."

"What department are you in?" Kirk asked.

"I'm in Sat-Design. Where do you work?"

"I just started working at JPL myself. I'm part of the SpaceX team that transferred here. Satellite design? You must be smart to get a job there."

Tammy laughed, "More like stupid. That place is a meat grinder for any life after work. Correct that; There is no after-work."

Kirk lifted his glass and said, "Yet here you are. Living proof JPL permits a life after work."

When Kirk finished his sentence, Alice exited the restroom and approached him. Looking at Tammy, she asked Kirk, "Who's this?"

A WEEK after meeting Tammy at Chamo's, Kirk saw her and Doris eating lunch at a cafeteria table. He approached them, holding his tray, and asked, "Mind if I sit with you folks?"

Doris quickly replied, "Take my seat. I have to get back to work." She got up, holding her tray, and walked to the exit. Looking at Tammy, she smiled as she left.

Tammy and Kirk ate lunch together for the rest of the week. Whenever Alice came into the cafeteria and saw the pair, she turned and left. On Friday, while eating lunch, Tammy asked Kirk, "Are you going to Chamos after work?"

Kirk replied, "I need some quiet time. My ears hurt when I go there. I thought we could get some dinner at Noodle House if you're not doing anything."

Gesturing her hand towards her head, Tammy said, "Look at this face and eyes. Would I pass up a chance to eat dinner at Noodle House?"

Kirk couldn't believe his luck. He just asked the most beautiful girl he had ever met to have dinner with him. It wasn't that he asked; it was that she said yes. The following Monday, Kirk couldn't wait to go to work. He thought about calling Tammy Sunday, but decided against it. He didn't want to seem too eager. For her part, Tammy must have picked up and then put down her phone several times on Sunday. She also couldn't wait for Monday.

Over the next few weeks, the couple regularly ate lunch in the cafeteria and fell into a routine. Lunch during the week, on Fridays, they would meet up at Chamo's. After a few hours of dancing and drinking with co-workers, they would get a late dinner at the Noodle House or the Mexican restaurant next door. After dinner, they would go to Kirk's apartment, ravaging each other until they fell asleep. One Saturday morning, Kirk turned in his bed to face Tammy. He said, "I have some vacation time left over from

SpaceX. JPL told me I could use it and not have it count against my JPL vacation time. I thought we could go somewhere."

Tammy said, "I only have four days. I got two weeks when I started. I have to use one of those weeks to help my sister and her husband open their new restaurant. It's a family thing, and I promised to help." Squinting her eyes and smiling, she continued, "Why? What do you have in mind?"

"My folks have a vacation house in Pebble Beach. I thought we could drive up PCH (Pacific Coast Highway) and spend some time there. They don't use the house very much these days."

"Wait. You have a vacation house in Pebble Beach? You didn't tell me you were rich."

"I'm not, believe me. My parents are. My dad runs a hedge fund and makes more money than should be legal. I don't think much of his job, even though it paid for a lot of things growing up. He takes other rich people's money and moves it from A to B, taking a cut in between. I don't know; I suppose there must be some value in what he does, but I don't see it."

Tammy said, "Pebble Beach isn't very far. I can use one of my days, and we could make it a long weekend."

Kirk smiled and said, "Well, okay then. I'll call my folks and make a reservation for two."

The following week, Tammy and Kirk left work early on Friday. It was two in the afternoon, and the four-and-a-half-hour drive would get them to Pebble Beach in time for dinner. After nearly five hours, Kirk took an exit off the highway. He turned right onto one street, then left onto another, drove a few miles, and repeated the process. After about fifteen minutes of this, Kirk pulled into the driveway of a house that astonished Tammy. The Spanish-style house wasn't particularly large compared to the others on the street, but it was much bigger than Tammy had expected. The cream-colored stone walls and orange-tiled roof made the house resemble a Spanish hacienda. What astonished Tammy was the view. The house was situated at the end of a cul-de-sac. The homes on the street gave a wide berth to each other, but Kirk's parents' house stood alone, with its backyard facing the Pacific Ocean and the beach a hundred feet below. The house was surrounded on three sides by a beautiful waist-high stone wall. After unloading the car, they entered the house and put their luggage in one of the five bedrooms. Kirk told Tammy it was too creepy to use the master bedroom. Tammy didn't care. The room Kirk chose was almost as big as her apartment. Tammy opened the back door and went to the stone wall that separated the backyard from the edge of the cliff. The sun was slowly sinking into the sea. Kirk came up to Tammy and wrapped his arms around her. Looking at the ocean, Tammy said, "Isn't this beautiful?

Kirk replied, "Well, it is for now."

"What do you mean?"

"Tammy, look at where we are, and look at that beach below us. That beach used to be up here. Someday, an earthquake or erosion is going to put this house down there."

"Why, Kirk, you're so romantic. I didn't know you were such a softy."

"I am. How about we get some dinner. "I'm starved. We can go to the store and stock up on some groceries on the way back.

Early Saturday morning, Tammy awoke. She glanced over and watched Kirk sleep. Tammy smiled from ear to ear. She had finally found the guy she wanted to marry and start a family with. Amy could bring her kids to their house on Thanksgiving, and she could bring hers to Amy's at Christmas. She leaned over and stroked Kirk's hair.

Andy Bui stood in the kitchen of his and Amy's second Thai Orchid restaurant. He wanted to open next month and was desperately trying to stay on schedule. He watched as five men moved equipment from the trucks outside to their places in the kitchen. He reached into his pocket and pulled out his ringing cell phone. He saw that it was Todd Hailey, his business manager, calling.

"Hi, Todd. What's up?"

"Andy, I still haven't received anything from the bank. The expansion loan was supposed to be a done deal by now."

Exasperated, Andy replied, "Well, why are you calling me? Amy works with Terry Harston at Providence Bank. I'm trying to get this place open. That's my focus."

"I did call Amy, and she told me to call you."

"Unbelievable, she knows I'm trying to get things ready here. She also knows I have to get the food recipes over to the co-packer by next week. The grocery meal kits need to start shipping by the end of the month. I can't do everything."

Todd replied with an edge to his voice, "Well, where does that leave me?

Frustrated, Andy said, "I'll call Amy and get this figured out. In the meantime, I'll have Terry call you directly so you can keep things moving."

Andy hung up and called his wife.

"Hey, beautiful. I just got off the phone with Todd. Why did you tell him to call me? You and Todd deal with all the financial stuff.

I'm just a worker bee. I'm up to my neck opening this place and getting the grocery meal kit recipes to the co-packer."

Amy had quit her hospice job shortly after she and Andy married. Andy's father had difficulty recovering from his bypass surgery and couldn't take care of the family restaurant's bookkeeping. Amy volunteered to fill in and soon discovered she must have some of her sister's math skills because she quickly saw the disarray in the restaurant's books and was able to sort it out. She haggled with vendors, reduced some of the overhead, and saved Thai Orchid almost eight hundred dollars a week.

"I'm sorry, babe. Juana is still sick, and the kids are taking full advantage of her absence. I caught Andy Junior playing with a lighter; I have no idea where it came from. Tessa is back, trying to lure stray dogs into the house. She took a pound of hamburger from the fridge and made a trail from the street to the front door. The only thing she lured were ants."

"I don't think Tess needs to lure a dog. We should go to the pound and get one for her."

Amy said nothing.

"Ok, we'll table that for now. Why can't you give Todd what he's calling me about?

Amy replied angrily, "Did you not hear what I just said? Besides, you know how I feel about Todd. I don't think he's qualified for what he does. Just because he's a good restaurant manager doesn't make him a good business manager."

"Well, you don't have to worry about it. I told Todd that I would have Terry deal with him directly."

"That's fine with me. I'll have more time keeping my eye on your pyromaniac son."

"I'm sorry, sweety pie. You know how much I love you. I love you more than anything in the world. You are so beautiful. It feels so hot whenever I come into the house, and then I realize it's you generating all that heat."

"Shut up, Andy. We're not getting a dog; you're the one with all the heat. Get your ass home so I can warm myself up."

Andy chuckled as he ended the phone call. He looked up from his phone and took in his surroundings. He couldn't believe he was opening a second restaurant. He remembered washing dishes and bussing tables when he was ten. He hated every minute of it, and his contempt worsened the older he got. He saw his parents as trapped in the family restaurant. They worked twelve and sometimes fourteen hours a day. They were rewarded for their hard work. His mother's native Thai recipes created a loyal customer base. The restaurant was always filled with diners. Thursday through Sunday nights were so busy that hour-long wait times for a table were the norm if you were dumb enough not to have a reservation.

When Andy turned sixteen and got his driver's license, his contempt for the restaurant got worse when his mother started sending him on errands. One such errand sent Andy to Costco to pick up the fifty-pound sack of Jasmine rice their wholesaler forgot to deliver. While looking for the rice, Andy passed by one of the freezer sections and noticed an Asian section that contained Panda Express dinners. The box said, "Enjoy our delicious restaurant meals at home." From then on, Andy decided to replace the Panda boxes with his own. Several months after Andy's father had bypass surgery, he suffered a fatal heart attack. It wasn't lost on Andy that his father's fourteen-hour days probably caused his death. Andy's dream of having a frozen food line would have to wait. He had to save the restaurant he had known since childhood.

Two weeks after Mike left Don's office at Digital Media, he was
finishing his first email marketing campaign. He provided Digital
Media with images and text, and they created a very professional-
looking email. "I would totally respond if I got this email." Mike
thought to himself proudly. "Who wouldn't?" The email
announced a ten percent ROI with a proven track record. It
featured an image of Mike sitting at his desk, talking to a client, a
link to Wolz's website, and a link to Mike's email. He logged into
his Digital Media account and selected the "Send to" option. Mike
had decided to send his email to men fifty and older who were
making two hundred thousand dollars a year or more. He thought
this demographic would give him the most opportunity to gather
new clients. He also sent it to business owners with ten to thirty-
five employees. When it came to scheduling when his email would
be sent, he chose Sunday at 7:00 PM. He thought this would be
when people would start thinking about the week ahead. The folks
suffering from a bad case of Sundaynightis would be especially
interested in managing their finances.

Mike got to his office early Monday morning before anybody
came to work. He couldn't wait to see how his email had
performed and how many new clients he would get. He logged
into his Digital Media account and selected "View results" from
his dashboard. He looked at the screen in disbelief. Out of the five
thousand emails he sent, six hundred and twenty-six recipients
had chosen to unsubscribe, which meant he could never send
them another email. Three hundred forty had bounced from bad
email addresses. What shocked Mike the most was the four thousand emails that arrived and were not opened. Four thousand
people were not interested enough to even open his email. Only
thirty-four emails were opened and read. He could see that all
thirty-four clicked on the company website link, and none clicked

on his email link. His inbox was empty. Mike got up and walked to Tim Halpern's office. He was surprised to see Tim sitting at his desk.

"Hey Tim, you're in early today, Mike said.

"Hey, Mike." Yeah, it's the end of the month, and I'm going over everybody's numbers. Except yours, of course. Knocking it out of the park as usual."

"I may be knocking it out of the park, but my numbers are starting to move in the wrong direction. I need to find some new and very rich clients. Speaking of which. Can you look at the website data and see if anyone's filled out the contact form?"

Tim stopped what he was doing and logged into the company website admin panel.

"Well, look at that," Mike Said. "Looks like we have a record. Twelve people filled out the form. Looking closer, Tim said. "That's weird. These forms were filled out last night. What's up with that?"

Mike said excitedly, "That's fantastic!" Mike proceeded to tell Tim about his email campaign and asked that he send the contact information to his email.

"You know I can't do that, Mike. Website leads are divvied up for the brokers. Their community property. You'll get your share. Don't worry."

Mike became apoplectic. "My share!?" Those are MY leads. I just explained to you what I did to get those!"

"Well, you'll have to take that up with Wolz. You report to him. Remember?

"You're an asshole, Tim. No wonder nobody likes you!" With that, Mike stormed back to his office.

Tim grinned. He despised that Mike reported to Wolz and not to him. He was going to take every opportunity to make Mike's life difficult. An hour later, Mike was sitting at his desk when Harry stormed in, brandishing a printout of Mike's email. He was fuming.

"What the hell is this?" Wolz demanded, waving the paper aggressively.

Mike responded, "I don't know. Can I see what you have there?"

Harry thrust the paper into Mike's hand. Mike glanced at it.

"This is a copy of the marketing email I sent. You must have been included in my demographic. We need to talk about this. Tim is being an asshole, and I need to set things straight. He..."

Wolz interrupted, "WE need to talk about this. Thirteen percent ROI? Proven track record? That's garbage, Mike. Where do you get thirteen percent? The company average is a little less than eleven."

Mike said defensively, "That may be true for the company, but I average almost twelve."

Harry shot back, "Twelve is still not thirteen. You can't tell people something that you know is not true. That's not how we operate here. From now on, any emails you send need to be cleared by me. Understand?"

Dejected, Mike said, "Yes, I understand. I'll clear them through you."

With that, Harry left, leaving Mike to contemplate his situation. First, Tim takes his hard-earned leads, and now Harry wants me to ask permission to breathe. Suddenly, Mike had an idea. Why can't I open my own brokerage business? I'm good at what I do. My clients are happy with me. Why am I settling for a measly commission when I can make more? Hell, the money Wolz Securities makes from MY clients would pay me enough to go on my own. Over dinner that night, Mike told Toni about his arguments with Harry and Tim. He also told her about going into business for himself. Mike was surprised when Toni thought having his own business was a great idea.

"I thought you wouldn't like me quitting my job and starting my own business," Mike said.

"Honey, it's been pretty obvious to me for a while now that you don't like Harry or working at HIS company. Besides, I make enough at my job to support us, and we have plenty in our savings accounts. We can buy the house after you get things going and start making money. How long do you think that'll take?"

Mike replied, "It wouldn't take long if I could get my clients to leave Wolz and come with me. I could get most of them, but Harry probably won't let me."

"What do you mean, let you? What's Harry got to do with you opening your own brokerage?"

"When Harry hired me, I had to sign a 'No-Compete' clause in my employment agreement. I can't do anything that would be competition for Wolz Securities. I can get around that, but there is no way Harry is going to let me take my clients. Even if they wanted to leave Wolz and come over to me, Harry would sue my ass and throw me in the ditch."

"You forget, my love, I'm an attorney at a big ass law firm. I can take care of Harry. Arnold and Little has a huge corporate litigation department. I know who to talk to, and it won't cost you a dime."

That Saturday evening, when Mike was sure nobody would be in the office, he unlocked the front door and went to his office. He turned the light on and logged in to his computer. He took his client's information, compressed it into a file, and attached it to an email he sent to his personal email account. He also sent an email to Harry. Mike turned off the computer and went to the storage room at the back of the office. He took several empty boxes to his office and filled them with his personal items. He put the boxes in Toni's Excella, returned to the front door, and tossed his key through the mail slot. He raised his arms and yelled as loud as he could, "FREE AT LAST!" With that, he got in the Excella and drove home. Mike had been home for barely an hour when his phone rang. It was Harry.

"Hey, Harry. I guess you're calling about the email I sent you."

"You're damn right I am," Harry retorted.

"Harry, I'm sorry things didn't work out between us. I've done a good job and made plenty of money for you. It's time for me to move on."

Harry replied, still angry, "Well, you do that. Just move on. You're not opening a brokerage in this town. I can tell you that right now. You signed a no-compete clause in your employment contract. You're out of the business. I'm going to drag your ass into court and watch you die."

"Harry, my attorney is in the other room. Let me get her on the phone so she can explain how things will play out. Talk as long as you want. My attorney doesn't charge me. I get everything free. You, on the other hand, will get buried in legal bills, and you're still going to lose."

———

SITTING at her desk in her home office, Amy yelled into the phone. "I told you, Todd. And for the last time, I'm telling you again. We don't buy from Vinh Thai anymore. Canton is better, and they deliver when they're supposed to."

Todd shot back, "Canton is more expensive. They charge at least four percent more."

"Todd, Vinh Thai is always out of something, so we end up going to Restaurant Supply or Costco. Both are expensive. Between what we buy elsewhere because Vinh Thai either doesn't have it or it's not delivered on time, we spend more than four percent. Todd, you need to look at the entire cost and not just the number on a price tag. How many times do I have to tell you that?"

Todd replied, "Ok. I get it. My bad. I'll go over the vendor list and send you the ones I'm having trouble with."

"Thank you. As long as I have you on the phone, I'm still waiting for you to send me the liquor license application for Thai Orchid 2. It doesn't do us any good having a restaurant that can't serve alcohol."

Todd said defensively, "I emailed it to you Monday."

"Well, I don't have it."

"Did you check your spam folder? I've been having a problem with my emails going to spam," Todd said."

Sarcastically, Amy replied, "Well, maybe somebody's trying to tell you something."

Scrolling through her spam folder, Amy said, "Hold on, I found it. I'm going to hang up and get this submitted to the state liquor people. Talk to you later." After finishing with Todd, Amy looked at the other emails in her spam folder. "What else is in here?" She asked herself. She noticed one that said in the subject line, "Watch your assets grow while keeping them safe. Invest with Caras Securities and Investments." Amy said out loud, "Investments? Who has any money to invest? Not me, that's for sure." She deleted the email.

ALAN BANNING WAS in serious trouble with his boss at On-Time Delivery. So far this month, Alan missed two "Priority Deliveries," a third one would cost him his job. He was still on probation and couldn't afford to lose his job. Full-time employees receive health insurance, but not if you're in the ninety-day probationary period. His newborn baby, Carmela, was sick and needed expensive drugs to boost her immune system. He needed the company's health insurance to pay for it. Alan had picked up the customer's package at six o'clock that evening, and it had to be at the delivery terminal in thirty minutes to meet the deadline for delivery the next day. He was on Colorado Avenue in Pasadena and needed to get to the 405 freeway if he had any chance of making the deadline. He saw the traffic light ahead turn yellow and made a decision. He pressed the accelerator as far as it would go. The twenty-thousand-pound van wasn't even close to making the light before it turned red. Alan's eyes saw a red Corvette enter the intersection to his right when he approached. Too late. He slammed the brake pedal as hard as he could and braced for the inevitable impact. The Corvette's fiberglass body was no match for the van. The back part of the car exploded as the van made contact. The Corvette's rear-mounted engine was catapulted to the other side of the intersection, hitting a stopped vehicle. The van skidded to a stop ten yards from the Corvette. Alan staggered out of the van and collapsed to his knees when he saw what remained of the sports car and the driver lying face down on the street.

AMY WAS HELPING their housekeeper and sometimes nanny prepare that night's dinner. She and Juana both heard the doorbell ring. "I'll get it, Juana. "It's probably somebody selling solar panels for the umpteenth time." Amy opened the door and saw a female police officer standing in her doorway. Before she could say anything, the officer said, "Please excuse me. Are you Amy Lin?" Amy became fearful. "Amy Bui. I'm married, but yes, I'm Amy Lin. What's going on? Did something happen? Why are you here?" The police officer replied in a sad tone, "Ms. Lin, my name is Officer Williams with the Pasadena police department. Your name was listed as an emergency contact on your sister's phone. I'm very sorry to tell you this, but there has been an automobile accident involving your sister."

Amy's eyes widened as she spoke, "Tammy? Something happened to Tammy. Is she ok?"

"It was a serious accident, Ms. Lin. Your sister sustained very severe injuries. She is alive and being treated at Huntington Hospital. I can take you there. You shouldn't drive yourself."

Amy left with Officer Williams immediately, forgetting to tell Juana what had happened and where she was going. On the way to the hospital, Amy called Andy. After telling him what had happened, she called her parents. Hours after arriving at the hospital, Amy was gathered with her family and close friends in the family waiting room beside the surgical suites on the hospital's third floor. Tammy had been in surgery for almost five hours when one of the surgeons left the operating room to talk to the family. Dr. Karen Donnelly was a neurosurgeon who tried to repair Tammy's severe brain injuries. Other surgeons were still working on repairing the rest of Tammy's multiple problems. Amy approached Dr. Donnelly as soon as he entered the waiting room.

"Is my sister going to be ok?" She asked.

The doctor spoke directly to Amy, not holding back, "Tammy has suffered some severe injuries. She has fractures to her legs, left arm, and multiple ribs. Those can be repaired. The injury to her head is the most serious problem. Her skull is cracked in two locations, causing her brain to swell. The swelling caused an aneurysm to form in a major artery. The only way we could prevent the aneurysm from bursting and Tammy bleeding to death was to tie the artery off, cut the aneurysm out, and sew the artery back together.

"Is she going to be ok?" Tammy's mother asked in a pleading voice.

The surgeon replied, "When we tied off the artery, part of Tammy's brain was deprived of its blood supply. Even though it was only for a very short period, her brain suffered more trauma from the lack of blood. If we didn't tie the artery, Tammy would die."

Amy started yelling at Dr. Donnelly, "Is she going to be all right? What are you telling me!?"

The surgeon replied, like she had so many times in her career, "We need to see how she does in the next two or three days. I'm very sorry to tell you that if she does survive, she will need constant medical attention. She might regain some level of consciousness, but not enough to be functional. I'm very sorry." Wanting to give some level of hope to the family, she continued, "Brain injuries are a puzzling science. People can have very different outcomes for the same type of injury. Medical science has made huge advances in treating brain injury. We're seeing outcomes that were impossible ten years ago."

Amy and her mother began wailing uncontrollably. Andy was frozen in his chair, staring at nothing. They all knew a significant part of their lives had just been ripped away, and nothing would ever fill the terrible and unbearable wound. This was especially true for Amy. Her twin sister would be alive but not present; the Christmas and Thanksgiving holidays would be spent with an empty chair at the table. Her children playing with Tammy's children would never happen. Amy's birthday will always be a terrible reminder of the sister she could no longer celebrate with for the rest of her life.

MIKE WAS SITTING at his desk, smiling in the office space he leased after moving out of his home office. His business was Caras Securities and Investments, or CSI, as he sometimes liked to say. He would follow that up with the phrase, "We investigate every investment opportunity." Toni thought it was corny and unprofessional, but he liked it. Mike was smiling because he was moving up, and having his business in a fancy office park proved it. The monthly rent was a stretch for his finances, but he wanted to project an impressive image when people Googled his company or visited in person. Mike hired his assistant/office manager, Marcy Bingham, from an online employment agency. Marcy was 5'7", had shoulder-length red hair, and was a regular at her gym. Like Mike, when he started, Marcy wanted a career in financial planning. Mike gave Marcy her first job. He wanted a good-looking employee because men traded stocks forty-five percent more than women. Men also checked their investment progress twenty-one percent more than women. These numbers were reflected in Mike's current client base. Mike wanted to close the "investment gender gap, so he skewed his email marketing more toward women than men. Mike didn't care if a man or woman responded to his emails as long as they responded.

When Mike officially opened for business, his first call was to his father's friend from Keystone, Jack Richardson. Jack was his first client at Wolz, and Mike wanted him to be his first client at CSI.

Jack was also a very active trader. He was always looking for a better ROI, no matter how well his portfolio was doing. Over the next several weeks, Mike brought most of his Wolz and Patterson clients over to CSI. Mike desperately needed the 1.5% management fee he charged his clients to pay the rent. Harry threatened legal action over Mike's "client stealing" but never followed through. The only thing he did was have his attorney send Mike a cease-and-desist order, which he promptly threw in the trash.

Mike realized he wouldn't make it if he didn't get new clients and get them quickly. With Marcy's help, he created a monthly newsletter with articles he copied from financial publications. He hoped to accomplish two things with this. The first was enticing his clients to trade, and the second was to remind them of their investments and spur referrals. Mike knew most of his clients only glanced at their monthly statements. As long as their investments were growing, they were happy and filed the statement away. Mike would send his newsletter email at the same time his client's monthly statement was sent. He hoped his clients would forward his newsletter to their friends. Mike quickly understood that sending emails to clients and hoping for referrals was not a sustainable strategy. He decided to max out his company credit card and buy an email mailing list from Digital Media. The list he bought contained twenty thousand email addresses. The demographic he chose consisted of people with incomes of one hundred thousand dollars or more. He didn't care if they were male or female as long as they responded.

Mike was sitting at his desk early one Monday morning, reviewing the results of his last email campaign. He was disappointed to see that only six hundred were opened and read. Worse, only four had filled out the contact form on his website. He considered buying more email addresses, but even doubling his initial twenty thousand wouldn't give him what he needed. He heard the front door open and looked up from his screen to see Marcy coming into work. She took off her coat and went into Mike's office. Standing before him, she asked, "How was your weekend?"

Mike replied, "I spent it getting my email campaign sent out."

"I know. You sent me one."

"Well, what did you think of it?"

"Honestly? I thought it was boring. You talk about how great CSI is, but you don't show people how that affects them. You don't give them a reason to trust you with their money or benefit by being a CSI client."

"Ok, that's fair. What would you do if you were me?"

"Well, the first thing I would do is mention how SIPC insures their money. Highlight the name, Securities Investor Protection Corporation, and that the federal government runs it. Emphasize Protection. Also, mention that their money is insured up to five hundred thousand dollars. The ROI you talk about isn't much different than any other brokerage. Instead of eight percent, make it, say, twelve percent."

"No, twelve is too much. I average eight. I can't advertise something I can't deliver on."

"Mike, you just said the magic word, Average. I'm sure you've had years where you made much more than eight percent. The market goes up and down like a Yo-yo. Everybody knows that. Besides, you're a small brokerage; tell people that. Tell them you personally watch over their money. You're not some online, over-the-phone, faceless person. They can always talk to you about their investments."

Mike stood up, raised his arms, and smiled, "Marcy, I knew I hit the lottery when I hired you."

A month later, Mike was in his home office preparing to send the new email he and Marcy had worked on. He hated waiting for an entire month between emails, but Don at Digital Media told him people unsubscribe more when they get too frequent emails from the same company. It was Sunday night, and as he clicked the send button, Toni entered the room. Mike looked up and saw Toni smiling and holding out her hand with something in it.

Mike asked, "Why are you smiling, and what's that in your hand?"

"Honey, we're having a baby!"

Mike looked closer at the pregnancy test Toni was holding and saw the symbol indicating a positive result.

"No way!" He said. "Is that thing accurate? Are you really pregnant?"

"Well, according to this, I am. We're going to need a bigger place to live."

Mike was overjoyed to learn he would be a father, but he couldn't help thinking of the added financial pressure he and Toni would face. He came into work on Monday and couldn't wait to see the results of his and Marcy's email campaign. The baby heightened his anxiety on the way, and the extra income he would need. Toni and Mike's discussion about buying a house and her desire to be a full-time mom increased his angst. He logged into his Digital Media account and was shocked to see how many people had opened his email. He checked his website contact form and saw that over a hundred people had asked for more information. It was going to be very busy this week.

SEVERAL MONTHS INTO HER PREGNANCY, Toni and Mike were actively looking for a house to buy. They chose the South Pasadena area for its beautiful homes and proximity to Mike's office. Their realtor took them to a house on a corner lot across from a small park. It was a large, stately house, as were all the other houses in the neighborhood. It had red brick with white trim and a huge front porch. They decided this was the house for them, and Mike immediately started thinking about how they would pay for it.

AMY AND ANDY stared at the check their attorney gave them several weeks after they appeared in court. They had sued On-Time Delivery on behalf of Tammy over the accident their driver had caused and received a settlement. It was a tremendous amount of money, but Andy and Amy knew Tammy would need all of it to pay for the care she would need for the rest of her life. They decided to set some money aside in a high-yield savings account that paid five percent a year. This would be used for her ongoing care, and they invested the rest in US savings bonds, earning a paltry three percent a year. Amy insisted on the savings bonds because of the safety they provided. Andy didn't think the savings bonds paid enough. He thought they should look for investments that paid more.

MIKE WAS in his home office trying to figure out how he and Toni would pay for their new home. Toni didn't want the stress of her job to interfere with her pregnancy, so she went on maternity leave. Though she wouldn't admit it, Mike knew her maternity leave would become permanent. Suddenly, Mike came up with a solution to his house problem. If he made a larger down payment on the mortgage, his monthly payment would be less. Getting the money for the larger down payment was simple. His business had it sitting in the bank. Security brokers are required to have a bank account called a "Special Reserve Bank Account." This account holds a portion of the money Mike's clients have invested. Mike didn't take all the money and immediately put it in the reserve account. The amount Mike was required to hold in the reserve account resulted from a complex calculation that considered many factors. One of those factors was the management fee that CSI charged its customers.

Mike would increase the management fee in the calculation but not reflect it on the client's monthly statement. The client's money in their account was unaffected, but the altered calculation resulted in a surplus in the reserve account. He would borrow the excess reserve money for the larger down payment. Mike figured CSI was growing enough that he could pay back the reserve money from the income generated by CSI's growing client base. Mike knew the Securities and Exchange Commission (SEC) wouldn't accept his smoke and mirrors act and land him in hot water. It was a risk he was willing to take. He knew he could have everything paid back before anybody found out. After Mike and Toni had signed the paperwork and made it official, they became proud owners of their first house in upscale South Pasadena. It didn't take long for another considerable expense for which Mike would have to find the money. Toni was spending money hand over fist, furnishing the house, and she wasn't going to the Palm Springs consignment stores to do it. When it came to furnishing the baby's room, Toni wanted to decorate it with a boy's theme. Mike disapproved.

"Buying baby stuff before he's born is bad luck," Mike said, standing in the empty baby's room.

Toni asked, "What's luck got to do with buying Robbie a crib and toys?"

"It just is. Harry Wolz would always say, "You never start spending your commission until the client's check clears the bank." I am a one-hundred-percent believer in that. Don't count your chickens before your eggs hatch. Buying Robbie, and that's another thing. Naming a baby before it's born is not good, either. Naming and buying invites bad luck. He could be born with two heads, and then we would have to come up with two names."

Toni shook her head and walked out of the room.

———

AMY WAS SITTING at the kitchen table when she hung up the phone and started crying. She had been speaking with Tammy's doctor at the long-term care facility where Tammy was a patient. Dr. James Wilcox had just told her that Tammy had developed a complication in her respiratory system. He assured her Tammy was not in any danger and that her condition was not uncommon. He went on to tell her Tammy would need an oxygen tent to help her breathe, along with a new and very expensive medication. Dr. Wilcox transferred Amy to the billing department, where she learned how much the new treatment would cost. Later in the evening, after dinner and when the kids were asleep, Amy told her husband the details of her conversation with Dr. Wilcox and Tammy's new expense.

"It costs that much?" Andy asked a little too loudly. How much will insurance cover?"

"Hush, you'll wake the kids, and yes, it's more money, but Tammy has to have it. We don't have a choice. Her insurance won't cover most of the cost because it's a new drug and classified as experimental."

Still speaking loudly, Andy said, "That's going to put her in the red each month. We'll need more money to cover the extra cost. That 'experimental' is crap, so the insurance can get out of paying."

"I know that, and keep your voice down. I've already started looking at Tammy's finances. We're going to have to do something with those savings bonds. The three percent they're earning isn't enough over time. We could put them in another high-yield savings account, but even the five percent in that isn't going to cut it. We'll need at least eight to cover the extra expense and give us some room if anything else happens."

Andy lowered his voice to a whisper. "We need to find some investment to give us the ten you're talking about. But it needs to be safe —really safe."

Amy said, "If we're going to get a decent return, we need to take some risks. I'm going to talk to Terry Harston at the bank tomorrow. Maybe he has some ideas."

The following day, Terry took Amy's call right away. Thai Orchid Restaurant Group was an important client, and Amy never let Bill forget it.

Terry put the call on speakerphone and spoke. "Hello, Amy. How are you today?"

"I'm good, Terry. Thanks for asking. Listen, I have a problem, and I need your advice." Amy told Terry about her sister's financial situation and that she needed to get a bigger ROI from the savings bond money.

"I'm sorry to hear that about your sister. You're in a tough situation. I must confess I don't know much about investing in the stock market. I have my savings in the bank's 401 (k). The bank matches my contribution, so it's a pretty good deal."

Amy asked, "Doesn't your bank have some kind of wealth management department?"

"No, I'm sorry, Amy. Providence is a savings and lending bank. Our highest-yield account isn't going to give you what you need. You know, I got this email the other day. Hold on while I get into my email account."

After what seemed like an eternity to Amy, Terry spoke, "Here it is. The company is called Caras Securities. Jeez, it says you can get a seventeen percent ROI. I need to tell my brother about this."

"Can you forward that email to me?" Amy asked impatiently.

"Of course. I'm sending it right now."

When Amy looked at the email, she thought it looked familiar. She clicked on the link to Caras's website and was impressed with what she saw. Then, she clicked the "Contact Us" button and completed the contact form.

MIKE WAS SITTING at his desk reading the online edition of Financial Times when Marcy walked into his office.

She said, "You're not going to like this. I came in this morning, and only five website contact forms were filled out. We're going to have to come up with something to get new clients. Of course, it doesn't help to be spending money on renovating this office and leasing the space next door."

Mike decided CSI needed a more impressive image, so he expanded into the space next door and completely redesigned his current space. He also "adjusted" the income and revenue reports for CSI so he could qualify for a bank loan. He knew he could offset the monthly loan repayment by adding the new brokers he had yet to hire. They would bring in the extra income.

Mike looked up at Marcy and said, "I'm working on a big project and don't have time. Why don't you work on those contact forms? You got your broker license two months ago. Time to start using it."

Marcy smiled. "Thanks, Mike! I wondered when you would let me start contributing to this place." Marcy started to leave but turned around to face Mike. "Don't forget, we have training on the new client management software tomorrow."

"I don't think I'm going to be able to make that. I'm having lunch with Willy Patterson tomorrow. I'm pitching CSI to manage Patterson Auto Group's executive 401K plan."

Marcy asked, "What's an executive plan?"

"It's for all of Patterson's top management. Employees with ten or more years with the company will get twenty-five percent of their salary added to their 401K's when they retire. It's going to be CSI's entry into the big leagues. Why do you think I'm expanding our office?"

Mike didn't tell Marcy that he was desperate for cash and needed the money Patterson would bring in to pay back the reserve account. He had just bought a second home in Lake Arrowhead and paid for it out of the reserve account. The project he mentioned to Marcy was setting up a separate business entity—an LLC called Caras Wealth Management. He would have his new clients make their deposits to the LLC so he could bypass CSI's books and keep the SEC from finding out about his "borrowing" from the reserve account.

"Well, good luck with Patterson. We need the business." Marcy returned to her office to follow up on the contact forms. She sent each one a boilerplate email inviting them to schedule an appointment to discuss their needs. Amy read Marcy's email and immediately scheduled an appointment.

Harry Wolz was sitting at his desk, fuming about the email he had received. Wolz was included in Mike's email demographic and regularly received his marketing emails. His first instinct was to unsubscribe from the list. He despised Mike and wanted nothing to do with him. He decided to keep receiving the emails as a way to spy on what Mike was doing. He might get some ideas about bringing in new clients himself. Harry walked into Tim Halpern's office, waving a printout of Mike's most recent email, and spoke, "I don't know where he comes off promising eighteen percent. It's beyond absurd. He's got to be up to something, and knowing Mike, it's probably not very Kosher."

Tim replied, "Don't you have a friend who works at the SEC? You went to school with him or something like that?"

"Lavar Bowers. We went to the same high school—Meadowdale High School in Dayton, Ohio. I saw him at a class reunion years ago. He's probably retired by now."

Tim said, "Hold on. I'm looking him up on LinkedIn." After a few moments, Tim said, "Nope, he still works at the SEC. He's a Director of Government Relations, whatever that is. I have a premium LinkedIn subscription, so I can send him an InMail. What do you want to say?"

AMY WALKED into Caras Securities and was greeted by Carol Sanchez, the receptionist who replaced Marcy after her promotion. Carol called Marcy on the intercom, and shortly after, Marcy came into the waiting area and spoke, "Hi, I'm Marcy Bingham. Thank you for coming in. You must be Amy."

"Hi, Marcy. Yes, I'm Amy."

"Why don't we go into my office, and you can tell me what your needs are?"

Amy followed Marcy into her office and sat down in front of her desk. She told Marcy what had happened to her sister, Tammy's financial problems, and the amount of money she had. Marcy spoke, surprised at what Amy had told her. "I'm very sorry about your sister. That is a considerable sum of money in bonds, which yields only three percent. Given your sister's ongoing health issues, I understand why you want asset safety. I think you should consider an Index Fund.

Amy replied, "I am new to all of this. What is an index fund?"

"Sorry, an index fund is a group of stocks that track the entire market's performance. If the stock market goes up ten percent, your fund goes up ten percent."

"Is that true if the market goes down?"

"Yes, it does, but you must understand an index fund is something you invest in for the long term. It's not something to trade back and forth. The S&P 500 is a good example of an index fund. If you had invested in the S&P twenty years ago, you would have a 345% ROI. If you reinvested the dividends, your ROI would be 546%. Given the large amount of money you have, you could take the yearly dividend to pay your sister's medical bills and not have to touch your principal."

Amy almost jumped out of her chair. "That sounds wonderful! I want to do that. What do I need to do to get started?"

"Well, the first thing we need to do is set up an account. I can do that now, but bear with me. We have this new software, and I'm still getting used to it."

Later that day, Mike sat in Toni's Excella outside the restaurant where he and Willy had just eaten lunch. He had been in the car for over half an hour, staring at the windshield. Willy had turned down Mike's offer to handle Patterson's executive package. Without Patterson's money, he could not pay back the reserve account he had been draining. His email marketing was not bringing in enough new clients, and his expenses from the office expansion were growing faster than he could keep up with. His house in Arrowhead had just closed, and he could look forward to another mortgage payment each month. When Mike finally pulled out of his trance, he returned to his office. When he got there, Marcy walked in with a huge smile.

"You're not going to believe this, Mike. I met with one of our website contacts, Amy Bui. She went on to tell Mike about Amy's situation and the amount of money she wanted to invest with CSI.

Mike rocketed up from his chair and yelled, "That's fantastic! Good job, Marcy!"

Marcy replied, "Well, it was just a contact form follow-up."

Several days later, Mike felt confident after Marcy told him about Amy and the money she would bring in. He would have Amy direct deposit her money into his LLC account. He could pay off some of his bills and mortgage payments and use the rest to make the reserve account whole.

LaVar Bowers heard his cell phone ring while washing his hands in the bathroom of SEC headquarters on F Street in Washington, DC. The sound told him he had a LinkedIn InMail message waiting to be read. He dried his hands and pushed the screen to read the mail. "Well, well," he said out loud. "Harry Wolz. Now, there's a name I haven't heard for a while." LaVar called the number on the screen and was immediately connected to

Harry's cell phone. Harry heard his ringtone, saw the caller ID, and answered.

"LaVar Bowers. As I live and breathe. How are you? The last time I saw you was at our twentieth reunion."

LaVar laughed and said, "You still telling people you're on the football team?"

Harry chuckled and said, "What do you mean? I was on the football team."

"I don't think being the team's videographer counts, Harry."

Harry, still chuckling, said, "Well, that line got me more than a few girls to spend some time with me."

"You still in the stock business? You were talking about starting your own company. Funny how things turned out. You're selling stocks, and I'm working for people who keep you guys honest. No offense, of course."

"That's why I'm calling, LaVar."

Harry went on to tell LaVar about Mike's advertising lies, and he didn't think his lies stopped at just advertising. He suspected Mike was not following the rules because of the rumors he had heard in the tight-knit Southern California broker community. Mike's start-up company didn't match the real estate he was buying. It didn't match anything he was buying.

After listening, LaVar said, "I hear you, Harry. Tell you what. I'll pass your information over to our enforcement people. They handle this kind of thing."

After catching up, Harry disconnected, sat back in his chair, and smiled.

RACHEL SIEGEL WAS an investigator for the SEC's Enforcement and Litigation Department in their Los Angeles field office. The SEC is the government's police force for the securities industry. They privately investigate possible wrongdoing so as not to disrupt the securities business's everyday operations. However, they were just the opposite when it came to charging the wrongdoing and the people behind it. After reading LaVar's email, she logged in to her computer and pulled up Caras Securities' website. The first thing that caught her attention was the ROI they were advertising. She clicked on the "Who we are" button and saw pictures and Bios of Mike and Marcy. She saw that Mike was the President and founder of Caras Investments and Securities. Rachel picked up her phone and called the number shown on the website. Carol Sanchez answered.

"Hello, thank you for calling Caras Investments and Securities. This is Carol. How can I help you?

"Hello. May I please speak to Mike Caras?" Rachel asked.

"I'm sorry. Mr. Caras isn't in right now. Would you like to leave a message? He checks his messages quite often."

"No, that won't be necessary. Is Marcy Bingham in? Can I speak to her, please?"

"Yes, she is. May I ask who's calling?"

"My name is Rachel Seigel. I'm with the Securities and Exchange Commission."

"I see. Can you please hold while I connect you?"

Carol called Marcy's intercom extension and told her who was on the phone and that she wanted to speak with her. Marcy nervously picked up and said, "Hello, this is Marcy Bingham. How can I help you?"

"Hello, Ms. Bingham. My name is Rachel Siegel. I'm with the SEC's enforcement commission. I have some questions about some of your advertising and the ROI you are promising."

"I see. Unfortunately, I'm not the person who handles our advertising. That would be Mike Caras. He's the owner and handles the advertising. He's not in right now. Can I take your number and have him call you back?"

Marcy wrote down Rachel's number and told her Mike would call her as soon as he could. Rachel disconnected the call and sat back in her chair. Rachel hung up and also sat back in her chair. She thought, "This is stupid. I have a million more important issues than somebody's advertising. Just because some low-level SEC employee sticks their nose in, I'm supposed to drop everything?"

The next day, after Marcy told him about Rachel wanting to talk to him, Mike was in his office when he picked up his phone and called her. He was so nervous that he had to take several deep breaths before punching in her number. He called Rachel's direct line, and she picked up after the third ring.

"Hello. This is Rachel Siegel."

"Hello, Ms. Siegel. This is Mike Caras from Caras Securities and Investments. My partner, Marcy Bingham, told me you wanted to speak with me."

"Hello, Mr. Caras. Thank you for responding to my request. I'm with the Division of Enforcement and have a few questions about your business. Specifically, the ROI percentages you are advertising."

After speaking with Rachel for ten minutes, he hung up and breathed a sigh of relief. Rachel only wanted to remind him of the penalties for misleading advertising. He was safe. They didn't know anything about his smoke-and-mirror activities. She did ask some weird questions, though. He answered them vaguely and didn't think much about them. His thoughts turned to a much more pressing item: More of his clients were taking money out of their accounts than usual, his personal expenses were growing because Toni was spending money on the Arrowhead house faster than a jackrabbit, and his LLC account was getting smaller. He was getting close to being unable to pay his clients the money they wanted to draw from their accounts. He still hadn't received Tammy Lin's money and was desperate to get it. He asked Marcy to find out where Tammy's money was. His anxiety was overtaking reality. It had, after all, only been a short time since Marcy had signed Amy up as a client. He was getting desperate because he wasn't bringing in new clients as fast as before. He wasn't sleeping well.

TWO DAYS after his talk with Rachel, Mike got a call from Jack Richardson while sitting at his desk. Jack had invested his parents' retirement money with Mike, and Jack's father took great joy in looking at his monthly statements.

"Hello, Jack. Nice to hear from you." Mike thought Jack was going to give him some more money to "invest," but he was wrong.

"Mike, I have some bad news. My father died two weeks ago."

"I'm sorry to hear that, Jack. How are you holding up? More importantly, how is your mother doing?"

"As expected. After you've been with someone for fifty-two years, she's the reason for my call. Dad handled all of the finances. Mom couldn't understand an ROI if you asked her to spell it. She doesn't want strangers handling her retirement, even after I showed her how well Dad was doing with it. Even after I showed her how well I was doing with you. Her best friend, Inez, showed her how she was doing, and it didn't make a difference. She only trusts the bank and won't hear of anything else. Even her sister couldn't make her understand."

Mike slumped in his chair. Cashing out Jack's mother would be a big hit, and he wasn't sure he could cover it. He said, "I'm sorry to hear that. Your family has done very well trusting their money with me. I hate seeing your mother put all her money into a five percent bank account. Is there any way you can talk her out of it?" Mike desperately hoped the answer was yes.

"I'm sorry, Mike. She's dug in. I'll send you an email with her bank account number. You wire her money into that. Will that work?"

Mike could barely speak. He said that was fine and that he would wire the money right away. He turned to his computer and pulled up Amy's account. He let out a sigh when he saw there was no money in it. Mike started to get Marcy on the intercom and find out where Amy's money was. After a moment, he decided to call Amy himself. Amy was in the grocery store, putting items in her cart, when her phone started playing her ringtone. She took the phone from her back pocket, looked at the caller ID, and sent the call to voicemail.

A week after leaving Amy a voicemail, Carol called Mike's intercom extension. It was Rachel Siegel. Mike picked up, thinking she was calling about his advertising. He had toned down the inflated ROI numbers in his ads. What did she want now? Mike picked up and said, "Hello, Ms. Siegel. If you're calling about my advertising, you can look at my website and see I don't advertise ROI anymore."

"Yes, I noticed that. That's not what I'm calling you about. I have a few questions I'd like to get answers to before I close your case."

Rachel asked Mike about his business and how he managed his client's money. Mike didn't understand why she was asking him things unrelated to his advertising, but he answered them anyway. He failed to be truthful in his answers. Rachel hung up her phone and turned to her co-worker Tom Edsall, who was listening to the conversation on speakerphone in her office's conference room.

Rachel spoke, "I didn't get anything from that. I don't think he knows anything about the emails we received."

Tom replied, "Well, I've had our IT techs try to track down the sender, but they tell me the email address is anonymous, and the encryption is too hard to break.

"Well, Tom, what do you think? Do we have enough from those anonymous emails?"

"I think we do. I'll send this to our friends at the FBI, and they can get things going on their end."

Two weeks later, Mike and Toni were jolted out of bed at 5:00 AM by somebody banging loudly on the front door. They could see flashing red and blue lights coming through the window blinds. As if the banging and lights weren't enough, someone yelled through a bullhorn, "This is the FBI. Mike Caras, come outside."

"Mike! What's going on?" Toni shouted over the bullhorn.

"I don't know! I don't know!"

Mike grabbed his robe, put it on, and raced down the stairs. He opened the door to find at least a dozen people wearing windbreakers with the letters FBI stamped in the back. Standing next to the man with the bullhorn, one of them stepped forward and asked, "Are you Mike Caras?"

Mike replied, barely audible, "Yes. I'm Mike Caras. What's going on here?"

"Mr. Caras, I'm Agent Fullmer with the FBI. You are under arrest for securities fraud, bank fraud, wire fraud, money laundering, and probably a lot more after the prosecutor gets done with you."

After he was handcuffed and placed in one of the FBI cars, Mike looked out the window and saw Toni, with a dazed look on her face, standing in the front yard, holding their baby while the FBI agents poured into the house to gather evidence.

MARCY DIDN'T GO to work that day. Instead, she sat at her kitchen table with her freshly brewed espresso. She opened her laptop, logged into her Digital Media account, and canceled her subscription. When Bull Software came to the office to install CSI's new securities software, Mike couldn't attend the training. Marcy had the tech set her up as an Administrator so she could learn how to use the software and go over it with Mike when he had time. When the data from the old software was imported into the new program, Marcy could see what Mike had been doing with the reserve account. When she found out Mike had asked Amy to deposit her funds into a different account, a clear violation of the law, she looked further and discovered Mike's LLC account. Marcy was stunned when she saw what Mike had been doing with the client's money. She made up her mind. She wanted a future in financial services and wouldn't let some crook ruin her career. She thought about calling the SEC directly, but decided they would probably ask her to gather documentation about Mike's activities. She didn't want to get involved in that. She contacted Don Wheelan at Digital Media and asked him how she could send an anonymous email so no one could find out where it came from. Don didn't ask any questions. CSI was a very good client.

She downloaded CSI's data and emailed it to the SEC.

AFTER MIKE'S CONVICTION, all his and Toni's assets were given a government ID number. These numbers were placed on each item in the form of stickers. One of those stickers was placed on Toni's Excella's windshield. Everything was going up for auction to help pay back the money he stole from his clients. Sitting at his desk, Harry Wolz grinned from ear to ear. He was reading an article in the Financial Times magazine.

3

BOOK THREE

THE EXCELA GETS A NEW OWNER

Quentin was promoted from Final Inspection to robot operator much quicker than he had imagined. He liked his new position very much. He suspected Mr. Sweeney had something to do with his promotion, but didn't know how. He remained in contact with Sweeney and talked to him several times a year. Their conversations were mostly about how Sweeney's dealership was doing and where Quentin was on his path to designing cars. Quentin didn't know that Clark Sweeney and Willy Patterson grew up together and remained close friends. In their last conversation, Quentin told Mr. Sweeney he was enrolled in Morriston Community College and was working on an Industrial Design degree. Quentin's mother, Mary, could pay for his education because of the success of her beauty business. She had just opened her third location and was considering franchising Jayvon Beauty Salons. Mary's devotion to Javon's memory drove the business's success. He gave his life for his family, and she wouldn't forget it.

PATTERSON AUTOMOTIVE GROUP had created a new division during the 2020 pandemic. The new division was for the rapidly expanding used car business. Used cars had a high profit margin, and Patterson couldn't get enough of them. Patterson had two supply sources: Trade-ins from its dealer network and auctions. There are two types of auctions: public and government. The public auctions are where car dealers buy and sell used cars. This is called the wholesale market. New car dealers use the estimated auction value as a basis for the amount they offer customers for their trade-ins. Government auctions are where government-owned vehicles are sold to dealers and the general public. Vehicles seized for criminal activity are also sold at government auctions. One vehicle in the seizure lot outside Los Angeles was a Blue Monarch Motors Excella. A sticker on its driver's side windshield read "Treasury ID: DR13256323M." The paperwork stated that the car had been sold to Patterson Automotive Group's used car division.

CLETUS BUREAUX WAS BORN and raised in Hattiesburg, Mississippi. He was 37 years old and married to his high school sweetheart, Susan. They had two children: Cletus Jr., who was six, and Karen, who just had her fourth birthday. Cletus and Susan briefly lived in New Orleans while he attended Tulane University Law School. Having a law degree from a school like Tulane meant he could land a job at any prestigious law firm he wanted. Cletus didn't like big city life and called Hattiesburg his home. He was an "ambulance chaser," and he was proud of it. He had nothing but disdain for lawyers, or attorneys, as they liked to be called, who worked for big corporate clients. He was all about helping the common man or woman get through their troubles and getting paid after his client was done with them. Most of his clients suffered personal injury, and Cletus was more than happy to sue

anybody who was even remotely involved. He liked suing companies because they always settled out of court, and he didn't have to
bother with all the work and upfront expenses necessary to bring a
case to trial. One hot and sticky summer Friday afternoon, Cletus,
his office manager, Stella Hardesty, and his investigator, Beau
Gaston, were celebrating in Cletus's office. Cletus had just won a
big award for his client, Maybelle Carver. Maybelle was sent to the
emergency room after a large can of tomato sauce hit her on the
head as she was reaching for it in the grocery store where she
shopped. It was cheaper for the grocery chain to pay Maybelle
rather than pay attorneys. After the celebration, Cletus walked
across the parking lot to his car. He stopped about ten feet from
his old car and looked at it. He had been driving this car ever since
he had graduated from law school. He decided it was time to trade
up to something more befitting a lawyer who just cashed in a big
check. His wife, Susan, didn't think much about his new car plans.
When Cletus arrived home, he told her what he wanted.

"Cletus Bureauex, what on earth are you thinking? You just came
into a pile of money and want to waste it on a new car? We got bills
to pay and children to feed and clothe. You're not buying a new
car!"

Cletus was very successful arguing in court the few times he was
there, but the same couldn't be said about arguing with his wife.
She did have a point, but he decided to press the issue anyway. He
wanted to ditch that old car.

"C'mon, honey, that old car is a wreck. I don't know how many
times Rufus Gadrey has gouged me at the service station fixing
that thing. It's always in the shop for something."

Susan started to say something but stopped herself. He did have a
point. She said in a quieter tone, "New cars are expensive. Why
don't we get a used one? A nice one that's not too expensive." Just
like someone on the witness stand, Cletus saw his opening. The

witness cracked, and he was going to take full advantage. Later that evening, after the kids were asleep, Susan was out in the garage, busy packing orders for her customers. She made beautiful scented candles, and her online business was booming. She was going to have to hire somebody to help her.

Cletus was sitting at the kitchen table with his laptop open. Susan said he could buy a used car, and one "not very expensive" was a relative term. He knew which car he wanted, and buying online would give him the best selection. He googled "Monarch Excella" and was greeted with a screen full of places to buy one. He clicked on "Patterson Pre-Owned Automobiles" and was taken to their website. He clicked on a car he thought would significantly enhance his image around town. Behind the scenes on Patterson's website, an order processor located Cletus's Excella. It was in Patterson's Beverly Hills dealership. The processor clicked on the car and arranged to have it shipped to Louisiana. Several weeks later, Cletus received an email telling him his car was ready to be picked up at Patterson Pre-Owned Automobiles' newest location in Belle Chasse, a few miles south of New Orleans. That Saturday, Cletus and his family got in his ancient car for the last time. They arrived at the dealership two hours later. When Cletus and Susan saw the blue Excella for the first time, they had two very different reactions. Cletus was elated. He worked hard and deserved to be seen driving this beautiful machine. Owning an Excella was a status symbol, even if it was two years old. Susan was shocked. She couldn't believe Cletus would waste so much money on this car. School started in a couple of months, and the kids needed everything.

"Cletus Bureaux. What have you done?" Susan loudly said.

Cletus knew he was in trouble. Whenever Susan said his last name, he had to brace himself. Cletus was ok; Cletus Bureaux meant he had to think fast or change the subject. Cletus thought fast.

"C'mon, honey pot, this is a terrific car. They make these things to last. No more Rufus Gadrey's repair bills; besides, I got us a great deal on this car."

Like speaking to the jury, Cletus knew he had to get his wife more involved with the car. He opened the driver's door and asked Susan to get in. He didn't notice that one of the driver's door rivets looked slightly different from the others. Susan sat in the car and had to admit that this was a very nice car. She smiled when she thought of taking the kids to school and having the other kids' parents see what she was driving. Especially Connie Haverson. "Wait till that bitch sees this," she said to herself.

JOHN ZSU and Travis Beloit were roommates at MIT and were studying to get their degrees in chemical engineering. They knew the world was a long way from kicking its fossil fuel addiction, and they wanted to make burning it much less stressful on the environment. John and Travis used MIT's vast resources to devise a way to burn oil and gas without producing hydrocarbon emissions. They knew this would upend how people drove their cars and heated their homes. They also knew their invention would help the environment immensely and make them fabulously wealthy. It was Travis's idea not to share anything with anybody, especially MIT. He convinced John they should quit school before graduating and start their own business. They were watching TV in the university student center when Travis turned to John and spoke.

"If we leave early and don't graduate, MIT can't claim any interest in our business. Besides, we don't need anything from them anymore."

John replied while looking at the TV, "I see your point. But we don't have the money to buy everything we need to get things going. We're talking some big bucks here for the lab equipment alone."

"How about your dad?" Travis asked. "He has to be rich for you to be here without a scholarship. Maybe you can get him to invest. He could be a silent partner, whatever that is."

John stopped looking at the TV and looked at Travis. "Well, I guess it doesn't hurt to ask."

John's parents, Zichen and Aihan, emigrated from China just before he was born. His sister, Beiye, who was seven, changed her name to Sarah after arriving in Chicago. Zichen was a minor government functionary in China and received permission to move his family to the US. China encouraged parents with children who had academic promise to move to the US and take full advantage of its universities. The Chinese government paid for everything. The only thing asked in return was for the children to bring what they learned back to China. This was non-negotiable and came with severe consequences if not obeyed. Six months after leaving MIT, John and Travis started their business. They called it SynCor, an acronym for Synthetic Correlation, which was what John and Travis called their invention. Several months after signing the office lease, John walked into their office's small, empty warehouse section. The only thing in the space was a wooden workbench with papers and technical drawings scattered on top. Travis stood over the bench, holding one of the papers.

"You're in early," John said, walking into the warehouse.

Travis replied, still looking at the paper in his hands, "I'm trying to put a list together of what we will need to build the correlator. Once I get that done, you can start sourcing the parts."

"Sorry, man, I have to get the patent applications filed. They should have been filed months ago."

Travis replied sarcastically, "Well, if you recall, we didn't have any money months ago. Without your dad, we still wouldn't. Speaking of money, we'll need more to pay for the refracture parts."

"I have a solution for our money problems," John said, rubbing his thumb and fingers together. We're going to get a bank loan and a line of credit. My dad is going to co-sign for the money. I'm tired of always going to him with my hand out."

Travis put down the paper he was holding and turned to face John.

"Damnit, I forgot to call Peter Murphy at Tennico. He wants to see our proposal before we meet with his engineering group." He pulled his phone from his back pocket and called Peter's number.

Tennico Oil and Gas was a huge energy conglomerate based in New Orleans. It had a presence in almost every part of the world. It owned oil and gas fields, refineries, and electrical power plants. Its gas stations were found in even the smallest towns around the country. Tennico had an oil refinery just outside Hattiesburg. It was called Tennico RD, which stood for research and development. The refinery was used as a laboratory to experiment with new refining technology. Cletus made a good chunk of his income from the personal injury cases the plant provided. Tennico never went to court. Marcus Hudsen was the general manager at Tennico RD. He was forty-three years old, divorced, and had two children in his ex's custody. His friends, the few he had, and his family, the ones who still spoke to him, told him he drank too much, but he didn't listen. His current flame was Darlene Moss, who ordered supplies and equipment in the refinery's procurement office. Darlene was eleven years younger than Marcus and knew he drank, but that didn't matter to her. What mattered were the gifts he gave her and the money she pried out of him. Darlene grew up in Tallulah, Louisiana, a tiny town with six thousand residents. She had three older brothers who never got past their second year in high school. When the nearby National Guard base moved to Leesville, many of the town's residents, including her three brothers, moved with it. The only employer left was a cotton processing plant that employed two hundred people. Darlene's parents, Atticus and Betsy, were born and raised in Tallulah and met in elementary school. Atticus owned a small hardware store that thrived before the Guard base moved. When that happened, Atticus could barely keep the doors open, and the family fell on hard times. Darlene was eight when the base moved. The family's financial downfall created a deep fear of not having money in her. She became obsessed with money and not having it. When she wasn't in school, Darlene and her mother made blueberry and peach pies in the kitchen during the summer. They sold them faster than they could make them, and all the money was used to help with the family's financial needs. However, Betsy made sure Darlene was paid one dollar for each pie sold. Darlene would deposit the day's earnings in her porcelain piggy bank on her dresser. She liked that the piggy bank had a slot to put money in, but unless you "broke the bank," you couldn't get it out. Darlene was the only child in the Moss family to graduate from high school. She knew her ticket to a decent-paying job required an education, even if it was only a high school degree. She also knew she wouldn't find that job in Tallulah. During her senior year, she would stay after class and fill out online job applications using the library's computer. One of those applications was for a job at Tennico RD as an administrative assistant in the procurement office.

Peter Murphy was Tennico's chief engineer. His department's current project was re-designing Tennico RD to accommodate the new emission reduction processing system, or ERPS as it was called. ERPS was two years behind schedule and cost more than double the initial projections. Peter wasn't entirely on board with the ERPS project. He didn't think the technology would be efficient when brought to scale. It worked great in the laboratory, but he didn't think it would work well in real-world production. That is why he wanted to meet with John and Travis and see what they were doing. He read about their start-up in the Oil and Gas Journal and wondered if they had something Tennico could use.

Hao Yang was another person who read the Oil and Gas Journal article about John and Travis. Hao was a senior director in China's National Energy Commission, or NEC, as it was called. He needed to learn more about these people. The Chinese government is very interested in anyone involved in technology who has a Chinese last name and lives in the United States.

A week after Travis called Peter to schedule a meeting, Travis and John made the eighty-mile trip from Slidell to Hattiesburg. They were nervous and couldn't stop talking about what they would say in the ninety minutes they spent in the car. At 2:30, they were escorted into Peter's office by his assistant. Peter had a large, well-decorated office with a beautiful mahogany desk. He got up from his desk to greet Travis and John and showed them to a separate area of the office with a coffee table, a couch, and two matching chairs. Travis and John took the couch, and Peter took one of the chairs. Peter said, "That was a heck of an article in the Oil and Gas Journal. You guys are the real deal. If you don't mind me asking, how far along are you with a working prototype?"

Travis looked at John, turned his head to Peter, and said, "Pretty close. We're in the diagnostic phase, working out some small kinks. We reserved a booth at the World Petroleum Congress's convention in Houston this November. We're going to have our prototype there." John was fighting to suppress a grin. He knew Travis was lying like a rug on the floor. He wasn't exaggerating; he was straight-up lying. They barely had enough money to pay the office rent, let alone pay for an expensive convention booth to show off a prototype they weren't even close to building. John and Travis were prime examples of the term "Fake it until you make it."

Peter replied, surprised at Travis's statement, "I didn't get you were that far along from the journal article. I thought you were at least eighteen months out. We'll be at the convention showing our ERPS system. ERPS doesn't do everything your system does, but it fits into our production model well."

John sat up and spoke, "I've heard about ERPS but don't know much about it. Can you tell me how it works?"

Peter stood from his chair and said, "I can do better than tell you. Come with me, and I'll show it to you. We installed it in one of our small-scale processors last week. It's not up and running, but you can see how it works." When they arrived at the building housing the ERPS, Peter pointed out the system and explained how it worked. When Peter mentioned its production capacity, John and Travis looked at each other. After about forty-five minutes, they said their goodbyes. Peter thanked them for making the trip and couldn't wait to visit their booth in November. On the drive back, Travis and John couldn't stop talking about Tennico's ERPS. Travis was driving and started talking as soon as they left Tennico's parking lot.

Almost shouting, Travis said, "I can't believe what I just saw. Those guys aren't even close to what we have. I'm convinced Peter set up this meeting just to pick our brains."

John also shouted, "They had that thing on a small production line because they know it won't work large scale. We have an expansion chamber that solves the production volume problem. They didn't even think of that."

"John, I think it's pretty obvious we have something amazing. The biggest player in the industry is so far behind us that they need a telescope to see our dust. We have to get things moving faster. If we're not at that convention, everybody is going to ignore us. We'll be dead in the water."

"Travis, I hate to tell you, but we're almost out of cash again. We've maxed out our credit line with the bank. I'm going to have to talk to my father. Once he understands what we saw today, his checkbook will fly out of his desk drawer faster than a rabbit running from a fox.

CALPURNIA BELL CAME into Cletus's office sitting in a wheelchair, pushed by her younger sister, Odette. Calpurnia was an older, heavy-set black woman with a cast on her left leg covering her foot up to her thigh and a cast on her left arm covering her hand up to her elbow. Her sister was much thinner and much more pleasing to look at. Stella got up from her desk and went over to greet the sisters.

Stella spoke, looking at Calpurnia. "Hello. My name is Stella, and you must be Calpurnia. How are you?"

Calpurnia responded in a raspy voice, "I'm in a wheelchair with a cast on my leg and one on my arm. How do you think I feel?"

Stella's eyes widened and she said, "I'm so sorry. I didn't mean to say-"

Odette interrupted Stella and said, "Don't pay her no mind. She's always that way. She don't need any leg cast to bring out the mean in her." Odette lowered her head and spoke directly into her sister's ear, "Now, Calpurnia, these people are going to help us, so stop being so damn unfriendly. That's why Clarence left. Everybody knows how you treated him. And Hadley. Never mind, Hadley. Your own daughter won't go near the house anymore. You can't even see your new grandkid because you're so mean to everybody. Now, go on and apologize to this woman. She ain't been nothin' but nice to you."

Stella just stared at Odette, not knowing what to say.

Calpurnia spoke quietly, "I'm sorry, Ms Stella. I shouldn't have said that to you. This whole thing has me worrying more than I should. Like to send me to an early grave." She raised her voice and said, "But I ain't mean. People treat me bad. I give them what they deserve. Odette here, don't know a damn thing." Turning to Odette, "Where did Hariss go? Tell me that. You can't keep a man either, so why're you telling me what to do?"

"You know where Hariss went. That fool never earned an honest dollar in his life, and he couldn't never keep his zipper shut. I kicked him out, and you know it.

Stella looked at the front door and was relieved to see Cletus entering the office. She immediately said, "Cletus, I'm glad you're back." Gesturing towards Calpurnia, she said, "This is Calpurnia Bell and her sister, Odette. Calpurnia was involved in that bus accident last March."

Cletus replied, "I remember that. Didn't everybody involved with that settle with the city?"

Cletus remembered that lawsuit very well. A city metro bus on its way to the maintenance facility crashed into another bus full of people. Cletus was madder than a wet hen when Cledale Ayres beat him in getting the class action suit.

Calpurnia said, "I didn't settle for nothin'. Those people made my momma ride in the back and give up her seat to some cracker carrying her shopping bags back in the day. They gonna pay me a lot more than what that Ayres fool got em. They all fools for accepting that piddly amount."

EVERY LAWYER in town knew Ayres was quick to settle with the city. He wanted his thirty-three percent as fast as he could get it.

Cletus said, "Why don't we go into my office and talk about this more?"

An hour later, Calpurnia and Odette left. Cletus asked Stella to come into his office.

He was sitting at his desk when Stella walked in.

"I don't know what I'm going to do with this one. The driver was speeding and had Marijuana in his system. The city admitted wrongdoing and paid everybody. The city got off cheap, but that's water over the dam. I could take them in front of a jury, but given what everybody else got, she would probably get the same."

Stella said, "Well, she's pretty adamant. I think the thing with her mother riding in the back is what's pushing her."

"Well shoot, thirty-three percent isn't much if we get what everybody else got. Especially after trial expenses."

"Well, this might help. When we talked on the phone, I gave her the usual speech I give everybody. When I mentioned the firm's rate is thirty-three percent of any award, she said that was too much. When I told her your hourly rate was one seventy-five, she said she would pay it."

"That's great, but it still brings us back to the same spot. I don't want to take her money if all I can get is what everybody else got."

Stella said nothing.

"Ok, go ahead and figure out the retainer amount and make sure we get it. I can use that to get started. Call Beau and fill him in. We need to give him some work anyway. Tell him to look at the bus. The city can't scrap it as long as there's litigation pending."

BEAU GASTON WAS sixty-three years old, with all his silver-gray hair perfectly quaffed. Three years ago, he retired from the Hattiesburg police department with a Detective third-grade pension from his years investigating homicides. His retirement lasted just three months. He couldn't stand another project on the house, and his wife, Judy, was ready to move in with their oldest daughter. She preferred spending time with their new grandson, Harley, than with him. He knew Cletus very well from seeing him in the courthouse. They both spent a lot of time drinking stale coffee in the cafeteria. Cletus ate regularly there, probably because it was cheap food. Beau wouldn't touch it if he was starving on an island. Beau started his investigation into Cletus' newest case by visiting his old stomping ground, the Hattiesburg police department. Specifically, the evidence locker at police headquarters. He took the elevator to the basement and saw a familiar face sitting behind the glass that faced the tiny entrance and waiting area. Beau stopped just inside the doorway, raised his arms, and said, "Well, well, look what I found." The red-headed woman behind the glass looked up and smiled. She spoke excitedly, "Beau Gaston! Look at you. Mr. Retirement. What are you doing here? I'm going to have to call security. They're letting civilians walk in off the street."

"Gina Miller, I missed you so much; I couldn't contain myself. I just had to see if you got kicked into retirement like I did."

"You didn't get kicked, Beau. When you hit your thirty-five years, you were out the door. Same as me. My twenty-five is eight months away, and I'm working the easy shift down here."

"Well, believe me, retirement wasn't anything like I thought. Judy was ready to divorce me. I'm working with Cletus Bureaux now. Somebody snitched here and told Cletus I applied for a Private Investigator license, and he called me right up."

"Well, Beau, I'm sure the pay is better. Ok, so down to business; what brings you here besides my ravishing, good looks?

"I need to look at the file on that bus accident a while back. I think Derrick Morgan was working that case. I don't have a file number, but I'm sure you know which one. It was a big deal."

"Of course, I know it. I thought that was a done deal. What do you need that for?"

"One of the victims is a holdout on that settlement the city coughed up. I don't know what I'm looking for, to be honest. Just going through the motions for my boss."

Gina started to get up from her chair at the window. "Ok. Take that clipboard over there and fill out the request. You know how it works. You're a civilian now, but I don't care."

Gina left the window and disappeared into the cavernous warehouse, filled with row after row of shelves containing evidence from decades-old crimes. After a few minutes, she returned, holding a thick brown accordion file. It wouldn't fit through the window's pass-thru, so she opened the door next to it and gave it to Beau. Gina spoke as she handed it to him, saying, "Here you go. Sorry, Beau. You know the rules. You can't take anything out of the room. You can use the table in the corner over there."

"Thanks, Gina. I don't think this is going to take very long."

Beau took the file, walked to the desk, and emptied its contents. The first thing he looked at were the eight-by-ten photos of the accident scene. He picked up one of them and looked at it. He didn't know what he was looking for, so he tossed it aside and picked another one. This one was taken by a drone flying over the scene. He was about to toss it with the other one when he noticed something. He was looking at the skid marks left by the bus just before impact with the other bus. The skid marks were about four feet long, but he noticed the left skid mark ended almost a foot before the right one. Speaking quietly to himself, he said, "That's odd. Why would one skid mark be shorter than the other?" He took out his phone and took a photo of the scene. He spent a few more minutes looking at the other photos. He noticed the detective notes were minimal at best. He asked himself, Why would Derrick not document this more thoroughly? This was a big deal accident the city was on the hook for. He made a note to call Morgan. Beau put everything back in the file and walked back to the window.

"THANKS, Gina. I'm done with this."

She opened the door, and Beau passed the file to her and said, "Find anything interesting?"

"Not sure," he replied. "I think I'll make a trip to the impound lot and look at the bus. Probably nothing, but I have to give Cletus his money's worth."

Beau left the building, checked the time, and decided to make the ten-mile drive to the police impound lot. The police impound lot was almost five acres of gravel surrounded by a chain-link fence with circles of barbed wire on top. Next to the sliding gate was a small office. Beau entered the office and saw a window just like the evidence locker. He approached the window and saw someone he recognized.

"Wonton!" Beau said out loud. "What the hell are you doing here?"

"Wonton" was Charlie Wenton's nickname in the department. He got the nickname because he was half-Asian. He was a heavy-set man with a bald head and a grey beard. He was a few years younger than Beau but didn't look it.

Charlie looked up and said, "Beau Gaston. What brings you here? I heard you were working for Cletus Bureaux."

"Yes, I am. I got my PI license to get out of the house. I just saw
Gina Miller over at the evidence locker. She's doing the easy shift
until she hits her twenty-five. Looks like you're doing the same."

"Damn right. Twenty-five years looking into murders is enough for
me. Say, how's the PI business? I'm thinking about following in
your shoes. How'd you get Cletus to hire you?"

"Long story. I'll buy you a drink at Taverns and tell you all
about it."

"There it is. You don't buy for anybody unless it's payback for
some off-the-wall favor you want."

"It's not a favor; I mean it about the drink. We were on the job for
a long time. Retirement isn't all it's cracked up to be. Getting away
from the department is fantastic, but not doing what you're good
at is not so much. Unless you're into woodworking and bowling
leagues."

"I tremble at the thought of making chairs in my garage. What can
I do for you?"

"Cletus has me looking at that city bus accident. The one with the
driver stoned on pot."

"I know about that. The bus is sitting out there in the lot. You here
to look at that or something?"

"Yeah, that's what I'm here about."

"No problem. I'll open the gate for you. I'm not supposed to, but
you can use the golf cart. Take the road to the very back, turn left,
and it's about fifty yards on the left. Keys in the cart."

"Thanks, Charlie. We'll talk about that drink when I come back."

Beau left the office, climbed into the golf cart, and followed Charlie's directions. After a few minutes, he saw the bus placed next to

the other bus involved in the accident. Beau got out of the cart and approached the bus's smashed front. Other than a crumpled front end, the bus looked perfectly fine. He walked to the rear and examined the tires on both sides. Not seeing anything of interest, he sighed and took off his suit coat. He grumbled, "I just got this suit back from the dry cleaner." He got down on all fours and crawled under the bus. He looked at the left wheel's brake and then turned his head to examine the right. He took his phone out of his shirt pocket and took pictures of each wheel's brakes. Beau returned to the golf cart and returned it to the impound office. Getting out of the cart, he entered the office and thanked Charlie.

Beau got back in his car and thought about calling Derrick Morgan, but he decided to wait until he could look at his photos more closely. He drove to his house on a sleepy residential street lined with trees. He walked into his ranch-style home and went to his home office. The office was a converted bedroom for their oldest daughter, who had moved into her own apartment after getting her first job. He took his phone and connected it to his big-screen computer monitor. He then pulled up images of the bus's brakes and placed the right and left brake pictures side by side. He squinted at the screen and noticed the left brake appeared newer than the right. It was hard to tell at first until he saw the left had much less grime on it than the right and had no grime where the axle connected to the wheel. He thought out loud, "I wonder if Morgan noticed this? It sure wasn't in his notes." Looking at the time, he decided to call him in the morning. He could smell the roast his wife was cooking.

The following day, Beau went into his home office and looked at the brake images again. He picked up the landline phone and called Derrick Morgan's cell. After a few rings, the call went to voicemail. Beau left a detailed message and went back to looking at the images. He decided to find out where the city had its bus maintenance done. Probably the garage where they worked on all manner of city-owned vehicles. Buses, police cars, and official vehicles. He was interrupted by his cell phone ringing. He looked at the caller ID but didn't recognize the number. He answered the call.

"Hello, Beau Gaston speaking."

"Beau Gaston, this is Derrick Morgan returning your call. I thought you were off the job. I was at your retirement party at Taverns, remember? I got your message. What's up?" Beau went on to give Derrick the same speech he gave everybody who asked about his retirement. When he finished, Derrick asked, "How much money are you making being a PI? I've been thinking about that myself."

"Not enough, that's for sure. I'm okay with my pension, so I shouldn't complain. Listen, Cletus Bureaux has me looking into that bus accident you worked a while back. One of the passengers didn't go for the settlement the city paid out. My boss knows he has a loser case but feels sorry for the old lady complaining about the money everybody got."

"I get it, but what's that got to do with me? I filed that away and moved on. My caseload is big enough. That was an easy one, and I closed it as fast as I could."

"I don't blame you one bit. I would have done the same. Caseloads are known to put people into early retirement or cause them to eat their gun. Listen, did you notice anything about the brakes on that bus? The different skid marks? Was some maintenance done on the left rear brake?"

Beau noticed a change in Derricks's voice when he said, "I didn't see anything with those brakes. The driver was high on weed, end of story."

"Understood. I'm just trying to give my boss his money's worth. Make him think I'm working my ass off. Sorry for the bother."

"No bother. Sorry, I don't have anything for you. Listen, I gotta go, but I'll let you know if I remember anything. Talk to you later." Derrick abruptly ended the call, immediately removed his burner phone from his coat pocket, and called a number he disliked using.

Beau took the phone from his ear and looked at it. He said to himself, "That's not right. Derrick said he didn't see anything regarding the brakes. I spotted a problem just by looking at a drone photo and getting my suit dirty crawling under that bus. On top of that, when I started asking questions, he got defensive and all but hung up on me. I need to find out who put that new left brake on."

THE ARYAN BRIGADE was a white supremacist organization based in Krotz Springs, Louisiana. Its leader, Harney DuBois, chose Krotz Springs for its isolation and small population. The Atchafalaya Bayou surrounded it on three sides and had Route 91 as its only major street. The brigade's compound sat on twenty-five acres located ten miles to the east of town. It was accessible by a dirt road off 91 that went two miles into the Bayou. The compound consisted of a main building that served as Harney's headquarters, two barracks that could house thirty people each, and a mess hall that could feed the entire compound when fully populated. A huge barn was filled with ATVs, all manner of survival gear, and three armored Humvees provided to the Krotz Springs Police Department as part of the Army's effort to rid itself of unused vehicles. The Armed Personnel Carrier was due to be delivered in three weeks. The department consisted of three people: the police chief, Grady Sutton, and two deputies. Grady, like his two deputies, was a proud Aryan Brigade member. The barn had a small hidden door built into the floor towards the back of the barn. Behind the door was a set of stairs leading down to a

concrete bunker the size of the barn floor. The bunker was separated by a concrete wall going down the center. One side had a
kitchen, bathroom, and bunk beds for ten people. The other side
was the brigade's armory. It was filled to the roof with M4A1 rifles,
M320 grenade launchers, 81mm precision mortar systems, MON-
200 directional anti-personal mines, and enough accessories and
ammunition to start a world war. At the back of the property that
abutted against the Bayou was a building separated from the rest of
the compound. It housed the brigade's methamphetamine lab.
Meth was a major source of income for the Aryan Brigade, so the
lab operated 24/7. Behind the meth lab was a boat dock with two
large airboats used to navigate the Bayou. The airboats transported
the meth from the compound to a pick-up location on the other
side of the bayou. During the week, the compound had a staff of
fifteen soldiers who lived there full-time. The compound was filled
to capacity on the last weekend of every month when the brigade
conducted paramilitary training.

Harney DuBois was only 5-8" and weighed a hundred forty-five
pounds soaking wet. He had dirty blond hair and a scraggly beard
that was barely visible. His small stature belied his meanness for
everybody who wasn't white and wasn't born in the US. Jews and
Muslims were also on his list. He was certain a civil war was
coming soon, and he was going to be prepared for it. So did every
other member of the Aryan Brigade.

He was sitting in his office in the main house when one of his eight
phones started ringing. He had each phone set to a different ringtone so he could tell who was calling. He picked up the phone and
heard Derrick Morgan's voice. Derrick knew exactly what Beau
Gaston had noticed. He had investigated the bus crash much more
thoroughly than his report showed. The police department's
higher-ups were getting calls from the mayor's office about the
accident. The mayor hoped the city wasn't responsible and
wouldn't have to pay a large lawsuit settlement. Once it was deter-

mined that the driver was stoned on pot, the pressure on the investigation stopped. Derrick could submit his sparse report because nobody would read it—until Beau Gaston showed up. He informed Harney about Beau's phone call.

THE CITY of Hattiesburg didn't maintain its own vehicles. A company called Hansen Vehicle Services placed the winning bid on the lucrative contract the city offered. One of the vendor requirements stated in the contract was to have a central location where city vehicles could be repaired. This location was required to work on city vehicles only. Beau decided to pay a visit to the service center and take a look around. He knew the location well. Detective Third Grades got their own city car, and his car always needed something fixed. Beau pulled into the service center's parking lot and exited his car. The building did not have a sign identifying it. It was a very large building with ten service bays. Each bay had garage doors in the front and back so vehicles could drive in one end and exit the other. In the center of the building, facing the parking lot, was a door with a sign over it that said "Office." He saw a bus in one of the bays and decided to take a look. When he entered the bay, he saw a service tech looking at a clipboard. There were several boxes of parts on a cart next to him. Beau approached the tech and introduced himself.

"Hello, I'm Detective Gaston. Beau left out that he was retired.

Would you mind if I asked you a few questions?"

The tech looked up from his clipboard and said, "You're not supposed to be in here. Detective or not. I guess detectives can't read the sign outside that says, "Employees Only."

"Sorry, I just have a couple of questions."

"I know you can't read, but there is a door over there with a sign that says, 'Office.' I suggest you go there because I'm busy here." The tech returned his attention to the clipboard, dismissing Beau.

Beau slummed his shoulders, sighed, and walked to the office door. He entered the office. Nobody was sitting at the receptionist's desk, so he started walking down the hallway to the right of it. The hallway had four small offices connected to it. He looked in the first office and saw it was empty. Must be break time, he told himself. He looked in the second office, and it was also vacant. He started to go to the third office when he heard a man's voice behind him.

"Can I help you? You're not supposed to be back here."

Beau turned and said, "Sorry, I didn't see anyone at the reception- ist's desk." I'm Detective Gaston. I'm looking for someone to talk to about that bus accident a while back. The one where the driver was stoned on pot. Do you know anything about that?"

Gary Burston, the service center's manager, was getting ready to tell Beau to leave. When he heard the word "Detective," he stopped and said, I'm Gary. I manage this place. Is there something you need?"

"Well, I'm not really sure. The case is closed, but one of the passen- gers didn't take the city's settlement money and wants to go to court. I'm just doing some follow-up. The D.A. wants to make sure there aren't any loose ends. My boss sent me here."

"Sorry, Detective. That bus went to the impound lot.."

"How about the maintenance logs? Do you still have those?"

"Sorry, when we remove a vehicle from inventory, we lose access to those logs. We got enough to do around here. We don't need scrapped vehicles cluttering up our database. Now, if you don't mind. We're having a meeting, and I need you to leave."

When Beau left, Gary went to his office to get his burner phone. He needed to make a call. When Beau got to his car, he took out his phone to make a call. It was time to have that drink with Charlie. Gary called when Harney was in his office with his lieutenant, Forrest Banks. Harney had put Gary's call on speakerphone so Forrest could listen in. Harney looked at Forrest and said in a deep southern drawl, Detective, my ass. That Gaston fella is sniffing around, and I don't like it one bit. Morgan told me about a conversation he had with that asshole. We gotta a big operation bout ready to start, and I don't need no nosey detective dumbass gitin' up in my business." He hung up.

Forrest said, "Not good timing, that's for sure. Whatya you goin' to do?"

"Right now, nothing. He can sniff all he wants. We gotta get those guns and ammo ready. Ole Pablo down in mexiland already paid upfront. I don't even wanna think about being late sending those damn things."

Pablo Hernandez worked for the Jalisco cartel, acquiring weapons. The Aryan Brigade was one of his biggest suppliers. The Brigade had more than a few loyal members in the military. Some of them worked at military ammunition depots. Unfortunately for the military, some of its larger depots were under the management of independent contractors and not the military itself. Pablo paid for the weapons using the vast wealth the cartel earned, selling drugs to anybody who wanted them. Jalisco was in a turf war with the Juarez cartel and needed as many weapons as it could get.

BEAU WAS SITTING in a booth at Taverns Bar and Grill when Charlie walked in. Beau waved him over, and Charlie sat down across from him. The place was crowded for a Wednesday night.

Beau didn't like having to raise his voice to be heard, but he had no choice.

"Hey, Charlie, thanks for coming on such short notice. I know you have things going on."

"Nothing going on that can't wait for free booze. What's IS going on? First, you come out to the lot looking for some wrecked bus, and then we're having secret meetings, and no, I didn't tell anybody I was talking to you."

"Sorry for the cloak and dagger. I'm looking into something that's getting more and more hinky the further I go." Beau went on to tell Charlie about what he saw at the impound lot and his conversations with Derrick Morgan and Gary Burston.

After Beau finished, Charlie said, "Well, I don't know much about Morgan. Never met the guy, but Burston must be drinking too much anti-freeze. The city keeps records on every vehicle, and they don't delete them once the unit is taken out of service. We have a public auction every year at the impound lot. We provide the maintenance history for any vehicle up for sale. Everything in impound, which that bus is, has a maintenance record."

"How can I see that? I'd like to take a look at that."

"Tell you what, when I go in tomorrow, I'll email you a copy of that bus's record."

True to his word, Beau checked his email in his home office the next day and saw Charlie's email. He opened the attached document and sent it to his printer. He looked at the printout and saw the bus had the usual maintenance one would expect: oil changes, tire rotation, belt tightening, and fluid replacement. At the bottom was the only unusual entry he saw: Left brake replacement. Next to this was the part number and the service tech's initials. The serial number for the new brake was in the notes section. Beau thought for several minutes and decided to make another trip to the impound lot. This time he would wear his yard working clothes.

He arrived at the impound lot and spent a few minutes talking to Charlie. Then, he left the office, hopped in the golf cart, and traveled to the bus. When he arrived at the bus, he let out a sigh. It had rained the night before, and there was a large puddle surrounding the wheel he needed to look at. Resigned to his fate, Beau got on all fours and crawled under the bus. Lying on his left side, he used his index finger to wipe away the grime on the brake and saw the brake's serial number. He pulled out his phone and took several pictures of it from different angles. He crawled out from under the bus and cursed. His pants were soaked through. He returned to the golf cart, traveled back to the office, and left the cart where he found it. Rather than go back and talk to Charlie some more, he went to his car and got in. He wasn't happy about putting his wet butt on the front seat. He reached into the glove box and retrieved Charlie's report. He selected the picture of the brake on his phone screen and held them both side by side. The serial numbers didn't match. When he scrolled through the images he took at different angles, he noticed some Chinese symbols on the brake drum where it connected to the axle. Beau put the phone and report in his lap and thought. He needed to go back to the service center and get an explanation about the serial numbers not matching from his good friend, Gary, and a service tech with the initials LH. Beau picked up his phone and started to punch in Cletus's number. He wanted to tell him what he found but stopped himself and decided to wait until after his visit to the service center. The serial number mismatch was probably something easily explained—no big deal. Lying about the maintenance records was probably some turf fight between city departments. He did introduce himself as a detective, after all. Beau had to admit to himself that his days in the department were over. His wife reminded him of that regularly. Having drinks with a fellow cop at Taverns and talking shop was like old times, and he missed them. He put the car in gear and drove home.

———

WHEN TRAVIS WALKED into Syncor's offices one morning, he was greeted at the front desk by Adelle LeBlanc, Travis's and Johns' newest employee. She was an attractive black woman with an unmistakable Cajun accent. She smiled and said, "Bonjou Travis, Ca va?"

Travis replied, "Adelle, please. Nobody around here understands you half the time. Everybody understands Truett. Why can't you talk like him? He's your cousin, after all. He doesn't have a problem being understood. I hope you're not answering the phone that way." Adelle's cousin, Truett Cook, was the first person John and Travis had hired when they started SynCor. He had a degree in structural engineering and knew his business. Truett's job was to design and fabricate the steel housing assembly where their synthetic correlator invention would process the oil that went through it.

After Travis scolded her, she lost her smile and said, "I'm sorry, Mister Beloit. I will remember not to speak this way." She had a crush on Travis, which was obvious to everybody in the company except Travis.

Travis sighed and said, "Ok, I'm sorry. I didn't mean to sound angry. I'm sorry about comparing you to your cousin. You're a very nice person and do a terrific job. We're lucky to have you and Truett."

Travis walked away, and she smiled behind his back. She knew saying "Mister Beloit" would turn him into putty. Worked every time.

Travis moved down the long hallway that led to the warehouse/engineering lab in the back when he stopped and poked his head into John's office. John was sitting at his desk with his eyes glued to one of the two large computer monitors in front of him.

Travis said, "I just got back from Johnson Hydro. I have the fluid tubes Truett ordered in the back of my truck."

"John replied, "Well, it's about damn time. We ordered those weeks ago. Just because it's a small order doesn't give them the right to jerk us around. We need to find somebody else."

"I know. It sucks, but Johnson is the only supplier that has the alloy we need. I think they know it. That's why they keep charging more and making us wait longer. They work on our orders when they get bored.

John replied angrily, "Well, guess what? I have a plan for them. When we get big enough, we're going to make our own tubes. I'm going to get rid of that pebble in my shoe."

Travis said, "Well, we need to make a decision now that we have the tubes. The deadline for reserving booth space at the Petroleum Congress's convention is coming up."

"I know. That's going to be a giant expense, but we need to be there. Thank God Chase gave us that line of credit."

Travis said, "I say we bite the bullet and go for it. I'll tell Adelle to fill out the paperwork and send it in with our deposit."

Travis approached John and held up his hand. John got up from his chair and high-fived Travis. John spoke excitedly, "We're doing it, man! We're punching our ticket to play with the big boys!"

"DAMN RIGHT, we are! We're going to show them how it's done!

We should ask for a booth next to Tennico. Make it easy for their people to ask if we're hiring."

PETER MURPHY angrily hung up his phone. He had just finished a call from the ERPS's project manager, who had told him the ERPS had failed its most recent test. Peter said out loud to himself. "I don't know why I'm mad. I've been telling everybody that damn thing won't work at high production levels. When are they going to figure that out?" He heard a voice say, "Are you talking to yourself again?" He looked up and saw Marcus Hudsen standing outside his office door.

"I'm talking, but nobody is listening."

"I heard that ERPS failed another test. Some of the guys in that department are starting to worry that their jobs might be getting cut. Not a good morale situation going on over there."

Peter replied, "Well, if we don't get something working, one of those jobs will be mine. I think we're going to have to go to the Oil and Gas convention with the small-scale version. I need to get the folks working that convention to come up with some BS explaining how we are going to revolutionize the oil industry with an ERPS that works like pushing oil into a fifty-five-gallon drum using a paper straw."

Marcus laughed. "Paper straw. I like that. Pretty accurate, too." He went on, "Seriously, there's a lot of worry going on over there. Those folks are working their butts off, and they ain't getting any overtime pay. It's hard to give a hundred and ten, wondering if you're not going to have a job and maybe not buying your kids Christmas presents this year."

"Don't even mention that Christmas stuff. I was let go twice when I first got into the oil business. I was just a kid the first time and didn't care much. I had a two-year-old the second time, and Sally was five months pregnant. It's a damn hard road not having work and trying to support your family."

"Well, Pete, I'm outta here. It's Friday, and Me and Darlene are goin to Nawleans for the weekend. I'm using my casino points. Got us tickets to a magician show.

"Well, you go ahead. I don't like casinos. I work too hard for my money to waste it like that. They only give you those points to bring you back and take your money again. Seems to have worked with you."

Marcus lost his excitement and said, "Well, we'll see about that." He left to pick up Darlene at six and make an eight o'clock check-in at the casino.

Darlene Moss was in her apartment, packing a large suitcase. She was humming a tune that had been going around her mind for the last hour. Spending the long weekend at Caesar's had been something she had been looking forward to since last week when Marcus asked her to join him. She had never been to a big fancy casino before and couldn't wait to get there. She was putting her beauty supplies in the suitcase when she heard the doorbell ring. Damn, she said to herself. He ain't supposed to be here for another hour. Now I'm gonna forget something because he's rushing me. Darlene left her bedroom to answer the front door. Marcus stood in front of her with a big smile and a cluster of flowers he had bought at the grocery store.

Darlene spoke before she fully opened the door. "Marcus, I swear, you're early, and I still got stuff to do."

"Well, hello to you too, miss, never on time. It's six o'clock. I told you I was pickin' you up at six." He held out the flowers and said, "These are for you. I know you like Carnations."

"That's sweet of you, Marcus, but what am I gonna do with them? They'll be dead by the time I get back."

Marcus pulled back his shoulders and said a little too loudly, "You can bring 'em with you and put 'em up in the hotel room."

"I'm sorry, sweetheart; you're so good to me. C'mon in and help me with my suitcase."

During the hour-and-a-half drive to Caesars Casino in New Orleans, Darlene couldn't stop talking. She kept looking at the brochure and commenting on what she saw. "Look at this, Marcus. Our room has the biggest beds I ever saw. And look at that big ole TV. There's even a sitting area with a couch and coffee table. My goodness, Marcus, the bathroom looks bigger than my apartment!"

Darlene flipped the brochure over and began her comments again. "This Casino is huge! Lookit all them slot machines, Marcus. I'm goin' to win a pile of money here, that's for sure."

Marcus replied just as excited as Darlene, "Damn right we're goin' to win some money. I don't care about the room. That's only a place to sleep when you get tired of winning money. Does that brochure show how many blackjack tables they got? I hate waiting for someone to leave so I can play."

"Doesn't say, but what are those things people are throwin' dice on?"

"Those are Craps tables, baby doll. You can win some really big money playin' on one of those things—big money. I'm goin' to take my Blackjack winnings and win more at one of them," Marcus said with a big smile.

"Think I'll do that with all the money I win at the slot machine," she said with a big smile. "I can't wait to see that magician show either. I ain't never seen one of them. Hell, I never seen anything like this period! Fancy hotel rooms with big bathrooms, glass showers, fancy restaurants, and all them slot machines." She leaned across the seat, kissed Marcus on the cheek, and said, "Thank you darlin. You're so good to me."

When they arrived at the casino, Marcus pulled up to the casino's main entrance. He gave the valet a ten-dollar bill and made sure Darlene saw him do it. He thought, "Shoot, I'll get that back in ten minutes." They walked into the casino, and Darlene was shocked at what she saw. Marble floors, massive chandeliers hanging from the ceiling, and people everywhere. She looked to her left and saw a casino floor so big she couldn't see the end of it. In front of her, she saw the colossal check-in counter staffed by people wearing fancy uniforms. Marcus stepped up to the counter and spoke to the brunette woman standing in front of her computer monitor. Her name tag said Helen. She looked up and said, "Welcome to Caesars. We're happy to make your visit as enjoyable as possible. Do you have a reservation with us?"

Marcus replied with a smile, Yes, Ma'am, I do. Names Marcus Hudsen, and I'm ready to be enjoyed myself."

Helen typed in Marcus's name and saw his reservation details. "Here you are, Mr. Hudsen. Your room is in the north tower. Room 1127. It's one of our premium suites. You're exchanging reward points, so there's nothing more to do. Here are your key cards. They open your room door but can also be used in any of our restaurants or shops. Your points will be deducted when you use the card."

Marcus turned to his left and spoke to Darlene with a huge smile: "Let's go, baby doll—it's time to start enjoying."

When Marcus and Darlene walked into their room, Darlene's jaw dropped. It was just like the brochure. Being in person only made the room more dramatic. Darlene turned to Marcus and embraced him tightly. She kissed his neck and said, "Honeybunch, this is beautiful. You're so good to me. I can't believe I'm here."

Marcus returned the embrace and gave her a long kiss on the lips. He looked around the room and said, "Jeeze. I been here many times before but never stayed in one of these PREMIUM rooms! Guess them points I got are comin' in handy."

"Honey bunch, I'm starved more than a dog lost in the woods. Let's leave the suitcases and go and eat."

Marcus said, "I say we go to the buffet. It's real good food, and we can try our luck after."

Walking to the buffet was like everything else. You had to travel through the massive casino floor to get anywhere. Even the bathrooms took a lot of work to find. It was deliberate. Casino owners didn't want you to have ANY distractions that would keep you from parting with your money. You could get your dinner sitting at the poker table if you wanted. Finding the elevator to your room required a map and compass. There are no windows to the outside and definitely no clocks. More than a few gamblers started playing after their dinner. When they left the casino to go outside, they were shocked to see it was morning. As Marcus and Darlene approached the buffet, they noticed a long line of people snaking through a maze of ropes. Darlene said, "Lord Marcus, it's gonna be midnight for we get anything to eat."

"Nope, baby doll, that lines for common folk, Darlene. "See that tiny line over there," Marcus said, pointing to a separate entrance to the buffet. "I got Ambassador status. We get to go in over there."

When Darlene entered the buffet, her jaw dropped again. She couldn't process what she was seeing. She said, "Jesus Christ on his throne, Marcus." Everywhere Darlene looked, she saw more food than she thought possible to make. Mexican food, Asian food, Creole food. A massive Prime Rib roast, a chef carving the most enormous turkey she'd ever seen. Table after table of every kind of food imaginable. A dessert section filled with cakes, pies, cookies, and ice cream with more toppings than a giant bag of M&M's. Tears started running down her face.

Marcus noticed the tears and said, "What's wrong, baby doll? Why're you cryin'?

Darlene replied, "Nothing, honeybunch. I'm just happy, is all." She didn't want to tell him she was thinking back to her childhood. She remembered her mother giving her a buttermilk biscuit just before bed some nights so her stomach wouldn't growl after eating the tiny portion of green beans and her mother's dirty rice recipe for dinner. Full and satisfying meals were scarce growing up.

"I'm glad you're happy, baby doll. I'm goin' over there, and get me some of that Prime Rib. How bout you?"

After thoroughly stuffing themselves with food, Marcus pushed back from the table and said, "Time to take some of this place's money, baby doll. I'm going over to the blackjack table. You wanna play some blackjack?"

Darlene pouted and said, "I don't like cards. I wanna play those slot machines."

"OK, I'll get you a player's card with some money on it. You just take the card, put it into the machine, and play all you want."

When Marcus returned from the cashier, he gave Darlene her player's card. "Here you go, baby doll. This card gonna be fatter than pregnant sow when you get done I hope."

"Thanks, honeybunch." She took the card and walked to the massive array of slot machines. Marcus went to the first Blackjack table with an open seat. The only open seats were tables with a twenty-five dollar minimum bet. He always played the five-dollar tables but didn't want to wait for a seat. He sat down and greeted the other people sitting at the table.

"Evening, folks. I hope this is my lucky table."

He took a hundred-dollar bill from his wallet and placed it on the table where the dealer would see it. The dealer took the bill and gave him four twenty-five dollar chips. Marcus looked at the tiny stack of chips. Usually, when he started playing at the five-dollar tables, he was used to seeing twenty chips for his hundred dollars. He nervously reached into his wallet, took out his remaining four hundred dollars, and placed it on the table. When the dealer gave him his chips, Marcus placed one closer to the dealer and anxiously waited for his cards to be dealt. The dealer dealt him an ace of clubs for his first card and a jack of diamonds for his second card.

"Blackjack!" Marcus yelled. "Winner, winner, chicken dinner! Cept I had the prim rib. Looks to be a good night, folks." He stopped the cocktail waitress passing him and asked for a double Jack Daniels neat. After several hours, Marcus felt a tap on his shoulder. He looked up and saw Darlene standing over him. She said, "Time to go, my dear. It's late, and I'm ready to go to bed."

"Baby doll! Lookey here!" Marcus said, pointing to his large stacks of twenty-five dollar chips. There were also two stacks of black one-hundred-dollar chips. "I'm killin' it here! We can't go now."

Darlene's eyes bulged when she saw the chips Marcus was pointing to. "Them's all yours?!" She gasped.

"All mine, baby doll, all mine. I ain't never been this hot!"

"You're hot, all right. You're also drunk as a moonshiner. You take them chips, and let's go. We got that riverboat cruise tomorrow, and I won't miss it because you're still sleeping it off."

The next morning, Marcus woke up in a haze. Lying on the bed, he looked to his right and saw that Darlene was not there. He smelled coffee, pulled himself out of bed, and saw Darlene eating at the small table in the room's lounge area. Next to the table was a room service cart with Danish, eggs, bacon, and fresh fruit on top. Darlene looked up and said, "Well, it's about time. You drank enough last night to sink a battleship. I swear, Marcus, you look terrible."

"Well, I may have sunk a battleship, but I won plenty of money doin' it. Lemme get some of that coffee."

Darlene poured him a cup and gave it to him. He took a sip, grimaced, and put it down. He entered the bathroom and reached into his kit, pulling out a flask filled with Jack Daniels. Hair of the dog, he thought, and took two long swigs.

Later that afternoon, Darlene and Marcus returned from their riverboat cruise. Darlene was annoyed with Marcus. He spent more time at the riverboat's bar than with her. Despite Marcus's behavior, she had to admit that she enjoyed the afternoon very much. She had never been on a paddlewheel boat before. She chatted up a newlywed couple from Cincinnati she met standing at the railing. When they returned to their hotel room, Marcus said, "Baby doll, we got a few hours before dinner. Our reservation isn't until seven, so I'm goin' to win some more money at the blackjack table. You want to join me? Bring some of that lady luck?"

"Naw, you go ahead. I'm plumb tired out. I need me a break, and I'm going to rest here a while."

Marcus smiled. "Well, you sure don't need any beauty rest. That's for sure. I'll be back in a while. I don't want to miss dinner at that fancy restaurant."

With that, Marcus left the room and walked to the elevator. He made a beeline for the table he sat at the night before. There were plenty of five-dollar table seats, but Marcus wasn't interested in them. He pulled a huge wad of hundred-dollar bills from his bulging pants pocket and placed it on the table. Darlene woke with a yawn and looked across the bed at the alarm clock. It was a little past six. She got up to get ready for dinner and noticed Marcus was not there. After she had dressed, Darlene left the room to find Marcus. "It don't take a genius to know where he's at," she thought. When she entered the casino's blackjack area, even a deaf person could hear Marcus's yelling.

"You took my queen!" Marcus yelled to the overweight woman sitting to his right at the table. "You didn't need to take that card! You're sittin' on seventeen! See that!?" Marcus pointed to the tabletop where a sign had been stenciled into the green fabric. "Dealer must stand on seventeen." "If they're tellin' the dealer not to take a card when they got seventeen, then why're you?! I got eleven here. That queen you took would've given me twenty-one!"

The dealer said, "Sir, please keep your voice down and not talk to the other players that way."

Marcus turned his attention to the dealer. "Well, listen to you. I done lost half my money sittin' here with people who don't know how to play. I want my money back! Y'all saw how much I was winnin' last night. You put these people next to me so you could get it back!"

Darlene was standing behind Marcus, watching him make a drunken fool out of himself. She slapped the back of his head and said, "Marcus Hudsen, you're drunk and out of control." The dealer and other players stared at the scene Darlene and Marcus were playing out. The woman who took Marcus's queen was smiling.

Darlene continued, "Git your drunk ass out of that chair right now! We got dinner waiting, and I'm hungry. I don't have time for your foolishness."

Marcus looked at the dealer and sheepishly said, "I'm sorry, folks. I didn't mean to be rude."

Darlene turned and started the long walk across the casino floor to the other end, where their restaurant was. Marcus got up and started following Darlene like a whipped dog. When they arrived at the restaurant, the female hostess checked off Marcus's reservation and led them to a table with a window looking out over the casino floor. After sitting down, Darlene looked at the menu and was once again shocked. Memories from childhood returned. She didn't understand the food's names and descriptions, but she homed in on the item that said lamb.

"I ain't never had lamb before. I'm gettin' me that."

After several minutes, their waiter approached the table and introduced himself. He stood over them and entered Darlene's order on an iPad. He turned to Marcus and waited for his order. "I ain't real hungry. I think I'm just getting me a couple of appetizers. I'll have the shrimp cocktail. That sounds good." Scanning the menu further, He said, "I always like to try new things. I don't know what this is, but it sounds good." He held up his menu to the waiter and pointed to the appetizer that said Escargot.

The waiter said, "That's a good choice." He entered Marcus's order and asked if they would like wine with their meal. Marcus said he did. When their waiter left, Darlene leaned into the table and said,

"Marcus, I swear. I'm madder than a wet hen at you. I ain't never seen you act like that before. What on earth were you thinkin'? Everybody at that blackjack table thought you were crazy."

Marcus spoke with a slight slur, "I'm sorry, baby doll. I was on a big losin' streak. I reckon I should have acted better. I'm glad you took me away. I need to re-group."

"Re-group nothin'. We're goin' to that magician show after supper here. You still got you some winnings. You don't need to go back there."

Marcus said nothing.

After a few minutes of silence, Darlene recounted her experience on the riverboat cruise. She chastised Marcus for spending most of the time at the bar rather than enjoying the sights. She was interrupted when their waiter brought Marcus his appetizers. Marcus pointed to the escargot and said, "What's that? Those what they look like?"

The waiter replied, "Yes sir, escargot is a French term for snails."

Marcus almost vomited and quickly lost any interest whatsoever in food. After dinner, Marcus and Darlene walked to the other end of the casino floor to the magic show Marcus had tickets for. They took their seats and waited to be awed by the magician who everybody was talking about.

After the ninety-minute spectacle, the audience didn't stop clapping for what seemed a very long time. Walking out of the theater, Darlene couldn't stop talking about what she had seen. She was giddy with excitement. "Marcus, how on earth did that magician get through that spinning wheel? I watched close and still couldn't figure out how she did it. And that table? How'd she make that table lift up off the ground? Lord have mercy."

Marcus said, "I don't know either. That was a really good show. I'm glad I got us tickets. I liked the card tricks the most."

In truth, Marcus was barely paying attention to the magic show. All he could think about was returning to the blackjack table and winning his money back. It didn't matter; he still had more money than when he started. He was fixated on getting back the money he had lost.

Looking at the casino floor filled with people, Darlene said, "I want to go play on those slot machines some more. Why don't you come with me and keep me company? You can win your money back on those. I won some money. You can, too."

"I don't like those things. All you do is push buttons and wait for the machine to decide if you're a winner or a loser. I like to have at least some control over my money. You go on ahead, baby doll. I'm goin' over to that roulette wheel. At least there, you don't have to worry about people taking your cards."

When Marcus arrived at the roulette table, he placed one bet and lost. He quickly started heading to the blackjack tables. Sitting in an open chair at the twenty-five-dollar table, he waved his hand at a passing cocktail waitress. "Double Jack Daniels, Neat," He said. Turning his attention back to the dealer, he asked, "Can I bet more than twenty-five dollars?"

Darlene was sound asleep when her cell phone started ringing. She rolled over and picked it up, noticing it was three-thirty-five in the morning. The number was blocked, and she started to silence the ring until she noticed Marcus wasn't in bed beside her. She answered the call and heard Marcus's voice crying. "Baby doll, I need you to come get me. Please come get me!"

"Marcus, what's goin' on? Where are you? It's three thirty in the morning. Why ain't you here?

"They put me in jail, baby doll! They took my money and put me in jail. I need to get out. Can you please come get me? Please, baby doll. I can't be here!"

"Marcus, what'd you do now? You don't get put in jail for nothin'."

"I didn't do a damn thing, baby doll! That damn dealer just straight-up stole my money. He took it all. That thieving no-account. He took it all!"

"You don't get put in jail for losing money, Marcus. What did you do?"

'That asshole sittin' next to me. He took my ace. Him and that dealer were in cahoots to take my money. I fixed that for sure. That no-account ain't goin' to be taking no aces for a while, that's for sure. I fixed him good."

"Marcus Hudsen, you're the no-account here. This whole trip, you ain't done nothin' but get drunk and gamble. You didn't give me any attention. The only thing you done right is them flowers before we left. I ain't leavin' this bed, traveling to some nasty jail. You can just stay there." With that, she hung up.

When Darlene woke up later in the morning, she ordered a large breakfast from room service. After eating, she packed her suitcase, called the concierge, and asked for a rental car. She said aloud, "I reckon I won me more than enough to pay for this rental. That fool can find his own way. I hope he rots in there."

BEAU WAS SITTING in his car at Hansen Vehicle Services' parking lot when he looked at the time on his Apple watch. It was nine-thirty in the morning, and Gary Burston had just pulled his car into the lot. Beau got out of his car and walked over to Gary.

He held the manila folder containing the bus's service report in his left hand.

Beau shouted, "Gary, nice of you to come to work so early. Listen, I have a couple of questions I'd like to ask. Do you mind if we-"

Gary interrupted, "Get the hell out of my parking lot. You're not a detective. You're retired and have no business here. That's right. I made some calls after you left. You're workin' with that lawyer. I got nothin' to say, and you can leave now, or I'm callin' the real cops."

"Well, you go ahead and call them. I may be retired, but I still have a lot of friends in the department. In fact, I'll call them for you. Save your phone battery."

Gary said nothing

"Look, I just want to ask you a couple of questions so I can tell my boss I did my job. That's all."

As he spoke, Beau opened the folder, pulled out his photo of the brake's serial number, and held it out so Gary could see it. He took the photo and looked at it.

"Do you see the serial number there? It doesn't match the number in this service report." Buau reached into the folder, pulled out the bus's service report, and passed it to Gary.

Gary said, "Look. Why do you care about some brake on a bus?"

"That brake was involved in an accident where a lot of people got hurt. Look at this photo."

Beau pulled out the drone image of the bus's skid marks and passed it to Gary.

"Look at the skid marks. Do you see that the right one is longer than the left? I think there was something wrong with that left brake. It failed halfway through the skid. That brake is different from what's in the service report. How come?"

"We probably didn't have the brake in stock, and neither did our normal supplier. We probably special-ordered it from a different company that had it. Somebody was too damn lazy to enter the different part number into the computer. They just used the one that was there. Doesn't matter. The price is the same. It costs the same as our regular supplier. There's no difference in price."

"Why did you lie to me about not having the service report? You told me once that something goes to the impound lot, the service records are deleted, and guess what? Here it is:" Beau passed the report to Gary.

"Look here. As far as I'm concerned, once something is out of service and going to the impound, the service records are deleted from here. It shows here that you got this report from the impound lot's database, not ours. Besides, the price is the same, so who cares?"

"It doesn't bother you that you are buying defective parts?"

"I didn't know anything about this until you brought it up. Now, if you'll excuse me, I have to get to work."

With that, Gary started walking away. Beau was left to think about what he had just heard. He thought, "Well, what he said makes sense, but why did he keep mentioning the price? I didn't even think about that. Who cares about what something costs?" He shrugged and started walking to his car. Before Beau turned the ignition, he wondered, "When does anything made in China cost the same as an American-made part? I remember buying that Chinese carburetor for my RV generator. I bought it because it was less than half the price of the one made by the generator manufacturer. I wonder if ole Gary there bought that brake cheap, billed the city for the same amount as the American-made brake, and pocketed the difference. The city controller pays the bills for the city. They should be able to tell me something. I think I'll give them a call." Beau decided to stop by Cletus's office and fill him in on what he was working on. He could use his tiny cubicle there to make his calls. When he walked into the office, Cletus wasn't there. He went to his cubicle and called the city controller's office. After getting his call transferred to what seemed to be everyone working there, Marcia Lyons was his latest call transfer.

Beau said, "Hello Marcia, my name is Detective Gaston; I hope you can help me. I've been transferred to all of your co-workers. I hope you don't transfer me."

Marcia replied, "Well, I'll try not to. How can I help you?"

"I need to see the financial records for one of the city's vendors. Hansen Vehicle Services. Do you have those?"

"I'm sorry, detective. We don't release that information unless it's part of an audit. I can't help you with that."

"Even if those records are part of an investigation?"

"Well, that's different. We need Form 291B filled out. The city attorney's office has those. You would need them to submit it to me. I handle those requests."

"Marcia, it's just a routine request. I'm just filling in some blanks. Is it really necessary to bring the city attorney in on this?"

"Sorry again, detective. I need that form."

Beau thanked Marcia and hung up. He asked himself, Do I need this? Cletus doesn't care about what something costs. Even he admits Calpurnia isn't going to get anything out of this. Why am I digging into this so much? As soon as he finished that thought, he realized again that he missed the job. I really miss the action. I like chasing the bad guy. I'm going to keep digging until I find out what Hansen's is up to. Something's hinky, and I'm going to find out what it is. Beau spent the next hour trying to get someone in the city attorneys to help him out. He'd lost count of the call transfers and finally gave up. He was just about to leave and go home when Cletus walked in. Cletus saw Beau in his cubicle and said, "Well, looky here. Beau Gaston in the flesh. How're things? Anything going on with that bus?" Beau told Cletus everything he had been doing for the last week, ending with his conversation with Marcia at the controller's office. He also mentioned his roadblock at the city attorney's office. Cletus thought momentarily and said, "Beau, this is important news." If we can show a conspiracy with Hansen and the city is using defective parts on its vehicles, that changes everything in Calpurnia's lawsuit. I can subpoena those financial records as part of our civil suit. That driver may have been stoned on weed, but if the city is using bad parts, that helps Calpurnia. Good for her, sticking to her guns and not taking the settlement. I'll have Stella draw up the subpoena so you can look into this more. Maybe we'll get some money with this suit after all. Good work, Beau."

BILLY LEBLANC and Alden Henry were inside the Aryan Brigade's meth lab. It was two in the morning, and they had been in the lab for almost eight hours. Billy stood over six feet and had long, greasy black hair. Alden was much shorter and had his head shaved. They were in the process of pouring the liquid meth they had just made into several drying trays where the liquid would dry into a fine white powder. When the trays were full, they placed them in a drying chamber, which was a gas kitchen stove in a previous life. Alden turned the stove on and set the temperature to two hundred degrees.

When he closed the door, Alden said, "Ok, we're done. It's gonna cook in there for a few hours. I think I'll head to my bunk and get some sleep."

Billy replied, "Yeah, I think I'll join you. Been a long day. What time is this stuff supposed to be ready to go on the airboat?"

"It's not going out until tonight. Forrest is sending the first batch of guns to the Mexicans, so space might be tight. We'll figure it out."

Billy and Alden left the lab and started walking to their bunkhouse. They returned to the lab three hours later and were shocked to find the oven cold. Alden opened the door and saw the meth had not dried to a powder. It had turned into a slushy liquid with congealed clumps of meth.

"Damnit to hell, Billy. This stuff is ruined. What's goin' on here? Why is this oven cold? I turned it on and set the temperature. I know I did. The dial here shows the stove is set to two hundred degrees."

Billy turned the dial on one of the stovetop burners and sniffed the air next to the burner.

"There ain't no gas, Alden. I don't smell or hear anything coming from this burner."

Alden left the lab and walked to the back, where the large propane tank that supplied the lab was located. He looked at the gauge and saw the tank was empty. He shouted, "Damnit to hell, Billy. The propane tank is empty. That fool Nash forgot to refill it from the last time."

Billy also left the lab and walked to the propane tank. He looked at the gauge and said, "Damn. We're gonna' git it from Forrest. That Crank was supposed to go out tonight. That's a lost pile of money sittin' in that stove, and I ain't takin' the blame. Forrest is gonna be pissed"

Jackson Forbes and Chad Curtis were in the Aryan Brigade's armory, packing Pablo's M4 carbine rifles into wooden crates. The rifles were courtesy of and stolen from the US Army's ammunition depot just outside New Orleans. The crates would be loaded onto the airboats and transported to the pickup point across the bayou that night. Jackson was very muscular. His head was shaved, and he had Nazi and Aryan Brigade tattoos all over his body. Chad looked like any other person on the street. He had a wife and twin seven-year-old boys. His day job was as an electrician for Palmers Industrial Electric in Hattiesburg. He knew a race war was coming and wanted to be part of it.

Chad and his wife, Marbella, were raising their children to continue the Aryan cause. For their birthdays, Marbella made them matching uniforms with Swastikas on the shirt collars.

Chad spoke to Jackson, "Who's taking the airboats tonight? I know you're in one. Who's driving the other?"

While packing a crate, Jackson replied, "It's supposed to be Nash, but after that propane tank fiasco, who knows?"

"Well, you better hope he's driving the other. He's lived here all his life and knows that bayou better than anybody."

Closing the crate's lid, Jackson said, "You're right about that. This is gonna be my first run at night, and I'm sticking to him like glue on a stamp. That's for sure. Them gators are big as houses out there."

Nash Alden was a big man. He stood 6-4 and weighed close to three hundred pounds. His head was shaved on the sides, and a mohawk went down the center. He was supervising the loading of the airboats for that night's run across the bayou when Chad and

Jackson approached him carrying the last crate from the armory. They set the crate down beside the other crates next to the dock, and Jackson said, "Hey, Nash. You driving one of these boats tonight?"

"Why wouldn't I? I always drive the boats. That the last crate?"

Jackson said, "Yep. That's fourteen crates total."

With a smile, Chad couldn't resist saying, "We don't have any crank to load. We might be able to squeeze another crate or two on these boats."

Nash shot back, "Well, ain't you the comedian. If some damn fool would've told me the tank needed fillin', I would have done it. My job is here and not looking after empty propane tanks." Staring at Alden, he continued. "Billy and Alden didn't bother to check their damn equipment before they started drying that stuff.

After checking the gas levels in the airboats, Nash handed Jackson a Nightfox 100V night vision goggles and said, "Here, take these. You're going to need them."

Jackson took the goggles and asked, "What're these for?"

Nash replied, "We can't use the lights on the boat. The law knows what's going on here, but Harney pays them enough to mind their own business. It's the damn feds that's the problem. They been caught more than once sniffing around here, and they got boats just like we do. Only theirs are faster. You need them goggles to look out for Cypress knees and gators."

Jackson asked, "What're Cypress knees?"

"They're like thick poles standing up out of the water connected to the tree and damn hard to see at night. Now it's time to git. I wanna get back before sunrise."

With that, Jackson and Nash got into the fully laden airboats and started the engines. Nash was the first to pull away from the dock. He pressed the throttle pedal forward, and the airboat responded with a loud growl. The six-foot propeller at the rear pushed the air like a hurricane, and the airboat moved quickly into the blackness. Jackson was right behind him. Cruising in the blackness, Jackson was astounded at how well he could see using the night vision goggles Nash had given him. He could see the big Cypress trees and the hanging moss all around him. He also saw the Cypress knees sticking out of the water several feet from the trees. A shiver went through his body when he saw multiple pairs of bright dots just above the water's surface. The dots were alligator eyes reflecting infrared light from the night vision goggles. Jackson was convinced they were all looking at him. After about an hour of cruising, Jackson noticed Nash was getting further away from him. His goggles had a limited range, and Nash was at their outer edge. He was having difficulty seeing him and had a choice: Accelerate to keep up and risk hitting something or keep his pace and risk getting lost. After several minutes, his choice was made for him. The low battery indicator on the goggles started blinking.

He yelled aloud, "Damn you Nash! You checked the gas and not the goggles?"

He reached under the console, pulled out the boat's walkie-talkie, rotated the power switch, and saw it had no battery power. Jackson cursed Nash again and tossed the walkie-talkie back under the console. He throttled back to a crawl, trying to decide what to do. After a few minutes, he decided to do nothing. He would either wait for Nash to come looking for him or wait until the sun came up. Half an hour later, while Jackson was smoking a cigarette, he saw a bright white light off in the distance, moving back and forth across the bayou. The sound of an airboat followed this. Jackson started yelling, "Damn you, Nash! Git your ass over here!" After about a minute, he saw the airboat start moving to the left, away from him. Jackson cursed and climbed over the crates to the front of the airboat to switch on the airboat's powerful light. The light came to life, and he started moving it rapidly from side to side. The airboat in the distance must have seen the bright light; it turned and started approaching him. As the boat drew closer, Jackson shined the light directly at the approaching airboat and shouted, "Nash! You dumbass, leaving me here! I swear I'm gonna knock you-" Jackson's words froze when he saw the airboat coming alongside him. Two people on board wore blue windbreakers with the letters FBI stenciled on the back. He thought about making a run for it but soon realized its futility. The fed's airboat was much faster than his, and he had no night vision. Off in the distance, Nash looked on in horror. When the FBI airboat was close enough to Jackson's boat, the agent driving cut its engine, filling the air with silence. Special Agent Ferguson, the agent in front of the boat, said, "Hello. Are you okay? Is there something wrong?"

Jackson replied, "Well, hi there. No, I'm good. Just havin' a smoke is all."

The agent driving the airboat, Special Agent Conrad, said, "Nothing wrong with that. What are you carrying there? That boat looks like it's ready to sink. Big gators around here, and I see you aren't wearing a flotation device. What's on that boat?"

Before Jackson could respond, he heard a loud sound and saw the top of SA Conrad's head transform into a red mist. SA Ferguson started to reach for his weapon when half of his neck disappeared. His head tilted from the missing support and fell into the water. Jackson stood on his airboat and started to hyperventilate. He was looking at SA Conrad, who had been driving the boat. He was strapped into the chair, his arms dangling, and the top of his head missing. Jackson came out of his shock when he heard an airboat approaching. It was Nash.

TRUETT STARED at the boxes in SynCor's booth at the annual Oil and Gas Journal convention in New Orleans. This was going to be the Journal's largest convention in years. Over one hundred vendors displayed their products in search of customers to buy from them. He checked his watch and wondered where Travis and John were. They should be helping set up the booth. While waiting for them, he visited the food court and got breakfast. When he returned to the, they still weren't there. Truett said to himself, "Well, I don't know where they are, but this booth needs to be ready by ten o'clock." That's when the doors open, and the hundreds of attendees flood the floor. Just as Truett unpacked the last box, Travis and John entered the booth. Truett looked at them and said, "Well, it was nice of you to show up. Too bad there isn't anything for you to do, seeing as I already got everything set up."

John replied, "Sorry, man. We were spying on Tennico over there. No one was manning their booth, so we took the opportunity to grab some of their marketing literature.

Truett said, "ok, well, I have almost everything done, but I'm going to need some help putting our correlator on this table." After the three had everything the way they wanted it, Truett asked John what he thought of Tennico's booth and marketing material.

John said, "Well, it's funny. They have their small-scale ERPS in the booth, but their literature is all about large-scale production. They're in the "Fake it till you make it" mode like we were. The only difference is we made ours, and here it is." John pointed to their correlator.

Truett turned his attention to the entrance to the convention floor and saw people flooding in. He said, "Ok, everybody. Time to make some sales."

Hours later, it was almost five-thirty when Truett finished his conversation with one of the attendees. Ahmed Sawaff was from Saudi Arabia. He had just come from Tennico's booth, listening to Peter Murphy talk about ERPS. When he left SynCor's booth, the convention floor was empty of people, and the lights were turned low.

Truett said to John and Travis, "That went well. It seems the Arabs are getting into the refining business. The guy I was talking to is from Saudi Arabia's oil ministry. He wants us to meet with his bosses. Can you believe it!?"

John started pumping his fist and said, "Damn, glad we spent the money to be here. It's been totally worth the cash, and it's only the first day.

Travis said, "I'm ready for a brewsky. Let's go back to the hotel and hit that bar across the street. They have food. I want a burger with my beer."

After going to their rooms and changing into more casual attire, Travis, John, and Truett walked into Cajun Willy's Pub and Grill. The place was packed with people from the convention. There was no hope of finding an open table, so they settled for standing at the end of the bar. As the three waited to get one of the bartender's attention, Travis saw a man waving at him from a table halfway down the bar. It was Peter Murphy from Tennico. Travis excused himself and walked over to Peter's table. There were several other people at the table. Travis recognized two of them. They had been talking to John at SynCor's booth earlier.

Travis approached Peter and said, "Hey, Peter. Nice to see you. I stopped by your gargantuan booth this morning, but no one was there. I guess when you're as big as Tennico, you can afford to sleep in."

Peter chuckled and said, "Nobody at Tennico sleeps. You can do that when you're dead." He went on to introduce the other people at the table. After the introductions, Peter said, "Travis, you probably noticed we don't have our large-scale ERPS in the booth."

"I couldn't help but notice that. Still having issues?"

"That would be an understatement."

Travis wanted to brag and said, "We had one of the Saudi folks come into our booth. They're getting into the refining business and want us to meet their oil minister."

"Yeah, Ahmed talked to me about what his people are planning. I had to tell him I would get back to him when our full-scale ERPS was ready. Looks like you beat us to the punch as far as the Saudis are concerned."

Travis and Truett stood in their booth the next day, talking to their neighbor on their left side. Stan Dober was a sales rep for Odessa Pipe and Valve. Truett was firing questions at Stan about how Odessa might be able to make the fluid tubes he needed. SynCor still couldn't make its own, and Truett was looking for a company to replace the ever-tardy Johnson Hydro. They were interrupted when a large Asian-looking man stopped in front of SynCor's booth. His name tag said Zhang Wei, but no company was associated with the name. He was large and heavy-set with a bald, shiny head. Travis turned from Stan and, reading his name tag, said to Zhang, "Hello, thanks for stopping by our booth, Mr. Wei. My name is Travis Beloit. I'm one of the founders of SynCor. Would you like to see what SynCor produces for oil refining? We developed a method to eliminate hydrocarbon emissions when oil and gas fuels are combusted. We've created an Eco-friendly fossil fuel."

. . .

WEI REPLIED in a thick Chinese accent, This is very interesting. Are you saying I can run my automobile in the garage with the door closed?"

"Well, I wouldn't advise it. The additives and chemicals in the gas aren't affected by our correlator." Travis continued, "Our system removes greenhouse gases and doesn't interfere with the refining process."

Wei asked, "Does your system have new technology, or are you using a variation of existing technology?"

"We developed the technology and have eight patents. More to the point, our correlator will be used in every refinery around the world. Nobody's going to want hydrocarbon-laden fuel anymore."

Wei picked up a brochure from the table before him and asked, "How much does this cost a refiner? How does your company make money?"

Travis proudly said, "We don't charge for the correlator. We charge the refiner by the barrel. SynCor gets a royalty for every barrel of oil a refiner processes. We provide, install, and maintain our system at no charge to the customer. We get a constant revenue stream."

Wei said nothing.

Travis continued, "May I ask what your interest in our correlator is? Do you work for a refiner?"

Wei replied, "Do you know John Zsu?"

Travis was taken aback. "Yes, he's my partner. We're co-founders of SynCor. Have you met him? Would you like to speak to him?"

"That won't be necessary. I know his father, Zichen. Zichen told me about how well John was doing. I am here on other business and thought I would visit your booth here." After a pause, Wei continued, "Thank you for your time." He turned around and walked away.

Travis watched Wei head to the exit and turned to look for John. He didn't see him in the booth, so he asked Truett if he knew where John was.

Truett said, "I saw him with Peter Murphy. They were walking to the food court. What's up?"

Travis looked puzzled and said, "Nothing. I just had a strange conversation with this Chinese guy. We talked about our system, and he asked if I knew John.

"What's so strange about that?"

"He didn't have a company on his name tag, and he said he knew John's father but didn't want to talk to John."

Truett started straightening the literature on the table at the front of the booth and said, "Did you get the guy's name?

"Zhang Wei. That's what he had on his nametag."

Truett said, "I don't know what John's talking to Murphy about, but he should be back pretty soon. He's scheduled to speak in an hour, and his notes are in his backpack under the table."

Zhang exited the convention's main room and went outside to the lounge area. In its former life, the lounge was filled with wall-to-wall pay phones and crowded with people engaged in important conversations. Now, it had couches, chairs, coffee tables, and soft music playing in the background. Wei pulled out his cell phone and called a number that was answered over seven thousand miles away. Wei was calling his boss, Hao Yang, at the Chinese National Energy Commission (NEC). Yang looked at his phone and saw that Wei was calling him. He picked up and said, "Zhang. How are things in New Orleans? Have you met with Zichen's son? John"

Wei, speaking softly, said, "I am at their convention and spoke to John's business partner. His name is Travis Beloit. I know nothing about their invention, but Travis said it would revolutionize the oil refining business and make very big profits for their company." Wei went on, "I think this is a significant invention. I will contact Zichen to find out what he knows about his son's invention. He is very much in debt to us, and I'm sure he will cooperate with our requests."

Yang replied, "Yes. Talk to Zichen and let me know the results." Yang disconnected the call without saying anything further.

Half an hour after Wei left the booth, Travis saw John walking down the aisle toward SynCor's booth with a big smile. When he arrived, Travis told him, "Truett said you were talking to Peter Murphy. Anything I should know?"

John could barely contain his excitement when he said, "Peter told his bosses what he'd seen at our booth. Tennico is pulling the plug on its ERPS system, and they want to discuss a partnership."

Travis exploded, "Are you serious!? We just knocked out one of the world's biggest oil and gas companies?" Travis and John high-fived each other and pretended to box each other. John dropped to the floor and shouted, "I give up! You're too good! SynCor rules!"

When he heard the commotion, Truett was talking to a sales rep in a booth across the aisle. He turned and saw Travis and John yelling at each other. Truett walked over and said, "What the hell are you guys doing!? What's going on?"

John yelled, "Tennico threw in the towel! They're bagging ERPS and want to go with us!"

Looking at John, Travis yelled louder, "We're going to be rich! I can see the headline: John Zsu and Travis Beloit are officially richer than God!"

Truett looked at the two and didn't know what to say.

BEAU WAS in his home office, going through emails. As he scrolled down, he saw what he was looking for. It was an email from the City Controller's office. Cletus's subpoena had done its work, and Marcia Lyons had complied with Beau's request for the financial transactions for Hansen Service. Beau opened the attached PDF file and sent it to his printer. Beau turned his attention back to his list of emails and started deleting the obvious spam. After a few minutes, Beau noticed his printer was still busy with the PDF file. He picked up the stack of printed paper and was shocked at what he saw. Hansen was being paid for hundreds of invoices submitted to the city. Beau quickly realized there was no way a vehicle service business the size of Hansen could handle the amount of work associated with the invoices it had submitted to the city. He sat in his chair, looking at the printout on his desk. He thumbed through the pages, looking for the invoice Hansen, or more to the point, Gary Burston, submitted for the bus involved in the accident. When he found it, he wasn't surprised at the amount billed for the brake Hansen's replaced. Beau took his phone and pulled up the photo of the brake's serial number. He googled "Chinese Bus brake" and added the serial number. Google responded with what appeared to Beau to be a list of unusable information. He did see one link that took him to a Chinese auto parts website. He opened the website page and found that everything was written in Chinese. What a surprise. He put the serial number in what appeared to be the "Search For" box and hit enter. The site returned a page with a product image of the brake he had seen on the bus. He converted the currency into dollars and found the price was less than a third of what Burston billed the city for. Beau thumbed through the invoice printouts, and it was evident that Hansen had been involved in a major financial crime. He picked up the phone and called Cletus. After listening to what Beau had to say, Cletus disconnected his call and sat back in his office chair.

The news Beau had just given him was incredible, to say the least. Cletus jumped from his chair and rushed to tell Stella the good news. Hansen and, by extension, the city were using defective Chinese parts and fraudulently billing the city. Calpurnia had just hit the jackpot. His joy was short-lived when Stella reminded him that Calpurnia was paying Cletus by the hour. He wouldn't get his customary thirty-three percent contingency fee. His disappointment was lessened because he would soon be all over the news. He'd just won his client a huge settlement, and everybody was going to be talking about it. He was about to get very busy with new clients. After Cletus presented what he'd learned about Hansen to the District Attorney, the police grapevine began to buzz. When he heard about Gary Burston's pending arrest, Derrick Morgan called Harney using his burner phone. Harney was walking to the airboat dock when he pulled the vibrating phone out of his back pocket. Ever since he was made aware of Beau's visits to Hansen's, he kept his connection to the Hattiesburg police department nearby.

Harney answered and said, "What's goin' on now?"

Derrick spoke, "I just heard Gary is going to be arrested. They found out what he was doing and proved it enough to bring charges."

Harney yelled into the phone, "Damnit to hell! What'd that fool do to get caught?"

Derrick replied, "That asshole Beau Gaston is to blame. Gary had some damn bad luck with that brake, but Gaston is the one who started asking questions."

Harney said quietly, "Now, what am I goin' to do? You're tellin' me I lost the money that fool Gary was gettin' us?"

"Sorry, Harney. I have more bad news. The FBI is getting a search warrant for the compound. Killing those agents was a very bad thing. They know you're behind their disappearance. What the hell were you thinking?

"Don't talk about that. I don't want to hear another word from your mouth about people getting killt. Harney disconnected without saying another word. He continued his walk to the boat dock and saw the FBI airboat Nash had towed back to the compound after making his and Jackson's delivery the night before. The airboat had blood all over it, and two Brigade members were cleaning it up.

Harney stood at the end of the dock and yelled, "Never mind cleaning that thing. Take it out and sink it. I don't want that thing cummin' to nobody's attention. Just git it on out of here. Sink it."

Harney wasn't worried about the FBI's search warrant. Morgan would give him a heads-up when he could expect visitors. Besides, being prepared for a law enforcement raid was a well-practiced drill at the compound.

Mason Campbell was pulling a cart filled with cleaning supplies to the meth lab. He was wearing white coveralls and was breathing through a painter's respirator. His job was to turn the lab into a storage facility and remove any traces of the meth produced there. Mason Campbell wasn't his real name. That was Matt Hollister. Matt's real job was working undercover for the Army's Criminal Investigation Division (CID), gathering intelligence on the Brigade and Krotz Springs's corrupt police department. Mason's concern for his safety was elevated considerably with the news of the FBI agent's demise at the hands of the people he was spying on.

CID recruited Matt after he graduated from Danver University. He was the ideal candidate for undercover work because he wasn't married and had no children. He was also white and didn't have a Muslim or Jewish-sounding name. He stood over six feet and weighed two hundred and twenty pounds, with blond hair and blue eyes. Mason joined the Aryan Brigade through the federal prison in Pollock, Louisiana. United States Penitentiary Pollock (USP Pollock). Mason was situated as a corrections officer, better known to the inmates as a hack. He worked in the medium security part of the prison and gave special treatment to members of the Aryan Brotherhood, a nationwide prison gang with ties to the Aryan Brigade. In addition to favors inside Pollock, Mason helped family members of inmates on the outside. A mother was having problems with her neighbor, or a sister needed her car repaired. These were favors that Mason could provide without bringing much attention to himself, and that meant a great deal to the inmates.

Mason had been working at the prison for over a year when he got "fired" for a made-up accusation. The "firing" was his next step in burrowing himself into the brigade. It wasn't chance that brought Mason to Harney's attention. Mason made sure the majority of his outside favors involved Aryan Brigade inmates. Mason had been a full-time compound resident for over six months and took his orders from Forrest. Currently, those orders were to clean out the meth lab. Mason was on the lookout for guns. Guns had gone missing from the Army's depot outside New Orleans, and the Army wanted them back. He needed to find out where the brigade kept their guns and copy the serial numbers off of them. Having the compound in "raid mode" gave him a greater opportunity to sniff around places he usually wouldn't be allowed. He had seen men moving crates from the barn and onto the airboats at the dock, but when he went inside the barn, all he saw were ATVs and survival gear. He noticed a large area in the barn was empty, but

you could see oil spotting where some type of large vehicle or vehicles used to be. Leaving the cleaning cart outside, Mason walked
into the meth lab and started collecting all of the lab's glassware
and carefully packing it into foam-lined boxes. He heard a noise by
the door and turned to see Alden Henry walking into the lab.

"Hey, Alden. What's up? I'm almost done packing this stuff. What
do you want me to do with it after I'm done?"

"Mason, I swear. You should be workin' for Amazon, quick as you
are packin' that glass."

Mason replied, "Too many coons working there. I'd be arrested for
murder before my first lunch break."

They both laughed until their sides hurt.

When he stopped laughing, Alden said, "We're goin' to take this
stuff to the barn. I gotta a special place for it. Sure as hell don't
need any of this glass breaking. C'mon with me, and I'll show you
where to put it."

Mason removed the cleaning supplies from his cart and placed the
boxes he was packing on it. They both started the long walk to the
barn. When they arrived, Alden walked to the back of the barn and
pointed to the floor. He said, "Bring that thing over here." Mason
pulled the cart over to Alden and watched him turn on a space
heater on a shelf on the back wall of the barn. He turned the heat
selector dial all the way to the left and then back to the right. He
did that three times. When he finished the third twist, there was an
audible thump. Alden used his foot to press on the floor, and a
section of it popped downward. The section was four feet square.
Alden grasped the top edge and pulled it towards him. The floor
section disappeared under the floor where Alden was standing,
revealing a staircase descending into darkness.

Mason, astonished, said, "Pretty cool. Until you pushed that down with your foot, there's no way I would have seen that."

"We got all kinna tricks round here. This one's Harney's doing. He's one damn smart dog, that's for sure."

Alden flipped a light switch at the top of the stairs and started walking down. When he got halfway down, he said, "Pass me one of them boxes. You take another and follow me."

Mason picked up a box and started down the stairs, following Alden. When he reached the bottom, Mason stared in disbelief at what he saw. He thought, "No wonder the Army is pissed, half of the Army's weapons are down here." He then spoke out loud, "Geeze, Alden, you guys really know how to play."

"10-4 on that. Harney and Forrest know how to git things done. That's for sure."

Mason followed Alden down a path lined with wooden crates and M4-Carbine rifles standing on end. At the end, Alden turned left and stopped in front of what appeared to be a concrete wall. He set his box down, put his hands and shoulder against the wall, and pushed with all of his strength. When nothing happened, Alden said to Mason, "Help with this. This damn thing gets more stubborn by the hour. I swear." Mason put his shoulder to the wall and pushed. A section of the wall the size of a door went in. Alden grabbed the side and pulled. Just like the barn floor, the door slid behind the wall. He reached inside, flicked a light switch, turned around, picked up his box, and went inside. Mason followed. They entered a room the size of a garden shed. The room was empty except for three small brown cases the size of a suitcase. Mason saw faded red lettering on the cases and instantly became alert. He'd spent enough time in CID training and watching TV to see the lettering was Cyrillic. These cases came from Russia.

"What're those?" Mason asked.

"Just never you mind. Forrest would piss a fit if he knowed you were down here. Hell, I ain't supposed to be here either, but I need a safe place for these glass items." Pointing to the cases, he continued, "That's Harney's and Forrest's business right there. Ain't anybody's concern. Now we got to go."

Mason walked back to the meth lab to continue his cleaning. He thought about those Russian cases and what he thought they were. He needed to get back there, take a picture, and send it to his handler at CID. The only problem was when he would get the chance. The compound was busy as live crabs in a pot. He couldn't risk sneaking out of the barracks at night. He would never get away with that. After a moment, an idea struck him. He would go to dinner when everyone would be in the mess hall. Nobody missed dinner. Mason continued cleaning for the next several hours. He had just finished spraying the lab with Ammonia to prevent the FBI's search dogs from being able to smell anything when he heard the ring of the mess hall bell. Mason went outside, removed his respirator, and suddenly realized he had a problem. Brigade members weren't allowed to have their cell phones inside the compound. They were locked inside Harney's office. He scanned the lab and then remembered what he had—a pen and notepad in his back pocket. The notepad had his cleaning checklist and notes on what he observed on the equipment being moved. Satisfied that he had what he needed. Mason walked into the mess hall and found it crowded with people. It was all hands on deck preparing for the FBI's visit. Mason took a seat at one of the dozen long tables. Looking at his tablemates, he didn't recognize most of them. This was a good thing because nobody would notice him leaving the table. After what seemed like an eternity of chattering with his neighbors, and as soon as the food started being served by the women in the compound, Mason excused himself to go to the bathroom. He made a show of going to the bathroom, turned, and walked out. He didn't notice Alden watching him leave.

He walked to his barracks, went inside, walked into the bathroom, opened the window, and exited the barracks. Dusk was setting in, so he would have some cover from the coming darkness. Taking as circuitous a route as possible to the barn, Mason walked in and went to the back. He looked at the space heater and mimicked what he had seen Alden do. Nothing. "Damn," he said in a whisper. He asked himself, "Was it two times left or three? Maybe it was three to the right. No, it was definitely to the left." He tried again and was rewarded with the floor dropping down. He grabbed the edge and pulled it back, revealing the staircase. He flew down the stairs and ran to the wall he and Alden pushed to reveal the room with the Russian cases. Mason put his shoulder to the wall and pushed. The wall didn't move. He tried again with the same result. He tried again, this time lowering his shoulder to give himself better leverage. The wall finally moved. Mason froze before he could grasp the edge to pull the wall section back. "What was that?" he asked himself. Spinning around to look behind him and holding his breath, Mason listened for the sound he heard. Nothing. After a few moments, he returned his attention to the wall. Time was racing by. Pulling it back, he walked up to the three cases and began examining one of them. It was heavy. Mason thought it must be around fifty pounds. The red Cyrillic letters were faded but still readable. He reached into his back pocket and pulled out the pad and pen he had. Squinting at the strange letters, he copied them, put the case back as he found it, closed the wall opening, and started up the stairs. He took the same route back to the mess hall. Mason didn't wear a watch, but he thought his absence from dinner lasted about ten minutes. When he got to his table and sat down, he was relieved that his tablemates only made jokes. One tablemate said his reason for being in the bathroom so long was because he was full of crap. Mason didn't notice Alden wasn't in his seat.

The next morning, Mason left the barracks at 4:45 AM. Revelry was at five, and he was raising the flag today. Brigade members considered it an honor to raise Old Glory on the new day, and everybody took turns. Mason was surprised when his bunkmate, three cots up from his, asked him to take his place. Early in his stay, Mason learned it was best to ask as few questions as possible, especially to senior brothers-in-arms. He walked to the flagpole and saw Horace Walters pulling his bugle out of his case. Mason moved to the box attached to the flagpole, removed the flag inside, and attached it to the rope going up it. At precisely 5:00 AM, Horace blew revelry while Mason raised the flag. When the flag was tied off, Horace started to put his bugle back in its case, and Mason heard his name being called. He turned and saw Jackson walking towards him.

"Mason, I need you to give me a hand with that FBI airboat. Harney wants it taken out and sunk."

"Sure, no problem. What do you want me to do? I still have more cleaning to do in the lab. Will this take long?"

"Naw. We're just goin' take it out a ways and sink it. Shouldn't take long. Follow me."

Jackson walked to the boat dock with Mason following behind him. When they got there, Alden was finishing filling the FBI airboat with fuel. One of the compound's airboats was next to the FBI boat. Alden looked up and said, "Well, c'mon there. I got things to do. "Mason, you'll ride with me. Jackson, you take our boat.

Alden went to the front of the dock, picked up a rope, and tossed it to Mason.

"Alden commanded, 'Take that and tie the front of that FBI boat to the back of our boat."

Mason took one end of the rope and tied it to the front cleat of the FBI airboat and the back cleat of the compound's airboat. Alden and Mason joined Jackson in the compound's airboat. Jackson pressed the throttle pedal down, and the airboat responded with a deafening roar as the prop blade created a hurricane-force wind that propelled the boat forward and pulled the FBI boat with it. Mason noticed he was the only one without headphones and saw Jackson and Alden talking into the noise-suppression mics attached to the headphones. After about twenty minutes, Jackson throttled back the airboat and brought it to a gentle stop so the FBI boat behind wouldn't hit them. Alden turned his head and yelled into Mason's ear. "Go back there and untie that boat. Take that gas can in the back and pour the gas out on the boat, and then git your ass back here." Mason walked to the back of the airboat, carefully slid around the prop cage, and stepped onto the front of the FBI boat. He felt the breeze from Jackson's idling prop and walked to the rear of the airboat to get the gas can Alden had put there at the dock. Halfway to the can, Mason felt the boat move up and down. He turned and saw Alden walking towards him with a gun in his hand. Mason felt every hair on the back of his neck come to attention as he watched Alden approach.

He yelled at Mason, "I seen you go into that barn when everbody was eatin' supper last night. What's so damn interesting about them cases that you took the time to write things down? Tell me that!"

Mason remembered what he had learned in training: If it's a knife, run away. If it's a gun, run forward. You can't run faster than a bullet. He lunged forward, grabbed Alden's hand, and pushed it up. The sound of a gunshot was lost in the noise created by Jackson's airboat. Alden kicked his leg out and struck Mason in the chest. Mason refused to release his grip. Doing so meant he was a dead man. He fell backward, pulling Alden with him. They hit the deck with a thud. Mason took his knee and rammed it into Alden's groin. He screamed in pain and released his grip on the gun. Alden got up and started to run toward Jackson's boat. He was at the front of the FBI boat when he felt his back being pushed. That was the last thing Alden felt as he was propelled into Jackson's prop blade. Mason flattened himself to the deck while parts of Alden flew past him.

Jackson was sitting in his pilot's chair when he felt a jolt, followed by the engine faltering and dying. Turning around, he saw the bloody scene behind him and Mason coming up from the deck. He looked for Alden and realized what had just taken place. They locked eyes on each other for a second before Jackson leapt from his seat to retrieve his rifle, latched to the underside of the passenger bench. Mason, wasting no time, ran to the front and untied the rope connecting the two airboats. He jumped into the pilot's chair just as Jackson released one of the two latches holding his gun. Mason stared at the console in front of him, not knowing what to do. He'd never driven an airboat. He did the obvious, turned the ignition key, and heard the airboat's engine roar to life. He stared at the console again, not knowing what to do next. He glanced up and saw Jackson pointing his rifle at him just as a bullet slammed into his seatback, missing him by inches. Mason frantically looked for a way to control the boat while Jackson refined his aim and prepared for another shot. He looked down from the console and saw a large black pedal. Jackson was adding pressure to his gun's trigger when Mason slammed his foot on the pedal. The airboat lurched forward and hit Jackson's boat just as his gun fired. Mason felt another bullet slam into his chair, missing him by a fraction of an inch. He kept the pedal pressed, pushing Jackson's boat to the side. Jackson toppled into the water as Mason roared away. Jackson felt an agonizing pain in his right shoulder. He turned his head and saw the eyes of a gigantic alligator. The alligator rolled on its back, pulling Jackson under the water's surface.

CLETUS' cell phone vibrated in his pocket while on the Meadowbrook Country Club golf course. He was its newest member. He was with Beau and Cletus' latest clients, Everette Rolms and Colton Ertz, who were owners of Towson Auto Parts. Towson had twelve locations between Hattiesburg and New Orleans. Cletus was moving up. He wasn't chasing ambulances anymore. Lawyering for business meant he could worry less about going in front of a judge and jury and more about his golf score. He became well-known after getting Calpurnia's massive settlement from the city. He became almost famous when the news media learned that he and Beau's work on Calpurnia's case resulted in the dismantling of a white supremacy organization over in Krotz Springs. Everybody was calling him. Calpurnia had insisted he should get his customary 33 percent commission from her settlement. He was the only lawyer who listened to her. Besides, giving back 33 percent still made her a very wealthy woman. Cletus remembered his father's advice when it came to finances: "Never turn down somebody giving you money." Cletus was in high cotton, and it felt great. He looked at his phone's caller ID and saw it was his wife, Susan. Concerned, he excused himself and walked off the putting green to his golf cart parked next to the green. After a few minutes, Cletus returned to see Beau sink a thirty-foot putt.

Beau yelled, "That's the one! That's what I'm talking about. Everette, you need to sink your putt, or I win the hole and twenty bucks."

Cletus grimaced. There are better ways to endear yourself to clients, especially new ones, than taking their money and rubbing it in.

Colton asked Cletus, "Everything good?"

"That was my wife. Her car broke down at the grocery, and she wants me to come get her. She's got the kids with her. I told her to take an Uber and that I'd take care of the car later. I need to win some of my money back. You and Everette are skinning me like that rabbit I shot last week." They all laughed.

Beau said, "I thought Excella's never broke down."

Colton said, "It's breaking down because that Monarch dealer doesn't buy their parts from us."

Everette chuckled as he started to line up his money-saving putt.

Several weeks after they returned from the convention, John, Travis, and Truett began preparing their Synthetic Correlator for installation in Tennico's R&D facility. When John walked in, Truett was in the back warehouse section of the office, unpacking the fluid tubes he had just received from Odessa Pipe and Valve.

John asked, "Are those the new fluid tubes you got from Odessa?"

Truett stopped what he was doing, turned to John, and said, "You bet they are. Stan Dober really came through. He sent us these five days after I ordered them. If you can believe it, Johnson Hydro keeps calling and asking when we will place our next order. I had to tell Adelle to stop taking messages from them. They're learning the lesson; you don't know how good you have it until it's gone."

"You cut a great deal with Odessa Truett. How did you get these tubes so cheap?"

Truett smiled and said, "I got them to give us a volume discount based on future orders. They're not stupid. They know the business we're going to give them. Stan told me Odessa is already ramping up production."

"Well, keep up the good work. Peter Murphy keeps bugging me about setting an install date for the Correlator. Have you talked to Travis about the controller?"

"He's over at Tennico as we speak. He's meeting with their engineers to go over the install procedures for our system. He'll be back Wednesday. I finished the software routines for the controller. Travis just needs to calibrate it for the correlator flow rate."

John turned to leave and said, "Ok. Thanks, man. Talk to you later."

In Tennico's conference room, Travis spoke to the engineers responsible for implementing SynCor's correlator into Tennico's refining system. The four engineers sat at a large table, and Travis stood before a large whiteboard, explaining the diagrams he drew. Marcus, Tennico's plant manager, was also present. Jim Swaney, the lead engineer, asked Travis a question.

"Your system is larger than our ERPS. How are you going to fit it in the same space?"

Putting his marker down, Travis reached for his Stanley thermos filled with Starbucks Veranda brewed so strong a spoon would stand up. After taking a sip, he replied, "Good question, Jim. One of the nice things about our system is its flexibility. We can adjust the size of the fluid tubes to fit any refinery. In your case, we'll extend them from here," pointing to one of the diagrams, "To here. This gives us plenty of room. We just need to source some fittings for the adjusted tubes."

Jim crossed his arms and said, "I see what you're saying, but I'm still not sure you'll have enough room."

Julie Whiton was one of the engineers sitting at the table. She looked at Jim and said, "If you reroute the pump pipe to the other side, it'll work. You'll have more room to work with." Everybody looked at Julie as she continued, "That pipe should never have been there in the first place. Whoever put it there was lazy and didn't want to build the ceiling suspension for the pipe to cross over. I looked at the original plans before the revisions were made and saw that the suspension was there. The revised plans don't show it."

Jim uncrossed his arms and said, "Good point, Julie. I hadn't thought of that."

Marcus chimed in, "I noticed that. I didn't want to say anything because it wasn't my place. I know everything about this refinery." Everybody looked at Marcus and said nothing.

Travis was in the office space Tennico had provided SynCor two weeks later. It had three desks with computer terminals, a countertop with a microwave and coffee maker on top, and storage underneath. Travis worked full-time at Tennico, and John spent most of his time there. The third desk was for Jing Mao. Jing had a master's degree in fluid dynamics from Stanford. Jing responded to John's job posting in an online engineering recruitment company. His job at SynCor was to design the correlator's flow controls so they matched up with Tennico's. Jing was skinny and medium height, had short black hair, and spoke with a slight British accent. His parents were Chinese, and his father worked at the Chinese embassy, assisting the ambassador. He grew up in London and moved to the States after being accepted into Stanford.

Travis was sitting at his desk and feverishly clicking his mouse when he heard a knock at the open door. He looked up and saw Darlene standing there. She held a notepad with a pen clipped to it. "Hello, Mr. Beloit. I'm Darlene Moss. I work in the procurement office. Mr. Swaney asked me to stop by and see if you needed anything." Travis couldn't speak. He just stared at Darlene. After a few uncomfortable seconds, Darlene asked, "Mr. Beloit, do you need anything for your office?"

Travis came out of his trance and said, "I'm sorry. What did you say?"

Darlene smiled and said, "I asked if you needed anything. Mr. Swaney wanted me to see if you needed anything. I work in the procurement office. People come to me when they need something. I git it for them."

"Oh, I see. Well, thanks for stopping by. I'm sorry I didn't get your name."

Darlene smiled. "It's Darlene, Darlene Moss."

"Hi, Darlene, I'm Travis, Travis Beloit, but my friends call me Travis."

"Well, silly you. Now, do you need anything? Cause I need to get back to my desk."

"I'm ok, Darlene. I don't need anything for now. Thank you. Can I ask if there is any place besides the cafeteria where you can get a decent hamburger? The bottom of my shoe tastes better than their burger."

Darlene chuckled, "There's Dora's Café. It's about three miles from the plant entrance. Turn left at the entrance. Their Hamburgers are ok, but they've got the best Po'boy for miles around."

She turned and walked away. Travis was left with a smile a mile wide. He asked himself, "I wonder if she's taken?"

An hour after Darlene left, John walked into the office. Travis looked up from his computer screen and said, "Where's Jing? He's supposed to finish the flow parameters." John went over to the coffee pot and started pouring himself a cup. "He finished those. He's with Jim Swaney's group, inputting them into the Tennico's system."

"Already?" Travis said, surprised. "He picks things up fast."

As if on cue, Jing walked into the office and said, "Hey guys, I finished with Swaney's group. They'll all set to go."

John looked at Jing and said, "Good job, man. Travis and I are happy you're part of the team." He looked closer at Jing and said, "Hey, you don't look so good. Are you OK?"

Jing replied, sitting down on his chair, "I feel like crap. I cut my finger on a valve handle. Then I accidentally got the Isoflurane valve flux they use for valve sealing on my hand."

Travis said, "Isoflurane? Nobody uses that stuff anymore. It's way old school."

John walked over to his desk and sat down. "We have a case of Isobutyl flux back at the warehouse. I'll call Adelle and have her drive it up."

Travis quickly rose from his chair. "No. Don't call her. I'll go to the procurement office and have Darlene order it."

John asked, "Darlene? Who's Darlene?"

Travis didn't answer as he walked out of the office. John looked at Jing, saw him make a face, and shrugged his shoulders.

Travis couldn't walk fast enough to Darlene's office. When he got there, Darlene was on the phone. She looked at him and waved to one of the two chairs in front of her desk. Travis sat down and noticed another desk behind Darlene's. A woman in her late forties with short red hair was tapping away on her keyboard. She looked at Travis and smiled before returning to the keyboard.

Darlene finished the call and said, "Well, hello, Mr. Beloit. What can I do for you?"

"Please, Darlene, Mr. Beloit was my father. Remember, I said my friends call me Travis."

"I do remember you saying that. Now, what can I do for you, Mr. Beloit?"

Travis sunk in his chair and said, "I need to get a case of Isobutyl Flux. The quart size, not gallons."

"I'll get that taken care of. You should have it by Thursday. Is that quick enough?"

"That'll be fine. Thanks, Darle-, Uh, Mrs. Moss. Thank you very much."

"ANYTIME. Now, if you'll excuse me, I have some calls to make. One of them is ordering your flux." She picked up the phone and started dialing.

Travis got up, and as soon as he left the office, Darlene and her officemate, Kimee Addison, burst into laughter.

Kimee said, "Mrs. Moss, can you get me some flux, too? I really need it!"

Darlene had to wait until she stopped laughing before she said, "Did you hear that? Mrs. Moss. Uh, thanks, Mrs. Moss." More laughter.

Kimee said with a big smile, "Mrs. Moss. That poor man is fishing like a boy skipping school. Him tryin' to see if you're married. I declare he's sweet as pecan pie over you. That's for sure. Hell, Darlene, you ain't seeing Marcus anymore. Why you given him such a hard time? Shoot, girl. You don't want him. Pass him to me. I'll git to his flux right quick."

They both erupted in laughter. The laughter stopped when they noticed Marcus standing in the doorway.

He said, "I saw that SynCor boy leavin' this place. What'd he want, Darlene?"

"What he wanted, Marcus, is no damn business of yours. Now, what do YOU want? Why're YOU interrupting my day?"

"I'm the one working with those SynCor boys. Anything they want comes through me."

"Well, listen to you, mister important. Don't step on nothin' because your nose is so high in the air."

Kimee giggled into her computer screen.

Marcus moved closer to Darlene and quietly said, "You keep it up, Darlene. Just keep running that dirty mouth."

"The only reason my mouth is dirty is because it touched you, and you can be damn sure that ain't never gonna happen again. Now git your feet to walking right out that door."

"Damn you to hell, Darlene. I ain't finished with you yet." He looked at Kimee and said, "Who you lookin' at bitch?

Kimee replied angrily, "I ain't lookin' at nothin', Nothin' t'all— just some fool who likes jacking off in the bathroom. You need to stuff some paper towels in your mouth so's nobody hears your squealing all the way down the hall. I swear, you squeal like a little piggy looking for his mama's teet."

The two women roared in laughter as Marcus stormed out.

THE NEXT DAY, Jing walked into Tennico's SynCor office and said, "John, I feel terrible. I think that flux really got to me. I'm going back to my apartment to get some rest.

John said, "Good idea. You are hereby ordered not to come back here until Monday. I'll have Adelle call you later to see how you're doing."

Back at SynCor's Slidell office, Adelle hung up her phone and looked at Truett sitting in a chair across from her desk. She said, "That was John. Jing got sick from something at Tennico and wants me to check in on him over the next couple of days and make sure he's ok."

Truett pulled out his phone and called John. When he picked up, Truett said, "Hey, John. What's up with Jing? He get sick on something?"

"Truett, my man, I was just getting ready to call you. Jing cut his finger and got isoflurane valve flux on it. I swear it made him sick as a patient in a cancer ward. He went back to his apartment, and I told him not to return until Monday."

"Isoflurane? Nobody uses that stuff anymore. See, that's why Tennico couldn't get their ERPS working. They're still in the past, using outdated everything. No forward thinking at all."

"Don't I know. Listen, I need you to take up what Jing couldn't finish. Can you come up here and do that? Maybe a couple of days to button up Jing's work."

"Travis, help me out. That's going to cut into the weekend. My brother invited Adelle and me to go deep-sea fishing off his new boat."

"Sorry, man. We're getting ready to finish this up. Once everything is up and running, I'm going to have a discussion with Tennico about how large of a check they're writing me. By the way, you'll like this: I have a meeting with your friend Ahmed Sawaff from the convention scheduled for next week. The Saudi oil minister is joining us and bringing his checkbook. Good job,

Truett. Listen, I need to go. I'll check in with you on Sunday. Thanks, man.

Travis disconnected. Leaving Truett to stare at his phone. Adelle said, "What was that about?"

"I'm going to have to work this weekend. Jing got sick, and John wanted me to finish what he was doing."

"That's not fair. Your brother will be disappointed. I will put a gris-gris on Mr. Travis." She smiled and continued, "It will be a not-so-bad gris-gris. Mister Travis is too cute and lovable for a bad gris-gris."

"Hilarious, Adelle. I don't think putting a curse on the guy who signs our paychecks is a good idea. Ok, I need to get my stuff and start heading to Tennico. At least the traffic is going the other way. See you Monday, cousin. Catch a big one for me."

Truett left the office grumbling, "What are you doing this weekend, Travis? If you need Jing's work to be done that bad, then why don't you do it? Better yet, if you want me to do Jing's work, then pay me for it. The fact is, if it weren't for me, this company wouldn't be close to where it is now." Continuing his thought, he said, "I'm tired of getting jerked around by these guys. I'm just sick of it."

When Jing returned to his apartment, he collapsed on his bed and didn't wake for almost six hours. He crawled out of bed, went to the kitchen, and drank half of the orange juice bottle in the refrigerator. Feeling better, Jing picked up his phone from the kitchen table and called a number. After a few rings, the call was picked up.

Zhang Wei spoke, "I have been waiting for your call. You were supposed to call me yesterday."

"Sorry. I got sick from one of the chemicals they use at Tennico and had to leave and rest. I'm feeling much better now."

"How is your work progressing? Is everything working?"

"We're getting close to finishing. John has a test of the completed system scheduled for next week."

Wei said, "Excellent. Contact me when your test is finished." Wei disconnected without waiting for Jing to reply.

Jing felt his sickness return, but this time, it wasn't the valve flux. He liked everybody at SynCor. They made him feel welcome and gave him important responsibilities. But his father made it very clear his tuition for Stanford had strings attached. If the government asked him for something, he must comply. Not doing so would have severe consequences. Not for him; he was valuable. His family would pay the price for his disobedience.

Before Jing could put down his phone, it rang again. The caller ID said SynCor, so he picked it up.

"Hi, this is Jing."

"Hello, Mr. Jing. How are you feeling today?"

"Oh, Hi, Adelle. I'm doing ok. Thanks for asking."

"Ça c'est bon. Mister John asked me to check in on you. Mr. John said you got poisoned. That was pas de chance for you."

Jing sighed. He couldn't have a normal conversation with Adelle because he didn't know what she was saying half the time.

"Yes, I got some valve flux on my cut finger. Tennico shouldn't have had that damn Isoflurane flux there. It's very toxic, as I definitely found out."

"I'm sorry, Mister Jing. I do not understand what you said, but I am glad you are doing ok."

"That makes two of us," Jing thought to himself. He said out loud, "Thanks. Tell John I'll be there Monday. Thanks for calling."

Jing disconnected before she could say anything else he wouldn't understand.

Monday morning arrived with Travis and John sitting at their desks. It was around ten when Jing walked in. He left the office door open and said, "Hey, guys. I'm back from the dead. Next time I'm near that stuff, I'll be sure to wear gloves."

Looking up from his keyboard, Travis said, "Glad to see you are okay, Jing. Truett filled in for you and finished the work you were doing. We're all set to begin testing our Correlator with their oil flow."

Jing asked, "When is that scheduled?"

John replied, staring at his computer screen, "It's Thursday. We're going to flip the switch at two in the afternoon. Truett double-checked everything over the weekend, and we're good to go."

Travis walked to the coffee and microwave station and retrieved his Stanley bottle from under the storage area. He placed it on top of the microwave, reached back into the storage area to retrieve his bag of Starbucks Veranda, and started to brew a pot.

Just before noon, one of the Tennico workers walked into SynCor's tiny office, pushing a cart with two medium-sized boxes. He looked at Travis and asked where he wanted the boxes placed.

Travis asked, "What're those?"

The worker replied, "I don't know. Darlene, over in procurement, asked me to deliver these. Now, where do you want them? I got places to be."

Travis got up from his desk and looked at one of the box labels. It was the Isobutyl flux that he had asked Darlene to order.

He said, "Well, they don't belong here. Can you take them to Marcus Hudsen's department? He'll know where to put them."

The worker sighed, turned around, and left the office.

Two hours later, Travis said, "I think I'll go down and thank Darlene for getting us that flux."

He dashed out the door, leaving John and Jing to look at each other. When Travis arrived at Darlene's office, he paused before opening the door. Taking a deep breath, he entered and saw Darlene and Kimee putting on their coats and getting ready to leave the office.

Kimee looked at Travis and said, "Well, hi, Travis. What brings you here?"

"Hey there." Travis couldn't remember Kimee's name and turned his attention to Darlene. "I wanted to stop by and thank you for getting me that flux. We're testing our correlator on Thursday, and we really needed it."

Kimee put a fist to her mouth, suppressing a giggle at the word flux.

Darlene said, "Well, that's very kind of you, but it's my job. Just doin' my job is all."

Travis didn't know what to say. He just stood there looking at Darlene when Kimee spoke.

"Travis, me and Darlene are goin' to get some lunch at Dora's. Why don't you join us? We're real curious what you SynCor folks are up to. Everybody is talking about SynCor and wondering if they need to worry about they jobs."

"No, it's nothing like that. We developed a system to remove harmful parts of the oil to help the environment. It won't affect anyone's job. The oil still needs to be refined."

Darlene said as she started to walk out, "Well, I'm ready to get some lunch. Y'all can keep chattering, but I hear a shrimp Po'Boy calling my name."

When they entered Dora's, Darlene and Kimee noticed many of their co-workers. Dora's was a popular lunch spot with Tennico employees. They found an open table and sat down. Travis saw the paper placemat double as the restaurant's menu. He looked up and spoke to Darlene.

"What's good here? What do you folks usually get?"

Darlene replied, "Well, I'm here to get me a shrimp Po'Boy. I love Dora's remoulade sauce."

Kimee said, "I like the Jambalaya. They make it spicy here. I like spicy food."

Travis said, "Well, a shrimp Po'Boy sounds good to me. I'll get one of those too."

After their waiter took the order and left, Darlene and Kimee started bombarding Travis with questions about how SynCor could affect workers at Tennico.

Travis said, "Ok. I get it. People get nervous when they think something will change with their job. They start to wonder if-" Travis was interrupted when he heard a loud voice behind him and felt his shoulder being grabbed. He turned to see that Marcus had a hold of him.

Marcus said, "Well, looky here. Darlene sittin down eating with one of them damn SynCor assholes. What's this, Darlene? You sweet on this couyon? You like fools?

Travis sprang from his chair, pushed Marcus away, and said, "You touch me again, and it'll be the last thing you touch." The dining room went silent.

Marcus noticed the silence and spoke loudly, pointing to Travis, "Everbody. This here is one of them SynCor people. He's gonna put us out. We gonna be in the unemployment line before long. Ain't that right, mister SynCor?"

As soon as Marcus finished, Darlene sprang up from her chair and yelled at Marcus, "Marcus Hudsen, you get your damn ass away from here. I've had enough of you. I can smell the alcohol comin' from you across the room!"

Travis spoke softly to Marcus, "I'd take the lady's advice and leave. Because if you don't, you and me are going to have a problem, and that's a problem you don't want."

"Well, mister SynCor, you and that bitch over there are the ones with the damn problem, and we'll see about that. Yes, we will." Noticing the stares of the people in the restaurant, Marcus turned and stomped out.

When Marcus left, Kimme said, "I'm reportin' that fool to HR as soon as I get back."

Darlene replied, "Don't bother. We're not on company property. Besides, he's got seniority runnin' the place and enough friends to make anything go away."

After his lunch and encounter with Marcus, Travis walked into his office and saw Jing sitting at his desk, tapping his keyboard. Travis noticed Jing had his laptop connected by a cable to Travis's PC. Travis asked, "What's up, Jing?

Startled, Jing looked up and said, "Oh, Travis. I thought you were having lunch." Thinking quickly he continued, "I wanted to look at the expansion tube calculations you did. I can't access them on the VPN (Virtual Private Network).

"They're not accessible for a reason, Jing. Our VPN is private and pretty bulletproof, but it's still connected to the internet. We keep sensitive data away from even the remotest chance of someone hacking into our system. You could have just asked me for the data."

Disconnecting his laptop, Jing said, "Sorry, Travis. You were gone, and I wanted to triple-check everything. We have a big day coming up, and I didn't want any surprises."

Jing walked back to his desk while Travis sat in his chair and thought, "How the hell did Jing get past my firewall? I was pretty sure even GOD couldn't do that." He decided not to ask Jing how he did it but instead, talk to John. Jing put his laptop in its case and turned his head to look at Travis.

———

JOHN AND TRAVIS met with Peter Murphy in his expansive office on Friday afternoon. They sat at a circular table in the conference area. All three were excited about the success of SynCor's Correlator processing Tennico's oil. Peter said, "Well, you guys did it. Refining oil is never going to be the same. It's a new day in the oil business, and that's for sure."

TRAVIS ADDED, "It sure is. Word travels fast. This morning, I got an email from some reporter at the New York Times wanting to come down here and write a story about us."

John put his hands on the table and said, "Well, that's great, but we really don't need the attention. Peter, we talked about Tennico buying SynCor when we completed a successful test, and I think we need to get into the details about that."

"Yes, we did talk about that, and we have a proposal for you to look at."

Peter got up, walked to his desk, and said, "I have a copy for you to look at right here."

He picked up the thick proposal and its electronic version on a thumb drive and put them in front of John. John was flipping through the pages when Travis spoke.

"Hey John, why don't we talk about this over the weekend? I want to spend some time going over this in detail. We should also get an attorney to look at this." Looking at Peter, Travis added, "I'm sure you guys had a whole legal department working on this. Am I right, Peter?"

"Travis, I learned a long time ago that nothing gets done in this world without lawyers. Why don't we get together next week and talk about this some more?"

John said, "Sounds good to me. The sooner we get this done, the better. I'm going to buy a sailboat and travel the world."

Travis replied, "John, you'll be calling the Coast Guard before you even leave the dock." Peter laughed.

After meeting with Peter, John, and Travis, they returned to their office. Travis asked John, "Dude, why do we want to sell? Why sell our business? We can make way more money getting royalties than selling it outright."

"Travis, you're right. We make more money, but it's over time. It could be five or six years of royalties before we get what Tennico will give us now. Plus, we still have to run the business and everything that entails. We cash out now and move on. Do whatever we want."

"What about the Saudis? We start getting royalties from them, and that five or six years gets cut way down."

"Travis. Dealing with the Saudis is going to be a nightmare. It's their country and their laws. Besides, Adelle would have to wear a burlap sack with holes for her eyes to see. Why do you think they call what women have to wear burkas?

Travis said nothing

Sunday evening, around eight-thirty, Travis called John to discuss Tennico's offer. He had spent the entire day reading every line in the proposal.

"John, I went through Tennico's offer line by line and have some serious questions about this thing."

"What questions? I went through it and didn't see anything terrible."

"Well, for one thing, it has a clause that says basically, we can't be in the oil business after we sell to them."

"What's wrong with that? I sure as hell don't plan to be in the oil business any longer than I have to."

"Well, that's great for you, but what about me? I'm too young to play golf or sail a boat for the rest of my life. I have plans. I want to stay in the oil business."

"Travis, I hear you. Why don't we get an attorney to look at this? We can always give them a counterproposal. We hold the cards here. How about I call my dad and see if he knows a good attorney we can talk to?"

"Ok, great. That sounds like a plan. Let me know what you come up with."

Monday morning, John walked into SynCor's Slidell office and gave Adelle the thumb drive containing Tennico's proposal.

"Adelle, my computer is acting up. I need to email the files on this thumb drive to our new and first attorney, Jason Wu."

John gave her the drive and a Post-it note with Jason's email address.

He said, "Just say, per our discussion, here is the proposal we talked about and the partnership agreement Travis and I have. Tell him to call me when he can."

She took John's drive and Post-it note. "Of course, Mister John. I will send it right now.

She inserted the thumb drive into her computer and opened her email program. She entered Jason's email address and pressed send. Nothing. Double-checking that she had the correct spelling of the email address, she pressed send again. Nothing.

Truett was going by Adelle's desk to go outside and smoke a cigarette when he heard her cursing.

"What's wrong, cousin?"

"There is something wrong with my email. Mister John wants me to send this file, and it will not go. Mister John could not send this file on his computer either."

"Here, let me take a look."

Truett checked the settings and internet connection on the computer and pressed the send key. Nothing.

"You said John couldn't send this on his PC either?"

"Yes. It would not work for him."

"Hmm. Okay, I have an idea. Give me the drive, and I'll try sending it on my laptop. It's not connected to the company network. Let's see if that works. If it does, then we know there's a problem with our network."

Truett took the thumb drive and Post-it note and returned to his office. He inserted the drive, typed in Jason's email address, and pressed send. After a few seconds, he received a confirmation that the email had been delivered. He spoke to himself, "Well, there you go. I guess that means we have an issue with our network. I'm going to have to track that down." Before Truett gave his cousin the good news, he became curious about who Jason Wu was and what John was sending him. He googled Jason Wu and saw he was a corporate attorney in San Francisco. His curiosity piqued, Truett imported the thumb drive files into the word processor on his laptop and began reading.

Two days after sending John's email to Jason, John and Travis were on a conference call with Jason in Travis's office.

Jason said, "Well, congratulations, guys. It looks like you're both going to be some very wealthy people."

John replied, "Thanks, Jason. It's been a long road, but we got here."

Travis chimed in, "Hello, Jason. This is Travis. Nice to meet you. What do you think about the offer we got? Can you tell us what we are looking at with Tennico? I want to know what we can do about that clause that says I can't be in the oil business."

Jason said, "That's called a 'no-compete clause,' and they're hard to enforce. In many cases, they're not enforceable at all. Companies put those in to see if they can get away with it. You put up a little fight, and they go away. It's nothing that should concern you. I can FedEx them a letter on my letterhead, asking them to remove the clause if you like."

Travis leaned into the speakerphone and said, "That would be great, Jason!" Looking at John, he continued. "Once that clause is gone, I don't see any reason not to go ahead with the sale."

John smiled and said, "Thanks, Jason; I knew my father would send us in the right direction. You've been a great help. Please email Travis and me a copy when you FedEx Tennico."

"Ok, will do. Send me the contact names, and I'll have it out by early next week."

Jason disconnected the call and looked across his desk. Sitting before him was Zhang Wei, who said, "It was nice of you to send a notice to Tennico for them. However, that won't be necessary. I want you to prepare a contract for John Zsu to buy Travis Beloit's shares in SynCor. I will discuss this with John's father, Zichen.

MARCUS WAS WAITING for the service elevator when one of his co-workers came up beside him. The elevator doors opened, and they both got in. His co-worker, Austin Mays, said, "That was a heck of a thing you got into at Dora's the other day. Me and Abbott were at the table next to that SynCor guy you were yelling at. I don't like those SynCor boys one bit. One of them is a damn Chinese.

Marcus replied, "Damn right. Somebody needs to set them in their place."

"Looks like that Travis fella is sweet on Darlene. I seen them talking all the time."

"Well, never mind him. That Travis fool needs to learn his place, and I'm gonna be the one who teaches him."

Arriving at their floor, Marcus and Austin left the elevator and started walking in separate directions. Marcus said to himself, "Darlene, you got sweet with the wrong guy. We'll see about that. That's for damn sure."

Two weeks after John and Travis spoke with their attorney, they were in SynCor's Slidell office/warehouse. John walked into Travis's office, holding a stack of papers. He said, "Well, here it is. I just got Peter's revised sales agreement. They took out the no-compete clause. We should send Jason a bottle of champagne.

"Let me see."

John handed Travis the papers and watched while he skimmed through them. After finishing, he returned the documents to John and said, "Looks good to me. I still feel bad about giving away SynCor to strangers. I remember that day in the student center when we started this. We were scared, like a cat being chased by a mean ass dog. Those were some days for sure."

"Well, for one, we aren't giving away anything. We're trading SynCor for a huge pile of money, and second, they're not strangers. If it weren't for Tennico, we wouldn't be where we are."

"Yeah, I get it. We should have a company meeting and tell everybody."

John enthusiastically said, "We'll have everybody here today. I'll have Adelle order up some lunch, and we can meet in the break room."

"Tell her to order from Pizzaro's. I want one of their meatball subs."

An hour later, the employees of SynCor were either sitting or standing in SynCor's break room after eating the lunch Adelle had ordered. John spoke, "Ok, folks. As everybody knows, Travis and I are selling our shares to Tennico. We got the final proposal from Tennico and are ready to sign on the dotted line. Thanks, guys, for bringing us to this point. When Travis and I started this thing, we never thought in a million years we would be here." John's voice quivered, "I'm really going to miss you guys. You all mean so much to me."

Travis spoke, "I second that." Looking at Truett, he continued, "Truett, you saved our ass more times than I like to count. You always answered the call. Turning his attention to Jing, "Jing, what can I say? You're one of the smartest guys I know. Getting that correlator working was genius, even if it did make you sicker than eating a rotten possum."

They all laughed.

Truett spoke, "We all owe you and John for bringing us along on your journey. I know I've learned more than I ever could have imagined."

Jing stood from his chair and reached across the table, shaking Travis's hand and then John's. He said, "I was so lucky to find a job with you guys. I had just about given up looking online. This has been a wonderful experience. Thank you so much."

Adelle stood behind Truett and said, "Mister John and Mister Travis, I am so happy for you. You are Toot Toot for me. C'est si bon in your new work."

She started to cry. Travis rose and hugged her, saying, "You are Toot Toot for me also."

Jing shook his head.

An hour after their meeting, John walked into the warehouse and saw Truett sitting at his desk. He said, "Hey Truett, I just got off the phone with Peter Murphy. He told me you have a job interview with him next week."

"Well, yes, I do. I wouldn't call it an interview, though. He wants me to meet with Jim Swaney and his engineering group.

I'm going to have my own group managing the correlator systems."

"Good for you. You'll be a great addition to Tennico's engineering department. I'm happy for you."

Jing walked into the warehouse to ask Truett a question when John asked, "Jing, what's up with you? What's your next career move?"

Jing replied, "I am going to China to work at the Energy Commission. They are building a refinery to lower oil import costs."

John said, "Going to China? That's going to be a big change for you. I know you're Chinese, but you've never lived in China. Don't tell Tennico. Murphy would squeal like a stuck pig if he knew you were going over there with all you know."

Jing said nothing. John was right. He grew up in England and had only visited relatives in China a few times, and he couldn't have waited for those visits to end. He despised Zhang and had little choice but to do what he asked. Jing didn't know how, but John would get Travis's shares in SynCor and then sell the company to China. John didn't realize it, but he was as much a prisoner to Zhang as he was. Zhang had told him about John's father and the money he loaned his son to start SynCor. Jing knew what borrowing money from Zhang meant. John was about to find out.

Three days later, John called Travis at the SynCor office in Tennico to ask why Travis hadn't signed the documents selling SynCor to Tennico.

Travis sat at his desk when his phone started playing his latest ringtone.

"John. What's up?

"Travis, why haven't you signed the sale docs? We need to get this done."

"I was just getting ready to call you. I got an email from Ahmed. The Saudis are willing to change the licensing agreement we talked about. They'll pay us a yearly fee. We do the initial installation and training. We can send Truett over there for a couple of months to do that. I already talked to him about this. Now, here's the kicker. We supply the expansion tubes. Those things wear out and need to be replaced. No money. No replacement tubes. The Saudi money brings in way more cash than we would get from Tennico."

"That's messed up, Travis. We have a deal that Tennico made in good faith. We, as in YOU and I, agreed to that. Now, YOU want to back out? No way, man. Not going to happen."

"Calm down, John. We're going to make a ton of money with the Saudis on board. I forgot to mention that they'll pay the first three years upfront. Why would we pass this deal up?"

"We pass it up because we agreed to sell to Tennico. End of story. Now, will you please sign those documents? I'm done talking about this."

Travis looked up and saw Darlene standing in the doorway. He waved at her and returned to his conversation.

"John, you forget. I own the same number of shares you do. We are EQUAL partners."

"Damnit, Travis, you're not going to do this!"

"Look, John. I'm going to get some lunch. We can talk about this later." Travis disconnected and looked at Darlene when she spoke.

"Well, that sounds like you and John aren't getting along."

"He'll come around. Let's go. I'm ready for a bowl of Dora's Jambalaya."

Travis and Darlene were walking out of Tennico's lobby while Marcus was coming in. Travis and Marcus stared at each other, but neither spoke.

Jing was driving to his apartment after dark when his phone rang. The caller ID said "Unknown Caller," but Jing knew who it was. He picked up and started talking immediately.

"Hello, Zhang. What is it this time?"

"I have heard some very bad news. It seems one of your bosses, Travis, has decided not to sell his shares. That is a big problem for us. We have given John's father the money to buy Travis's shares, and we must move forward. Travis must sell his shares.

"Well, what do you want me to do? I don't have anything to do with what Travis does. I just work there."

"I must remind you. You are working at SynCor because we paid for your education, so you could do just that. You will do what I want you to, and there is no choice. John must have Travis's shares.

Zhang went on to tell Jing about his duty to the Chinese government and the severe consequences for not doing what was asked of him. Zhang disconnected the call without waiting for Jing to respond to what he had just told him. Jing had to pull over and stop on the side of the road. He started to hyperventilate, and sweat began to form on his forehead. He asked himself how things could have spiraled so out of control.

An hour after his argument with Travis, John was at his desk googling sailing lessons when his phone rang. John looked at the caller ID and saw that his father was calling. He picked up and listened to what his father was telling him. After a twenty-minute conversation, John disconnected and stared into space. He looked at his phone and asked himself if he had really heard what his father had just told him. He started to feel nauseated and began to sweat. John pulled the trash can from under his desk and vomited.

Two days later, Travis, John, Truett, and Jing were in their Tennico office packing up Syncor's computers and equipment. John and Travis could barely look at each other, let alone talk. Travis had continued his conversations with the Saudis, which incensed John. Travis didn't care. Once John saw the money coming in, he would thank him. Truett picked up the last box and started to walk out of the office to the van he had rented. He said to Travis, "I'll talk to you tomorrow. Tell Ahmet I said hello."

"Will do. Talk to you later."

Travis sat at his empty desk, looking around the office he had spent so much time in. He noticed his thermos next to the coffee pot and decided to brew a pot. It was two-thirty in the afternoon, and his scheduled call to Ahmed wasn't for another half hour. Jeddah was nine hours ahead, and he thought about how he and Truett would schedule their Zoom meetings.

Darlene and Kimee were in SynCor's cafeteria having a late lunch when Kimee said, "I'm for sure glad those SynCor boys are leaving. Everybody can get back to normal around here."

Darlene replied, "I guess. But it was nice having some new faces around here."

"Well, I know what face you liked seeing."

"Shut your mouth. Just because I want to talk to somebody new, don't mean a thing. Now, c'mon, we got to get back to work."

Walking out of the cafeteria, Darlene said, "You go on. I'm gonna see if them SynCor people are gone yet."

Darlene started to walk in the opposite direction of her office, leaving Kimme smiling as she went. She got on the elevator and pressed Travis's floor. Exiting the elevator and walking down the hall, she noticed SynCor's door was closed. She felt her shoulders sag and started to walk back to the elevator. She stopped halfway and decided to look inside and see if Travis and his people were really gone. Darlene knocked softly, opened the door, looked inside, and screamed. She saw Travis on the floor in a horribly contorted position with a black foam around his mouth. It was obvious he was dead.

TWO DAYS after Travis's funeral, John, Truett, and Adelle sat at Syncor's Slidell office's break room table. It was mid-afternoon, and the two empty chairs at the table were the elephants in the room. With tears streaming down her eyes, Adelle said, "I cannot understand why this would happen. Everybody liked Mister Travis. He always brighten my day with his smile. Who would do this? Who is so evil?"

Truett reached over, held Adelle's hand, and said, "It's ok, cousin. I know you liked Travis very much. We'll get through this. I know Travis is looking down and smiling at you. He wouldn't want you to be sad."

John stood up and walked behind Adelle. He put his hands on her shoulders and said, "Travis didn't show it much, but he was happy you worked here. I know you miss him—we all miss him—but Truett is right. We'll get through this."

Truett said with an angry voice, "Where the hell is Jing? Why isn't he here? Has anybody heard from him?"

John removed his hands from Adelle's shoulders and said, "I have no idea where he is, and I'm not real happy about his being gone. Makes no sense. Travis hired him, and he couldn't come to his funeral?" John didn't say it, but he knew precisely where Jing was.

Truett replied, "I don't know what's going on, but it sure doesn't look good for Jing to do a disappearing act right after Travis is killed. So help me; if he killed Travis, I'll be the one tying the noose."

John asked, "If he did kill Travis, why? What would cause him to do something like that? It doesn't make sense."

Adelle said, "Maybe Mister Jing is the same as Mister Travis. Mort.

John looked at Adelle and said, "I'm sure the police will find out about Jing."

"What happens now, John?" Truett asked. "Are you going to go ahead with your original plan and sell SynCor to Tennico?"

"I really can't think about that now. Travis didn't want to sell his shares to Tennico. But now, I don't know. I really can't think about that stuff right now." John looked at his watch and said, "Sorry, I have a five o'clock flight and need to leave. I'm going to see my parents and get out of here for a while. Truett, I talked to Peter Murphy and told him I would keep him in the loop until things settle down. I told him you would call him when you're ready to meet with him."

"Of course, John. I'll get in touch with him tomorrow."

John put his hands back on Adelle's shoulders and said, "Adelle, Travis wouldn't want you to be sad. I know he meant something to you. I'm so sorry."

Adelle put her hand on John's and said, "I know he would not want me to be sad, but I cannot help it."

"Me neither, Adelle. Me neither."

DERRICK MORGAN WAS SITTING at his desk reviewing the autopsy report of Travis Beloit. Derrick had been promoted to homicide detective despite his sparse report on the bus accident that had cost the city enough to put the Spruce Street bridge repair on hold. The vague rumors he knew in advance about the FBI's raid on the Aryan Brigades compound and the deaths of two FBI agents didn't seem to matter. Everybody knew he was one of the best detectives in the department. He laughed when one of his new co-workers gave him a present at the promotion party his wife, Miki, had organized at their home. It was a paperweight with the slogan "Welcome to homicide. Our day begins when your day ends" inscribed on a brass plate. The report Derrick was looking at said Travis had died from Isoflurane ingestion. He didn't know what that was, other than it was obviously a deadly substance. He tapped on his keyboard and searched for the chemical. The results showed that it was an ingredient commonly used in valve flux sealant. He made a note to see if any of that was present near the murder scene. He sat back in his chair and asked himself the same question every homicide detective asks when they first start investigating: "Cui Bono?" Latin for "Who benefits?" Travis wasn't married, and he only had a small amount of life insurance, of which his father was the beneficiary. He didn't have a criminal record, and he was killed at his workplace, which indicated to Derrick that this might be some kind of work-related offense. He made a list of the people Travis worked with. Somebody will talk. Somebody always talks.

Derrick's first stop was to revisit the crime scene. He had been there when the crime scene investigators (CSI) processed the scene, gathering evidence of which there was very little. Travis was poisoned, so there was no murder weapon, such as a gun or knife. The CSI team collected a metal thermos that was lying next to the body. He would have that checked for fingerprints and test for the presence of Isoflurane. Since this was an office, checking for fingerprints was a daunting task. There would be dozens of fingerprints to check among the people who worked there, the cleaning staff, and visitors. Lots of fingerprints. He went to Tennico's HR department. He wanted to know the names of everybody who worked in Travis's office. He would start with them. He opened the door to Tennico's HR department and saw a man and two women sitting at their desks. He pulled out his badge and said, "Excuse me, I'm Detective Morgan, and I'm investigating the death of one of your employees. Can I speak to someone about that?" All three people sitting at their desks looked up. Jamis Westbrook spoke, "That's that SynCor guy. Right? He wasn't a Tennico employee, but him getting killed here sure has everybody looking over their shoulder. Terrible thing. What do you need?"

"Do any of you have any ideas on who might have killed Travis Beloit? Anybody here who might want him dead?"

Shirley White replied, "Marcus Hudsen did it. I know he did."

Darrick asked, "Marcus Hudsen? He work here? Why do you think Marcus would kill Travis?"

One of the women replied, "I saw him fightin' with Travis at Dora's a while back. Travis and Darlene, Darlene Moss was getting sweet on each other, and Marcus didn't like that. Marcus and Darlene used to be a pair until that drunk fool got thrown in jail for fightin' in the casino."

"Darlene Moss? She work here too?"

Jamis interjected, "Yes, she does. She works over at procurement."

Looking at Jamis, Derrick said, "I need the names of everybody who works here that would have come into contact with Mr. Beloit. Can you get that for me?"

Leaving the HR department, Derrick took the list of names he had gotten and put it in his coat pocket. He took the elevator to

Travis's floor, walked down the hall, and stopped at the closed office door. The door had crime scene tape and a paper seal covering the edge of the doorframe. Derrick took his pocketknife, cut the seal, removed the tape, and walked in. He noticed the office was empty except for a few cleaned-out desks and chairs. He saw the white tape the CSI team used to outline Travis's body next to a desk. Not much here, he thought. Derrick turned to leave and saw a man standing in the doorway. It was Marcus.

Marcus asked, "Can I help you with something?"

"Who are you?"

"I'm Marcus Hudsen. I'm the general manager here. I keep this place running."

Derrick took out his list of names and saw Marcus's name. He asked Marcus, "What was your relationship with the decedent?"

"Decedent?"

"The dead guy. What was he to you?"

"Travis was one of them SynCor boys. I was helping them put their invention into our refining process. Terrible thing, him gettin' himself killed and all. They were clearing out of here. I guess they was done with their work."

"Do you know anything about Isoflurane? Any of that around here?"

"What? Why do you want to know about that?"

Derrick could see Marcus becoming tense, and his demeanor began to change. Raising his voice, Derrick said, "Just answer the question. Do you know anything about isoflurane, and is there any of it around here?"

"Well, yes. We use it to seal valves."

"Show me where you keep it."

"I'm sorry, I didn't get your name. Why are you here?"

"My name is DETECTIVE Morgan, and I'm the one asking the questions. Now, I'll say it again: show me where you keep it."

"I'm sorry, detective. We don't keep it in one place. It's all around this refinery. If there's a valve problem, we don't want to walk ten minutes gettin' it."

"So everybody that works here has access to it?"

Marcus put his hands in his pockets and said, "Well, yes. I reckon so."

Terrific, Derrick thought. He looked at his list and said, "Where can I find Darlene Moss? I want to talk to her."

"Darlene? What do you want to talk to Darlene about?"

Derrick noticed Marcus was becoming agitated, and his forehead began to glisten. He spoke, "Like I said, I'm the one asking the questions. Now, where is she?"

"She works in the procurement office. I can take you there if you like."

"That won't be necessary. Just tell me how to get there."

"You go down to the second floor and take a right off the elevator. It's two doors down on the left."

"Got it. Now, I'm going to ask you to leave. I need to reseal the door." Before starting, he asked Marcus, "Do you have a cell phone number in case I need to talk to you again?"

"Talk some more? Why do you need to talk to me some more?"

"Again, I ask the questions; now, please give me the number."

Derrick followed Marcus's directions and walked into Darlene's office. He saw two women sitting at their desks and asked, "Excuse me. Sorry to interrupt. Are either of you Darlene Moss?"

Darlene looked up and said, "I'm Darlene. What can I help you with?"

Kimee looked up, also.

"I'm Detective Morgan with the Hattiesburg police department. I'm investigating the death of Travis Beloit."

Kimee said, "Bout time somebody showed up."

Darlene turned to face Kimee and said, "Shut your mouth, Kimee. This man is here to see me. We don't need no interruptions from you." Turning back to Derrick, "I'm sorry bout that detective. Now, what do you need? Travis was one of the sweetest men I've known. I can't wait for you to find out who killed him." Darlene reached across her desk and pulled a tissue from the box beside her phone.

"How well did you know him? Were you involved in any way?"

"We was friends is all. We'd eat lunch at Dora's or the cafeteria. I'm gonna miss him terribly." Darlene's eyes filled with tears.

"I'm sorry. I know this is difficult. Do you know anyone who might want to harm the deceden-Travis?"

Kimee spoke loudly, "I know who killed Travis. Marcus Hudsen is the one who did it. That damn no-account hated Travis. He hated Travis for spending time with Darlene."

Derrick looked at Darlene and asked, "That true? You and Travis were seeing each other? What's Marcus's connection to that? To you and Travis."

"Like I said. Me and Travis would have lunch. It weren't nothing more than that. Marcus and I used to date."

"Used to date? You're not dating him anymore? Why is that?"

Darlene sighed and said, "Marcus is a drunk. When he gets drunk, he turns to mean. He also gambles his money away. I didn't see any future with him, that's for sure."

"Do you think Marcus killed Travis?"

"Kimee loudly said, "You're damn right. I think Marcus killed Travis. He had a fight with him at Dora's diner a while back. Everybody saw it. Me, Darlene, and Travis was havin' lunch. Marcus came to our table and grabbed Travis by the shoulder. He threatened him. He didn't like him being round Darlene. Everybody saw it. Yes, they did."

Darlene turned to Kimee and shouted, "Kimee! Shut your mouth. This man is talkin' to me, not you. If he wants your conversation, I'm sure he will tell you. Turning back to Derrick, "I'm sorry for the interruptions. Do I think Marcus killed Travis? If he was drunk, it's a damn certainty to me."

"I just spoke to Marcus before coming down here. I think I have some more questions for him. Where can I find him?"

Kimee said, "He's on the third floor, right across from the elevator. He's the General Manager here, and that's his office right there. Lemme know if you need any help puttin' your handcuffs on him. I'm happy to help in any way."

Following Darlene's directions, Derrick made his way to Marcus's office. He opened the door without knocking and let himself in. Marcus wasn't there. He looked around the office and saw it was a disorganized mess. He could smell alcohol. Derrick walked over to the desk and started opening the drawers. He picked up a pen and used it to poke around the drawers, not looking for anything particular. He walked over to the wall file cabinets, opened the drawers, and thumbed through the folders inside. He heard a noise behind him and turned towards it.

Marcus asked in a loud voice, "What're you doin' here? This ain't your place."

"I'm here because I have some more questions for you. I had a talk with your girlfriend, or should I say, your ex-girlfriend, Darlene. It seems you two don't get along anymore. Seems you didn't like her new friend, Travis. That true? You didn't like Travis spending time with Darlene. He make you jealous?"

"Darlene and I stopped seein' each other because of work. Tennico don't like employees dating each other."

"Darlene says different. What was that thing at Dora's? Why did you assault Travis? Were you drunk at the time?" Derrick was firing questions at Marcus to keep him defensive while letting him know he was well-informed and that lying would be difficult. Derrick went on, "You didn't like Travis, did you? Did you kill Travis? He make you so mad you killed him? Is that what you did?"

"I didn't kill Travis. If that's what Darlene is sayin', it's a lie. She's a damn liar!"

"Darlene isn't the only one who believes you killed Travis." This made Marcus stop talking. He could see Marcus's mind working on his face. He understood why Marcus was such a lousy gambler. At least playing poker, anyway. He saw Marcus start to sweat. "Tell you what, Marcus. Why don't you stop by the station tomorrow? The one on Finch Street across from the church. Say, about eleven? That work for you?"

Marcus wanted Derrick to leave. He needed a drink and couldn't get one with Derrick there.

"Fine. Eleven. I'll be there. Now git out of my office. I got work to do."

The next morning, Derrick was sitting at his desk. Marcus would be there in another two hours. Derrick couldn't wait to get him in the interrogation room. Detectives in the department called it "The Box," as in "boxing the suspect in." He was reviewing the list of names he had received from Tennico's HR department when he asked himself again, "Who benefits?" Business partners in small companies are like spouses in a marriage. They argued and fought about things just like anybody else. Spouses were always the first to look at when murder is involved. After he finished with Marcus, he decided to pay this John Zsu a visit. He put the names list down when he heard his computer chime telling him he had a new email. Derrick wiggled his mouse to turn off the screensaver and saw the new email was from Marilou Watson. Marilou was the lead CSI investigator assigned to Derrick's case. The email said trace amounts of isoflurane were found in Travis's Stanley thermos. Derrick looked at his list of names again and asked himself, "Which of you poisoned Travis's coffee?" Continuing his thought, "I'll find you. Nobody gets away on my watch. Nobody."

Eleven o'clock came and went. Marcus was a no-show for his conversation with Derrick. Marcus's failure to appear only heightened his suspicion about Marcus. This guy was hiding something, and Derrick was going to find out what it was. He picked up his phone and called Marcus's cell phone. Marcus picked up almost immediately. He saw the caller ID was from the Hattiesburg police department.

DERRICK SPOKE FIRST, "Marcus! It's Detective Morgan. I'm very disappointed you didn't come in for our chat this morning. I was looking forward to it. If you weren't going to be here, you should have called. It was very rude not to call."

"I ain't gotta talk to you. No, sir, I don't."

"Well, Marcus, that's not entirely true. We need to discuss your involvement in Travis's murder. I think you might be hiding something from me. Are you hiding something, Marcus? You gotta secret you don't want anybody to find out about?"

"I ain't talkin' to you. I talked to my cousin, Eustis. His friends got caught makin' shine over in Lamar County, and the law thought he was part of it even though he wasn't there. Eustis got himself a lawyer, and that ended things with the law right then and there. So, mister detective, if you want to talk to me, I want a lawyer with me. I'll hire Eustis's. Yes, I will."

Marcus disconnected the call, leaving Derrick as mad as a hatter. The worst four words a detective could hear are, "I want a lawyer." Everything stops when those words are spoken. Any opportunity to talk to a suspect without someone telling him not to answer the question is gone. He looked at his list of names and saw three who worked with Travis. They were the "SynCor boys" he'd heard about when he visited Tennico the day before. He decided to visit SynCor's office in Slidell rather than call. Showing up unannounced was a tried-and-true method of gauging someone's reaction when they find out they're "under the eye." They're being looked at.

Slidell was a ninety-minute drive from Hattiesburg. Derrick spent some of the drive talking to Marilou Watson about the email she had sent earlier in the day. He wanted to know more about Travis's Stanley thermos. He called Marilou and asked, "Marilou, what can you tell me about that thermos? How do you think that iso stuff got in there? Could it have accidentally gotten in there?"

Marilou responded, "It's doubtful. We didn't find any traces of isoflurane in the office. Not anywhere. It only takes a tiny drop of that stuff in your system to kill you, though. You certainly wouldn't taste it."

"Anything in that office you found interesting?"

"It was pretty empty except for the desks and chairs. We tested the coffee maker and found nothing. We did get a hit on the thermos, but it's going to take more testing for that. Your perp, whoever that is, probably spiked your victim's coffee. That's my opinion."

"Ok, thanks, Marilou. I'll talk to you later."

Derrick disconnected the call and thought about what Marilou had just told him. His suspicion about Marcus's involvement ticked up a notch. He had plenty of opportunities to put a drop in Travis's thermos, and his motive was as common as finding sticks in a forest. As he continued his thoughts about Marcus, something in his brain asked him for attention. How does Marcus benefit from Travis's demise? He eliminates a rival for Darlene's attention, but it's evident that the relationship is not returning, and Marcus knows it. Besides, Travis was leaving Tennico. Marcus would probably never see him again. Marcus's possible involvement in Travis's murder ticked down several notches.

DERRICK WALKED into SynCor's Slidell office and was immediately greeted by Adelle, who was seated at her desk. She looked up from her computer screen and greeted Derrick.

"Hello, may I help you?"

Derrick replied, "Hello. My name is Detective Morgan. I'm with the Hattiesburg police department. This is where Travis Beloit worked. Is that correct?"

Morosely, Adelle said, "Yes, this is where Mister Travis worked. Are you here to find out who killed him?"

"Yes, I'm looking into his death. Do you know anyone who might have wanted to harm him? A friend, a co-worker perhaps."

"Mister Travis was a nice man. I do not know anyone who would hurt him. He was good to everybody."

"Does John Zsu work here? He was in business with Mr. Beloit. Is that correct?"

Adelle reached for a tissue, started to dab her eyes, and said, "Yes, Mister John is here. He and Mister Travis were partners. Would you like to speak to Mister John?"

"Yes, I would. That would be nice."

Adelle picked up her phone and punched in John's extension. After a moment, she said, "Mister John. There is a detective here who wants to talk to you. He is looking for the person who killed Mister Travis."

Adelle looked at Derrick and said, "He is coming now. You don't think Mister John killed Travis? That is not correct. They started this company together. Mister John would never hurt anyone. No, he would not."

Before Derrick could reply, John entered the lobby and said, "Hello, I'm John. Are you looking for Travis's killer? Are you going to find out who killed him?"

Pulling out his badge and showing it to John, Derrick said, "Hello, John. I'm Detective Morgan with the Hattiesburg police depart-ment, and yes, I have been assigned to Travis Beloit's case. Were you his business partner?"

"Yes, I am, err, was I should say. We are all very heartbroken. He didn't have anyone who didn't like him. Listen, why don't we talk in my office? Follow me."

Walking into John's office. There were two chairs in front of John's desk. John sat in one, and Derrick sat in the other. Derrick asked, "What was your relationship with Travis? You were partners in your business, correct?"

"YES, Travis and I founded SynCor. We were equal partners."

"Did you and Travis get along? Did you ever argue over anything?"

"No, not really. We're in the process of selling SynCor. There wasn't any need to argue about anything."

"Not really? So, you did argue? There was some friction between you two."

"We didn't argue. We may have disagreed, but we didn't argue."

"Who stood to gain from Travis's death? You were equal partners, right? What happens to Travis's part of the business now?"

"Our partnership agreement has a clause. If anything happens to either of us, the remaining partner gets the other's shares. That would change, obviously, if either one of us got married. There are other details, but that's the gist of it."

"So, you do stand to gain from Travis's death. You get his shares now. Correct?"

"I didn't kill Travis. We are selling SynCor, and my half alone will give me more money than I could possibly spend. I don't need Travis's money."

"How about this partnership agreement? Do you have it in this office? Can I get a copy of it? I'd like to take a look at that."

"Listen, Detective, I didn't kill Travis, and I don't know who did. I don't see how giving you confidential company documents will help you find out who killed Travis."

"Listen, John, and I do mean listen. You don't have to see anything. I'm the one asking questions here, and I'll decide what I need to help me in this investigation. Now, you can give me a copy now, or I can ask a judge to make you. I have to say, John, I don't think you're cooperating too much. You got something you're hiding from me?"

"I'm not hiding anything, and I don't like your tone. I didn't kill Travis, and the more time you waste on me, the person who did kill Travis is getting away. I want to know who killed Travis."

"So do I, John. That's why I'm here talking to you. Now, are you going to give me that copy or not?"

"Fine. I'll print you a copy right now, and then I'm going to ask you to leave. You need to spend your time looking for Travis's killer."

"John, I'll tell you what I need or don't need, not the other way around. I'll decide when it's time for me to leave, not you. Do you understand that, John?"

Not giving John a chance to reply, Derrick pulled out his list of names and said, "I need to speak to Truett LeBlanc and Jing Mao. Are they here?"

"Jing's not here. I don't know where he is. He didn't come to Travis's funeral. He might be at his apartment in Hattiesburg. I'll write his phone number and address on the agreement when it's done printing. Am I cooperating now, Detective?"

"The jury is still out on that. We'll see. Now, where can I find Mr. LeBlanc?"

"Go out my door and take a right. Follow the hallway till it ends and go through the door. His office is in the back of the warehouse on your left. I'll tell him you're coming."

"That won't be necessary. I can find my way."

With that, Derrick left and went looking for Truett. Following John's directions, he found Truett sitting at his desk, tapping away on his computer keyboard. Derrick knocked on the open door and asked, "Pardon me. Are you Truett LeBlanc?"

Truett turned his head and looked at Derrick. He said, "Who are you, and how did you get back here?"

Pulling his badge from his jacket pocket, Derrick said, "Mr. LeBlanc, my name is Detective Morgan. I'm with the Hattiesburg police department, and I've been assigned to investigate Travis Beloit's death. John told me I could find you here. Mr. LeBlanc, do you know anybody who may have wanted to harm Travis? Somebody angry enough to kill him?"

"Everyone liked Travis. Travis got along with everybody. I can't imagine someone wanting to kill him."

"Well, someone did. How long have you worked here?"

"I was the first person Travis and John hired. I do everything here. I designed the Correlator housing and the expansion tubes. I also set up the flow parameters Travis worked out. Travis and I were like hand in glove, getting everything to work at Tennico. I still can't believe he's gone."

"So, nobody comes to mind. You can't think of anyone who would want Travis dead? How about John? Those two get along?"

"Well, yes, for the most part, they got along."

"Most part? They had disagreements? Arguments?"

"John and Travis were in the process of selling SynCor to Tennico. Travis wanted to back out because he thought they could make more money with the Saudis. John was all set to sell because he wanted to retire and buy a sailboat. Travis wanted to keep the company and not sell it."

DERRICK TOOK ALL this in and said, "So John and Travis did argue about selling SynCor. Would that be a correct assumption? John wanted to sell, and Travis didn't?"

"Well, I guess so. If you put it like that."

Derrick pulled out his list of names and said, "How about Jing Mao? Did he work with Travis like you did? Did he get along with Travis? What was his role here"?

"You ask a lot of questions, Detective. Jing was a technical whiz. He picked things up fast. He got the Correlator to work with Tennico's systems. I can't see Jing harming a fly, let alone Travis. I haven't seen him since Travis was killed, though. He didn't come to the funeral. You think Jing had something to do with Travis being killed?"

"I'll ask the questions."

Derrick didn't see much going on with Truett, so he said goodbye and returned to John's office. John was walking to Truett's office, carrying a copy of his and Travis's partnership agreement. They met in the hallway, where John said, "Here's the copy you asked for. Now, will you please leave and start looking for Travis's killer?"

Derrick replied, taking the papers from John, "Working on that as we speak. Thanks for the copy. I'll be in touch if I have any further questions." Derrick walked past John and out to his car. He got in and started thumbing through the agreement. After about thirty seconds, Derrick gave up trying to understand it and decided to give the agreement to the District Attorney. Derrick knew the DA, Glena Olsen, would be handling such a high-profile case. Looking at the agreement again, he decided to pay Jing a visit.

When Derrick left, John sat at his desk and thought about what had just occurred. He didn't like Detective Morgan's questions, and John thought the detective had too much interest in him. Usually, John would talk to his father about this, but he wasn't talking to his father. He didn't know if he ever would again. He thought about calling Jason Wu but decided against it. Jason was connected to his father, who was two thousand miles away. He googled "Lawyers in Slidell" and saw that most of the lawyers were in New Orleans. He keyed "Lawyers in Hattiesburg" and was amazed at how many there were. John looked through the names and saw one he recognized. He said out loud, "I've seen this name before. This guy's been in the news. John picked up his phone and called Cletus Bureaux's office.

DERRICK PULLED into the parking area in front of Jing's apartment. Cedar Grove apartments looked like a thousand other garden apartment complexes. There were 20 identical buildings that had two floors. The buildings were red brick with two sides and a staircase up the middle. Derrick walked up the stairs, found Jing's apartment, and knocked on the door. No answer. After a few moments, he knocked again, still no answer. Since Jing was on the second floor, there was no window for him to look inside the apartment. He called Jing's cell and heard a message that his number was no longer in service. Derrick looked at his phone and decided to visit the leasing office. He walked down the stairs and took the short walk to the office. Derrick stepped inside and started talking to the first person he saw.

He asked, "Excuse me. I'm Detective Morgan with the Hattiesburg police department. I'm conducting a welfare check on one of your residents. His name is Jing Mao, and he's in apartment H-12. I knocked on his door, but there was no answer. Pulling out his badge, he continued, "I need to gain entry to his apartment. Can you help me with that?"

"Hello, Detective. I'm Casey Lynn, the Assistant Leasing Manager. Is there something wrong with one of our residents?"

"That's what I'm here to find out. I need entrance into that apartment, and I need that now. Will you please unlock his door? It's an urgent matter."

Flustered, Casey said, "Yes, of course. I'll get the master key. I hope everything is alright."

Casey retrieved the master key and walked towards Jing's apartment with Derrick at her side. When they arrived, Casey unlocked the door and stepped aside. Derrick told Casey to wait by the door as he entered. Entering the apartment, he noticed nothing out of the ordinary. It was a standard one-bedroom apartment with a living area, bathroom, and kitchen. Walking into the kitchen, he noticed dirty dishes in the sink. There was nothing special about the bedroom other than an unmade bed. He walked into the bath and was struck by something; He didn't see any personal items. No toothbrush, no shaving kit, nothing other than a used bath towel. Puzzled, he walked back into the bedroom and opened the closet door. When he looked inside, Derrick realized he had a problem. The closet was empty of any clothing. Jing was in the wind.

The following day, Derrick was sitting in the lobby of DA Glena Olsen's office. He was there to give her the partnership agreement that John had printed for him. Almost before he could cross his legs, Glena opened her door and asked Derrick to come inside. Glena was a tall woman with short blond hair and black-framed glasses. She sat at her desk while Derrick took one of the three chairs in front. Glena spoke first, "Well, Detective. How are things going with the Travis Beloit case? Where are we at?"

"I've interviewed most of the suspects (Everybody was a suspect in a homicide case), and I have a problem with one of them. His name is Jing Mao. He worked at SynCor and was one of their top people. A real tech whiz, his co-workers said. Trouble is, when I went to interview him at his apartment, he'd cleared out. He's in the wind."

Glena responded, "Well, that is a problem, Detective. I'm getting a lot of heat from Mayor Poteet. SynCor represented tech growth and jobs for Hattiesburg. Having one of the founders murdered is not good publicity. We need to find out who the perp is and find out fast. I'm going to try this case myself. That's how important this is."

"I get it. Nobody wants this case closed more than me."

"I must tell you, Detective, this is your first homicide case, and I'm concerned about that. We can't afford any mistakes. Now, besides this Jing fella, who else are you looking at?"

"Well, at first, I thought I had it easy. This guy who worked at Tennico, Marcus Hudsen, seemed like a good fit. The victim was going out with his ex-girlfriend, Darlene Moss. Marcus didn't like that. He's a drunk and assaulted the victim in a restaurant. His ex said he was a mean drunk and wouldn't be surprised if Marcus had killed the victim. The more I thought about it, though, I decided he didn't do it. Just not enough motive there.

"Anybody else, Detective?

"The victim's business partner, John Zsu. He's the one who most benefits from the vic's demise. They were 50-50 partners. If something happens to one, like drinking poison and dying, the one left gets all the goods. At least, that's what I could gather from this partner agreement I brought you." Derrick handed Glena the manila folder he held and said, "You can better understand this than me, but I think I got that right. Also, he wasn't too forthcoming in my interview. I had to threaten him with a judge to get that."

"You're getting warmer, Detective."

"I did some poking around Tennico. Darlene Moss told me John and Travis were selling their company to Tennico. Darlene was sweet on Travis. Those boys hit the lottery with that one. They were going to be richer than God."

Glena put her elbows on the desk and leaned closer. "Going to be richer? What happened with that?"

"Our victim backed out at the last minute. Not sure of the details, but it put the brakes on John's plans. He was royally pissed."

"What about this guy who flew away? Jing, did you say?"

"Yeah, that's a tough one. From what I gathered, talking to the folks at SynCor, he was a stand-up guy. A real brain amongst brains. He got sick with that stuff that killed our vic. Got some on a cut on his hand and went ill for three days. He certainly understood the effects of that stuff. I have no idea why he bolted— drawing a blank on that one. What I do know is he moved here from London and went to Stanford. Young guy with nothing to gain as far as I can tell."

Glena leaned back in her chair and said, "Well, this John Zsu guy certainly earns a closer look. See if you can get him in the box and find out what he knows."

STELLA PICKED up the ringing phone on her desk and said, "Cletus Bureaux Law offices, how can I help you?"

"Hello, my name is John Zsu. I'd like to speak to Cletus Bureaux."

"Hello, Mr. Zsu. Thank you for calling. May I ask if you are an existing client of Mr. Bureaux?"

"No, I'm not a client. I need some legal advice."

"I understand. Can you tell me the nature of the advice you need?"

"Some detective came into my office asking questions about my business partner's murder. I didn't appreciate how he talked to me and thought I should get a lawyer."

"I see. I'm sorry, Mr. Zsu. Mr. Bureaux does not handle murder cases. He primarily works with corporate clients."

"Well, it's not about a murder. I just need to get some advice."

"I'm sorry, Mr. Bureaux specializes in corporate law, not murder investigations."

"I understand. Would it help that I am the President and founder of SynCor? You might have heard of SynCor. We've been in the news quite a bit these days. I just need some advice. Nothing more."

This got Stella's attention. Everybody knew about SynCor in Hattiesburg. News of Travis's murder at Tennico and Tennico buying out SynCor was everywhere. John and Travis were very familiar names. "Yes, of course. I'm very sorry about Travis Beloit's death. Unfortunately, Mr. Bureaux isn't in his office right now. Can I have a number where he can contact you as soon as he's available?"

Stella wrote down John's cell number and hung up. She said out loud, "Damn you, Cletus. This is the third time this week you're playing golf. We got things going on here, and you're out hittin' a little white ball into the water." She picked up her phone and called Cletus's cell phone.

Cletus felt his phone vibrate in his back pocket just when he started his downswing to hit the bright yellow golf ball. Bright yellow balls were easier to find than white ones. His club connected with the ball, and he watched it sail to the left into the trees lining the number 12 fairway.

Cletus heard his golfing partner, Mays Alan, say, "Cletus, you need to add a hatchet to your bag. As many times as you've been in that forest."

Cletus responded, "Mays, I did that deliberately. I want you to think I'm a no-account when it comes to golf, so I can sucker you into doubling our bet."

Mays was the chairman of Standard Drilling. The second-largest oil-drilling bit manufacturer in the country. He laughed at Cletus's remark.

Walking off the tee, Cletus looked at the caller ID on his phone and saw it was Stella calling for the umpteenth time. He'd call her when he was back in the clubhouse. After six more agonizing holes, Cletus watched Mays sink a twelve-foot put on the eighteenth green. He said, "Damn you, Mays Alan. You don't have enough money, so you need to take mine?"

"Don't complain to me. You're the one who kept losing those side bets. You need to get yourself a new putter or stop making side bets."

After Cletus and Mays settled up their bets, Cletus sat down on a bench in the men's locker room. He took his phone from his pocket and called Stella.

Stella answered, "Well, mister hole in one...Not. You won't believe who called here looking for you today."

Cletus joked, "It's about time Exxon called."

Stella said, "John Zsu. The owner of SynCor. The company in the news about that murder at Tennico. He called."

"Why would he call me? I don't handle criminal cases. You know that. Not as much money as civil and corporate business. Besides, you actually have to go to court for most criminal cases. What'd he want? He get himself charged for that murder?"

"No, nothing like that. He said he didn't like the way some detective was talking to him, and he wanted some advice on how to handle this detective asking questions about him."

"Advice is the same as representing. I don't want any part of criminal. Call him back and tell him to call Legal Referral. They'll find him a lawyer."

"Ok. If that's what you want. I thought you'd be interested in a company like SynCor. Lot in the news about them. High profile, free publicity, and all that."

Cletus thought for a moment. John Zsu and SynCor were big items. He'd get plenty of attention from that. He just wants some advice, after all. He hasn't been charged or anything like that. Thinking further, Cletus decided it wasn't worth the effort. He had things right where he wanted.

Cletus told Stella, "Yes, that's good and all, but we got enough goin' on. Tell him to call the referral service."

"Ok, I'll call him back." Stella discontented from Cletus and called John's number.

John was in the kitchen of his spacious condominium when he

answered Stella's call. John lived in a luxury condo complex in the Oak Grove section of Hattiesburg.

John picked up and said, "Hi, this is John."

Stella replied, "Hello, Mr. Zsu. This is Stella Hardesty from Cletus Bureaux's office. Did I call at a good time for you?"

"Yes! Yes, this is a good time. Thank you for calling me. I really appreciate it."

"I'm very sorry, Mr. Zsu. Mr. Bureaux's current client load prevents him from engaging any new clients at this time. I have a number for the Legal Referral Service in Hattiesburg. They will be more than helpful in finding representation for you. Shall I text you the number?"

John took what Stella said in and thought, "I don't want some random lawyer on a list of who is next up. This Bureaux guy, everybody knows him. He's got some weight. I have to get him on my side."

John told Stella, "Thank you, but I really want Mr. Bureaux's advice. I can pay whatever you need. I need his advice very much."

"I'm very sorry, Mr. Zsu. We give our clients a great deal of attention. We make sure their needs are well and promptly met. Taking on more clients would mean less time for our current clients. If I may, the referral service does have some very fine lawyers."

John said with a touch of desperation, "Look, Ms. Hardesty, I really just need a few minutes. Can I please make an appointment to see Mr. Bureaux? It would only be for a short meeting."

Stella started to talk but hesitated. She thought to herself, "SynCor is a very big deal. Cletus just wants to spend his time on the golf course anyway. He should at least talk to this guy. Getting a client like SynCor would be a nice addition to the company bank account and my paycheck."

She said to John, "Mr. Zsu. If it's just a short consultation, I can have you meet with Mr. Bureaux tomorrow at ten o'clock tomorrow morning. Will that work for you?"

"I'll be there at ten. Thank you very much!" John disconnected the call and ran around the kitchen, fist-pumping and yelling, "Yes! Yes!"

The following morning, Cletus walked through the front door of his office. Stella greeted him and said, "You have a ten o'clock with John Zsu. The one that owns that SynCor company that's been in the news."

"John Zsu? SynCor?"

Stella, annoyed, said, "Yes, we talked about him yesterday. You were playing golf. His business partner got murdered over at Tennico."

"I thought I told you I wasn't interested in talking to him. What's he coming here for?"

"It's a consult. Nothing more. I told him to call the referral agency, but he wouldn't have it. These are important people. You should at least listen to the guy."

"Well, I reckon I don't have a choice now. Do I?"

"Like I said, it's just a consult. Nothing to sign."

Looking at his watch, Cletus said, "Damn, it's almost ten now. I got work to do."

Stella retorted, "Well, if you come to work when you say you will, that shouldn't be a problem."

Cletus said nothing, walked into his office, and closed the door. Several minutes later, Stella knocked and opened it. "John Zsu is here. Do you want to greet him in the lobby, or do you want me to show him in?"

"The lobby is for paying clients. I'll stay right here."

"Fine. I'll get him and stop acting like a child who didn't get their way. You may be Mr. Big Shot now, but just you remember how we started. We were begging for anybody to call us. You couldn't pay me sometimes, but I stayed. Now, here we are, you playin' golf while I'm here making things work. This John Zsu might just bring us in some good money, and you're acting like this?"

Sitting at his desk, Cletus lowered his head. She was right. He was poor as a church mouse when he hung out his shingle. Nothing would erase those memories. He said, "I hear you, and I'm sorry. I'll come out and meet him." He got up and followed Stella into the office lobby, where he saw John sitting in one of the waiting chairs. Cletus held out his hand and said, "Mr. Zsu. I'm Cletus Bureaux.

John stood, took Cletus's hand, and said, "Thank you for seeing me. I have a small matter that I hope you can help me with."

Cletus turned and said, "Well, follow me into my office, and let's talk about it."

Entering Cletus's office, he said, Take a seat, young man, and tell me what's got your cage rattling."

"Thank you, Mr. Bureaux."

"Call me Cletus. Everybody calls me Cletus under this roof. I'm real sorry to hear about your business partner getting himself killed. That's a damn shame in our town. Yes, it is. Now, tell me about this detective that's been asking you questions."

"His name is Detective Morgan. He thinks I killed Travis, killed my business partner and friend."

Cletus moved in closer. The name Morgan got his attention. He investigated that bus accident. He was in with those white supremacist folks over there in Krotz Springs.

"Did he say he thinks you killed your partner? Did he accuse you?"

"No, it was nothing like that. He threatened me with getting a judge if I didn't give him a copy of my partnership agreement with Travis."

"Did you? Give it to him?"

"Of course I did. I don't have anything to hide. I don't want a judge getting involved. Besides, he was very insistent."

"I'll bet he was. John, listen very closely to what I am about to say. Unless you're under arrest, you don't give or say anything to him or anybody else. Givin' him that agreement was a big mistake. Now, I'm not holding you to account, I'm just telling you for the next time he comes calling. He starts knocking on your door again. You tell him to talk to your lawyer and slam that door right in his face. That man is after your freedom, and don't you ever forget it."

John was stunned by what he had just been told. The room felt like being inside a furnace, and he began to sweat. He could barely utter the words, "I didn't kill Travis. Why does he think I killed him? Travis and I started our business from our dorm room at college. We've been through everything. I don't need his money. What reason would I have?"

Cletus didn't care if John was guilty or innocent. No good lawyer lets that train of thought enter into their case preparation. The lawyer's job is to gather enough evidence and present it to a jury so they can answer that question. Nothing more.

John continued, "You said I should have Detective Morgan talk to my lawyer. That's why I'm here. I want you to talk to him."

"I understand that, but I must tell you, I don't handle murder cases. I don't have much experience in that area of the law. You should find somebody who does. I believe my assistant gave you the number of the legal referral agency here in town."

John began to panic. "Murder case? What murder case? I haven't been arrested. I just need advice. Somebody to talk to this detective. I didn't kill Travis!"

Cletus sat back. "I understand that. But I can't help you. You need a more qualified lawyer."

John pleaded, "I can pay you whatever your fee is. I don't have any actual money right now, but I will as soon as the sale goes through. I can pay you then."

"Like I said, you need someone more qualified."

"I'll pay you with stock in SynCor. Having some of that will give you more money than you've probably made in your lifetime. Much more. I need you to help me with this detective."

When Cletus heard John's words, he felt the earth shake, and he almost fell backward out of his chair. Did he just hear what he thought he heard? Even a tiny amount of SynCor stock would mean fabulous wealth for him and his family. Generation upon generation of wealth. He didn't know what to say. He was frozen like an iceberg and couldn't speak. He heard John ask him if he was alright through the frozen mist in his mind. After the mist cleared enough, Cletus spoke, "That's very generous, John. But, as I said, I don't handle murder cases. What I can do is have my investigator look into this. In the meantime, if this detective has any more questions, you tell him to talk to me."

"So, you'll be my lawyer?"

"I will have my investigator look into this, and I will deal with Detective Morgan."

"I'm sorry Mr. Bureaux, Cletus. That's not good enough. I want you as my lawyer. You'll be one of the highest-paid lawyers in the world. I need your help."

Cletus's mind raced while images of his wife and children flashed at him like bullets coming from a gun at night. He began to sweat. Thoughts of his early days with Stella, asking her if it was ok for her to miss another paycheck, hit him like a jackhammer. He needed to let go. Cletus pressed the intercom button on his phone and asked Stella to come in. A moment later, Stella opened the door and stepped in.

Cletus looked at John and said, "Stella, would you please help John fill out our client acceptance documents? We will be representing him from here on. We'll need to add a separate document outlining the payment arrangements."

Stella asked, "Payment arrangements? You want a separate doc for that?"

Looking at Stella, Cletus said, "Yes, John will be paying us with stock in his company. Also, have Beau set up a meeting with John. He'll need to hear what John has to say. I also want you to call Jesper Keyes. He's tried more murder cases than anybody in this town. I need him as co-counsel. I'm sure he won't have a problem with what I have to tell him.

Stella could barely speak. She said, "Well, Mr. Zsu. We're happy to have you as a client, and we'll do everything we can to help you."

Cletus stood and walked around his desk to shake John's hand. "John, my investigator's name is Beau Gaston. He'll be in touch as soon as you want. Don't worry, we'll get this detective out of your world so you can go on without worrying about him."

Shaking Cletus's hand vigorously, John said, "Thank you. Thank you very much."

Two days after John had retained Cletus, John received a phone call from Derrick asking him to come into the station to "help clear a few things up." John gave him Cletus's phone number and told him to "Talk to my lawyer." After disconnecting from John, Derrick cursed. He called Cletus's office. Stella answered the call and transferred it to Cletus.

Sitting at his desk, he picked up and said, "Hello, Cletus Bureaux speaking."

Derrick, sitting at his desk, said, Hello, Cletus. Derrick Morgan. It's been a while. Last time I saw you, you were eating a slice of thing they called pizza at the cafeteria."

Cletus laughed, "I remember that pizza. I think I ate it just about every day I was in that place. Cheapest thing on the menu. How can I help you? I bet I know why you're calling me after all this time."

Derrick picked up his pen, getting ready to take notes. Good detectives write plenty of notes. He said, "I have a few questions I want to ask your client. Not a big deal. Just checking some boxes. Can you bring him to the station so I can move on to other things? It won't take long."

"I see. Well, tell you what, Derrick. All that pizza made me stiff. Why don't you come over here? We can discuss things here. I'll talk to my client and see what a good time for him is. He's a busy man, but I think he can spare a few minutes tomorrow afternoon at five. That sound good?"

DERRICK COVERED the phone and cursed. Cletus deliberately chose the end of the workday. He wants me worn down before I talk to John. "That's fine, Cletus. I'll see you then." They both disconnected without saying another word.

The next day, Cletus, John, and Beau sat in Cletus's conference room. The room had a large table in the center with six chairs surrounding it. The back wall was a bookcase filled with matching law books. These were for show and to impress clients. Everything was online today. Cletus and Beau had notepads in front of them. Cletus said to John, "Now, John. I don't want you to say a word until I tell you to. Don't answer any questions unless I say so. Nothing. Not a single word. Do you understand that? It's very important you understand that."

John replied, "I understand. I'll have no problem keeping my mouth shut."

Beau was about to say something when Stella opened the door and said, "That detective is here. Want me to bring him in?"

Cletus answered, "That's fine, Stella. Bring him on in."

Stella left and quickly returned with Derrick. He stood in the doorway and was surprised to see Beau. Outnumbered, he thought.

Cletus waved to an empty chair at the far end of the table. He wanted as much separation as possible from his client. He said, "Have yourself a seat, detective. I think you know everybody here."

Derrick and Beau looked at each other, but neither spoke. They didn't need to. They both understood the game they were about to play.

Sitting in his chair, Derrick pulled a small notepad from his suit coat and placed it on the table. Getting down to business, he looked at John and said, "You and the victim, I mean, you and Travis were equal partners in SynCor, correct?"

John looked at Cletus and saw him nod his head slightly. This went on with each question Derrick asked.

"Yes. We started the company together and were equal partners."

"Now that Travis is dead, what happens to his half?"

"Travis wasn't married, so his shares passed to me."

"I see. So, you benefited quite well from your partner's death. Is that correct?"

"Nobody benefits from their best friend being killed."

"Where is your employee Jing Mao in all of this? He have a reason to kill Travis? Why'd he disappear? Maybe you and he had something going on?"

Cletus interrupted before John could speak, "Next question, detective."

Derrick continued, "Seems suspicious if you ask me. Both you and Jing's parents are from China. Both work for the government. That right?"

Cletus interrupted again, "Next question."

Derrick said, "That's something your company has. Special technology, for sure. Maybe China would be real interested in that. Maybe Travis got in the way of that?"

Cletus spoke again, "Is there a question there? I thought you were here to ask questions, not make ridiculous innuendos.

Beau sat back in his chair, taking it all in. He remembered days like this when he fired questions at a suspect. The questions revealed information as much as they elicited it. These guys think John and Jing were in this jackpot together. What he couldn't figure out is why. Why couldn't Jing steal whatever this thing was and take it back? What's the reason to kill Travis? John wanted to cash out, and Travis didn't. That's the play here. What's all this China stuff about? He was pulled from his thoughts when he heard Derrick ask John, "Travis didn't want to sell his shares to Tennico. Would he sell them to somebody else? Somebody who would pay more than Tennico?"

Cletus rose from his chair and said, "That's all, folks. Time to go home."

THREE DAYS before his meeting with John, Derrick found a FedEx envelope addressed to him on his desk. He looked at the sender's name and address and saw it was his. Very clever, he thought. He opened the envelope and pulled out a thick stack of papers that looked like some kind of legal document. The top page said, "SynCor Partnership Dissolution and Share Settlement." He thumbed through the pages, seeing the usual legal mumbo jumbo. When he got to the last page, Derrick let out a whistle. He saw John's signature, but the line for Travis to sign was blank. He picked up the phone and called Glena.

Beau drove to SynCor's office a day after John and Derrick were in Cletus's conference room. He wanted to talk to Truett and hear his thoughts about Jing. Beau preferred to speak to people in person. He walked in the door and saw Adelle sitting at her desk. He approached her and said, "Hello. My name is Beau Gaston. I work for Cletus Bureaux, who is John Zsu's lawyer. I'm looking for Truett Beloit. Is he here?"

Adelle looked up and said, "Hello, Mister Gaston. Are you here to find out who killed Mister Travis? It is a terrible thing here. C'est pas bon."

Beau had to think for a moment before he said, "Yes. I'm investigating Travis's death. May I ask your name? Do you know of anybody who would want to hurt him?"

"I am Adelle. Everybody liked Mister Travis. Who would do such a thing?"

"That's what I intend to find out. Is Truett Cook here?"

"Yes, he is my coosan."

"Excuse me?"

"Truett is in the back. His office is in the back. Take this hallway and go through the door. Walk back, and his office is on the left. He is there. I will tell him you're coming to talk to him."

"Thank you, Adelle." Beau reached into his suit coat pocket and handed Adelle one of his cards." He said, "If you think of anything that might be important, please give me a call."

Adelle took the card, placed it in her desk drawer, and said, "Yes, of course. Of course, I will."

Beau turned and followed Adelle's directions. He found Truett sitting at his desk, tapping away on his keyboard. Truett looked up from his screen when he felt a presence in his doorway.

Beau knocked on the door frame unnecessarily and said, "Hello, I'm Beau Gaston. I work for John Zsu's lawyer. Are you Truett Cook?"

"Truett replied, "Yes, that's me. Is there something I can help you with?"

"Do you know anybody who may have wanted to hurt Travis?"

Truett immediately said, "Jing. Jing Mao. I think he killed Travis."

"Why do you say that? Why do you think he killed Travis?"

"Travis told me he caught Jing loading data from his computer to Jing's laptop. Travis asked me to check for any vulnerabilities in his firewall. He wanted me to find out how Jing was able to bypass it. Next thing you know, Travis is killed, and Jing disappears."

Beau took this in and said, "Did you tell Detective Morgan this?"

"Well, no. I didn't think of it at the time."

"Do you know where Jing is right now?"

Truett responded, "I have no idea. Probably somewhere in China."

Beau thought about what Truett said. He pulled a card from his pocket, handed it to Truett, and said, "Here is my card. If you think of anything that might be important, call me. I would appreciate it."

"I certainly will. I want you to find out who killed Travis. We had a lot of plans."

Beau sat in his car, thinking about what Truett had just told him. He thought, "Morgan is going down this Chinese road. It certainly looks bad for Jing, so why do they like John? Maybe there is some connection with John and Jing after all. They both had Chinese backgrounds, and their parents worked for the government. Maybe Morgan has something, and that's why he likes John. Things are starting to look bad for John.

DERRICK WAS in Glena's office the day after he told her what had appeared on his desk. They were discussing the sale agreement between John and Travis when he said, "This agreement says John is buying Travis's shares. If that's true, where's he getting the money to do that?"

Glena said, "That's a huge amount of money. I got a warrant to look at John's financials, and nothing shows up with that kind of money. No offense, detective. This is your first homicide case. I've been doing some digging myself."

Derrick felt offended but said, "Well, it doesn't matter; the vic wasn't going for it. He didn't sign this."

Glena said, "Think about this: John wants to cash out and sell to Tennico. Travis isn't interested. John comes up with this agreement to buy Travis's shares for much more money than Tennico was paying. There's only one place I can think of with that kind of money."

"You think the Chinese are part of this?"

Glena replied, "Think about it. SynCor has this technology that anybody would want, including the Russians, China, and any other country with big energy needs. These Chinese hear that SynCor is selling out to Tennico. Travis doesn't bite on Tennico's deal, so they decide to put in their bid. The vic doesn't bite on that apple either. The partnership agreement John was so generous in providing says that John's father gets control if anything happens to John. Maybe these Chinese have John's father in the mix. I got a warrant for his financials and found that he put up a lot of cash to help SynCor get started. His tax returns don't show anything about that money. Where'd he get the money to loan John to start SynCor?"

Derrick asked, "Ok, where does this guy Jing fit into all this?"

Glena said, "I think Jing did the hit on Travis. Jing's father works in the British embassy. He works for the Chinese government. Jing went to Stanford. I got a warrant for his admission application. It showed he paid for his tuition himself. No scholarship money. Where'd that come from?" Leaning forward and lowering her voice, Glena continued, "I think John is being framed. Here's how:

Jing kills Travis and goes into the wind. The mysterious sale agreement you found on your desk suggests that John was going to sell his and Travis' shares to the Chinese. It gives us evidence about that and helps the Chinese frame John. Think about it. Travis doesn't sell to Tennico. This gives the Chinese their opening. They know John's father will take over the company if Travis and John are gone. Jing kills Travis, John gets framed, and John's father gets control of SynCor. We tell the jury that John is guilty by showing that his motive was money and selling the company to the Chinese.. First, Travis blocks the Tennico deal. Then, he balks at the sale agreement to John. We don't have to say anything about where John is getting the money to do this. John pops a cork when Travis doesn't sign the agreement you found on your desk, and kills him, thinking he gets the company after Travis is gone. That's what the jury will think."

Derrick asked, "Where does that leave Jing? You know, Bureaux is going to bring that up. That's his reasonable doubt play for the jury."

"The jury won't buy it. We have more explanations and evidence that John killed Travis, not Jing. Bureaux can't prove anything about Jing. I'm going to get an indictment and charge John."

Derrick said, "You just said Jing is the perp, not John. Why are you charging John?"

Glena replied, "I know there's a connection between Jing and John. I can't prove anything about Jing any more than Bureaux can. Somebody is going down for this. I have a slam dunk against John.

Two days after John's indictment and arrest, John, Cletus, and Beau were seated at John's kitchen table. Part of the bail agreement required John to wear an ankle monitor and be confined to his condo. Cletus had a stack of papers in front of him. He looked at

John and said, "John, I've been going over the prosecution's evidence, and it doesn't look good for us."

John rocketed up from his chair and yelled, "I didn't kill Travis! Why won't anybody believe me?!"

Cletus replied, "John, it doesn't matter if you killed him or if you didn't. It's what the jury believes. Nothing else. Right now, the prosecution has enough evidence to make the jury believe you did."

Hearing this made John wail even louder. He collapsed on the floor and went silent. Cletus and Beau looked at each other, not knowing what to make of John's collapse. Beau rushed out of his chair and over to John. He put his fingers on his neck and felt a pulse. He could see John's chest rising and falling. Beau said, "Well, he isn't dead. He's had a lot thrown at him over this jackpot he found himself in. No wonder he passed out."

Cletus said, "I'm going to call Stella. I want someone to be with him when he wakes up."

Three days after Adelle heard about John's collapse at his condo, she was sitting at her desk, wondering why she was there. She didn't see any future with SynCor. With Travis gone and John going to jail, she didn't want to be there anymore. After finishing her third bout of crying that morning, she decided to change her situation. At least half a dozen temp agencies were in the sprawling business park SynCor was in. Adelle could easily walk into any of them, hand them her resume, and start applying. She knew she was well qualified for any administrative job. Adelle didn't want to go in person because she knew people had difficulty understanding her. She had just started attending an English class at Pearl River Community College, but still wasn't confident enough to talk to people professionally. Adelle spent the next two hours polishing her resume. She found the various temp agencies in the business park's directory and wrote down their email addresses. Then, she pulled up her email program on her computer, composed an email to the first one on her list, and pressed "send." Nothing. She pressed the key again- Nothing. Adelle let out a long sigh and started to call Truett's office on the intercom. She stopped dialing when she remembered he had left to pick up the lunch order she had placed at Pizzaro's. Frustrated, she copied her resume to a thumb drive, picked up her email list, and walked to Truett's office. She was going to use his laptop to send her emails. When Adelle opened his laptop, she was asked to enter a password. Frustrated, almost to tears, she sat back in the chair and tried to think about his password. Birthdays and pet names were too simple for a technology person like Truett. After thinking a little more, she had an idea. Truett's first real love was a girl named Chrissy. Chrissy Cartwell. Truett loved her very much, and she had accepted his marriage proposal only to back out at the last minute. To Truett's humiliation, the wedding invitations had already been sent. The invitations had July 12th as the wedding date. Some in the family didn't believe Truett's explanation for the wedding cancellation. Chrissy never spoke to Truett's family about it. He never got over Chrissy's last-minute refusal and embarrassment. He hasn't asked anyone to marry him since. He hasn't asked anyone because he's never dated anyone. Family members would ask, "Why would such a smart and handsome man not be married?" He would always answer, "His work was his love." Truett called Chrissy "Syrup." Because she was so sweet, he would say. Adelle was rewarded with access to the laptop after trying several variations of the nickname and wedding dates. She pulled up the email program and saw something she didn't understand. It was an email with the subject line, "Payment receipt-Odessa Pipe and Valve." She didn't understand because she handled the vendor transactions for SynCor. Adelle was an excellent bookkeeper and was strict on employee vendor purchases. She was going to have to have a talk with Truett. She clicked on the attached invoice PDF to see how much Truett had spent without her permission. Adelle looked closer at the screen and saw that the shipping address was Truett's home. Next, she saw what Truett had bought: Isoflurane valve flux. She said out loud, "What is this?"

"What is what?"

Adelle, startled, looked up and saw Truett standing in the doorway. She said, "My email is broken, so I am using your email program. What is this you ordered from Odessa, and why was it sent to your house?"

Truett felt his heart stop, and the room turned into a furnace. He didn't know what to say.

Adelle continued, This is the thing that killed Mister Travis. Why are you ordering it?"

Truett still wasn't able to speak, and he started to sweat.

Adelle asked, "Did you hurt Mister Travis? Why do you have this thing delivered to your house? What did you do?"

Truett gathered himself and started to get angry. He said, "Adelle. I worked my ass off for these guys. This company would be worth nothing without me. I was at that convention putting our booth together while those guys were having drinks at the bar. I was the one who got the Saudis involved. Me. I was the one who worked out the deal with Odessa for the expansion tubes; I was the one who got everything to work at Tennico. I was the one who trained their engineers. I had it made. They were selling the company to Tennico, and I would have my own engineering department. Travis ruined my future with Tennico by not agreeing with John to sell SynCor to them. Travis was shipping me off to Turbanville to work with the Saudis. With Travis gone, John can still sell to Tennico. I read their partnership agreement. Travis is gone, so John owns the whole company. I would have my engineering group, and I could take you with me. Think how great that's going to be."

"Great!? Great!? I loved Travis. He was very special to me. You killed him. You killed the man I loved. You un méchant homme! You are evil, Truett Beloit. What happened to you? Why are you this way now? I don't care what you say." Adelle got up and left Truett standing there. She went to her desk, opened the drawer, and picked up Beau's card.

Two days after Adelle had called Beau, Cletus, Beau, Stella, and John were in Cletus's law office. John was there to finalize his stock agreement with Cletus, but really, it was a celebration of John's freedom. Susan watched Cletus sign his stock certificate and said, "It's a good thing we're rich now. We're going to need it."

Cletus asked, "Why is that?"

Susan took Cletus's hand, placed it on her stomach, looked at him, and said, "Take a guess." Everybody roared and congratulated the couple on their new addition. Cletus looked at Susan and said, "Well, I guess we're going to have to trade the Excllea in for an SUV."

4

BOOK FOUR

THE EXCELA MEETS IT'S END, BUT IT'S PARTS LIVE ON

D r. Cade Fortnoy walked out of Harrah's Casino on the New Orleans waterfront a beaten man. He was surprised to see the sun coming up. Was he really in the casino that long? Cade was a serial loser when it came to playing cards. He looked at the sun coming up and thought to himself, "How could it have gone so wrong? How bad did I screw my life up?" Cade was a forty-six-year-old Plastic Surgeon with a once-thriving practice. He was a short man with brown hair and silver-rimmed glasses. He always laughed when his patients said the worn-out phrase, "Why do they call it a practice? Shouldn't you know everything by now?" Those patients were gone. He had recently settled a malpractice suit from one of his more famous patients. Lilly Hammond was a well-known television personality in New Orleans who was in a coma at Carlisle Extended Care. She had undergone facelift surgery and Liposuction at Cade's surgical facility attached to his office. His Anesthesiologist, Bryce Young, cautioned against performing both procedures simultaneously, but Cade went ahead anyway. He needed the money to continue fueling his gambling problem. If he performed the surgeries separately, it would cost him more. He would have to pay twice for his anesthesiologist and surgery tech. It also meant he would have to wait for the money on the second procedure while Lilly healed from the first.

Lilly's facelift took longer than usual. In addition to her face, Lilly wanted her nose bump removed and implants in her cheeks. She was trying to add as many years as she could to her TV career. Before Cade started the Liposuction procedure, Bryce cautioned Cade again about performing another procedure. The Anesthesia gas he was using was not recommended for lengthy operations. Cade went ahead anyway. A little over an hour into the liposuction procedure, Lilly began to have problems. Her heart started racing, and she began to bloat from the fluid being pumped into her body for the liposuction. The bloating increased her blood pressure and, coupled with her rapid heart rate, caused a blood vessel in her brain to rupture. Lilly would never regain consciousness.

Cade's marriage had been on the rocks for quite some time. He spent more time on his patients than his family. His gambling problem didn't help. Lilly's demise was big news in New Orleans. His practice disappeared overnight, and his wife filed for divorce. He took the elevator up to the third level of Harrah's parking garage. Getting off the elevator, he clicked his key fob, listening for the sound of his car. He walked towards the sound and found his car—a blue Excella he had purchased used from Patterson Pre-Owned Automobiles. Cade couldn't afford the lease payments on his Mercedes and needed to keep up his appearance, so he bought the Excella. Cade sat in his car and pondered his situation. He was renting a condo that he couldn't afford. His medical practice disappeared when the Louisiana Medical Board suspended his license, and his children weren't speaking to him. He was deeply affected by what he had done to Lilly, and yet, he was sitting in a casino's parking garage where Lilly's money had been lost on a lousy poker hand. Cade thought about all of this and decided he needed a fresh start. He wanted out of New Orleans. After spending almost nine hours in the casino, he drove home to get some sleep.

Cade woke up, looked at his phone, and saw it was nearly four p.m. He laid back on his pillow and, after a few moments, pressed the number to his older sister's phone. Peggy lived in Centreville, Virginia. A suburb of Washington, DC, and was divorced from her husband of twenty-five years. Peggy's children were grown and living their own lives. Cade and Peggy were close growing up, and she frequently asked Cade to stay with her while he got his life back together after his divorce. She had plenty of room for Cade to stay as long as he liked. A week after calling his sister, Cade loaded his Excella with what was left of his life and started the thousand-mile drive to Centreville. He got an early start and left his Condo garage at six in the morning. He had about an eleven-hundred-mile drive in front of him. Cade decided to drive as far as he could that day.

He was surprised he had made it as far as Marshall, Virginia, on his first day. He saw the sign for a hotel and decided to sleep there. He parked his car in the Hampton Inn parking lot and entered the lobby. It had been a long day, and he was as tired as an one-arm wallpaper hanger. He checked into his room and walked across the street to the twenty-four-hour Denny's to eat a late meal. Cade had a long and restful sleep. When he looked at his phone, he saw it was almost nine a.m. He took a shower, dressed, and walked towards the Denny's for breakfast. After his meal, Cade collected his things from the room and checked out of the hotel. He started walking to his car when he noticed something: His blue Excella was not where he had parked it. Confused, Cade looked around the parking lot and didn't see his car. After several minutes of contemplating where he may have parked it, Cade began to panic and returned to the hotel lobby to call the police. His blue Excella and everything in it had been stolen while he slept.

RUSSELL COSGROVE and Josh Millgrim were cruising the streets of Marshall while Cade slept. They were looking for a late-model Ford F-250 truck. They weren't interested in the truck; they wanted its parts. Josh and Russell were part of a gang called "The Company," which specialized in stolen auto and truck parts and mainly operated in the Washington metro area. Josh was looking for a catalytic converter for his brother, Derris, who lived in Marshall. They stopped at the local Denny's for a late dinner after working on Derris's truck for most of the day. The converter was Derris's last part to make his truck street-legal. Josh prided himself on being able to remove a catalytic converter from any vehicle in less than five minutes. Russell spotted Cade's Excella in the hotel parking lot as they left the Denny's after a late-night meal. He said to Josh, "Hey Josh, look at that blue Excella over there."

Josh replied, "Yeah, I see it. What do you think?"

"It's the right year for sure."

New, high-end luxury cars were not a good fit for parts thieves. Wealthy people usually owned these. The car would probably still be under the factory warranty, and the owners would take it to the dealership for any needed service or repair. The dealership would purchase parts directly from the manufacturer, and the cost would be covered under the car's warranty. Dealers wouldn't buy parts from a stranger opening his trunk at the service center. Older high-end cars were a much better fit for what Josh and Russell did. These cars would most likely have been traded in for the latest model by the original owners. The new owners would have purchased them as used, and they would not have any warranty coverage. These car parts were expensive, and owners would likely take them to privately owned repair shops rather than the more costly dealers. Plenty of private repair shops were willing to buy parts from somebody's trunk. High-end car parts were much sought after.

"Go over and park next to the car," Russell said. "We can use our car to block the view from the lobby."

Josh parked, opened the trunk, and retrieved his tools to gain entry into the Excella. He took a screwdriver and pried the touchpad key panel off the driver-side door, exposing the wires connecting the panel to the car's computer. He placed a small box with four wires coming out of it on the hood. He had bought the box off the dark web and put it to good use. When he connected the wires from the box to the panel wires, the red light on the box turned green. Josh pressed the ONE button on the car panel four times and heard the door lock click open. Once he gained entry, Josh opened the car's hood so Russell could disable the car's GPS and thwart any tracking by the owner or police. While Russell was disabling the GPS, Josh took his screwdriver and pried the ignition button away from the dashboard, exposing its wires. He, once again, took the box's wires and connected them to the ignition wires. When the green appeared, he waited for Russell to finish and close the hood. When Russell did this, Josh pressed the ignition button, and the Excella started. Josh closed his door and drove off with the Excella while Russell returned to his car and followed. Josh and Russell drove their vehicles approximately twenty miles to Centreville, where the company had one of it's "Chop Shops." Chop shops were garages where stolen vehicles were disassembled for their parts. Josh didn't drive directly to the shop but rather to a side road from the main street in Centreville, five miles away. Here, Josh parked the car. A hunter's trail cam was hidden in a tree across the street. Even though Russell had disabled the Excella's GPS, there might be some other tracking device, like an Apple AirTag, hidden in the car that Russell couldn't see. Josh would leave the Excella parked for four days, with the trail cam activated every time a car drove past. Josh would retrieve the trail cam and view its recordings over the last four days. If anything was out of the ordinary or a police car drove past, the vehicle would be abandoned. After four days, Josh saw nothing on the trail cam and drove the Excella to the garage for disassembly. When he drove into the garage, Josh saw a buzz of activity, with gang members working on stolen vehicles and taking them apart. Any parts with serial numbers or factory identification were put in a bin next to the car. These parts were marked with a red Sharpie—only service and repair shops the gang trusted and had a relationship with received these parts. Josh parked the Excella under one of the several hydraulic lifts and got out. Two gang members approached the Excella and began taking it apart. While one of them was getting the car's engine ready for removal, the other started taking the door panels off to remove the power windows, motors, and brackets. When a gang member removed the driver's side door panel, a white piece of paper dropped to the floor. He picked it up, unfolded it, and read what was written on it. He said out loud, "Quentin Waters? I don't know who you are, but you better build another one because this one here doesn't exist anymore."

As he removed the water pump, the other gang member asked, "What did you say? Who's Quentin?"

WALT INGRAM WAS a family man who lived in Columbia, Maryland, thirty miles north of Washington, DC. He was thirty-nine years old, with sandy brown hair and a mustache. He lived with his wife, Olivia, and their 11-year-old son, Liam. Walt worked at the Air Force's Materiel Command (AFMC) in Laurel, Maryland, a twenty-minute commute from his house in Columbia. His job was to evaluate the defense contractor's product against the specifications in the contract and recommend whether the Air Force should proceed and pay the contractor, request changes, or,

in some cases, terminate the contract. He was driving home after
leaving his office late. It was almost seven o'clock on a frigid
January night. He was driving his seven-year-old Monarch
Catalina when he noticed the "check engine" light come on, and
the engine temperature gauge start to rise. This was the third time
his car had acted like this in as many weeks. The other times, the
car corrected itself. After driving another ten miles, he realized his
car was losing power. He pulled to the side of the road, where the
vehicle gave up and went silent. He hit the wheel and cursed. The
Christmas bills were coming due, and the last thing he needed was
a car repair bill being added to the mix. He picked up his cell
phone and called his wife to give her the bad news that he would
need a ride home from the repair shop. After disconnecting, his
next call was to Triple-A to have his car towed. After waiting
almost half an hour, the tow truck arrived. The signs on the truck
doors said, "Robinson Towing." There was a AAA decal next to
the name. The driver jumped down from his truck and
approached Walt, standing beside his broken car. He greeted Walt
and asked him to open the hood of the Catalina and try to start the
vehicle. After several attempts to start the car, he said, "I see some
coolant seeping out of the water pump gasket.. I can tow you to
Robers Service Center if you like. Your membership level would
cover the towing distance." Walt's shoulders slumped. He had
been to Robers Automotive Service before. He called them
Robbers when he used them the last time the Catalina needed
fixing, but they were close to his house, and Olivia wouldn't have
to drive far to pick him up. He gave the driver the go-ahead and
started to call his wife. The tow truck driver pulled into Robers's
overnight parking lot, got out, and punched in the passcode to
open the gate. He didn't mention to Walt that Robers gave him a
kickback for any customers he towed to them. After the driver
"dropped" Walt's car, he said, "There you go, Walt." He pulled one
of Robers business cards and handed it to Walt. "Here's their card.
They open at eight."

The following morning, Walt called Robers to relay what Lucas had said about his car. The receptionist took down his information and told him to expect a call from the service manager after his car had been looked at later in the day. He disconnected the call, selected the Uber app on his phone, and sighed. He was going to be late for work. At 9:25, Walt finally made it to his desk. Walt's office mate, Ellie Taylor, looked up from her screen and said, "I was just getting ready to call you." Ellie was twenty-four years old and stood five feet two inches tall. She had long blonde hair and wore pink-framed glasses.

Walt said, "My car died last night on the way home. I had to take an Uber this morning and walk in from the front road because the driver didn't have clearance to get through security.

"That sucks. Don't forget we have a project meeting with Owen at eleven."

"Damn. I left my notes at home."

"I didn't hear that. You know the rules about taking stuff home."

After lunch, Walt got a call from Robers service manager, Clay Helton. Walt answered the call, dreading what he would hear after Clay introduced himself. Clay said, "Hello, Mr. Ingram. This is Clay Helton from Robers Auto Service. We've looked at your car, and it appears you have a bad water pump. There's coolant leaking from the pump seal, and it's not building enough pressure to feed the radiator. You're going to need to replace it."

Sitting at his desk with one hand on his face, Walt groaned and said, "Ok, how much will that cost?"

Clay replied, "I can email you an estimate if you like. Once you approve the work, we can get started. The pump is in stock, so we don't have to order it. That's going to save a lot of time. I can have your car ready for pick-up tomorrow afternoon if that works for you."

Walt's face was inches from his desktop when he said morosely, "Go ahead and send me the estimate, but I don't want to waste time. It is what it is. I need my car back as soon as possible."

"Will do, Mr. Ingram. If anything comes up, we'll give you a call."

"Anything comes up? What do you mean, if anything comes up?"

Clay replied, "Well, sometimes we find other issues after we start working on the vehicle. Probably not, in your case, but you never know."

Walt groaned again and said, "I understand. Let me know as soon as possible if you find anything else."

Walt hung up, picked up his cell, and selected his bank's app. He saw the balance in his and Olivia's joint account and groaned some more. Their Christmas bills were due, and Walt wasn't sure he could cover the car repair bill. He said to Ellie, "Every time I turn around, I have another bill. I think Christmas should be canceled next year."

Clay hung up and left his office to give one of the service techs the work order for Walt's car. The tech looked at the work order, walked to the parts department, and began collecting the parts he needed to fix Walt's car. He put the parts on a small steel cart and pushed it over to a separate section of the parts department. He scanned the shelves, looking for a Monarch Catalina water pump. After several minutes of looking for the pump, he saw a Monarch Excella water pump. The tech had worked on dozens of Monarchs and knew an Excella pump was the same one used in a Catalina. He pulled the pump from the shelf and used his hand to wipe the accumulated dust that had accumulated over time. He smiled when he saw the red Sharpie mark on the pump. He would make more commission on this part rather than one ordered new. Robers had a big supply of parts with red Sharpie marks.

JANICE COLLINS WAS PARKING her car at the Washington Metro Station in Vienna, Virginia, when she heard her phone's ringtone. She looked at the caller ID and saw that her daughter, Cheri, was calling. Janice sighed and decided not to pick up. Cheri was in the middle of a divorce and called her what seemed like every thirty minutes. Janice was fifty-three years old, and Cheri was her only child. Her husband, Max, died of a heart attack five years ago, and she lived by herself. She had been taking the Orange Line train to work in Rosslyn, Virginia, for the last eight years, where she was a senior department manager at Carnegie National Bank, the third-largest bank in the US, with offices nationwide. Her department managed abandoned demand accounts. Demand accounts were checking and savings accounts that owners could deposit or withdraw funds without giving the bank any notice. Almost all checking and savings accounts were in this category. Accounts were classified as abandoned if they had had no activity for the last four years. They usually had small balances, but some could be quite large. The money from the abandoned accounts was sent to the state where the account was opened as unclaimed property. Banks had thousands of abandoned accounts each year, totaling billions of dollars. Janice had twelve people in her department assigned to different parts of the country. Each month, she would combine their reports that showed the total dollar amount discharged as unclaimed property from each region in the country and forward them to the bank's accounting department. At her age, Janice knew she had peaked with the bank, career-wise. She thought about one of her employees, Lexi Walker. Lexi was, by far, the most dedicated employee she had, and Janice wasn't shy about letting her know that. Janice marveled at Lexi's attention to detail and looked for any possible reason not to close an account and send its balance to the state. This was almost to a fault because Lexi was always the last to submit her monthly report. Janice saw Lexi as the person she wished she had been in her younger days. Lexi was an average-looking woman, twenty-five years old, with red curly hair. She was sitting in her usual spot at the Starbucks next to her work. She lived in Alexandria, Virginia, a city on the Potomac River, a few miles south of Washington. Her condo was in the tony Old Town section of the city. Lexi could afford to live in Old Town because of her Family's wealth. Walker Financial was one of the largest financial companies in the country, with interests in insurance, banking, and financial services. Lexi was a very bright student in high school and college and could have had a career working at Walker Financial. Her parents were dismayed when she became a junior accountant at a bank after graduating from Columbia University. Lexi wanted to be her own woman and not follow the easy route of joining the family business like her older brother, Brooks, did. Lexi was a creature of habit. The clock dictated her strict schedule. She woke up at six-thirty each morning, whether it was a workday or a weekend. On workdays, she was dressed and out the door by seven-fifteen. She walked two blocks to the King Street metro station and took the Blue Line train to her job.

She arrived at her desk at eight-thirty. As a junior accountant, Lexi was given responsibilities nobody else in her department wanted. After reviewing a list of abandoned accounts, Lexi's job was to transfer the money into one of several accounts at the Virginia Comptroller's office. She would receive a receipt from the Comptroller's office of the transfer, which she added to the notes in the now-closed account. It was a tedious and time-consuming process, so it was considered one of the less desirable jobs at Carnegie. It wasn't undesirable to Lexi. She enjoyed digging into the more personal side of banking and often wondered about the person who abandoned their money, especially the accounts with large balances. One such account was Emily King's. Lexi saw that Emily's account was opened almost thirty years ago. The last activity was a direct deposit from the Social Security Administration nearly five years ago. The notes on the screen showed the bank had sent two letters to Emily, notifying her that her account would be closed unless she contacted the bank. There obviously had been no response to the letters. Lexi had seen quite a few accounts that matched Emily's history. She felt sad for every one of them. The account owners probably died and had no family to look after their affairs. After spending the morning reviewing and marking accounts for transfer to the Virginia Comptroller's office, Lexi's cell phone started playing its ringtone. She looked at the caller ID and saw her boyfriend's name. Lexi met her current significant other, Elliott Cole, while waiting for the Blue Line metro to work. She noticed the tall, handsome guy a few months back, standing on the platform, waiting for the same train as Lexi. Lexi didn't see a wedding ring but assumed that someone who looked that good probably had a girlfriend. Over the next several weeks, like clockwork, Lexi would arrive at the station, see him standing in the same spot, and sit in the same seat. Several times, Elliott caught Lexi glancing at him. She averted her eyes each time, but one day, she knew she had been caught. She didn't look away on the day Elliott saw her. He gave a slight wave of recognition and returned his gaze to his phone screen. When the train arrived at the Rosslyn station, Elliott got off, and Lexi saw him start up the same escalator she took every morning. When she reached the top of the escalator, there was Elliott with a smile that melted her like butter in a microwave.

Elliott was raised by his Aunt Farah and Uncle James in St. Louis because his parents couldn't get a visa to emigrate from Iran when he was six. He lost contact with them shortly after his seventh birthday and has never found out what happened to them despite his unrelenting efforts to learn their fate. He and Farah were bonded by their despair at finding out what happened to them after Immigration and Naturalization denied their visas. Elliott obtained a degree in mathematics from George Mason University. His advanced math skills landed him a position as a software engineer for the Department of Transportation. His current task was updating the software for Air Traffic Controllers to display alternative flight paths for planes encountering high wind turbulence.

A month after meeting Elliott at the metro station, Lexi answered her phone at work and said, "Hi there, good-looking. Are we still on for lunch?"

Elliott replied, "Sorry, babe, my boss just put a load on me, and I'm going to have to cancel."

Disappointed, Lexi said, "That's too bad. Why don't you tell your boss you would love to do the work, but you have more important things to do?"

"What a great idea! Why didn't I think of that? I wouldn't have a job, so I couldn't pay my rent and would have to move in with you."

"Not so fast, light of my life. I think Charcoal would have a fit if somebody moved into his territory. He just got neutered, and he's probably not in the mood for any more disruptions in his life."

"Ok, I wouldn't want to be disruptive. I wonder, since he got his balls cut off, does that mean he'll stop humping my leg when I come over?"

"Well, I don't know. Why don't you stop by tonight and find out?"

"Sounds like a plan. I'll pick up a pizza from Fresno's."

"Don't forget the garlic knuckles."

"With extra sauce, I know. I'll call you when I get out of here."

"You're so good to me. I'll talk to you later."

An hour later, Janice called Lexi into her office and asked, "Lexi, can you take this folder over to Patti in legal for me?"

"Sure thing, Janice. I need to go that way anyway." She pointed to the coffee mug on her desk and said, "That's a cool mug, Janice."

"My gym across the street gives those out to new members. I go in the morning before work. By the way, how are you and Elliott getting along? You know how much I enjoy office gossip."

With a broad smile, Lexi replied, "He's coming over for dinner tonight."

"Well, make sure you tell me all about it tomorrow."

Later in the evening, Elliott knocked on Lexi's condo door with one hand while trying to balance a pizza with a bag of garlic knuckles on top with the other. Lexi opened the door and said, "Oh, thank you, mister delivery man. Why don't you come inside so I can give you a tip?"

He replied, "Well, thank you, ma'am. I like delivering here. You tip better than anybody." He came in, and Lexi took the pizza and bag from him and entered the kitchen.

"Where's Charcoal? My leg isn't getting humped."

"He's on his bed in my bedroom. I don't think he's in the mood for company right now. My neighbor gave him a couple of cannabis gummies to ease the pain from his vet visit, and he's sleeping like a dog who ate cannabis gummies. Poor boy."

"Well, if I had my boys cut off, I'd need a whole bag of gummies."

Lexi smiled and said, "I'll put these in the oven for a few minutes to warm up. The microwave dries everything out." After putting the pizza and knuckles in the oven, she walked over to Elliott and wrapped her arms around him. She looked into his eyes and said, "I'm so glad you're here. How did your day go?"

"Pretty good, except having to stay late. Writing code is like reading a good book for me. You get into the zone of a good story. I look at the time and see I've been at it for hours."

She unwrapped herself and said, "Talk to me in the kitchen while I make a salad."

When they entered the kitchen, Lexi went to the refrigerator and opened the door, while Elliott went to the oven, opened its door, and took the pizza out. Several minutes later, they sat at a small round table in the kitchen, eating their meal, when Elliott asked, "So, how are things at work? Are you still taking people's money and giving it away?"

"Shut up. It's sad when people don't have anyone when they die. I think their money should go to a charity rather than some government that'll waste it on God knows what.

Elliott picked up a slice of the pizza and said, "This smells great."

Lexi said, "How are things at your work? The next time I get on a plane, I'll be thinking about you."

"I love it. My boss leaves me alone. As long as I meet my deadlines and don't have many revisions, he's cool. How about your boss? Janice, right?"

"I think she likes me. We talk, but sometimes she can get a little personal."

"How so?"

"Oh, I don't know. I feel bad for her. Her husband died a few years ago. She has a daughter, but I don't know how close they are. She doesn't have any pictures or personal items on her desk. Sometimes, I think she's going to be one of my abandoned accounts someday."

Reaching for another slice of pizza, Elliott asked, "I still can't understand how your bank decides someone doesn't want their money. You told me you send them letters and try to contact them, but what if someone's been in a coma for five years and wakes up to find their money gone?"

"The bank has the account holder's Social Security number and uses it to verify death certificates, passports, and any financial activities like credit card transactions or loan payments. The bank's computer system manages that. Letters and personal contact attempts are considered a last resort. That's my responsibility before I close the account and transfer the funds. If no letters receive responses, I change the account from abandoned status to closed and begin the transfer process." I suppose if someone comes out of a coma, they could get their money back from the state. Shifting topics, she asked, "How are you doing with finding your folks? I know that's a big deal for you."

"Nothing new. I've been looking since I was old enough to start. Not giving up any time soon. If the asshole who decides who gets a visa had done their job, I wouldn't have to look."

'I'm so sorry for you. It's terrible not knowing what happened to your parents."

Lexi got up to take their plates to the sink when she stopped and saw Charcoal enter the kitchen and sit in front of his bowl. Elliott said, "I think he has the munchies and caught a whiff of the pizza." He tore off a small slice, removed the toppings, and dropped it into Charcoal's bowl. He added a garlic knuckle after the pizza had vanished in one gulp.

JANICE PARKED her car in the garage of her house after working all day at the bank and staying late once her co-workers had left. She stayed late for two reasons: to avoid traffic and delay coming home to an empty house. Another reason she stayed late was that she had befriended one of the cleaning staff, Manuela, who was teaching her how to speak Spanish. Manuela had recently lost her husband to cancer and enjoyed her sessions with Janice. Janice's house was in a neighborhood where every house looked the same. Ranch-style homes with a driveway and a mailbox at the beginning of that driveway. She closed the garage door and went inside. She immediately heard her parrot, Maestro, loudly reacting to her coming home. Janice smiled, entered the kitchen, retrieved a stalk of celery from the refrigerator, walked to the TV room, and placed the celery in the bird's giant cage. Max bought Maestro shortly after they were married, and it was Janice's living connection to him while she was home. The one drawback was cleaning the cage every two weeks. She returned to the kitchen, opened the fridge again, and sighed. She didn't feel like cooking dinner, so she opened the freezer door, took out one of the dozen or so frozen dinners, and placed it in the microwave. When the frozen dinner wasn't frozen anymore, she put it on a plate, took a bottle of white wine from the fridge, and walked back to the TV room. "Another day in paradise," she said to Maestro as she put her plate on the TV tray.

WALT PARKED his car in the garage and entered his house after a long day of work. It was Friday, and he was ready for the weekend. He entered the kitchen and saw Olivia pulling a pan out of the oven and testing the temperature. He said, "That smells good, what is it?"

Olivia replied, "It's my lasagna."

Walt looked at the kitchen table, noticed four place settings, and said, "Someone else coming to dinner?"

"Ivey and Braden are joining us. We owe them a dinner for Ivey helping me stuff envelopes for the school's fund drive."

"I see. Well, good call on the lasagna. I can't wait to dig into that. Why only four plates?"

"Liam is over at the Bennets. He and Finn are working on their project for the school's science fair next month."

"I hope they win. I need to see a return on all the money you spent helping them."

"First of all, it's WE spent, and if you want a return on investment, how about he does well enough to score some points when it's time to apply for college?"

"Well, I agree. It might score some points for him to get a scholarship. His college fund isn't doing so well these days. It's been at least three or four years since we've been able to deposit anything into his account."

"Don't I know."

Walt said nothing.

"Walt, I've been thinking about getting a job. Liam is old enough to be alone, and I spend so much time volunteering between the school, church, and the HOA. I should use that time to help us out."

"Well, I can't argue with that."

As soon as Walt finished, the doorbell rang. He left Olivia, opened the door, and said, "Well, look who's here." He turned his head towards the kitchen and shouted, "Hey, Olivia, those people looking for a free meal are back. Should I let them in?" Turning back to Ivey and Brandon Price, he motioned them in and said, "Bran, I took your money last week, so treating you and Ivey to dinner is the least I can do."

"Brandon said, "You got damn lucky with that field goal. Besides, that off-side call was the worst example of officiating I have ever seen."

Walt smiled and said, "You're just ticked because you gave me that half-point on the spread, and it cost you."

Ivey said, "I'll leave you two gambling addicts while I go see Olivia."

Ivey entered the kitchen and saw Olivia making a salad. She held up a bottle of red wine in each hand and said, "I brought the good stuff."

"Thank God, Ivey. Pour me a glass as fast as you can."

After putting the wine on the counter, Ivey looked through the oven window and said, "I could smell your Lasagna as soon as I walked in the door."

"The wine, Ivey, the wine, please."

After finishing their meal, Brandon sat back in his chair and said, "Olivia, I swear that's the best food I've ever eaten."

Ivey said, "You made this Lasagna last month at the church's potluck. People were mad you didn't make more."

Brandon asked, "How do you make it? What's in it?"

Olivia said, "That's a state secret, but I'll tell you, all pasta is the same if it's made fresh, and cheese is the same if it's made with good ingredients. What makes it taste so good is the sauce. Making a really good sauce is an art form. You go to any good Italian restaurant, and you'll notice they use the same sauce for their lasagna, spaghetti, ravioli, you name it. Their sauce is what makes them stand out. It's what a good Italian chef works on the most to perfect."

Ivey said, "Well, it's obvious you perfected yours. I think you should sell it. How cool would seeing your sauce on a grocery shelf be?"

Brandon said, "I'd buy it for sure."

Olivia said, "I don't have time for that. Besides, I wouldn't know where to start. Now, who wants cheesecake?"

Later in the evening, when they were getting ready for bed, Walt said, "You know, Ivey has something there. You could sell your sauce. It is really good. Everyone thinks so."

"Walt, I don't know the first thing about selling anything."

"What about that Farmer's market on Sunday? People are selling their stuff there. Barbeque sauces, hot sauces, all kinds of different foods. We have two bottles of Mr. B's hot sauce in the pantry right now. I love that stuff."

"You have a point. I didn't think about that farmer's market."

"I have an idea. I'll make some Jar labels on my PC and get them printed. You find out who we need to talk to about getting a booth at the market. How many bottles of sauce can you make?"

"I don't know. How many should I make? I have that big crab pot I could use. I think twenty-five or thirty bottles."

"Well, ok then. We have a plan. What should we call it?"

"I think we should call it 'Lucy's' after my mom. It's her recipe. I just made a few changes."

"It needs to sound Italian. How about "Lucia's?" "Lucia's, the sauce your mother made."

"Walt, that sounds great. I'm getting excited about this."

"I'm getting excited, too. Turn off the light."

NOAH CLYBURN STOOD on a wooden platform in the middle
of the Mojave Desert, watching his company's latest self-guided
missile test. Noah was the lead administrator for Warner Systems'
Air Force division. Warner had invested hundreds of millions of
dollars in developing the missile and was over a year behind
schedule in delivering it to the Air Force. Noah's role at Warner
was making sure his company received payment for the time and
resources it had invested in the Spear Missile system. He needed to
demonstrate to the Air Force that the missile met all the requirements in the contract, and it was time to pay Warner. After the
test, Noah took a van from the test range to Warner's office at
Edwards Air Force Base, which was twenty-five miles away. When
he entered the office, one of his assistants, Margie, was waiting for
him. Margie pointed to a large computer monitor on her desk
without saying a word. Noah bent down to look at the screen,
which displayed the results of the test he had just witnessed. After
a moment, he cursed out loud, "Damn! We're still slow." He
turned to Margie and said, "We missed the speed by six miles an
hour. Can you believe that? Six freaking miles. I don't care; they
need to change the contract specs. We can't keep doing this. That
thing is going five hundred and seventy-five miles an hour, and
they're going to complain about six miles? Give me a break."

He left the office and told the van driver to take him to Warner's
company jet. He needed to find a solution to his problem. Noah
was in the air and had another hour before his plane landed. He
was on the phone with Warner System's president, Mack Gilliam.
Mack was an Air Force Colonel who retired early to join Warner.
Mack had connections with the Air Force's decision-makers that

go way back to his early days flying F-15 Eagles, and he was in high demand with Air Force defense contractors. Sitting at his desk, Mack said, "Noah, I heard about the test today—same results as the last two. What are we going to do about that?"

"Colonel, these guys are being unreasonable. We've passed every benchmark except this one. I can understand if it's twenty-five or thirty, but six is ridiculous. Besides, when the missile goes into production and real-world use, there's going to be a variance. Some of them will go faster, and some slower. It depends on the air conditions in flight."

"Do we know who is making such a big deal out of this? Who is holding our feet to the fire?

"I know it's the Air Forces, Contracts Administration in Materiel Command. They call it AFMC. Those are the folks responsible for making sure we live up to our end of the contract. They have the ultimate say in this. I don't know the actual person."

"Well, somebody has to be in charge of that. Find out who it is. Find out why they're being such a dick."

"I was thinking the same thing. I'll get back to you as soon as I find out."

Noah disconnected the call and sat back in his seat. After a few moments, he called his administrative assistant, Simon Foster. Simon was a bull when it came to getting things done. After a few rings, the call went to voicemail. Frustrated, Noah left him a message, looked at his watch, and realized he had forgotten the time change. The following morning, after an abbreviated sleep, Noah entered his office suite and saw Simon sitting at his desk in the outer office. His eyes were fixed on his computer screen. He looked up and said, "Morning, boss. I got your message. I printed out what you wanted and put it on your desk. I heard about the test yesterday. I was talking to one of the engineers on that project this morning. He said the missile's propellant system was maxed out. The only way to get more speed is to redesign it with a larger nozzle."

Noah said, "No way that's going to happen. We'd have to abandon the project if it comes to that. Our stock price would go to zero, and we'd be out of a job."

Noah turned, entered his office, and saw the printout Simon had put on his desk. He picked it up and saw what Simon had found: Walt Ingram, senior contract administrator at AFMC, was causing Noah's problem.

Noah returned to Simon and said, "Find out everything you can about this guy. I want to know what he puts in his coffee and everything else about him."

SUNDAY EVENING, Elliott was in his apartment on the seventh floor of a high-rise building four blocks from the metro station where he met Lexi. In addition to the usual furniture, his spacious bedroom featured a desk with two computer monitors and a fold-out keyboard. Elliott had a second source of income, assisting small businesses in his area with their computer needs. He had just finished designing an inventory system for Delta Liquor stores. His phone rang at seven-thirty, and he answered without checking the caller ID. His Aunt Farah called him every Sunday at the same time. He was very close to her; even though she was his aunt, he regarded her as a mother figure. He had called her "Auntie Mom" since he was ten. Farah missed her sister, and she and Elliott were determined to discover what had happened to her, even after all the years that had passed. It was even more personal for Elliott since he was also searching for his father. He picked up and said, "Hi, Auntie."

"Hello, son. How was your week?"

"It was ok. I finally got paid by Logans Dry Cleaners."

"Well, how did you manage that?"

"I told them if they didn't pay me by Friday, I would take down their website."

"That's nice. Now, tell me about this girl you met."

Elliott knew his Auntie couldn't care less about somebody paying him. She was calling to see if he was any closer to getting married. If he told her a girl his age knocked on his door selling cable and internet service, she would ask when the wedding was.

"Lexi is great. Same as the last time you asked about her."

"Well, I only want what's best for you. How's your job? I tell everybody you make it safe for people to fly."

Before he could answer, He heard a knock on his door. He got up, opened the door, and saw his neighbor from three doors down, Serene Hadid, standing there with a jar of sweet relish in her hand. Elliott told his mother to hang on and made a show to Serene of being on the phone. Holding the phone to his ear, he opened the jar. He returned the jar and mouthed, "I'll talk to you later." Serene smiled and said, "Thank you." Elliott chided himself for being so helpful to his neighbor. He had work to do, and Serene's interruptions were getting in the way. He started placing a towel on the floor to block out any light from the gap between the door and the floor. He used Apple AirPods while watching TV, so she couldn't hear his TV. Returning to his mother, he said, "I have to go, Auntie. I have a presentation to give my boss tomorrow, and I need to polish it up."

"Ok, dear. I don't want to interfere with your work. Tell Lexi I said hello."

Elliott didn't have a presentation to give to his boss; he just wanted to return to the work he was doing before his mother called. His newest client was very demanding, but he couldn't complain. The money was too good to pass up. He would need to use some vacation time next week to finish. Then he thought, "What's the use of making extra money when you don't have any vacation time?" Thinking further, "Check that. I need permanent vacation time."

MONDAY EVENING, Janice parked her car in the garage, grabbed the bag of groceries from the back seat, and entered her house. She set the bag next to the refrigerator, opened the door, and put away some of its contents. She took the remaining cans and boxes, opened the pantry cabinet, and stored them. After doing this, she looked down at the countertop and noticed a thick white envelope. Puzzled, she picked it up and turned it over, searching for any writing. Seeing none, she opened the envelope, gasped, and dropped it to the floor. She stared at it for a few seconds, bent down, and picked it up. Looking inside, she exclaimed, "Oh my gosh! What's this?" She pulled out a stack of one-hundred-dollar bills and stared at it. The paper wrapper around the money read five thousand dollars. It was then she realized the envelope didn't appear out of nowhere. Someone had been in her house and placed it there. She began to panic, thinking the person who had put the envelope on the counter was still in the house. Janice started to flee back into the garage and out its side door. Halfway to the garage door, she stopped, thinking the person who put the money on the counter was probably long gone. It was left for her to find, but why? Janice went to get her phone and call her daughter. After a few rings, the call went to voicemail. She left a message. As a precaution, Janice began to look in every room and closet in the house, looking for anyone and to see if there were any more envelopes. She decided to call her daughter again and leave a message. Cheri was the only other person who had a key to her house. Two hours later, Cheri returned her mother's call. Janice was sitting in her recliner beside Maestro's cage when she picked up and said, "Cheri! Thank God you called."

Concerned, Cheri said, "What's wrong, Mom? Did anything happen?"

Janice told her daughter about the money and how she found it. After she finished, she said, "I wonder if I should call the police."

Cheri said, "I don't know. What are the police going to do?"

"Why would somebody do this?" Janice asked.

"Mom, I'll admit it's a little weird. Maybe it's a debt or something being repaid. Maybe it's something Dad was involved with."

"Cheri, your father has been gone for five years."

"I know, but maybe it's taken that long for somebody to make good on the debt. You know how Dad was. He was always helping people. You even had arguments with him about it."

"Cheri, I get what you're saying. I do remember telling him to stop being so generous. If this was someone repaying a debt, they sure have a strange way of doing it."

"Well, I can't argue with you there. I don't know what to tell you, Mom. There's nothing you can really do. You know what? You should put Ring cameras on every outside door and change the locks. You could call the police and tell them about your house being broken into. Don't mention the money. That way, you have a police report in case anything else happens."

"You're right. I'll do that after we hang up."

"You know what, Mom? I'll stop by this weekend to help you set up the Ring cameras. It's simple—I installed mine."

"Thank you so much, Cheri. I'll get the cameras tomorrow."

Janice disconnected the call and immediately returned her thoughts to the money. When she went to work tomorrow, she decided to open a savings account in Cheri's name and adopt a dog from the animal shelter. She'd been thinking about it for a while. Janice woke the following morning and thought about calling in sick. The memory of finding the envelope and someone in her house roared back. She was afraid to come home after work and have the same experience. Worse, the envelope person would be there waiting for her. Suddenly, a thought occurred to her: they had left her money. If they wanted to hurt her, they would have done so last night. Her fear quickly turned into excitement. She couldn't wait to come home tomorrow night. Maybe she would find another envelope waiting for her.

Saturday morning, Cheri entered her mother's side entrance and saw a large Best Buy bag on the floor. She said in a loud voice, "Hi, Mom. I'm here."

Janice called back, "Hi, sweetie. I'm in the TV room."

Cheri walked through the kitchen, entered the TV room, and saw her mother cleaning Maestro's cage. The parrot spotted Cheri and immediately began bobbing its head and making sounds only a parrot could, saying, "Cheri here, Cheri here."

Cheri said, "Hey, Tweety. How's my girl?" She walked over to Maestro's cage, placed her hand inside, and watched Maestro climb onto it. Cheri brought her close to her face and used her thumb and index finger on her other hand to gently squeeze and pull the back of her neck. She said, "What do you say to people?"

The parrot responded, "Give me a treat, give me a treat."

Cheri bent down and took a "Parrot stick" out of the box beside the bird's cage. While doing this, she said, "I saw the Ring Cameras."

"I got one for the front door, one for the side door, one inside the garage, one for the kitchen, one for this room, and one for my bedroom. I got a price break for six or more."

"Well, that ought to cover everything. Do you know what your WI-FI password is?"

"I have no idea."

"It's on the side of your router. Where is that?"

"It's on the floor next to the TV stand."

Cheri walked over to the TV and saw the router on the floor. Using her phone, she took a picture of the password and said, "OK, Mom. Give me your phone. I'm going to download the Ring app and get everything set up." After placing the cameras around the house, Cheri showed her mother how to use the app on her phone to monitor the cameras. After familiarizing herself with the app, Janice said, "This is terrific! I feel so much safer with this. Thank you, Cheri."

"You're welcome, Mom."

"Let's go to Clyde's, and I'll buy you lunch. I'm so happy you did this for me."

LEXI AND ELLIOTT were leaving the cabin they rented at a small resort in Cobbs Creek, Virginia, fifty miles south of Washington. It was Elliott's idea to spend the weekend getting some alone time with Lexi. For her part, Lexi was thrilled at the idea of spending the weekend with her man and shacking up in a cabin with the Chesapeake Bay, a short drive away. The coming fall colors were just starting to make an appearance. Today, they were going to the small marina on the bay to rent a sailboat. Elliott had spent several summers at a summer camp growing up and learned to sail there. He hadn't been sailing since then, but sailing was like riding a bike. You don't forget. After signing way too many forms and paying for three hours, Elliott and Lexi walked down the dock and saw the boat Elliott had requested. It was a thirty-four-foot Wayfarer. Lexi looked at the boat and asked, "This is the boat you rented?"

Elliott said, "Yes, it certainly is. Go ahead and get in, and I'll get us out of here."

Lexi stepped onto the boat while Elliott untied it from the dock. After getting in, he pulled out two life jackets stored under the transom and gave one to Lexi. Lexi put it on and said, "I sure as hell hope we don't need these."

Smiling, Elliott said, "If we do, I'm going down with the ship."

"That's encouraging."

Elliott began showing Lexi the different parts of the boat and explaining how they worked. Then, he pulled on the start cord of the small outboard motor attached to the stern and started down the narrow channel that would take them to the bay. When the boat cleared the channel, the wind picked up dramatically. Elliott cut the engine and said, "Ok, Lex, come over here and put your hands on the tiller while I open the mainsail." Lexi did as she was told and watched Elliott untie the sail from the boom and start pulling a rope. The mainsail started climbing the mast, and Lexi could feel the power of the wind take hold of the boat. After the sail had reached the top of the mast, Elliott tied off the rope he was pulling and grabbed another one attached to the boom. He pulled the rope tight and let the wind fill the sail. He tied that rope off and returned to Lexi. He pointed to the tiller and said, "This steers the boat. Pull it towards you."As soon as she moved the tiller, the boat turned direction and accelerated. Thrilled at the power of the wind she felt, she exclaimed, "This is amazing, Elliott! I can't believe I'm doing this!"

"Pretty cool, huh?

For the next two hours, they sailed up and down the coast. Lexi gazed out across the water. The whitecaps in front and the autumn colors in the background took her breath away. She glanced at Elliott, who was managing the sails while she steered the boat, and thought, "How lucky am I? I love this man. I love him so much." Sunday morning, they were eating breakfast in the resort's rustic restaurant. Lexi said, "I don't want to go home. I really don't want to go back to work tomorrow."

"Me neither, but such is life. My boss is a real pain on Mondays. How about yours?"

"Janice is always the same. Every day is the same as the next for her." After a pause, she continued, "Although she was acting pretty weird last week."

"How so?"

"She seemed hyper. She seemed distracted. I think maybe her daughter is bugging her."

"Her daughter? What's up with her daughter?"

"She's getting divorced and keeps calling her at work."

"Does she talk to you about it? Does she talk to you about personal things?"

"Sometimes, she talks to me about personal stuff. I think she wishes I were her daughter."

"Well, enough about work. We still have the rest of the day before we have to go back. They have horse rentals here. Why don't we do that?"

"I don't know how to ride a horse."

"No problem. I'll teach you."

AT 12:30 in the afternoon, Olivia unloaded the four grocery bags she had brought into the house onto her kitchen table. Liam was at school, and Walt was at work. She decided that today marked the beginning of "Lucia's Italian Sauce." Finally, she was doing something for herself and not for someone else. After sorting the groceries, she entered the large pantry and took down her crab pot from the top shelf. Every family had a crab pot if they lived in the Washington-Baltimore area. Summer crab feasts with Maryland Blue Crabs from the Chesapeake Bay were a staple. Her pot had been passed down from her grandma to her mother, and now it was hers. Looking at it, she estimated it could hold enough for twenty-five jars of sauce. When she placed the pot on the stove, she heard a familiar voice: "Hi, Olivia. Sorry, I'm late." Ivey had let herself in and was walking toward the kitchen.

Olivia turned from the stove and said, "Thank God you're here. This is going to take more work than I thought."

'What do you need me to do?"

"Why don't you chop the garlic and onions, and I'll get these tomatoes pureed?"

An hour and a half later, Olivia and Ivey had a crab pot full of sauce simmering on the stovetop. Ivey said, "That smells fantastic."

Olivia said, "Sorry, Ivey. I'm going to have to kill you now that you know my recipe."

Ivey said, "Not so fast. I don't have the most important ingredient: you."

"Well, flattery will get you everywhere with me. Help me with these jars. Walt printed some labels Liam designed."

Olivia opened the dishwasher, took the Ball canning jars out, and placed them on the counter. She went to the little kitchen desk and took the printed labels to the jars. Ivey looked at the labels and said, "Lucia's Italian Sauce. The sauce your mother made." This label looks great. I didn't know Liam was such an artist. He did a really good job on these."

"I was surprised myself. Here, take these and stick them on the jars while I check the sauce."

After adding water to the pot, Olivia returned to help Ivey with the jars. When they finished, Olivia said, "Ok. That's it for now. The sauce has to simmer for the next four hours. Then, it needs to cool for another two hours before it's ready for the jars. Then I have to put them in the canning pot for an hour."

"Geez, Olivia. I had no idea it would take so much time and effort."

"Tell me about it. I hope people will buy them. If they don't, our families will be eating it for the next five years."

"You'll be fine. People will buy these up faster than a bullet leaving a gun."

Shortly after Ivey left, Liam came home from school, smelled the air, and said dejectedly, "Mom, we're not having lasagna again." He walked into the kitchen and said, "Wow, Mom. Look at all this stuff." Olivia was putting the jar tops together when he picked up one of them, admired it, and said, "These turned out great."

"You did a terrific job with the labels, Liam."

He walked over to the stove and looked into the pot. He said, "You sure made a lot of this, Mom. I hope somebody buys it."

A couple of hours later, Walt came home. He entered the kitchen and saw Liam looking at take-out menus. Olivia was at the stove when Walt said, "Honey, you've got quite a project going on here."

Olivia said, "Don't I know it. I've been at it since noon. Ivey came over to help me."

Noticing the jars on the kitchen table, Walt picked one up and said, "These look great. Good job, Liam." He turned to Olivia and said, "That's a lot of jars to fill. I hope people will buy them."

"Shut up, Walt."

Saturday morning at seven, Walt, Olivia, and Liam were setting up their stand at the Fairfax Farmer's Market. The market occupied most of the parking lot at the city's government center. About forty stands filled the lot, selling everything from locally produced goods like honey, hot sauce, produce, craft items, and more. Olivia's stand was in the middle of a long aisle, with a stand selling Kettle Corn on one side and one selling Jams and jelly on the other. Liam had made a sign that was an enlarged copy of the jar labels, which he placed in front of the stand. While Olivia was putting the jars on a red and white checkerboard tablecloth, Walt was walking around the market to see if anybody else was selling something similar to Lucia's. Not finding any competitors, Walt set his sights on seeing if Mister B's was here. He wanted to buy some more hot sauce.

Olivia looked at her watch, wondering if anyone was going to buy a jar. It was Ten-thirty, and she hadn't sold anything. She turned to

Walt and said, "I don't know about this. Plenty of people are walking by, but that's all they do."

Walt said, "I know. Doesn't look promising. What if you lower the price?"

"I already priced it really low. I have to make some money."

Liam was sitting on a box at the back of the stall when he said, "I have an idea, Mom. Why don't you let people taste it?" He pointed to the jam and jelly stand next to them and continued, " See, they have their jars open, and they have those little spoons."

Walt and Olivia turned and looked at Liam. Olivia said, "Well, that's something to try."

Liam got up and turned to the woman at the jelly stand, asking, "Can we use some of your spoons?"

The woman said, "Of course you can, young man." She reached into the box of spoons next to her samples and gave Liam a handful."

Olivia, watching this, said, "Thank you. This is my first time coming to one of these. My name is Olivia."

"Hi. Olivia. My name is Betty. You'll do fine. It's only ten-thirty. It starts picking up in about an hour."

"I hope so. Thank you again."

Olivia turned and saw Walt opening one of the sauce jars while Liam placed a small pile of spoons on the table. All three of them went back to sitting in their chairs. Several minutes later, a young couple stopped at the booth. They both took a spoon and dipped it into the jar. The woman said to Olivia, "This tastes really good. Did you make this?"

Shooting up from her chair, Olivia said, "Yes, I did. It's a variation of my mother's recipe. This is my first time here."

The woman said, "Well, I need to have this for dinner tonight. Can I get two jars?"

SIMON ENTERED his boss's office, carrying a thick manila folder. Holding it up, he said, "Here's everything you wanted about Walt Ingram. Our head of security used to be a detective in New York. He put this together."

Sitting at his desk, Noah took the folder, opened it, and began thumbing through the pages. One page caught his attention. He said, "I see Mister Ingram likes to go to the MGM casino over in Oxen Hill. He's been there three times in the last month."

Simon replied, "Yeah, but his player card shows he spends all of his time at the slots. His wife, Olivia, is the same."

"I see that. Small-time stuff. He only goes down a hundred or so. I see a couple of decent wins, but he gives a lot of that back."

"He gets a fair amount of comps from the casino. A concert here, a buffet there. Pretty average stuff."

Noah put down the folder and said, "I have an idea. This is what I want you to do."

A WEEK LATER, Olivia was going through the mail when she saw an envelope from the MGM casino, which she and Walt liked to visit. It was addressed to Walt. "Probably another buffet," She thought. She pulled out the contents of the envelope and noticed something unusual. It was a black MGM debit card with Walt's name stuck to a letter. The letter congratulated Walt for winning a slot tournament and said the card had a thousand-dollar balance and could be used for anything in the casino. Later that evening, when Walt came home from work. Olivia handed him the letter he had received from MGM. Walt said, "I don't remember being in a slot tournament. When was I in a slot tournament?"

Olivia said, "Who cares? There's a thousand dollars on that card. Our last visit there emptied our gambling fund."

"Tell me about it. That free dinner at their new steakhouse was pretty expensive."

"Let's go Saturday. We can go early and beat the buffet crowd."

MONDAY MORNING, Walt entered his office and saw Ellie sitting at her desk, pecking away at her computer keyboard. She looked up and said, "Hey, Walt. How was your weekend?"

Walt replied, "Not so good. MGM clipped me for six hundred bucks."

"Geeze, Walt. That's why I don't gamble."

"Well, it wasn't that bad. I had a thousand-dollar comp card, so I lost their money."

"Losing is losing, Walt."

An hour later, Walt hung up his phone after talking to one of the engineers at Warner Systems. Warner had been bombarding him with emails about getting a contract variation for the missile they were selling to the Air Force, and now they were calling him on the phone. Walt gave Warner a six-month extension but remained committed to the contract details. Two days later, he walked across the parking lot at work to head home. He got into his car, turned the key, and heard the engine crank but not start. Walt tried this several times without success. He began cursing and banging his hands on the steering wheel. After he calmed down, he dejectedly picked up his phone and called AAA. The next morning, Walt went through the same routine as the last time his car broke down. He called Robers and explained what happened when he tried to start his car. He hung up and anxiously waited for a return call about the cost this time. An hour later, he received the dreaded news from Clay. Clay informed him that the fuel was contaminated. He couldn't determine the contaminant, but the fuel pump needed to be replaced. The fuel line and engine would also have to be flushed. Clay shocked Walt by telling him the estimated cost. He said Walt's car should be ready late tomorrow afternoon, just before Robers closed. The next day, Ellie gave Walt a ride to Robers. Robers wasn't out of the way for Ellie, and she felt bad for Walt. She knew how strapped for money he was. Walt entered Robers, approached the customer counter, and told the attractive customer representative he was there to pick up his car. She replied, "Hello, Mr. Ingram. Let me grab your paperwork." She left the counter and retrieved Walt's paperwork from a file holder attached to the wall. Returning to the counter, she handed Walt his bill and said, "There you go, Mister Ingram." Walt looked at the bill, dreading what he was about to pay, and noticed the zeroes on the 'Amount Due" column. His eyes widened, and he said, "This shows zero for what I owe. What's with that?"

"You pre-paid Mister Ingram. Do you see the payment at the top of the bill?"

Walt looked at the bill again, saw the payment, and asked, "How was this paid? I didn't pay this. Not that I'm complaining or anything."

"The last four digits of the card you used are shown next to the payment amount."

Walt looked at the card numbers. After a moment, he pulled out his wallet to check his credit cards. None of them matched the numbers on the bill. He returned the cards to his wallet and noticed the black MGM card in another slot. He took it out, looked at the numbers, and almost dropped his wallet. The numbers on the MGM card matched those on the bill. Walt drove home in a daze. "That card could only be used in the casino," he thought. "Besides, he and Olivia had used up most of the thousand dollars on it at the casino." Walt knew he hadn't used the card to pre-pay his bill. He couldn't. So, who did, and how did they do it? More importantly, why? When he got home, he told Olivia what happened at Robers. She asked, "How can a casino comp card be used to buy other things?"

"I don't know. Maybe it's not a comp card. Maybe you CAN use it for other things."

"No way. That's the casino's money. They don't want you spending it anywhere but there."

"I'm going to call the casino. They should have some answers." Walt took his phone and called the customer service number on the back of the card. After a couple of rings, his call was answered.

A female voice answered, "Visa Card services. This is Livia. How may I help you?"

"Hello, Livia. My name is Walt Ingram. Did you say Visa card services? Is this MGM Casino? I'm calling about my Player's Card. Sorry. I mean, debit card, credit card, or whatever the hell this card is."

"This is card services, not a casino. Can you provide me with the card number, sir?"

Walt gave her the number, and then she asked for the last four digits of his Social Security number and his mailing address. After several moments, the service representative said, "I'm sorry, Mr. Ingram. The information you gave me doesn't match our records. Are you sure you have the correct information?"

Walt repeated the same information.

"I'm sorry. That information does not match our records."

"I'm confused. I received this card in the mail, it's an MGM casino card. It says so on the card, but someone used it to pay for my car repairs. You can only use these cards in the casino. How is that possible?"

"Our records indicate that it's a credit card, Mr. Ingram. What you have is a vanity card. It's a new product we offer. Customers can use personal photos or designs for their cards. You can customize your card to look any way you prefer."

"I didn't apply for this card. I have enough of them already. Can you tell me what the balance is?"

"The card has no balance due.

Walt hung up without saying anything. He turned to Olivia, standing next to him, and said, "I don't know what the hell is going on here."

"I have an idea. Walt, give me the card."

Olivia took the card and entered their tiny home office. She turned on the computer on the card table, which served as a desk, and typed in the website for Ball Canning Jars. She selected a package of twenty-four and placed it in her cart. She used the card to finalize the sale. They both looked at the screen and then at each other. The card had been accepted.

Walt said, "What the hell? That's a legitimate credit card."

He took his player card from his wallet and called the casino's Players Club. After talking to a representative, he said to Olivia, "They don't give out credit cards."

Three days later, Walt was in a Home Depot looking for sheet metal screws. He noticed the patio furniture was on sale and decided to take a look. Not that he could afford any of it, but he wished he could. Buying patio furniture in the fall was like buying Christmas decorations the day after Christmas. They wouldn't get any cheaper. He was sitting in a patio chair in front of an umbrella table when a man in a brown sweater sat down in one of the chairs across from Walt. He laid a large manila envelope on the table and said, "Hi, Walt. Thinking of buying some patio furniture?"

Walt said, "Thinking about it. I'm sorry, do I know you?"

Simon replied, "We haven't met. We're meeting now. You know my boss, though. He works at Warner Systems. You know Warner, Right?"

"Warner? Who are you? What do you have to do with Warner? Why are you talking to me?"

"That's a lot of questions. You and my boss are having a disagreement over the Spear Missile System. You know about that, don't you? Six miles an hour. Does that ring a bell?"

"Listen, I don't know who you are or why you're here, but if your boss has any issues, this is not the place to discuss them."

"I'll get to the point, Walt. Warner needs you to forget the contract extension and just give us the variance. It's only six miles. Quit being an asshole."

"I've made the Air Force's position very clear. You coming here is a waste of time and pretty weird if you ask me."

"Not a waste of time at all."

Simon opened the envelope he had brought, took out three sheets of paper, and gave them to Walt.

"Those are your credit card statements for the past three months."

Walt picked up the papers and glanced at the top of the first page. It showed his name along with an address he didn't recognize. Scanning down the list of transactions, he noticed nothing but cash advances. These advances were from an ATM located inside the MGM Casino. He turned to the next page and found the same thing. At the bottom of the third page, he saw the payment to Robers."

Walt angrily said, "What is this? What the hell is going on here? Damn it! Who are you!"

Simon calmly said, "Walt, it seems you have a gambling problem. It's a pretty bad one, as you can see. Just take a look at that card balance. How are you ever going to pay that down on your salary?"

Walt, seeing the balance due, said nothing.

"Walt, I don't need to remind you of the Air Force's policy regarding security clearances. Employees with gambling issues are considered at risk for interference from bad actors aiming to harm the United States. You can, correction, you will lose your clearance over those casino cash advances. I don't need to explain what that means for your job."

Walt said, "This is bogus. No way anybody would believe this. Nice try, asshole."

Simon pulled another sheet from the envelope, passed it to Walt, and said, "That's a copy of your most recent credit report. It's real. You can check it."

Walt looked at the report and said, "I can't believe this. How did you change my credit report? Nobody's going to believe this either."

Simon returned to the envelope, took another sheet, and passed it to Walt. He said, "That's a letter to the Air Force Inspector General. Do you really want to risk that letter being sent?"

Walt looked at the letter and said, "I don't know why you think any of this is going to get you something from me. You obviously put a lot of energy into this, but it won't work. Besides, I'm not the only one who decides what goes in or out of a contract.

"Walt, we know you're the lead on this. No one in your department is going to object to the variance." Simon reached into the envelope, pulled out a stack of hundred-dollar bills halfway out so Walt could see it, and said, "Walt, Warner understands you're having some financial issues at home. We can help you out with those. We help you; you help us. What's the harm?"

With that, Simon got up and left. Walt opened the envelope and looked inside. He saw the money and thought, "I've heard about this kind of thing. People being caught in bribery schemes. I should write my own letter to the Inspector General." He looked at the money again, picked up the envelope, and left. He got in his car and sat there for a few minutes in thought. He picked up the envelope from the passenger seat, looked at the money, and thought about how it would help with the bills dragging him down. He also thought about the contract variance. That guy was right. I do have the final say. Besides, maybe I am being a dick. Six miles is not that much. If you take in atmospheric conditions while the missile is in flight, it's nothing. Maybe he was mad about his and Olivia's financial situation, and he was letting it affect his work. He put the envelope down and drove home.

JANICE ENJOYED her time at work, glancing at her phone to see
live images from her ring cameras. She finally understood how
Maestro escaped her cage while she was away—clever girl. But the
novelty of the cameras wore off after a couple of weeks, and she
stopped looking at them during work. Her routine was to view
what the cameras had recorded during the day, fast-forwarded,
before she pulled into her garage after work. Some days, she even
forgot to do that. This was the case one night after a particularly
rough day at work. The bank's accounting department had an
issue with its software for managing abandoned accounts that day.
The software engineers took the whole morning to fix the problem, so everybody in her department was behind in getting their
reports ready for the end of the month. Janice closed the garage
door, entered her house, and heard Maestro welcoming her home.
She smiled, reached into the refrigerator, and took some lettuce for
the bird. She shut the door and screamed. On the counter next to
the fridge was another envelope and a roll of red masking tape. She
dove into her purse, took out her phone, and viewed the day's
recordings. She viewed the entire day without seeing anyone enter
her house. She viewed it again and saw the same thing. Watching a
third time, she noticed something. She saw Maestro outside her
cage for most of the morning, and then she suddenly was in her
cage as if by magic. She continued watching and saw Maestro
escape her cage for what seemed like the second time that day.
Janice didn't understand at first but soon realized her cameras had
been turned off and then back on. She knew she didn't turn them
off; why would she? Then it dawned on her; Cheri had taken a
picture of her WI-FI password while setting up the cameras. When
the intruder came the first time, he probably did the same.Janice
returned to the envelope and opened it. She saw another stack of
money, but she also saw a note inside. She took out the note and
read it.

· · ·

JANICE, I am very sorry to disturb you like this, but entering your home was the safest way for me to communicate with you and also leave a large amount of money unattended. I need your help to further my plans. The money I left you is a small portion of what you can have if you decide to help me. If not, the cash is yours to keep. If you do decide to help me, take the tape and place an X on your car's rear bumper when you park at the metro station tomorrow. If I see the X, check your mailbox when you come home.

Janice put down the letter and went to sit at the small kitchen table against the wall. She reread the letter and decided to call her daughter. She picked up her phone and then put it down. She thought, "I don't know what this is all about, and it's crazy as hell, but I am ten thousand dollars richer. Besides, I don't even know what whoever is leaving this money wants me to do." Suddenly, she became intrigued. Whatever this was about, it was pretty exciting. She reread the letter again, got up, and picked up the roll of tape. She decided to see where this was going to go. The next day, Janice parked at the station, just like every other day, going to work. She got out with the tape and looked around, feeling a mix of fear and excitement. She tore the tape into two small strips and placed an X on her rear bumper. She looked around again, looking for the person entering her house. After a moment, she walked to the train and tried to concentrate on the workday ahead of her. Throughout the day, Janice kept looking at the video from her cameras. The only camera she looked at was the one on her front door with a view of her mailbox. Her habit of looking at her phone every half-hour changed to looking at the clock. At four-thirty, she couldn't wait any longer. Feigning an upset stomach, she left to go home. As the metro train took Janice to her parked car, she viewed the camera's recordings that day on fast-forward. She saw Maestro switch positions and knew the cameras had been turned off. When she pulled into her driveway, Janice stopped and got out. She opened her mailbox and saw the day's mail. Pulling it out and thumbing through it, she saw an envelope that looked identical to the ones left in her kitchen. She raced into her house, not bothering to put her car in the garage. Closing her front door, she put the stack of mail on a small table in the foyer and opened the envelope.

It read, "Wear the red scarf you have and go to work one hour early tomorrow."

Janice walked into her TV room and sat down. She thought, "Is this some kind of joke someone is playing on me?" How does he know I have a red scarf? Then it hit her: "Is he following me?" "He knows where I live, where I park, and where I work. He's been inside my house and knows my Wi-Fi password. Most people would be terrified at the idea of some stranger knowing so much about them and being in their homes while they weren't there. Not Janice. She had never felt so alive and excited.

⸻

OLIVIA WAS in her kitchen with Ivey, making her third batch of sauce this week. Every time she took her sauce to the Farmer's market, it was sold out before noon. Word spread, and people started lining up to purchase her sauce as soon as she arrived. Olivia told Ivey, "You know, I was in Gleason's yesterday getting the oregano I use for the sauce, and Bob Gleason asked me if I wanted to sell my sauce in his store." Gleason's was a small neighborhood grocery store that sold organic foods and locally made specialty products.

"That's great, Olivia!"

"I'm tired of going to the Farmer's market every other weekend. Selling this in a store would be much easier, and I think we can sell more."

"We?"

"Ivey, I couldn't do this without you. I think we make a good team."

"Well, thanks, Olivia. I like being a part of this. Gleason's sounds like a good thing. Why don't we take this last batch and put it in the store?"

"That's what I was thinking. Let's take ten jars and see what happens." Five days later, Bob Gleason called to say the sauce was sold out and asked if she could bring more. It wasn't long before Olivia stopped going to the Farmer's market, and she and Ivey spent all their efforts keeping their sauce on Gleason's shelves. One day, Olivia and Ivey were at Gleason's, bringing more sauce jars, when Bob approached them and said, "Thanks for bringing those. I have some good news. We're opening a new store next month in Bethesda, and I want to stock your sauce."

Olivia and Ivey looked at each other and said nothing.

Bob said, "Well, that's not the reaction expected."

Olivia said, "Bob, that's great you're opening a new store, but Ivey and I can barely keep up with what you're selling here. We wouldn't be able to make enough for another store."

Bob asked, "Have you thought about using a co-packer to make your sauce?"

Ivey replied, "What's a co-packer?"

Bob said, "Co-packer is short for Contract Packer. You agree on a contract, and they will take your recipe and instructions and make the sauce for you. They even provide the ingredients. Co-packers can make, bottle, and label as much as you want. It's very common. A lot of the stuff you see on shelves comes from a co-packer." He picked a can of tomatoes off the shelf and showed it to

Olivia and Ivey. He said, "You see here on the label, it says,'
Produced for Nester Foods.' That means somebody made this for
Nestor Foods.'

Olivia asked, "So ours would say, "Produced for Lucia's?"

"Exactly."

"Do you know any co-packers we could talk to?"

"Sure. Let's go to my office, and I'll give you a couple I know do a
good job and don't cost an arm and a leg."

TWO MONTHS after Simon met Walt at Home Depot, he sat in
Noah's office, reviewing a stack of papers. Noah said, "The Secret
Service is requesting some security upgrades for Air Force One.
They have an identical copy of the plane, so we're bidding on two.
The Air Force also wants to upgrade the aircraft's communications
system. This is a great opportunity for us, but there's a problem:
we're competing against Boeing and Lockheed. I'm not too
concerned about Lockheed. They always bid high for contracts,
they don't have the same tech capabilities as Boeing and us."

Simon said, "Boeing's a bitch to go up against. We've lost the last
two to them."

"I need you to get in touch with Walt Ingram. He helped us with
that variance for the Spear Missile contract. If he can get us a copy
of Boeing's bid, that could give us an edge."

"I don't think that's going to be an issue. You should've seen him
when I cornered him at Home Depot."

Noah said, "Don't threaten him so much this time. Make him
comfortable and give him double the money he got last time.
Money makes everything feel better."

SATURDAY MORNING, Walt was setting up the stall at the Farmer's market with Liam. Olivia was focused on finding a suitable co-packer, but both parents believed Liam could gain first-hand experience in the business world by selling Lucia's sauce at the market. Liam loved buying his own things with the money he earned. The only requirement was that he had to save twenty-five percent. When Liam left to retrieve another box of sauce from the car, Simon approached Walt. Walt looked up from what he was doing and said, "What are you doing here? I did what you asked. Angrily, he continued, "Get the hell out of here. My son is here."

"Calm down. If your son comes back, I'll buy some sauce and leave. I came by to show you something in case you're having second thoughts about helping us. Simon took his phone from his back pocket, started a video, and pointed the screen at Walt. Walt looked at the screen and saw himself and Simon sitting at the umbrella table at the Home Depot. Walt hadn't noticed the person standing off to the side, looking at their phone with the camera lens pointing at him.

"I like the parts where I show you the money, and you leave with the envelope."

I brought you some money today. I put it under your car seat. Besides the cash, they're instructions for what we need this time. I'm sure you're aware of the Air Force One upgrades."

When Simon left, Walt was surprised by how he felt. He felt calm and thought about the money under his car seat. He didn't know what Simon's instructions were, and he didn't care. As he thought more about the money, he grew concerned. "What am I going to do with this cash? I can't just deposit it in the joint account. Olivia would be all over me in a second." Suddenly, he had an idea. He would go to the casino, exchange the cash for chips, and play blackjack. After a few hands, he would cash in the chips for a casino check made out to him. Soon, he realized this plan wouldn't work. All he was doing was converting the cash into a check; he wasn't hiding anything. Worse, the casino would have a record of his transactions for his Players Club account. His thoughts were interrupted when Liam returned with a fresh supply of sauce for the stall.

———

JANICE ARRIVED at the top of the escalator at the metro station an hour early, as instructed, wearing her red scarf. She noticed a boy, about ten, selling newspapers, just like every morning. This time, however, a homeless man was a few yards away from the paper boy, holding a sign asking for money. Janice reflected on the irony of one trying to make money while the other was asking for it to be given. The fact that it was a grown man asking for a handout and a small boy earning his own money heightened the irony. She saw the boy look at her with a surprised expression. He left his papers behind and approached her. Reaching into his back pocket, he pulled out an envelope that looked like the others. He handed it to her and said, "I'm supposed to give this to you."

Janice took the envelope and said, "Who gave this to you?"

The boy replied with a huge smile, "Some man paid me to give this to you. I can sell papers all week and not make that much."

"What did he look like?"

"He had black hair and glasses. Sorry, I have to get back to my papers before anyone steals them." With that, the boy left Janice standing, holding the envelope. She didn't notice the man with black hair and glasses standing several yards away, pretending to read one of the boy's newspapers and watching the transaction.

When Janice started walking to work, he took off his glasses, threw them in the trash, and walked in the other direction. When she arrived, none of her staff were in the office. She closed her office door and sat down at her desk. She pulled the envelope from her purse and read the note inside.

"Take the memory card and insert it into your computer. Wait for the blinking light to stop, remove it, and flush it down the toilet."

She looked inside the envelope and saw a black memory card. She placed the card on her desk and thought, "I don't want to do this. It's not what I expected." Then she realized she wasn't sure what she had expected. She enjoyed the money and the thrill, but now she felt uncertain. She contemplated what would happen if she kept the money and didn't follow through on her end. Then, she remembered how it all started: Someone had entered her house, obtained her Wi-Fi password, interfered with the Ring cameras, and followed her without her knowledge. "Hell, they're probably still following me," she said aloud. She picked up the memory card and tapped it on her desk several times, considering what she wanted to do. After a moment, she inserted the card into her computer, waited for the light to stop flashing, took it out, and headed for the restroom.

Walking back to her office, she checked the time and decided to go downstairs to grab a Grande Mocha from Starbucks before the line started to form. Sitting at a table, she noticed Lexi in the line that had formed since her arrival. She waved, and Lexi returned the gesture. After getting her drink, Lexi joined Janice at the table and said, "I thought I was the early bird this morning."

Janice said, "I had something I needed to get done before our staff meeting this morning."

"Everything ok? You seem a little down."

Janice said, "My daughter and her soon-to-be ex want me to referee their divorce. They both keep calling me. I'm also worried about catching up with our money transfers after that accounting software glitch."

"Oh, I'm sure it'll be fine. By the way, did you hear Martha is pregnant?"

IT WAS Sunday evening at the usual time when Elliott's ringtone started playing. He quickly answered, saying, "Auntie, I have some news about Mom and Dad."

Excitedly, Farah asked, "What? What have you heard?"

I met a guy who works at Homeland Security at a government software development conference in Baltimore. I told him about my parents, and he wanted to help me out. He downloaded and sent me the list of employees from the Immigration and Naturalization Department who were there around the time Mom and Dad applied for their visas. There were way too many employees for it to be of any use, so I emailed him asking if any of those employees would have been involved with visas and if he could get me a list. I got it on Friday and spent the whole weekend writing code for a program that'll take the names and search the internet for their email address if there are any. Once I get those, I can send a bulk email asking them for information about Mom and Dad. I'm tempted to ask in the email why they were so intent on killing my parents by denying them a visa."

"You don't know if they're dead."

"Auntie, how long have we been trying to find them? After all this time, they would have figured out a way to contact us."

"I know. Sometimes, not hearing anything gives me hope, but other times, I want closure."

"I want more than closure, Auntie. I want accountability. They're not getting away with killing my parents and not having to answer for it."

Changing the subject, Farah said, "So, how are you and Lexi getting along?"

Sighing, Elliott responded, "She's great, Auntie. But I think she might be getting a little tense with me."

"Oh?"

"I've been spending a lot of my free time working on this thing for my new client. It's more than just writing code. I have to manage some elements that go with the code."

"Elliott, there are much more important things than working for something that will be gone as soon as you finish it. Friends and family will always be with you."

"It's not like that. She understands how important this client is to me and the money I'm making. I don't want to work for the government the rest of my life. My problem is that Lexi wants to spend any free time returning to that cabin we rented."

"Cabin? What cabin? Tell me about this cabin."

"I have to go, Auntie."

SEVERAL WEEKS after her conversation with Bob Gleason, Olivia was inspecting a jar of sauce at Iverson Foods. Iverson was on the list of co-packers Bob had provided her, and she had chosen them to produce, bottle, and distribute her sauce. She opted for Iverson because they distribute her sauce directly to stores rather than storing cases of sauce in her garage. When Olivia and Ivey first visited Iverson, she was amazed by what they saw. They met Derek Anderson, Iverson's General Manager, who gave them a tour of the facility. The tour began at the receiving area, where produce and ingredients are brought into the facility. "These are sorted by customer," Derek explained. He then showed them the production area where the sauce would be made. Continuing deeper into the facility, they arrived at the packaging area, where the sauce was poured into jars with precise amounts in each one. After this, a machine vacuum seals the jars and twists the lids on. The jars are then sent to another machine that places the labels. The final step involves the jars being placed into cardboard cases, which are then set onto a conveyor belt that leads into a large warehouse, where they are taken to the customer's storage area.Olivia's inspection was interrupted when her ringtone began playing. She looked at the caller ID, picked up, and said, "Hi, Archie. What's up?" Archie Colson worked at T.A.B.S., Tax and Bookkeeping Solutions. T.A.B.S. was another suggestion from Bob Gleason.

Archie replied, "I have your 'sole proprietorship' documents ready for your signature.

Olivia smiled and asked, "So Lucia's is a real company now?"

"Well, it's not a corporation. It's a sole proprietorship. You're personally responsible for any taxes and liability. If Lucia's were a corporation, you wouldn't have any personal liability. You'd be an officer of the corporation, but your personal assets wouldn't be exposed. Once you get bigger, you should convert Lucia's to a corporation."

"Well, let's hope I need those corporate documents sooner rather than later. I'll stop by around three if that's okay."

"No problem. I'll see you then."

A little after three, Olivia was sitting in Archie's office, signing the documents he had for her. After she finished, she said, My partner, Ivey, told me I have to have some kind of special tax form for my business. Is that something you can help me with?"

"Your partner is correct. It's not a complicated form. As much as I would like some extra business, you can fill it out and file it yourself. I recommend you get some small business accounting software to keep track of your business finances. It's very easy to use."

"What do you recommend?"

"I'll email you a link to this company we recommend for our clients. When your business grows enough to need our services, we can import your company information into our software."

"Thanks, Archie. Now, I just have to find the time to use the software."

LATER THAT EVENING, Olivia, Walt, and Liam were having takeout for dinner for the third time that week. Olivia said, "I was at that accounting firm I told you about today to make Lucia's official. They told me to get this accounting software, but I'm not good with that kind of thing, and I don't know when I'm going to find time to use it."

Walt said, "Let me take a look at it. It couldn't be too hard. You're just selling sauce. It's not like you're a big company selling all kinds of things."

After dinner, Walt and Olivia were in their tiny home office, following the instructions to use the accounting software. Walt said, "This isn't hard at all. I can do this."

Olivia said, "Not hard for you, maybe. Tell you what, I'll take care of the sauce, and you take care of all of this accounting stuff."

Looking at the monitor, Walt said, "Sounds like a plan. Ok, it's asking for bank information. We should have a separate bank account for Lucia's.

"Yes. We definitely should."

"Let's use the same bank where we have Liam's college fund."

"You mean the one we haven't made any deposits to in the last four years. I even got a letter from them telling me they're going to close the account if we aren't using it."

"Well, I have an idea. We use the same bank. We can make transfers from Lucia's account directly into Liam's. We can set up automatic deposits for Liam. Lucia's can pay for Liam's college." Walt moved the mouse cursor to the bank field and typed in Carnegie National Bank.

TUESDAY AFTERNOON, Noah was in his office reviewing the specifications for the Air Force One contract. Given Walt's compliance with his last request, he felt confident that he would come through with providing Boeing's bid. Today, his thoughts shifted to something else: making some money for himself. Warner Systems used many subcontractors to fill its customers' orders. Like the Air Force, Warner sent out RFB's (requests for bids) to its suppliers for the goods and services Warner needed. The Air Force One project required a specialized digital radio switch made by two companies, Arinc and Astra Radio. Airinc was the larger of the two companies and had an office near Tinker Air Force Base, the Air Force's largest repair facility. Noah was on the phone speaking to Kyler Bradley, Astra's president, when he said, "Kyler, what do you think of that RFB we sent you last week?"

"It's a tall order, Noah. We can supply the switch, but its processing speed will be slightly slower than Airinc's. I'm not sure we can pass the sniff test with the Air Force's requirements. I don't think Warner will let us slide on that."

"You let me worry about Warner. I'm the one with the final say here. I can get the Air Force to change the contract requirements."

"Change the requirements? How can you do that?"

"Not a concern for you. I can do it, but I'll need some help."

"Help?"

"Yes, I need you to help me like the last time."

"Oh. Sorry, Noah, I haven't had my coffee this morning. Yeah, no problem. We can help you. I appreciate Warner's business. I also appreciate sticking it to Airinc."

They both laughed.

"Tell you what, I'll have Simon get in touch. Sound like a plan?"

"You bet, Noah. Thanks again."

Noah called Simon into his office after finishing his conversation with Kyler. He said, "Astra's on board. Get in touch with Kyler and work out the details. The price is double this time."

Simon asked. "Double? Why double?"

"Because we have to pay Walt."

"He's already been paid. I saw him at that farmer's market."

"I know. Tell him how much we appreciate his help, and we're putting him on the payroll. I want to make sure he's on our hook.

Giving him more money is like increasing the limit on a credit card. The bigger the balance, the bigger the minimum monthly payment."

———

WEDNESDAY MORNING, Lexi sat at her desk and logged into her computer. It was the end of the month, and she was preparing her report of abandoned accounts to be closed and their balances transferred to the state in which they were open. She had more accounts than usual this month and resigned herself to working late the rest of the week. She pulled up her first account and looked at the screen. The account holder was Edie Simmons, who had opened her account twenty-eight years ago. Lexi looked at the balance and sighed. She thought, "How sad. This money could be put to a lot better use than going to some state to be wasted on some, who knows what." She selected the state where the funds would be transferred and clicked on the account number. She saw the fields that concerned the state fill up the right side of her screen. She was getting ready to click on the transfer button when she noticed something bizarre. The dollar amount on the left side of her screen, which contained the bank's number, was a penny higher than what was being transferred to the state. She had never seen this before. After a moment, she thought this might have something to do with last week's accounting software problem. Before she could click the transfer button, she saw the bank's amount suddenly switch back to the state's amount. She clicked on the transfer button, and the transaction was accepted. After seeing this, she decided to get a report for this account. Usually, she would finish all of her transfers and run a batch report for Janice, but she was curious. She sent the report to her printer and looked at the amounts. They were the same. Lexi brought up another account and saw the same thing. She pushed her chair back to talk to her cubicle neighbor, Khloe.

"Khloe, I just had the weirdest thing happen when I tried to transfer an account. At first, the amounts were different by a penny. Before I could click the transfer button, the bank's amount switched and matched the states. Like a penny just disappeared."

"I'm having the same issue. Probably that software problem last week. I don't care. My job is to transfer accounts. As long as I can close the account, that's somebody else's problem. It's probably showing up on everybody's computer. You should talk to Janice."

Lexi tapped on Janice's office door frame and said, "Hey, Janice, I'm having some kind of issue when I try to close an account."

Janice said, Yes, I know. Marla came to me and told me about it. Don't worry. As long as we can close the accounts, it's not our concern. We need to plow ahead and finish this month's accounts."

Several hours later, Lexi pulled up another account to close. She didn't feel bad about this one. It was a custodial account and had a very low balance. She figured whoever opened it deposited the minimum required to open an account, made a few deposits, and then withdrew them. She clicked the button to select the state, and suddenly, her screen went blank. After a few seconds, her screen came back on, but the account she was working on wasn't there. She selected a list display of all her accounts to close and didn't see the account she was working on. After a moment, she thought, "This is pissing me off. I want to see Elliott tonight, and this damn thing is slowing me down." An hour later, she picked up her phone and called Elliott. When he answered, she said, "Hi, dearest, I'm going to be late. This thing at work came up, so why don't you order some take-out, and I'll be there in an hour."

"No problem. Sorry about work. I'll see you when I see you."

True to her word, Lexi parked her car in the parking lot of Elliott's Hi-Rise. She rode the elevator and got off on his floor. She took two steps and saw Serene leaving Elliott's apartment. She watched her walk to her door and enter her apartment. Confused, she knocked on Elliott's door and let herself in. She heard Elliott clattering in the kitchen and said, "Hey, Elliott. I'm here."

"I'm in the kitchen."

She walked to the kitchen and saw him placing their take-out in the microwave. "Was that your neighbor I saw coming out of your place?"

"That's Serene. Pain in the ass. She keeps coming over with lame excuses to see me."

"She's very pretty."

"Forget it, Lex. I went out with her one time, and now she keeps angling for me to ask her out again. This time, she wanted me to show her how to program her new thermostat. Enough about her. Let's eat." After their meal, they sat on the couch, and Elliott said, "You know what? I have something I want to show you."

"Lexi smiled and said, "I bet I know what it is."

SATURDAY AFTERNOON, Elliott was in the back office of Delta Liquor, showing the owner, Titus Rollins, and his daughter, Lana, how to use the inventory software he had customized. Although Elliott didn't design the software himself, he tailored a generic, off-the-shelf product to their needs. Titus was fifty-two and significantly overweight, with a head that had seen far more hair than what was currently present. Lana was thirty-two and getting close to the overweight part of the spectrum, but her striking good looks diverted attention from her weight. She removed her wedding ring whenever Elliott visited to show his progress with the software and get Titus and Lana's feedback. For his part, Elliott visited the liquor store a couple of more times than necessary. He couldn't get enough of Lana's perfume. However, this Saturday was strictly business. He was deleting Delta's old inventory system and replacing it with his own. Once that was accomplished, Elliott planned to leave only after receiving a check. This had become his new policy after Logan's took an unacceptably long time to pay him. He didn't want to take the money and run with Delta, so he decided to stop by and check on things every once in a while. Saturday evenings were usually spent with Lexi at home, making dinner and Elliott choosing the movie. Elliott loved playing with Charcoal. His apartment didn't allow dogs, and he was thinking about moving to a place that did. Moving sounded like a great idea. This Saturday, however, he was flipping the script. Lexi was coming over for Chinese takeout, and then they were going to an art gallery that was showing the work of an artist Lexi liked. Elliott dreaded spending a perfectly good Saturday night looking at paintings where it was obvious to Elliott that the "Artist" went to Home Depot, bought some paint and a big brush, splattered the canvas, signed their name, and charged a million dollars to some idiot with too much money. Tonight, he figured the sacrifice was worth it. Elliott was stopping Serene from ever bothering him again, and Lexi was all in. No more towels covering the door crack and AirPods watching TV.

At almost six, Lexi began loudly knocking on Elliott's apartment door. She raised her voice and said, "Elliott, my darling. I decided to come by early. I brought Charcoal with me."

Elliott opened the door. Raising his voice, he said, "Charcoal!" Lowering himself to one knee, he took Charcoal's head in his hands and said, "How's my best buddy?"

He rose and hugged Lexi, saying, "I'm glad you're early, love of my life. I hate it when we're not together. He released Lexi, made a gesture for her and Charcoal to enter the apartment, and said,

"You're going to love the dinner I made for you." Just before he closed his door, he looked down the hall and saw the crack in Serene's door disappear.

FRIDAY AFTERNOON, Walt was getting ready to leave work early when he received a text from another number he didn't recognize. "Damn that asshole, Simon, he said under his breath. The text told him to look inside his trunk when he got to his car. Another text quickly followed. This one said, "We need you to move faster on that thing I told you about when I saw you at that market."

Walt sighed and put his phone back in his pocket.

He thought, "This is getting out of hand. How did that asshole get inside my trunk?" Thinking further, he said to himself, "Probably the same way he screwed up my fuel pump." Walt knew he was dragging his feet getting Boeing's bid to Warner. Approving a variance on a contract was one thing; passing confidential information to a rival bidder was next-level bad. Taking money for it was next-level jail time. When he got to his car in the parking lot, he looked around and opened the trunk. Inside was yet another overstuffed envelope. He didn't bother to look inside it. He tossed it back in the trunk and covered it with his golf club bag. He closed the trunk and got in. Walt thought about his situation. "What am I going to do with this cash? I can't hide it forever in my workbench drawer in the basement. I thought I had a great plan with the casino until it wasn't. Suddenly, he had an idea: Olivia's business was doing really well. She had just signed a deal with Whole Foods to put Lucia's in six stores in the Baltimore and Virginia suburbs, and the money was pouring in. He was managing the books while Olivia and Ivey concentrated on sales. He said out loud, "I know what I can do. I'll create a separate income category in the accounting software. I'll call it "Farmer's sales." Then, I'll create an expense category and call it "advertising." I'll make deposits to the income category, then make fake invoices and put them in the expense category. The fake invoices can come from a company that I set up." Walt Googled "How to set up a company" and saw the screen fill with companies offering their services. He chose one and began the process. He'd call it "College Fund Inc." After he'd created his company, Walt sat back and contemplated his situation. He had to figure out a way to get the Boeing bid to that asshole Simon. He couldn't email it; that was obvious, or was it? He said out loud, "I can create a fake email account and call it 'boeing.services@gmail.com,' email the bid to it, and then forward it to asshole." He knew Simon wouldn't give him his email address, but that wasn't a problem. He knew how to get it. Walt was jarred out of his thoughts when he heard Olivia's voice behind him.

"Who are you talking to, Walt?"

Walt whirled around his chair and said, "Nobody. Just thinking out loud."

"Who's an asshole?"

"Just some guy at work."

Olivia said, "Oh." Without saying anything else, she turned and walked away.

Walt was frozen. He thought, "How long has she been standing there? How much did she hear? Damn it!"

Two days later, Walt came to work early to email Simon. It wasn't that he didn't want anybody around; he just wanted to get it out of the way. He had a meeting with his boss that morning and needed time to prepare. He logged into his department's secure server, copied Boeing's bid, and attached it to the fake email address he created, forwarded it to Simon, and pressed send. "How easy was that?" He thought.

After work, Walt pulled into his driveway just as the rain started to fall. He cursed, knowing he would get wet. The garage was packed to the rafters with things Walt couldn't remember the last time he used. Only one car could fit, and that was Olivia's. As soon as he opened the door, the rain poured down heavily. When he stepped out, he heard a horn from the car parked in front of his house. Then, he noticed the car flashing its lights. Walt didn't recognize the vehicle; it wasn't one of his neighbors'. He saw the driver's door open, and Simon got out. He gestured for Walt to get in the car. Taking a moment to think and being encouraged by the rain, Walt ran to Simon's car and got in. Getting in himself, Simon slammed the door, turned to Walt, and yelled, "What the hell? How did you get my email address? That's not how we do things!"

Walt yelled back, "Asshole! You've got a lot of balls coming to my house! How else was I supposed to get you the Boeing's bid? Mental telepathy? It's not like I can print a copy and walk out the door."

"We could have arranged something. If you're having a problem, we need to know."

"We, We, We. Just who is We, exactly? You keep saying we, but all I see is you."

"As long as you're getting paid, it's no concern of yours."

Walt calmed down and said, "Fine. But I need a better way to contact you and Mister We."

"You don't contact us. We, I contact you."

"Well, that's too bad because I have something you'll be very interested in."

Calming down himself, Simon asked, "And what would that be?"

"Besides Air Force One, the Navy is upgrading Marine One. The president's helicopter and the other two duplicates. It hasn't been announced. I can get the contract to bend in your direction."

"Bend?"

"Parts of the contract can require things that Warner has an advantage in. The contract can specify parts that only Warner has—parts you make and don't subcontract. Any other bidders will have to substitute and apply for variances. Guess who decides variances?"

Walt had Simon's undivided attention when he continued, "I want to be paid big-time for this. Not some puny ass cash in an envelope."

"Very good, Walt. I'm impressed. Didn't know you had it in you. Okay, I need to work on this. Can you get a copy of the Marine One requirements that the Navy is asking for?

"I can get those."

"When"?

"I need some time to figure it out. I'll let you know."

When Walt got out, Simon picked up his phone and called Noah. When he picked, Simon recounted his conversation with Walt. Noah said, "I think we landed a bigger fish than we thought."

AFTER LEXI MENTIONED EXPERIENCING the same issue with closing accounts as others in her department, Janice became alarmed. She was convinced it was related to the memory card she had inserted into her computer. With only two days left before she had to compile her department's reports and send the results to Accounting, she didn't want to wait that long. Instead, she compiled what had already been done to check for any issues.

Three hours later, Janice was reviewing the final report she had created. She looked over the totals, and everything matched correctly. Letting out a sigh of relief, she thought, "Whatever that memory card was about, it's not affecting me." Before closing the final report, she noticed something unusual: the report listing the accounts marked as abandoned included one that didn't appear in the closed accounts report. She moved her cursor to the account number and clicked. After a few seconds, the account information appeared. It was the custodial account Lexi had been working on earlier when it suddenly disappeared from her screen. She was surprised to see that the previously abandoned account was now active. She concluded that the account holder had likely generated some activity, such as a deposit or withdrawal, causing the account to no longer be considered abandoned. This was strange since such activity should have immediately removed the account from the abandoned list and shouldn't have shown up in her reports. She didn't mind; as long as her reports matched, the people in Accounting could sort it out. Before leaving the account information page, her curiosity got the best of her. She moved her cursor to the account balance button and clicked. "Oh my God," she said aloud. She was astonished by the amount of money in the account. Her curiosity grew when she saw this, so she clicked on the account holder's button. The screen displayed "Walt and Olivia Ingram, custodians for Liam Ingram."

SEVERAL DAYS after his conversation with Simon outside his house, Walt was driving around the Capital Beltway, thinking about how he would get Simon the initial draft of the Marine One contract so Warner could figure out what parts they could insert to gain an advantage over the other bidders. Walt did his best thinking while driving, and he was on his third lap. The contract was stored on a secure server to which Walt had access. The only problem was that a log was kept of anyone accessing the contract. At this stage of development, Walt would have no explanation for why his name would be on the access log. Then he realized he could use his office mate Ellie's password. The only problem with that is that if someone questioned Ellie, she would immediately know it was Walt. Not a problem. He was going to make too much money on this. Now, he had to figure out how to get her password.

Ellie always went to lunch with her partner, Fay O'Connell, who worked three floors above in the Logistics office at the same time each day. She would typically be away from her desk for about forty minutes. Walt knew that was more than enough time to get a copy of the contract proposal on a memory card. The real challenge was obtaining her password. Employees were required to change their passwords every sixty days. Walt updated his by adding a number in sequence at the end of the password each time a change was needed. He wondered if Ellie did the same. Thinking some more, He didn't want to wait for Ellie to leave for lunch and spend forty minutes searching her desk. He could stay late and wait for Ellie to leave for the day or come in early on the weekend, but he didn't write his password down on anything, and she probably didn't either. Walt figured he would try some social engineering.

The next day, Walt and Ellie returned to their office from a staff meeting that morning that went way too long. Walt was at the coffee maker on a small table in the office when he said, "Password changes are coming up, and I've run out of numbers."

Ellie asked, "What do you mean you ran out of numbers?"

Walt explained his system to Ellie. When he finished, Ellie said, "I let the computer auto-generate my password. That way, I don't have to deal with my new password being declined because it wasn't secure enough."

"I tried that once. The only problem with it is that if I want to work remotely, I can't remember the complex password the system generates for me."

"Don't tell anybody, but I take a picture of the password with my phone."

"What a great idea. Just don't let the Gestapo in security find out."

Ellie put a questioning look on her face and said, "Find out what?"

After Ellie told Walt how she remembered her password, he still had difficulty getting it. Ellie was glued to her phone, which never left her. He decided to do a bit more social engineering. An hour after he and Ellie had their password discussion, Walt sat at his desk and cursed, looking at his phone.

Sitting at her desk, Ellie asked, "What's wrong?"

"My phone died, and I can't find my charger. I need to check my bank balance."

She remembered Walt's constant talk of his financial difficulties and said, "Here, you can use mine."

Walt got up, took her phone, and returned to his desk. Pretending to log into his bank, he opened Ellie's photo album. He felt guilty about intruding on her personal life, but had no choice. The last password change occurred three weeks ago. He selected a date range for that period and started scrolling through the photos. After a few seconds, he found what he was looking for. Using the AirDrop feature on her iPhone, he sent a copy of the image to his phone. Then, covering his tracks, he opened her phone's web browser and logged into his bank account. If Ellie checked, she would see his bank's web address in her browser history. He got up and returned her phone, smiling on his way back to his desk.

Saturday afternoon, after Walt and Liam returned from the Farmer's market, Walt entered his office and logged into Ellie's computer, looking at his phone for the password. He was nervous beyond belief and kept listening for any sound outside the office. He was also anxious that Ellie's password wouldn't work. When he pressed the return key, he let out a sigh of relief when the screen filled with Ellie's home screen. Without wasting any time, he quickly navigated to the secure server that held what he was looking for. He found the folder that contained the Marine One contract and copied it to the memory card he had inserted after logging in. Once the light on the card stopped blinking, he removed it. Just as he did this, he froze. He heard footsteps coming towards him, getting louder with every step. He looked at Ellie's computer and then at the door. The footsteps were almost at his door. Panicking, he knew he didn't have time to log out. He reached for the screen button and turned the monitor off. He bolted to his desk. Ellie and a security guard came through the door just as he sat down. She said, What brings you in on a Saturday? I thought you and Liam sold your sauce on Saturdays." Before Walt could answer, the security guard said, I'll be outside the door when you're ready to leave. Ellie had a lower security clearance than Walt, so she had an escort after hours.

WALT SAID, trying to sound calm, "Things were a little slow at the Farmer's Market, so we decided to leave early. Lying, he said a little too quickly, "Olivia has her card club over, and I wanted to get out of the house." Rattling on, he said, "I need a hobby. I should probably be one of those guys who dress up in Civil War clothes and pretend to annihilate each other." He forced himself not to look at Ellie's computer. Beads of sweat on his brow began to form as he watched Ellie walk to her desk and sit down. Wanting to shout at her to get out, he asked, "What brings you here?"

Reaching into the bottom drawer of her desk, she replied, "I'm getting Fay's birthday present." She took a small box wrapped in gift paper from the drawer and placed it on her desk. She continued, "I didn't want to risk her finding it, so I kept it here." She got up and said, "That's it for me. I have a strict policy about coming in on a weekend. I don't." Walking out of the office, she said, "See you Monday. Have fun with whatever you're doing today." With that, she left. When he stopped hearing Ellie's and the security guard's footsteps, he leaped from his desk to log out of her computer. Ellie, walking to her car, thought, "Damn Walt. What the hell? You could have given me a heads up. Security guards around here do a lot more than stand around. It's a damn good thing I kept Fays' present in my desk drawer. Now I have to find another hiding place for it. Thanks, Walt."

IT WAS Thursday at ten o'clock in the evening, and Elliott was home and had spent the last two hours typing away on his computer. He didn't have a towel plugging the door crack. He had just finished transferring the money from the account Lexi told him to use to collect the money he'd stolen to an offshore account he'd set up months ago. When he saw the word "Custodial" on the account, he didn't know what that meant, but didn't care. His bank scheme was working perfectly. He had written a small piece of computer code and, thanks to Janice, inserted it into the bank's accounting software. The code was designed to shave one percent of the balance from each abandoned account. Lexi had given him her username and password, so he had access to the bank's growing list of abandoned accounts. Dozens were added each week from the bank's offices around the country. He couldn't have the amount taken reflected in the reports Janice compiled for the bank's accounting department, but he couldn't completely mask the discrepancy. However, he could mask the transaction down to a single penny. Accounting software bugs were easy to find and fix if the amount was large enough. A one-hundred-dollar error can be easily spotted. Something as small as a penny indicated a bug deeply embedded in the software. Elliott knew his scheme would eventually unravel, but not before he'd stolen a considerable amount of money. Janice and Lexi were just collateral damage in Elliott's mind.

Lexi was easy to bring into his plan, which he thought of shortly after they met. She always hated the idea of people's money being returned to a state so it could waste it on some courthouse with a politician's name stamped all over it. He fought not to laugh when Lexi gave him a list of charities to donate the money he stole. Elliott had only one charity in mind, the state of Israel. Israel was a bitter enemy of Iran. Elliott wanted to strike a blow at Iran for killing his parents, and he wanted to hurt the country that denied his parents a visa. Israeli intelligence found it easy to recruit him out of college and use him to infiltrate the US Government. The bank scheme was Elliott's idea. His masters in Israel were more than happy to take the money to fund their infiltration into the US government.

Lexi was riding the metro home from work when she checked her phone for the umpteenth time that day. Elliott had told her he was going to visit his parents over the long weekend and be back Monday night. Today was Tuesday, and her last text from him was Sunday morning. She had called him several times over the weekend but was sent to voicemail each time. Instead of going home, she decided to go to his apartment. She arrived at Elliott's door, knocked, and said, "Elliott, are you home?" After waiting a moment, she did the same, only louder. After another moment, she raised her voice and asked, "Elliott, why haven't you called me?" Suddenly, she heard a voice coming from her left. Serene had opened her door and said, with some satisfaction, "If you're looking for Elliott, he moved out Sunday."

AFTER PUTTING the Marine One contract specifications on the memory card, Walt was getting in his car when he realized he had almost made a huge mistake, and Ellie saved him. Anybody sniffing around would see Ellie accessing the secure server on the weekend. The only problem was that the building entry security log would show only Walt using his ID card to enter the building. Ellie, showing up, fixed that problem. He realized he wasn't very good at being a spy, since what he was doing was about as serious a crime as there was. Purging the thought, he started thinking about a way to get the memory card to Simon and Noah and, most importantly, get paid. It didn't take a rocket scientist to figure out Noah Clyburn was behind everything happening to Walt. Simon was just his henchman. Because the Air Force frowned on its personnel having unofficial contact with contractors, Walt didn't want to risk showing any involvement with Warner outside normal channels. Driving home, he came up with a solution to pass the memory card to Simon and get paid at the same time. He remembered a book about an FBI agent who betrayed his country by passing classified information to the Russians. The agent used a dead drop, leaving his stolen information at a pre-arranged location and returning to collect his money. He and his Russian handler never met face-to-face. Walt decided that his car at the Farmer's market was the perfect spot. He would tape the memory card to the bottom of a sauce jar and leave it in the trunk. Simon didn't seem to have any trouble getting into his car. Once he and Liam finished selling for the day, he would find an envelope much larger than the others that Simon had left him. He smiled at the thought. He still needed a way to contact Simon and let him know about his Farmer's market plan.

When he got home, Olivia called him into the home office, where

Olivia was at the computer. She said, "Take a look at the new Lucia's website."

Walt bent over Olivia's shoulder to look at the screen and said, "This looks great. You did a great job with this. I'm assuming Liam created all of the graphics."

"Of course he did. He told me he wants to be cut in on Lucia's profits since he's responsible for creating Lucia's brand."

"Smart kid. He's probably right about creating the brand."

"Take a look at this." Olivia moved the mouse cursor to the menu selection that said "Order Online." When she clicked on it, the screen filled with different-sized jars and discounts for buying more than one. The website also offered subscriptions to have the sauce delivered to your home regularly. The website also provided a gift service. Customers could send Lucia's as a gift with a personalized note emailed to the recipient. The email also notified the recipient about the arriving package. When Walt saw this, he knew how to notify Simon and exchange the memory card for his money.

The next day, he purchased a prepaid debit card online and sent it to himself at his office address. When the card arrived, he went to his computer and ordered a gift pack that included four jars of Lucia's. He sent it to Noah using the email address Noah had used to inundate him with his constant stream of complaints. In the personalized card section, he wrote, "You can buy Lucia's every Saturday at the farmer's market. The first Saturday of every month is "Buy three and get the fourth free."

Next week was the first Saturday, so Walt chose "next-day delivery" as the shipping option. When he reached the payment section, he used his pre-paid debit card to finalize the transaction. After doing this, he sat back, smiled, and said to himself, "Maybe I'm not such a lousy spy after all." Saturday morning arrived, and Walt and Liam were loading the car with Lucia's sauce. After putting his last case in the trunk and closing it, Liam said, "What are you doing, Dad? Today's the first Saturday. We need to take more sauce.

"Oh. Sorry, I'm a little distracted today."

Liam went to the back of the garage, picked up a case of sauce, and brought it to Walt. He said, "Giving away a jar is stupid. We gave away six jars last time. That's money out of my pocket."

Walt looked at Liam and said, "Well, listen to you, mister capitalist. You're going to do well in life. That's one less thing for me and your mother to worry about. Get in; I want to get there early so we can get a good parking spot." Walt pulled into the market's parking area and cursed. "Damn it. This place is becoming a hassle. Look at this. Every space near the stalls has already been taken. The place doesn't open for another hour and a half. Who do these people think they are going to sell to?"

"Each other. If it's ok, Dad, can you set up? I want to take a jar and some spoons and get people to stop by. I bet a lot of them are finishing setting up their stands and probably just sitting there."

Walt shook his head and said, "Now I know you'll do well. Go ahead. That's a great idea, Liam."

Walt parked the car, cursed again, and got out. He opened the trunk and started carrying the jars to the stall. After two trips, he grabbed the last case and set it on the ground. Looking around, he pulled a baggie from his pocket, examined the memory chip inside, and placed it in the trunk. After closing the trunk, he glanced around once more and returned to the stall. He didn't see Simon sitting in one of the parked cars near the stalls. Simon was one of the first to arrive at the market that day. After waiting several minutes, Simon got out to check if Walt was done with his trips to the car. He noticed Walt reaching into the cases of sauce and placing them on the stall's table. Satisfied, he returned to his car and retrieved a large, fat manila envelope from the glove box.

He walked to Walt's car, took his lock-picking tool from his pocket, and opened the trunk. Smiling, he took the baggie and replaced it with the envelope. He closed the trunk and started walking to his car. He took half a dozen steps when he heard somebody yelling behind him, "Freeze asshole!!" Simon turned and saw two people with guns pointed at him. He looked past the people shouting at him and saw police cars coming from every direction, flashing their lights and blaring their sirens. He turned to his left and saw more people screaming at him and holding guns. He noticed all of the people with guns were wearing the same color windbreaker. One of them turned, and Simon saw the letters FBI on the back. Simon started to panic and looked around for an escape path. He noticed immediately that he was surrounded by people holding guns and yelling at him to get down on the ground. He let out a groan and did as he was told. One of the FBI agents approached Simon, grabbed his arms, and hand-cuffed him. Two agents walked past Simon and entered the market, looking for Walt. They began scanning the market when one of the agents spotted Walt. He said, "That's him. His kid is wearing a red baseball cap."

When Walt and Liam arrived at the market that morning and pulled into the parking lot, Walt's heart started pounding. He knew what was going to happen, and he wanted it over with as quickly as possible. He thought back to the day Simon cornered him at the Home Depot. After Simon had left him, Walt raced home and told Olivia what had happened. He showed her the envelope with the money, credit card statements, and letter to the Inspector General. Olivia didn't hesitate to tell Walt he needed to take the envelope and bring it to the FBI. It was the FBI that had coached Walt on what to do next.

When he and Liam returned home from the market, Olivia rushed to the garage and said, "Thank God you two are home. What happened?"

Walt said, "I heard the noise when they arrested that asshole, Simon. I didn't go to watch, because Liam was with me. I wish I could be there when they cuffed that other asshole, Noah."

————

Lexi turned to face Serene when she heard Elliott had moved; she said, "Do you know where he went?"

Serene replied, "I didn't talk to him. A couple of movers showed up and emptied the apartment. Sorry."

Without saying another word, Lexi turned and walked to the elevator. When she got home, Lexi went to her bedroom, fell on the bed, and began crying. Lexi loved Elliott. They had plans to spend the rest of their lives together. Why did he leave her? Suddenly, Lexi stopped crying. As if a camera flash had gone off, she realized she had been used. "He never loved me," she thought. Thinking back to the time they met, she remembered their first couple of dates. After their first date, she thought Elliott was more interested in getting her in bed than having a genuine relationship. Par for the course. She was actually surprised Elliott had asked her out a second time. Lexi knew she wasn't very attractive, and second dates were rare. What was weird about the second time they went out was Elliott's questions about her job. He seemed more interested in it than her. The next day, Lexi went to tell Janice what she had done. She walked into her office and began telling Janice everything she and Elliott had done." Astonished at Lexi's revelation, Janice said, "Lexi, I don't know what to say. Elliott scared the hell out of me. I can't believe you were a part of this, this, whatever it is. What were you thinking?"

"I'm so sorry, Janice. I loved Elliott. He gave me so much attention. I thought we were going to help people with the money. I didn't think it was so bad taking money that the states wasted and giving it to charity."

"I don't know what to say, Lexi. I'm not sure what to do."

"I've thought about this, Janice. The bank is going to find out. That's what Elliott told me. Once they dig into the software, they're going to find what he did. It has nothing to do with us. They'll assume it was some Russian hacker stealing money. The money was abandoned, so nobody is going to miss it. The States certainly won't miss it because it was never reported to them."

"Well, Elliott has the money. Where'd he go with it?"

"He transferred it offshore, so it's gone. I don't know where his. His parents live in St. Louis, but I doubt he went there."

"Hold on a minute. I have an idea. What was the account Elliott used to receive the money he took?"

"It was a custodial account. The custodial account he used to collect the money is still an open account. Do a name search for Ingram."

Janice began typing on her keyboard. She said, "Here it is."

Lexi moved around the desk and looked at the monitor. Janice pointed to the screen and said, "The account hasn't shown any activity for four years. That's why it showed up in our abandoned accounts. Then you can see where Elliott had some money transferred into it, and the account switched from abandoned to active."

Lexi, shocked, said, "Oh my God. Look at how much money there was."

"My goodness, Lexi. What did you and Elliott do?"

"I'm so sorry, Janice. I didn't know it was that much."

"Look, you can see it accumulating each time an account goes from active to abandoned. Then you see it being transferred offshore. Once the money is transferred, the account switches back to abandoned."

"Never to be seen again," Lexi said ruefully. Then she pointed to the screen and asked, 'What's this?"

The screen showed a six-hundred-dollar transaction to American Airlines.

Janice said, "I don't know, but it sure stands out."

"Well, it looks like he took a plane to somewhere. I wonder where."

"Hold on, I think we can find out."

Janice picked up the phone and called the Airline's customer service. She explained she was from Carnegie National Bank and was investigating some irregular activity on one of their customer's accounts. She gave the service rep the date and amount of the transaction and the bank's routing and account number. After a moment, the rep said, "Thank you for waiting. Our system shows two first-class tickets to Tel Aviv, Israel, departing Washington Dulles on that date."

"Do you have the names on those tickets?"

WATCHING Lexi leave after telling her Elliott had moved out, Serene turned and said, "Okay. I don't think we'll have to worry about her anymore."

Elliott said, "Thank God. That woman was more work than I thought possible. Let's get out of here. Your contacts in Tel Aviv are waiting for us."

IT WAS two-thirty in the morning, and Walt was wide awake. It had been an extremely stressful day, and he couldn't fall asleep. He turned his head and saw Olivia sleeping. He got up, walked to the home office, and turned on his PC. He opened the web browser and typed in Bank of East Asia, and waited for the bank's website to appear. He logged in to his account and displayed a satisfying grin when he looked at the balance. Everything had worked out exactly as Ellie planned it. The only hiccup was her surprising him that Saturday when he was using her computer to get the Marine One contract specs. She was there to begin work on another project, her Israeli handler had requested. Warner Systems had promoted an employee to Noah's job after he was arrested and carted off. The newly promoted employee had been sufficiently groomed to take over Noah's job, both inside and outside of Warner. Noah had become greedy and self-important and needed to be replaced. His biggest sin was contacting Walt and trying to get him to provide information that he had other plans for. Plans that would enrich him behind his handler's back. Ellie learned of this and decided to go all in and try to recruit Walt into working with her and Israeli intelligence. It was easier than she could have imagined. Looking at the balance in his account, Walt decided he would wait for the dust to settle before transferring some of the money into Lucia's account. Olivia was adding another sauce to the business, which was doing very well. The money he laundered wouldn't be noticed.

QUENTIN CAME into work Monday morning earlier than usual. He was wearing the new suit his wife, Sonia, had bought him for his first day at his new job. He got off the elevator in Monarch Motors' company headquarters and walked to his new office. He stopped at the door and smiled at what was on the door. "Quentin Waters, Vice President of Design." He thought back to the day he put a note inside the door of that car on his first day of work. "It's been quite a journey since that day," he thought. Now, here he was, Vice President of Design. Monarch was entering the EV market and coming out with a car designed like no other on the road. When the first new EV car came down the assembly line, Quentin would make sure he was in the same position he was on his first day at Monarch. He had another note ready to be put inside the door.

THE END